KU-777-156

COLTON'S SECRET SERVICE

BY
MARIE FERRARELLA

Marie Ferrarella has written more than one hundred and fifty books, some under the name Marie Nicole. Her romances are beloved by fans worldwide. Visit her website at www.marieferrarella.com.

To
Patience Smith,
who makes being an author
such a pleasure

Chapter 1

His neck was really beginning to ache.

It amazed him how these last ten years, after steadily climbing up the ladder, from cop to detective to Secret Service agent, Nick Sheffield found himself right back where he started: doing grunt work. There was no other accurate way to describe it: remaining stationary, hour after hour, waiting for a perpetrator to finally show up—provided he did show up, which was never a sure thing.

But, at least for now, Nick had no other recourse, no other trail to pursue. This lonely ranch was where the evidence had led him.

He'd always hated surveillance work. Ever since he'd been a young kid, patience had never been in his nature. He was much happier being active. *Doing* something instead of just standing as still as a statue, feeling his five o'clock shadow grow.

However, in this particular instance, it was unavoidably necessary. He had no other way to capture his quarry.

Nick supposed he should consider this a triumph. After all, less than twenty-four hours ago, he still hadn't a clue where all those threatening letters and e-mails aimed at the man whose life he was to safeguard, Senator Joe Colton, came from. These days, it seemed like every crazy malcontent and his dog had access to a computer and the Internet, which made tracking down the right crazy malcontent one hell of a challenge. One that fortunately, he was more than up to—with a healthy dose of help from the reformed computer hacker, Steve Hennessey, who now worked for his security staff.

Technically, it was the Senator's staff, but he ran it. Handpicked the people and ran the staff like a well-oiled, efficient machine ever since he'd been assigned to the Senator. He liked to think that he was doing his bit to help the Senator get elected to the highest post of the land.

There was no doubt in his mind that unless something unforeseen or drastic happened, the Senator would go on to become the next President of the United States. In his opinion, and he'd been around more than a little in his thirty years on earth, there was no other man even half as qualified to assume the position of President as Senator Joe Colton.

He didn't just work for the Senator, he admired the man, admired what he stood for and what he hoped to accomplish once elected. In the last few months, he'd seen Senator Colton up close and under less-than-favorable conditions. In his opinion, they just did not come any more genuine—or charismatic—than the Senator.

Nick doubted very much if he would have spent the

last eight hours standing behind a slightly open barn door, watching the front of an unoccupied, ramshackle ranch house for anyone else.

Damn it, where the hell was this creep? Was he going to show at all?

He didn't want to have to do this for another hour, much less entertain the prospect of doing it for another day.

Nick's temper was getting frayed. It was late and humid, and the mosquitoes kept trying to make a meal out of him. He waved another one away from his neck even as he felt sweat sliding down his spine, making the shirt beneath his black jacket stick to his skin. Talk about discomfort.

Nick blew out a frustrated breath.

Why couldn't this crazy be located in one of the major cities, living in a high-rise apartment? Why did it have to be someone who lived the life of a hermit? The IP address that Steve had miraculously tracked down had brought him to a town that barely made the map. A blip of a town named Esperanza, Texas.

Esperanza. Now there was a misnomer. His Spanish wasn't all that good, but he knew that *esperanza* was the Spanish word for "hope" and in this particular case, Nick had no doubt that the hope associated with the town was reserved for those who managed to escape from it. If it wasn't for the fact that Esperanza was a sub-suburb of San Antonio, Nick doubted that he and his GPS system would have been able to even locate it.

And this person he was after didn't even reside within the so-called city limits. He lived in an old, all-but-falling-down ranch house that stood five miles from the nearest neighbor, and was even farther away than five miles from the town.

Hell, Nick thought impatiently, this character could be cooking up bombs and nobody would ever be the wiser—until the explosion came.

Nobody but him, Nick thought. But that was his job, tracking down the crazies and keeping them away from the best man he'd met in a long, long time.

"You're sure?" the Senator had asked him when he'd walked into his office with the news yesterday that his hacker had finally managed to isolate where the e-mails originated. He'd quickly given him the exact location.

For the most part, Nick didn't even bother telling the Senator about the nuisance calls, e-mails and letters that had found their way into the campaign headquarters. Anyone in public office, or even the public eye, was a target for someone seeking to vent his or her discontent. It came with the territory.

But this was different. These e-mails and letters smacked of someone dangerous. Someone seeking to "take you out" as one of the last ranting communications had threatened.

Nick had learned a long time ago to take seriously anything that remotely resembled a threat. The risk was too great not to.

He'd just informed the Senator that the sender was someone living in or around Esperanza, Texas, and that he intended to confront the man face-to-face. It was against the law to threaten a presidential candidate.

"That it's coming from there?" Nick asked, then went ahead as if he'd received a positive response. "I wouldn't be coming to you with this if I wasn't sure," he told the Senator simply.

Between them, on the desk, was a thick pile of papers

that Nick had emptied out of a manila folder. Letters that had arrived in the last few weeks, all from the same source. All progressively angrier in nature. It couldn't be ignored any longer, even if he were so inclined.

"We've tracked him down," Nick repeated. "And, unless you have something specific that only I can take care of here, I'd like to go down to this little two-bit hick place and make sure that this nut-job doesn't decide to follow through with any of his threats." He had no qualms about leaving the Senator. He was the head of the Secret Service detail, but by no means was he the only one assigned to the popular Senator. Hathaway and Davis were more than up to watching over the man until he got back.

"These are all from him?" Nick nodded in response to the Senator's question. "Sure has spent a lot of time venting," Joe commented. He picked up a sheet of paper only to have Nick stop him before he was able to begin to read it.

"No need to read any of it, Senator." Nick wanted to spare the man the ugliness on some of the pages. "It's pretty awful."

Joe didn't believe in isolating himself, but he saw no reason to immerse himself in distasteful lies and name-calling, either. He let the letter remain in Nick's hand. "Then why did you bring it to me?"

In Nick's opinion, the volume of mail spoke for itself. No sane person invested this much time and effort in sending vicious missives, and the future actions of an insane person couldn't be safely gauged. It would take very little to push a person like this to where he would become dangerous.

"To let you see that the man could be a threat and that

I'd like the chance to stop him before he becomes one," Nick stated simply.

In the short time they had been together, Joe had learned to both like and rely on the head of his Secret service detail. Nick Sheffield had impressed him as a hard-working, honorable man whose interest was in getting the job done, not in gathering attention or praise for his actions. He more than trusted the man's instincts.

Joe liked the fact that Nick always looked him in the eye when he spoke. "When would you leave?" he asked.

"Tonight." Nick saw a glint of surprise in the Senator's eyes. "I should be back in a couple of days— a week at most," he promised, although he was hoping that it wouldn't take that long. He intended to locate the sender, take him into custody and bring him back. The federal authorities could take it from there.

Joe nodded. There had been mutual respect between the two men almost from the very first day. Their personalities complemented one another. Joe trusted Nick not only with his life, but, more importantly, the lives of his family who meant more to him than anything else in the world, including the bid for the presidency.

"All right," the Senator agreed. "Go if you really think it's necessary."

There was no hesitation on Nick's part. "I do."

"That's good enough for me," the Senator replied. And then he smiled that smile that had a way of cutting across party affiliations and verbose rhetoric, burrowing into the heart of the recipient. "Just get back as soon as you can, Nick. I feel a whole lot better knowing that you're on the job."

Nick knew the man was not just giving voice to empty words, that praise from the Senator was always heartfelt and genuine. While exceedingly charming, with a manner that drew people to him, the Senator was not one to toss around words without thought or feeling behind them, like so many other politicians.

"I'll be back before you know it," Nick had promised, taking his leave. At the time, he sincerely meant what he said.

Georgeann Grady, Georgie to everyone who knew her, struggled mightily to keep her eyes open. For the last twenty minutes, she'd debated pulling over to the side of the road in order to catch a few well-deserved winks before falling asleep at the wheel. But she was only five miles away from home. Five miles away from sleeping in her own bed and after months of being on the road, sleeping in her own bed sounded awfully good to her.

She told herself to keep driving.

Digging her nails into the palms of the hands that were wrapped around the steering wheel of her truck, Georgie tried to shake off the effects of sleepiness by tossing her head. It sent the single thick, red braid back over her shoulder. Squaring them, she glanced into the rear-view mirror to check on her pint-sized passenger.

Big, wide green eyes looked right back at her.

Georgie suppressed a sigh. She might have known that Emmie wasn't asleep, even if her nonstop chatter had finally run its course. Ceasing about ten minutes ago.

"Why aren't you asleep?" she asked her precocious, almost-five-year-old daughter.

"Too excited," Emmie told her solemnly in a voice that could have easily belonged to someone at least twice her age.

Emmie sounded almost happier to be getting back home than she was. Sometimes, Georgie thought, it was almost as if their roles were reversed and Emmie was the mother while she was the daughter. There was little more than eighteen years between them. They could have just as easily been sisters instead of mother and daughter.

And, as far as daughters went, she couldn't have asked for a better one. Raising Emmie had been a dream, despite the unorthodox life they led. A good deal of Emmie's life had been spent on the road, as a rodeo brat. It was out of necessity so that Georgie could earn money by competing in various rodeo events—just as her mother and her grandfather had before her.

At all times, her eye was on the prize. The final prize. Not winning some title that would be forgotten by the time the dust settled, but amassing as much money as she could so that she and her daughter could finally settle down and live a normal life.

She owed it to Emmie.

Her mother, Mary Lynn Grady, had quit the life, walking away with nothing more than medals and trophies, as she took up the reins of motherhood. But she intended to be far more prepared than that. It took money to make dreams come true.

Emmie was coming of age. She'd be turning five next week and five meant kindergarten, which in turn meant stability. That translated into living in a home that wasn't on wheels, nestled in a place around people who loved her. That had been the plan for the last four-something years and Georgie was determined to make it a reality.

Every cent that hadn't been used for clothing and feeding them, or for entrance fees, had faithfully been banked back in Esperanza. By her tally, at this point, thanks to her most recent winning streak, the account was exceedingly healthy now. There was finally more than enough for them to settle down and for her to figure out her next move: finding a career that didn't involve performing tricks on a horse that was galloping at break-neck speed.

Any other career would seem tame in comparison, but right now, tame was looking awfully good. The accident that she'd had a few months ago could have been disastrous. It made her very aware that she, like so many other rodeo competitors, was living on borrowed time. She wanted to get out before time ran out on her—and now, she could.

Independence had a wonderful feel about it, she thought.

Emmie's unbridled excitement about coming home just underscored her decision. There'd be no pulling over to the side of the road for her. Not when they were almost home.

Leaning forward, Georgie turned up the music. Tobey Keith's newest song filled the inside of the cab. Behind her, in an enthusiastic, clear voice, Emmie began to sing along. With a laugh, Georgie joined in.

In the overall scheme of things, eight hours was nothing, but when those hours peeled away, second by second, moment by moment, it felt as if the time was endless.

He wanted to get back to the action, not feel as if his limbs were slowly slipping into paralysis. But he didn't even dare get back to the car he'd hidden behind the barn. He might miss his quarry coming home. The man *had* to come home sometime. The e-mails had been coming fairly regularly, one or more almost every day now. Because there hadn't been anything yesterday, the man was overdue.

Nick took out a candy bar he'd absently shoved into his pocket last night. It was just before leaving Prosperino, California, the Senator's home base, to catch the red-eye flight to San Antonio. After checking in with his team to see if there were any further developments— there hadn't been—he'd rented a car and then driven to this god-forsaken piece of property.

He'd found the front door unlocked and had let himself in, but while there were some signs here and there that the ranch house was lived in, the place had been empty.

So he'd set up surveillance. And here he'd been for the last interminable eight hours, fifteen minutes and God only knew how many seconds, waiting.

It would be nice, he thought irritably, if this character actually showed up soon so he could wrap this all up and go back to civilization before he started growing roots where he stood.

How the hell did people live in places like this? he wondered. If the moon hadn't been full tonight, he wouldn't even be able to *see* the house from here, much less the front door. Most likely, he'd probably have to crouch somewhere around the perimeter of the building as he laid in wait.

He supposed that things could always be worse.

Stripping the wrapper off a large-sized concoction of chocolate, peanuts and caramel, Nick had just taken his first bite of the candy bar when he heard it. A rumbling engine noise.

Nick froze, listening.

It was definitely a car. From the sound of it, not a small one. Or a particularly new one for that matter.

Damn, but it was noisy enough to wake the dead, he thought. Whoever it was certainly wasn't trying for stealth, but then, the driver had no reason to expect anyone to be around for his entrance.

Because he was pretty close to starving before he remembered the candy bar, Nick took one more large bite, then shoved the remainder into his pocket.

All his senses were instantly on high alert.

He strained his eyes, trying to make out the approaching vehicle from his very limited vantage point. He didn't dare open the door any wider, at least, not at this point. He couldn't take a chance on the driver seeing the movement.

It suddenly occurred to him that if the driver decided to park his truck behind the barn, he was going to be out of luck. That was where he'd left his sedan.

Nick mentally crossed his fingers as he held his breath.

The next moment, he exhaled. Well, at least one thing was going right, he silently congratulated himself. The vehicle, an old, battered truck, came into view and was apparently going to park in front of the ranch house.

A minute later, he saw why the truck's progress was so slow. The truck was towing an equally ancient trailer.

As he squinted for a better view, Nick tried to make out the driver, but there was no way he could see into the cab. He couldn't tell if the man was young or old. The vague shadow he saw told him that the driver appeared to be slight and even that might have just been a trick of the moonlight.

Nick straightened his back, his ache miraculously gone. At least the ordeal was almost over, he told himself.

The truck finally came to a creaking stop before the ranch house, but not before emitting a cacophony. It almost sounded as if it exhaled. Straining his eyes, Nick still heard rather than saw the driver getting out of the truck's cab.

Now or never, Nick thought.

"Stop right there," he shouted, bursting out of the barn. He held up his wallet, opened to his ID. As if anyone could make out what was there, he thought ironically. To cover all bases, he identified himself loudly. "I'm with the Secret Service."

In response, the driver turned and bolted back toward the truck.

"Oh, no, you don't," Nick shouted.

A star on his high school track team, Nick took off, cutting the distance between them down to nothing in less than a heartbeat. The next moment, he tackled the driver, bringing him down.

"Get the hell off me!" the driver shouted.

Nick remembered thinking that the truck driver had a hell of a feminine voice just before he felt the back of his head explode, ushering in a curtain of darkness.

Chapter 2

It was only through sheer grit that Nick managed to hang on to the fringes of consciousness, gripping the sliver of light with his fingertips and holding on for all he was worth. He knew that if he surrendered to the darkness, there would be no telling what could happen. In his experience these last ten years, death could be hiding behind every conceivable corner. Even in tiny, off-the-beaten-path burgs that made no one's top-ten list of places to visit.

Falling backward, Nick teetered, then managed to spring up, somehow still miraculously holding on to his wallet and displaying both his badge and ID.

Not that anyone was looking at it.

"Striking a Secret Service agent is a punishable offense that'll land you in prison," he barked at his assailant.

Swinging around to face the person who'd almost

bashed in his head, Nick struggled to focus. Everything appeared blurred, with images multiplying themselves. This intense ringing in his ears jarred him down to the very bone. But even though it was wavy, the image of his assailant was legions away from what he had expected.

Was he hallucinating?

There, standing with her legs spread apart and firmly planted on the ground, clutching a tire iron that was close to being half as big as she was, was—

"A kid?" Nick demanded incredulously when he could finally find his voice. "I was almost brained by a little kid?"

"I'm not little! And you stay off my mama!" the tiny terror shouted. She held on to the tire iron so hard, her knuckles were white and she'd lifted her chin like a pint-sized, old-fashioned prize fighter, daring him to try to touch her.

His head throbbed and the headache mushrooming over his skull threatened to obliterate everything else. *Focus, Nick, focus!*

"Your mama?" Nick echoed. Well, that explained it all right. His ears hadn't been playing tricks on him. The driver he'd tackled had sounded like a woman for a very good reason. "He" was a "she."

Even as he fought to clear his brain and try to keep the headache at bay, he saw the woman—and now that he looked, he could see that she was a petite, curvaceous woman whose body could *not* be mistaken for boyish— move swiftly to stand beside her daughter. She rested her hand on one of the little girl's shoulders. The woman had lost the ridiculous, oversized cowboy hat she'd had on. Without it, he saw that she had red hair. It was pulled back and tucked into a long, thick braid that ran down to the small of her back.

The fiery-looking, petite hellcat didn't look as if she could weigh a hundred pounds even with her daughter perched on her shoulders. He should have easily subdued both of them with no trouble, not find himself at their mercy.

This wasn't going to look good in the report.

The woman took the tire iron from her daughter. But rather than drop it, the way he expected her to, she grasped it like a weapon while gently attempting to push the little hellion behind her. The girl didn't stay put long. It reminded Nick of a painting he'd once seen in a Washington museum, something that had to do with the spirit of the pioneer women who helped settle the West.

For one unguarded moment, between the monumental headache, the intermittent confusion and the anger he felt at being caught off guard like this, the word *magnificent* came to mind.

The next moment, he realized this was no time for that kind of personal assessment.

He found himself under fire from that rather pert set of lips.

"Who the hell are you?" she demanded hotly, moving the tire iron as she shot off the words. "And what are you doing, sneaking around on my land, attacking defenseless women?"

"I already told you who I was," he reminded her tersely, "and I'd hardly call you defenseless."

As he said that, he rubbed his chin and realized belatedly that the woman he'd inadvertently tackled had actually landed a rather stinging right cross to his chin.

Maybe he was damn lucky to be alive, although he probably wouldn't feel quite that way if word of this incident ever really got out: Nick Sheffield, aspiring Secret Service agent to the President, taken down by two females who collectively weighed less than a well-fed male German shepherd.

He eyed the tire iron in her hand. "I feel sorry for your husband."

"Don't be," Georgie snapped. "There isn't one."

Once upon a time, during the summer that she'd been seventeen and full of wonderful, naive dreams, she'd wanted a home, a husband, a family, the whole nine yards. And, equally naively, she'd thought that Jason Prentiss was the answer to all her prayers. Tall, intelligent and handsome, the Dartmouth College junior was spending the summer on his uncle's farm. She'd lost her heart the first moment she'd seen him. He had eyes the color of heaven and a tongue that was dipped in honey.

Unfortunately, he also possessed a heart that was chiseled out of old bedrock. Once summer was over, he went back to college, back, she discovered, to his girl-friend. Finding out that their summer romance had created a third party only made Jason pack his bags that much faster. He left with a vague promise to write and quickly vanished from her life. In the months that followed, there wasn't a single attempt to contact her. The two letters she wrote were returned, unopened.

Georgie had grown up in a hurry that summer, in more ways than one. Eighteen was a hell of an age to become an adult, but she had and in her opinion, she and Emmie were just fine—barring the occasional bump in the road.

Like the one standing in front of her now.

Sucking in his breath against the pain, Nick rubbed the back of his head where Emmie had made more than gentle contact.

It was a wonder she hadn't fractured his skull, he thought. As it was, there would be one hell of a lump there. Probing, he could feel it starting to form.

No husband, huh? "Killed him, did you?" he asked sarcastically.

He saw the woman's eyes flash like green lightning. Obviously, he'd struck a nerve. Had she really killed her husband?

"I don't know what you're doing here, but I want you to turn around and get the hell off my property or I'm going to call the sheriff," she warned.

Nick held his ground even as he eyed the little devil the woman was vainly trying to keep behind her. He was more leery of the kid than the woman. The little girl looked as if she would bite.

"Call away," he told the woman, unfazed. He saw that his answer annoyed her and he felt as if he'd scored a point for his side. "It'll save me the trouble of looking up his number."

"Right." She drew the word out, indicating that she didn't come close to believing him. Inclining her head slightly toward her daughter, she nonetheless kept her eyes trained on him. "Emmie, get my cell phone out of the truck." Her eyes hardened as she turned her full attention back to him. "We don't like people who trespass around here."

Okay, he'd had just about enough of this grade B western clone.

"Look, I already told you that I'm a Secret Service agent—" Nick got no farther.

Georgie snorted contemptuously at what she per-
ceived to be a whopper. Anyone could get a badge off
the Internet and fake an ID these days. "And I'm
Annie Oakley."

"Well, *Ms. Oakley*," Nick retorted sarcastically,
"right now, you're interfering with a federal matter."

When it came to sarcasm, she could hold her own
with the best of them. Growing up with no father and
her lineage in question, the butt of more than one joke,
she'd learned quickly to use the tools she had to deflect
the hurtful words.

"And just what matter would that be?" she asked.

Although he rarely justified himself, he decided to
give this woman the benefit of the doubt. Maybe she
wasn't playing dumb, maybe the more-than-mildly
attractive hellcat really *was* dumb.

So he spelled it out for her. "Obstruction of justice,
harboring a criminal—"

She stopped him cold. "What criminal?" Georgie
demanded angrily.

This man was *really* getting under her skin. God,
but she wished she had her shotgun with her instead
of this hunk of metal. Wielding a tire iron didn't make
her feel very safe.

"Georgie Grady," he answered. He had his doubts
that she was innocent of the man's activities. Not if she
lived here as she claimed. Even so, Nick decided to
cover his bases and give reasoning a try. "Look, your
boyfriend or whoever Georgie Grady is to you is in a
lot of trouble and if you try to hide him, it'll only go
hard on you as well." Needing some kind of leverage,
he hit her where he assumed it would hurt the most. "Do
you want Social Services to take away your daughter?"

He nodded at the returning child holding on to the cell phone she'd been sent to get. "I can make that happen."

"Can you, now?" He was bluffing, Georgie thought. The man didn't know his ass from his elbow, he'd just proven it. "Somehow, that doesn't fill me full of fear," she informed him coldly.

"Mama?"

There was fear in Emmie's voice. Georgie's protective mother instincts immediately stood at attention. She slipped one arm around her daughter's small shoulders to give her a quick, comforting squeeze.

"But someone upsetting my daughter does fill me full of anger and I promise you, mister, when I'm angry, it's not a pretty sight." Her eyes became glinting, green slits as she narrowed them. "You'd do well to avoid it if you can."

What the hell was he doing, standing in the middle of nowhere, going one-on-one with some misguided red-headed harpy? He'd had enough of this. "Just tell me where I can find this Georgie Grady and I'll forget this whole incident."

Emmie tugged on the bottom of her mother's shirt to get her attention. "Is he simple, Mama?" she asked in what amounted to a stage whisper.

Georgie stifled a laugh. "It would appear so, honey."

He was not here to entertain them, nor did he appreciate being the butt of someone's joke, especially when he wasn't in on it. "Look, call the damn sheriff so we can get this over with."

To his surprise, she took a step toward him, lifting her chin exactly the way he'd seen her daughter do. "I will thank you not to use profanity in front of my daughter."

Of all the hypocritical— "But you just cursed," he pointed out.

Georgie allowed a careless shrug to roll off her shoulders. "That's different."

Of course it was. "God, but I hate small towns."

"And using the Lord's name in vain's pretty much frowned on around here as well," Georgie told him, not bothering to hide her disdain.

Well, it was obvious that no matter what she said, she wasn't calling the sheriff and he wanted this thing brought to a conclusion. "Fine, tell me the sheriff's number." He began to reach into his suit jacket pocket. "*I'll* call him and we can get this over with."

Alarmed that he might be reaching for a concealed weapon, Georgie raised the tire iron threateningly. "Put your hands up!" she ordered.

Abandoning his cell phone, Nick did as she said. "I can't dial and put my hands up," he protested. He was miles beyond annoyed now.

The woman seemed to relax, lowering the tire iron again. She raised her eyes to his and he could have sworn he saw a smirk. Her next words did nothing to dispel that impression.

"Don't do your research very well, do you, Mr. Secret Service agent?"

No matter how he focused, he hadn't a clue what she was driving at and he was very tired of these mind games. She was undoubtedly stalling for time. If he didn't know better, he would have said she was trying to give her boyfriend time to escape—except that he already knew the man wasn't in the ranch house.

"What are you talking about?" he asked.

She debated stringing him along for a bit, then

decided that more than wanting to get to him, she wanted him *gone*. There was only one way that was going to happen. "Well, for one thing, Mr. phony Secret Service agent—" she'd seen more convincing IDs in Howard Beasley's Toy Emporium "—*I'm* Georgie Grady."

"No, you're not." If ever he'd seen someone who *didn't* look like a "Georgie" it was this woman in the tight, faded jeans and the checkered work shirt that seemed to be sticking to every inch of her upper torso like a second skin, thanks to the humidity.

Georgie shook her head. Talk about a blockhead. Too bad he was so damn annoying, because, all things considered, he was kind of cute—as long as he lost the black suit and stopped using so much of that styling goop on his hair.

"Then the people who put that name on the trophy I just won at the last rodeo competition are going to feel pretty stupid," she told him.

Nick had to consciously keep his jaw from dropping. He eyed her incredulously. This was just outlandish enough to be true. "*You're* Georgie Grady."

"I'm Georgie Grady. I guess you've got a hearing problem as well as lacking any manners," she surmised. She looked down at her daughter. "Gotta feel sorry for a man like that, Emmie. He doesn't know any better."

He was hot, he was tired and his head was splitting. He was in no mood to be talked about as if he wasn't standing right there. Especially by his quarry if this woman really was Georgie Grady.

"Look," he said waspishly, "this is all very entertaining, but I don't have time for an episode of *The Waltons*—"

The woman watched him blankly. It was obvious that the title of the popular classic TV show meant nothing to her. "Must've been before my time," she commented. She nodded over his shoulder. "The road's that way. I suggest you take it."

She still had him holding his hands up. "Can I put my hands down?"

She pretended to think his question over. "Only after you start walking."

"Fair enough."

As if complying, Nick turned away from her, took two steps, dropped his hands and then turned around again. This time, instead of his ID, he had his service revolver in his hand.

And he was pointing it at the woman.

Startled, Georgie took a firmer grip on the tire iron. Seeing the gun, Emmie screamed and this time, the little girl allowed herself to be pushed behind her mother's back.

"Drop the tire iron," Nick ordered. His tone brooked no nonsense. "Now!" he barked when she didn't immediately comply.

Letting the tire iron fall, Georgie bit off a curse that would have curled the hair of the most hardened bronco buster had it made it past her lips. She should have known this was all a ruse. Served her right for taking pity on him because he was cute. When was she going to learn that cute men meant nothing but trouble in the long *and* short run?

"I don't have anything worth stealing," she told him between clenched teeth. She just wanted him gone. He was scaring Emmie and for that, she wanted to rip out his heart.

Nick took a step closer. Although small, the gun felt heavy in his hand. He didn't like pulling his weapon on a woman and even though he found the child annoying, he definitely didn't care for having to train a weapon around the little girl, but the firebrand who claimed to be her mother had left him no choice.

"As I was saying," he went on as if nothing had happened, "I'm here to arrest Georgie Grady and take him—or her—into custody. Put your hands up," he told her.

Georgie raised her hands. Out of the corner of her eye, she saw Emmie mimic her action.

You'll pay for this, mister, she silently promised. Her brain worked feverishly to figure a way out of this.

"So," Georgie began slowly, "you really are a Secret Service agent."

"That's what I told you."

Georgie nodded her head, as if finally believing him. "And why would a Secret Service agent want to take me into custody?" she queried, doing her best to hang on to her temper. He had the gun, shouting at him wouldn't be advisable.

"Mama, is he going to shoot you?" Emmie cried, suddenly sounding like every one of her four years and no more.

Georgie's heart almost broke. Barely holding up her hands, she bent down to Emmie's level.

"No, honey, he's not going to shoot me. He's not that dumb," she assured her daughter. Raising her eyes to his, she sought his back up. "Are you, Mr. Secret Service agent?"

He'd only discharged his weapon three times, and never in his present position. But saying so might sound weak to the woman. Who knew how these backwoods people thought?

"Not if you cooperate."

She rose to her feet again, but this time she wasn't holding up her hands. She was holding Emmie in her arms, determined to calm the child's fears despite the fact that beneath her own anger was a solid band of fear. She had no idea who this crazy person was, only that she doubted very much that he was who he claimed to be. Secret Service agents didn't come to places like Esperanza.

She wished now that she'd stopped at her brother's place instead of coming here tonight. Clay's ranch wasn't home, but it did have electricity, something her house didn't at the moment because she'd shut it off before she'd gone on the trail. And more importantly, Clay's place didn't have someone holding a dingy looking revolver that was pointed straight at her.

She shifted her body so that she was between the gun and Emmie. "And just how do you expect me to 'cooperate'?" she asked.

"By letting me take you into custody." He began to feel as if he was trapped in some sort of time loop, endlessly repeating the same words.

He'd already said that, and it was just as ridiculous now as when he'd first said it. "Why, for God's sakes?" she demanded.

"I thought you didn't believe in taking the Lord's name in vain," Nick mocked, throwing her words back at her.

"It's okay when I do it," she informed him coolly, tossing her head in a dismissive movement. "God likes me. I don't point guns at little girls."

Damn, how the hell did this woman manage to keep

putting him on the defensive? She was the criminal here, not him.

"I'm pointing the gun at you, not her." He saw the little girl thread her arms around the woman's neck in what could only be seen as a protective action. They were some pair, these two. "And I'm doing it because you left me no choice."

All right, she'd played along long enough. She wanted answers now. "What is it that I'm supposed to have done that has gotten your Secret Service agent shorts all twisted up in a knot?" she demanded.

She knew damn well what she'd done. He had the utmost faith that the hacker on his team had given him the right information. Steve'd had one hell of a reputation before he'd gotten caught.

"Don't act so innocent," he accused.

"Sorry," she retorted sarcastically, "but it's a habit I have when I haven't done anything wrong."

"I wouldn't call sending threatening letters to Senator Colton not doing anything wrong," Nick informed her.

Georgie felt as if someone had just hit her over the head with a nine-pound skillet. "Senator Colton?" she echoed.

He saw the look of recognition flash in her eyes. She'd just given herself away. He was right. She *was* the one sending the threatening letters. The innocent act was just that, an act. While he felt vindicated, the slightest ribbon of disappointment weaved through him. He had no idea why, but chalked it up to the blow on the head he'd received.

"Yes."

"Senator *Joe* Colton?" Georgie enunciated in disbelief.

Why was she belaboring this? What was she up to? He wondered suspiciously, never taking his eyes off her face. "Yes."

"Well, that cinches it," Georgie said with finality, unconsciously hugging Emmie closer to her. "You really *are* out of your mind."

Chapter 3

Nick bristled at the insult. "My state of mind isn't in question here."

It was on the tip of her tongue to tell him that he was crazy if he thought she would have anything to do with another Colton after her mother's experience. But that would lead to questions she didn't want to answer. "And mine is?"

His eyes met hers. "You're the one sending the threatening e-mails."

If she weren't holding Emmie, she would have thrown up her hands. "*What* threatening e-mails? I've been too damn busy working to pick up a phone, much less waste my time on the computer."

When she came right down to it, Georgie didn't care for the Internet. To her, it was just another way for people to lose the human touch and slip into a vague pea soup of anonymity. The only reason she kept a computer and maintained an Internet account was because she didn't want to fall behind the rest of the world. Once Emmie started going to school, she knew that a computer would be a necessity. In no time at all, she was certain computers would take the place of loose-leaf binders, notebooks and textbooks. She wanted to be able to help her daughter, not have Emmie ashamed of her because she was electronically challenged.

But that didn't mean she had to like the damn thing.

Her protests fell on deaf ears. The venom he'd seen spewed in those latest e-mails wouldn't have taken much time to fire off. She hadn't even bothered with spell-check, as he recalled. And the grammar in some of the messages had been pretty bad.

"My tech expert tracked it to your ranch house, your IP account."

She had no idea what an IP account was, but wasn't about to display her ignorance, especially not in front of her daughter. But she did know one thing. "Your tech expert is wrong."

"He's never wrong." It was both the best and the worst thing about Steve because his results could never be challenged.

Georgie was unmoved and unintimidated. With her mother the butt of narrow-minded people's jokes because all three of her children had been fathered by a man who was married to someone else, she'd had to stand up for herself at a very early age. That tended to either make or break a person. She'd always refused to be broken.

"Well, he just broke his streak because he *is* wrong and if the messages were traced to my ranch house, he's *doubly* wrong because I haven't *been* in my ranch house for the last five months."

Something told him that he should have investigated Georgie Grady a little before catching the red-eye to San Antonio, but time had been at a premium last night and he'd wanted to wrap this up fast.

His eyes swept over her. "Is that so?"

She rocked forward on the balls of her boot-shod feet. "Yes, that's 'so,' and I resent your attitude, you manner *and* your manhandling me."

"Lady, you got in a right cross and your daughter almost cracked open my skull with that tire iron of hers. If anyone was manhandled, it was me."

He saw a grin spread over otherwise pretty appealing lips. "Is that why you're so angry? Because you were bested by a woman a foot shorter than you and her four-year-old daughter?"

Not only was she cocky, but she wasn't observant either.

"You're not a foot shorter than me, more like eight inches," he estimated. "And I'm angry because I'm here in this one-horse town, wasting my time arguing with a pig-headed woman after waiting for the last eight hours for her to show up when I should be back in California, with the Senator."

"Well, go." Tucking Emmie against her hip, she waved him on his way with her temporarily free hand. "Nobody told you to come to Esperanza and harass innocent people."

Nick rolled his eyes. "This isn't getting us anywhere."

"Finally, we agree on something." She blew out a breath. One of them would have to be the voice of reason and because he didn't know the meaning of the word, it would have to be her. "You really a Secret Service Agent?"

"Yes."

"Can I see that ID again?"

Reaching into his pocket, he took out his wallet. "Not very trusting, are you?" He'd always thought that people in a small town were supposed to be incredibly trusting, to the point of almost being simple-minded. Him, he trusted no one. When you grow up, not being able to trust your own parents, it set a precedent.

She raised her eyes to his. "Should I be?" He was a stranger, for all she knew, he could be some serial killer, making the rounds.

His eyes slid over her. Someone as attractive as this woman needed to be on her guard more than most. That body of hers could get her in a great deal of trouble.

"No, I guess not." Opening his wallet to his badge and photo ID, he held it up for her to look over again.

Still keeping Emmie on her hip, Georgie leaned slightly in to peruse at length the ID he showed her.

As did Emmie. She stared at it so intently that Nick caught himself wondering if the annoying child could read. Wasn't she too young for that?

Georgie stepped back and looked at him with an air of resignation. The ID appeared to be authentic after all.

"I guess you are what you say you are." He felt her eyes slide over him. "You've got the black suit and those shades hanging out of your top pocket and all." There was that smirk again, he thought. The way she described him made him feel like a caricature. "And your hair's kind of slicked back, the part that's not messed up," she added.

Without realizing what he was doing, Nick ran his hand through his hair, smoothing down the section where the kid had hit him.

He saw the woman shake her head. "You'd look better with it all messed up. The other way looks like it's been glued down."

He knew what she was doing. She was trying to undermine him any way she could. Well, it wasn't going to work.

"We'll trade hairstyling tips some other time," he told her sarcastically.

Rather than put her in her place, his response seemed to amuse her.

"Touchy son of a gun, aren't you? Don't take criticism well, I see," she noted, as if to herself. She cocked her head, as if taking measure of him and trying to decide some things about him. You'd think he was the one in trouble, he thought, annoyed.

"You the one they used to make fun of when you were a kid?" she asked.

The exact opposite was true. He'd been more than half on his way to becoming a bully, threatening other kids at school. Smaller, bigger, it didn't matter, he took them all on because he could. In school and on the streets, at least some things were in his control. Not like at home where an abusive father made his life, and his alcohol-anesthetized mother's life, a living hell.

But then, one day, for reasons he had yet to completely understand, he suddenly saw himself through his victim's eyes. Saw his father as Drake Sheffield must have been at his age. Sickened, Nick released the kid who'd come within a hair's breadth of being pummeled to the ground because he'd mouthed off at him and just walked away.

After that, his life had turned around and he put himself on the path of protecting the underdog rather than trying to humiliate and take advantage of him.

"Well, were you?" Georgie queried, although, she couldn't quite see him as a classic ninety-eight-pound weakling.

"No" was all Nick said.

Her arms began to ache, reminding her that until this man had jumped out of the shadows, tackling her and causing her adrenaline to register off the charts, she'd been dead tired. It was getting really late.

Georgie decided to appeal to his sense of decency— if he had any. "Look, would you mind if I put my daughter to bed? It's been one back-breaking long day."

"I'm not tired," Emmie protested.

It was obvious that she didn't want to miss a second of what was going on. Because of the life she led, a child thrust into a world populated predominately by adults, Emmie thought like a miniature adult. Georgie was positive that if she'd elected to remain on the rodeo circuit, Emmie would have been thrilled to death. The little girl would have loved nothing better than to live in the run-down trailer amid her beloved cowboys forever. Especially because so many of them doted on her.

"That's okay," Georgie told her, "I am, pumpkin."

Emmie pulled her small features into a solemn expression. "Then you go to bed," the little girl advised her.

Georgie glanced at the dark-haired stranger. Yes, she was exhausted, but she was also agitated. There was no way she could have closed her eyes with this man around.

"Not hardly." She raised her eyebrows, silently indicating that she was still waiting for him to respond to her question. She didn't expect him to say no.

Nick gestured toward the door. "Go ahead."

Setting Emmie down, Georgie fished her house key out of her front pocket.

As she raised it to the keyhole, he said, "It's not locked."

She looked at him accusingly. Secret Service Agent or not, the man had some nerve. "You broke in?"

"No," Nick corrected patiently, "I found it unlocked."

The hell he did, she thought. "I locked up before I left," she informed him. In her absence, no one would have broken in. Everyone around here knew she had nothing worth stealing. He *had* to have been the one jimmying open her lock. How dumb did he think she was?

Pushing the door open, Georgie took Emmie's hand in hers and walked inside.

Nick followed in her wake. "Aren't you going to turn on the light?" he asked when she walked right by the switch at the front door.

"No light to turn on," she answered. The shadows in the room began to lengthen, swallowing up the pools of moonlight on the floor. She turned to see he was automatically closing the front door. "Keep the door open until I get the fire going," she instructed. Georgie quickly crossed to the fireplace.

Obliging her, Nick pushed the door opened again. He saw her squatting down in front of the fireplace, bunching up newspapers and sticking them strategically between the logs.

"In case you haven't noticed, it's June," he protested. A damn sticky June at that. "Isn't it too hot for a fire?"

"Not if you want coffee."

Finished, she glanced over her shoulder at him. The Secret Service agent was still standing in the doorway. The moonlight outlined his frame, making him seem a little surreal. He was a powerful-looking man, even in that suit. She supposed she should have counted herself lucky that he hadn't broken any of her bones when he tackled her in the yard.

"Don't you law enforcement types always want coffee?" she asked, trying her best to maintain a friendly atmosphere. Her mother always said that honey worked better than vinegar. "Or is that against some Secret Service agent code?"

Another dig. Still, after standing there for eight hours, he was hungry enough to eat a post. Coffee would help fill the hole in his stomach for the time being. "Coffee'll be fine" Nick heard himself saying.

With the fire illuminating the living room, he shut the door behind him. As he did so, he flipped the light switch.

Nothing happened.

Rising to her feet, Georgie paused, one hand fisted at her hip. Rather than be angry, she found herself mildly amused at this overdressed, albeit fine specimen of manhood.

"You want to play with the other switches, too?" she asked. She pointed to the kitchen and then down the hall. "There're about six more. None of them will turn on the lights either."

This was just getting weirder and weirder. "Why isn't there any electricity?"

"Because I don't have money to throw around," she suggested "helpfully." "There's no phone service either, so don't bother picking up the receiver." She nodded toward the phone on the kitchen wall. "If it makes you feel any better, they'll both be on in the morning. I got home ahead of schedule."

Ahead of schedule. That meant that he would have gone on waiting for her to arrive all night until the next morning.

The very thought of that intensified the ache in his shoulder muscles.

Of course, she could just be making the whole thing up and she and the pint-sized terror could have been coming back from visiting someone. "So you're sticking to your story about being out of town?"

"It's not a story, it's the truth," Emmie insisted angrily, stomping over to him, her hands on her hips, her head tilted back like a miniature Fury. "Mama doesn't lie. She says only bad people lie."

Georgie had her back to him. He watched the way her long braid moved as she arranged something in the hearth.

"No," he told the child while watching the mother, "sometimes good people lie, too."

Georgie straightened to go get the coffee pot from the cabinet in the kitchen. He was trying to trip her up, and he was just wasting his time. Because he had the wrong person. The sooner she convinced him of that, the sooner she could get down to the business of settling in.

"Ask anyone in town," Georgie urged him. The warm glow from the fireplace cast itself over her, coloring her cheeks, lightly glancing along her frame. "They'll all tell you the same thing. That I was out on the rodeo circuit. Around here, everybody knows everybody else's business." That used to annoy her. It didn't anymore. Now it just gave her a feeling of belonging.

"And what is it you do on the rodeo circuit?" Nick asked, not that he really believed her. Men who wore oversized hats and walked as if born on a horse hit the rodeo circuit, not a little bit of a woman with a big mouth and a child in tow.

"Win," Georgie answered tersely. "You'd better like your coffee black," she informed him, raising her voice as she walked into the small, functional kitchen and poured water into the battered coffee pot. "Because I don't have any milk handy. The last of it was used to drown a few chocolate chip cookies who were minding their own business about five hours ago."

Georgie looked at her daughter and grinned, remembering the snack they'd shared during the impromptu picnic she'd arranged for the little girl. She'd done it to lift Emmie's spirits because her daughter had been so sad about leaving the rodeo circuit. Georgie had talked at length about the ranch in glowing terms, reminding her daughter about all the people who loved her and were looking forward to celebrating her fifth birthday next week right here in Esperanza. By the time the cookies were gone, Emmie couldn't wait to get home.

"Black'll do fine," he told her.

As he watched, he saw Georgie stretch up on her toes, trying to reach the two white mugs on the top shelf. Crossing over to her, he took the mugs down and placed them on the counter. Georgie scooped them up and made her way back to the hearth.

He found himself following her.

Nick could feel Emmie's eyes boring into him, suspiciously watching his every move like some stunted hawk.

"This doesn't change anything," he warned Georgie,

referring to her effort at hospitality by making him something to drink.

"It's coffee, not a magic elixir," she responded. "I didn't think it was going to turn you into a prince. I'm just being neighborly."

"I'm not your neighbor."

"And for that, I am eternally grateful," Georgie told him. With the coffee brewing, she turned her attention to the center of her universe, her daughter. "Okay, Miss Emmie," she took Emmie's hand, "time to get you ready for bed."

But Emmie wiggled her hand out of her mother's grasp. Her large green eyes darted toward the stranger in their house, then back at her mother. "Mama, please?" Emmie pleaded.

In tune with her daughter, Georgie didn't need Emmie to spell it out for her. She could all but read her mind. Tired or not, there was no way the little girl was going to fall asleep a full three rooms away from here. Emmie was far too agitated about what was going on. She stood a better chance of having her daughter nodding off here, safely in her company.

Georgie surrendered without firing a shot. "Okay, pumpkin, take the sofa."

Relief highlighted the thousand-watt smile. Emmie wiggled onto the leather couch. "Thank you, Mama," she said happily.

Other than his own horrific childhood, Nick hadn't been around kids for more than a minute here or there. He had absolutely no experience when it came to dealing with them. Nor did he really want any. Kids had their own kind of logic and he had no time to unscramble that.

But his gut told him that what had just transpired was wrong from a discipline point of view. "You always let her win?" he asked Georgie.

Georgie watched him for a long moment, debating whether to tell him to butt out. But saying so wouldn't be setting a good example for her daughter. "I pick my battles," she told him. And, to be honest, she felt better being able to watch over Emmie right now. She didn't fully trust this character, Secret Service agent or not. "Arguing over everything never gets you anywhere."

"You could have fooled me."

"I have no desire to fool you, Mr. Secret Service agent—"

"My name's Nick Sheffield." He knew he was telling her needlessly. After all, she'd read as much on his ID—if she bothered reading it.

Georgie started again from the top. "I have no desire to fool you, Nick Sheffield," she told him. "I just want you to go away."

That made two of them, but under a different set of circumstances. "I'm afraid that's not going to happen right now," he informed her tersely.

Georgie sighed. "So much for *my* lucky streak continuing."

Behind her, the coffee pot had stopped percolating. She turned toward it, and, taking the two mugs she'd brought with her from the kitchen, she poured thick, black liquid into both. She set the pot back on its perch and brought the mugs over to him. Georgie offered him one.

He took it from her a bit leerily and she laughed. "Don't worry, I'm not going to pour it onto your lap." She couldn't resist a quick glance in that area. "Although the thought did cross my mind."

Thank God for small favors, he thought. But she'd stirred his curiosity. "Why not?"

"Because if I did that," she said only after she'd paused to swallow a mouthful, "then you'd think I was guilty. And I'm not," she pointed out.

"What if I think it anyway?"

"Then you're dumb," she told him simply. "Because that means that you're either not looking at the evidence—or ignoring it."

No, he thought, wrapping his hands around the mug, he had to admit that he wasn't looking at the evidence at the moment. He was looking at her. And God help him, he did like what he saw.

Chapter 4

Moving back toward the fireplace, Georgie pushed the coffee pot back on the grating. He heard her ask, "To your liking?" The woman didn't even bother looking over her shoulder as she carelessly tossed the words at him.

The question, coming out of the blue, caught him completely off guard. Was she referring to herself? Did she somehow sense that he was watching her, or was his reflection alerting her to the fact that he was studying her?

"What?"

"The coffee." Turning around, she nodded at the mug he was still holding in both hands. "Is it to your liking?"

Lost in his thoughts, some of which he shouldn't be having, Nick hadn't sampled the coffee yet. To rectify that, he took a sip—and discovered he had to practically chew the mouthful before he could swallow it. Accustomed to the coffee from a lucrative chain this offering she had prepared tasted almost raw to him. It certainly brought every nerve ending in his body to attention.

Nick cleared his throat after finally swallowing what he had in his mouth. He looked at her incredulously as she sipped, unfazed, from her mug.

"It's a little thick, don't you think?" he asked, pushing out each word. Was it coffee, or had she substituted tar?

Georgie seemed mildly surprised at his comment. "Most men I know like their coffee strong."

"You might not realize it, but there's a difference between strong coffee and asphalt."

Georgie lifted one shoulder in a careless shrug. "You don't have to drink it if you don't want to," she told him, reaching for the mug.

He drew the mug back out of her reach, knowing that to surrender it would somehow diminish him in her eyes. Nick had a feeling he was going to need all the edge he could get.

"That's okay," he assured the woman. "I'll drink it."

Nick saw a slight, amused smile curve the corners of her mouth. He had the uncomfortable feeling she was looking right through him. "Nobody said 'I double-dog-dare you,' Mr. Secret Service agent—sorry, 'Mr. Sheffield,'" she corrected herself. "If you don't like the coffee, don't drink it."

He held on to the mug anyway. "Just takes some getting used to." *Like you,* he added silently. Looking around at the darkened room, he changed the topic. "You really turned off the electricity."

A little slow on the uptake, aren't you, Sheffield? But she kept the observation to herself and replied, "That's what I said."

Then how had she sent those e-mails? he caught himself wondering. Eyeing her thoughtfully, Nick came up with the only alternative he could think of off the top of his head. "Then you took your computer with you?"

She thought of the refurbished tower and monitor she'd bought roughly six months ago, a couple of weeks before she'd gone back on the road with Emmie. She'd had the previous owner set it up for her, but personally had no interest in exploring its properties. It was like an alien entity to her.

She looked at him as if he'd lost his mind. "Now why would I do that?"

It took him a moment to realize she was serious. His own computer was almost an appendage with him. He took the notebook everywhere he went and couldn't conceive of a day going by without his checking his e-mail account. In his opinion, doing so was what kept the world small and manageable. He liked being in control, in the know. This was the best way.

"To stay in touch," he finally said when he saw that she was waiting for a response.

Georgie frowned. The man was obviously just another drone. Too bad, but then, what had she expected? He worked for the government. A clone without an imagination—except where it didn't count.

"They've got phones for that, Sheffield." She could see that her answer didn't make an impression on the Secret Service agent. "As I said before, I don't believe in computers," she told him. "I don't believe in sitting on my butt, sending messages to people I don't know—" what the hell was a "chat room" anyway? "—and living vicariously through someone else's stories. I'm out there, every day, experiencing life, I don't have to get mine secondhand." And then she gave him a reason she was certain he couldn't argue with. "Besides, my computer is too damn big to cart around across the state."

It was time he stopped trading words with this woman and start investigating. He was better at that anyway.

He'd already given the inside of the house a once-over when he'd first arrived on the property. "That tower in the bedroom room is the only computer you have?"

"Yeah. Why? How many computers do you have?"

Presently, he owned three. He had the one in his office at the Senator's headquarters, plus a full-sized one in his apartment. And, of course, there was the one that he always took with him, the notebook that contained everything the other two did, plus more. But he had no intention of telling her anything.

"This isn't about me," he reminded her.

Georgie lifted her chin defensively. Every time she started to think that maybe the man was human, he suddenly sprang back to square one all over again. It was like trying to take the stretch out of a rubber band and having it snap back at you.

"It's not about me, either," she retorted tersely. "Whoever you're looking for," Georgie informed him, "it isn't me."

What else could she say? He laughed dryly. "Mind if I don't take your word for that?"

"I'd like to say that I don't mind—or care—about anything you do, but because it affects me and mine—" she glanced over toward the sofa and Emmie, who, by virtue of her silence, she knew to be asleep "—I do. I mind very much."

"Afraid of what I'll find?" Nick asked. He was

already on his way to her bedroom. The fact that she had it set up in her bedroom rather than out in plain sight told him that she was probably trying to keep her little girl away from it and unaware of what she was doing. From what he'd observed she was a decent mother.

"No, I'm afraid that you'll plant something," she shot back, abandoning her mug as she hurried after him. "Hey, do you have a search warrant?" she challenged, suddenly remembering that on the TV dramas she'd occasionally watched, they always asked for a search warrant before allowing the police to turn their homes upside down. "Well, do you?"

"*Patriot* Act," Nick cited, reaching her bedroom. The existence of the act allowed for shortcuts and he mentally blessed it now. "I don't have to have one."

"That has something to do with finding suspected terrorists," Georgie remembered. The second the words were out of her mouth, her eyes widened in utter stunned surprise. She could only come to one conclusion. "So now you think I'm a terrorist?" This was becoming too ridiculous for words.

"Lots of definitions of a terrorist," he told her, pushing open her door. The small bedroom had only moonlight, pouring in through the parted curtains, to illuminate it. "Not all of them come with bombs strapped to their chests. The definition of a terrorist is someone who brings and utilizes terror against their victim."

This time, when he entered the room, Nick noticed something that had escaped his attention the last time he'd looked around the bedroom.

The computer tower and small monitor were set up on a rickety card table with a folding chair placed before it. The set-up stuck out like a sore thumb. What hadn't stuck out—at first glance—was the rectangular item stashed underneath the table. Pushed far back, it was attached to both the computer and the monitor.

"What's that?" he asked her.

"What's what?" she snapped. Was he talking about the computer? He would have had to have been blind to miss it. Just because she had a computer didn't mean she was guilty of sending threatening e-mails to his precious Senator Colton.

Damn it, Clay had told her to keep a gun in the house and she would have, if Emmie wasn't around. Not that she thought the little girl would play with it. Emmie knew better than that. But she knew her daughter. In a situation just like the one that had gone down in the front yard, if there'd been a gun around, Emmie would have grasped that instead of the tire iron—and used it. Emmie was very protective of her.

Almost as protective of her as she was of Emmie.

As she watched, Sheffield toed the rectangular object under the card table she'd put up. "This."

She looked down at it, then at him. Georgie shook her head. This was the first time she was seeing it. "I have no idea."

Squatting down, he used what moonlight was available to examine it. "Well, I do."

"Then why d'you ask?"

He ignored her annoyed question as he rose again to his feet. Nick dusted off his knees before answering. "It's a generator."

"No, it's not," she countered. She jerked her thumb toward the back of the house, beyond the bedroom. "The generator's outside, just behind this room—and it's broken," she added before Sheffield was off and running again. Repairing the generator was one of the things on her "see-to" list. The one that was almost as long as Emmie was tall. The house needed a lot of work, but because she was going to be home from now on and she was pretty handy, she figured she'd be able to finally get around to getting those things done.

If she could ever get rid of this man.

"Yes, it is," he informed her. "It's a portable generator."

As if to prove it, he switched the generator on. It made a churning noise, like someone clearing his throat first thing in the morning. The uneven symphony took a few minutes to fade.

Once all the lights on the machine's surface had come to life and ceased blinking, remaining on like so many small, yellow beacons, Nick rose and turned on the computer. It made even more noise than the generator, including a grinding noise that didn't sound too promising.

Georgie stared angrily at the portable generator. Sheffield had to have planted it earlier. There was no other way it could have gotten into her house. "That's not mine."

He ignored her protest. It was in her house, in her bedroom. Whose would it be if not hers?

The tower's hard drive continued grinding as it went through its paces. He half expected it to freeze up on him.

"You really should think about getting a laptop," he commented.

"What I should get," Georgie retorted, gritting her teeth, "is a gun so that I could keep trespassers off my property."

He wasn't listening. The grinding noise had finally abated and the hourglass had faded from the screen. Sitting gingerly down on the folding chair, he began to type. Braced for resistance, Nick found he was able to logon with no trouble. No password was necessary. The woman hadn't even taken the simplest of precautions. Go figure.

"And when you get that laptop," he commented, "you need to think about getting it encrypted."

Georgie watched him intently, convinced he would do something to her machine to make her look guilty. She only hoped she could stop him before he did it—not too likely because she had absolutely no idea what she was looking for him to do. "Encrypted?"

"Yes." He glanced at her for a second. She didn't know what he was talking about or she was pretending not to. "You know, password-access only. That way people wouldn't be able to get onto your computer."

She'd heard that if someone was really determined to get into your computer, they'd find a way. "But you would."

Nick couldn't help the tinge of satisfaction he felt from surfacing. He'd come a hell of a long way from that bully in the school yard.

"Yes," he agreed, "I would."

She crossed her arms before her, watching his fingers fly across the keyboard. Something was not right about a man being able to type that fast. Hands like that should be roping in a steer, not typing.

"So the people I should be protecting myself against with that password thing could still—what's the word? Hack?—into my computer."

"That's the word," he confirmed. "Hack." Nick laughed under his breath, although there was no humor to the sound. She played the innocent well, he'd give her that. "Guess you're right. Having a password wouldn't help. It would be pointless."

An uneasiness descended over her as she listened to

the keys clicking on the keyboard. "So is your nosing around on my computer," she insisted.

Bingo, he thought. He'd gotten into her online account and accessed her recent activities. It was right there in living color.

"Oh, I don't know about that." Rising from the chair, he started to turn the monitor toward her so that she could see what he knew she was already familiar with. He felt the card table begin to wobble.

Quickly bracing it, Nick muttered a few choice, ripe words under his breath. They mingled with his suppressed sigh.

Well, that hadn't taken very long, he thought sarcastically. And he had just begun entertaining the idea that maybe, just maybe, she was telling him the truth about not having sent those e-mails. Just went to show that con artists came in all sizes and shapes. Even pleasing ones.

Especially pleasing ones, he reminded himself. People like the Grady woman capitalized on their looks.

So much for believing in fairy tales, he thought. He raised his eyes to hers. Tapping the screen, he asked, "Do you know what this is?"

Georgie narrowed her eyes into angry green slits. "A frame-up."

Not by a long shot, he thought. "It's the Senator's Web site. And these," he pointed to communication at the bottom of the screen, "are the e-mails you sent to him just in the last couple of days."

Georgie forced herself to look at the screen. The e-mail Sheffield was pointing to was particularly venomous and it was signed "Lone Star Girl." But that was no proof that it was her.

This was surreal, she thought, fighting off a feeling

of desperation. This wasn't happening. She was asleep, that was it. She'd fallen asleep behind the wheel of the truck and maybe even crashed into a ditch. She was having hallucinations.

This *had* to be a hallucination.

This was real. He was real. And he was lying. She didn't know how he'd managed to do it while she was watching him, but somehow, he'd gotten that e-mail onto the computer.

Her jaw hardened. "No, I didn't." And there was no way he was going to get her to say that she did.

No more games, Nick thought. It was time to wrap this up. He pointed to the screen again. "Proof's right here. This is your computer, your account."

"I don't care if that damn message is painted across the Grand Canyon," she informed him hotly, tired of being intimidated. "I didn't write to your precious Senator. I don't even *have* an e-mail account."

"Then what's this?" he asked.

She threw up her hands. How the hell did she know how it got there? "A mistake. A glitch. I don't know. Machines are prone to errors." Her eyes blazed as she glared at him. "Nothing is foolproof and this proves it."

She'd emphasized the word "fool." Another dry laugh escaped his lips as he shook his head. "Calling me names isn't going to help you."

But strangling him might, she thought angrily. Georgie struggled to draw her patience to her and sound calm. "Look, I'm only going to say this one more time. I haven't been home in the last five months. The computer has. Somebody—"

Georgie clamped her mouth shut as her own words and the thought behind them resonated in her head. Sheffield hadn't planted this. Somebody had broken in. That had to be it. And if they broke in, there had to be evidence that they'd been here, right? Things would have been moved around, maybe the drawers had been ransacked. Something, anything, to show that someone had trespassed on her property, maybe even stolen her identity.

The idea took root, shaking her down to her very toes. Her throat tightened. Maybe she was overreacting. Oh, God, she hoped so.

Without another word, Georgie spun on the worn heel of her boot and hurried from the bedroom. The second she was out in the hall, she made a beeline for the kitchen.

Catching him off guard, it took Nick a second to realize that she'd bolted. He immediately hurried after her. Unable to refute him, she was making a break for it, he thought. Not on his watch. Not after he'd stood all those hours in this god-forsaken place, waiting for her.

"You can't run!" he called after her.

The woman didn't bother to answer him.

Expecting her to dart into the living room to grab her daughter, Nick was more than a little stunned to see Georgie run into the kitchen instead.

Was there a back door? Was she abandoning her daughter and making a run for it?

Nick strode into the kitchen after her and grabbed her by the wrist just as she'd reached the counter, spinning her around.

"Let me go!" she cried in outraged frustration. She struggled to yank her wrist out of his grasp.

For a little thing, she was pretty strong, he thought. Had to be all that rodeoing stuff she claimed to be doing.

Well, it wasn't going to do her any good. As a girl, she was strong, but she was no match for him.

"It'll go a lot easier on you if you surrender," he counseled.

"The hell it will."

Ever since she was a little girl, she'd hated the word "surrender." It meant weakness to her and she would rather die than admit to that.

Still trying to pull out of his grasp, Georgie raised her knee the way instinct and her older brother Clay had taught her, determined to award Sheffield the kind of pain that would make him set her free.

But Nick anticipated her move. "Oh, no, you don't," he cried.

Twisting, he jerked out of the way, throwing her off balance, then bodily pushed her against the wall. Pressed up against her, with his adrenaline running high and her breath hot against his chin, it took Nick a second to catch himself because his body was reacting to hers, taking him to places that his training did not allow for.

For two cents, he'd kiss that mouth of hers into silence.

It would have been the costliest two cents he would have ever had to pay and he knew it.

"You can't run," he told her, his breath coming in short spurts.

"I'm not running, I just want to get a damn flashlight," she cried.

Everything inside of her was scrambling madly—and anger had very little to do with it.

Chapter 5

Georgie's words burrowed through the wall of preconceived notions in his head. This matched none of them.

"A flashlight?" he asked.

Georgie glared up at him, doing her best not to think about the havoc his closeness caused within her. How could she be so angry and react to him on a far different level at the same time?

"Yes," Georgie hissed. "A flashlight."

Nick released her and took a step back—as much for her sake as his own. He wasn't the kind who usually entertained temptation, much less succumbed to it, but right now, he had to admit temptation was an irritating and unwanted guest.

"Why didn't you say so?" he fairly growled at Georgie.

She tossed her head, trying to ward off the effects of being so close to him. "I didn't realize I had to ask for permission to get something in my own house."

"We Secret Service agents are a jumpy lot," he told her drily. "Sudden moves make us nervous."

She looked at him for a long moment, unable to gauge whether he was serious. "I guess that means you don't attend many rodeos," she finally said.

"Never felt the urge." Although he found himself oddly curious about the events that would entice the likes of someone who looked like her to participate— if she was telling the truth and that was a big "if." He asked a question that was more to the point. "What do you need the flashlight for?"

Turning around, Georgie opened one of the drawers beneath the counter and took out the flashlight she kept there. She flipped it to the On position and it cast a waning beam.

The batteries were running down, she thought. Something else she needed to see to. The mental list was growing.

"So I can tell ghost stories." For a second, she put the flashlight beneath her chin so that it cast an eerie illumination on her face. And then she lowered it, as well as her sarcastic tone, again. "What do you think I need it for?"

He laughed drily. The woman was one for the books. "With you, my first guess probably wouldn't be the right one."

She had no patience with playing games, not with him, not now. She pointed the flashlight away from him. "I want to look around to see if anything's been taken or misplaced."

Again, she couldn't begin to imagine why anyone would want to break into her ranch house, other than for shelter during a storm. She had no hidden money stashed away in a wall safe, no valuable pieces of jewelry stuffed beneath her mattress or even any high-tech electronic equipment lying around. Everything she had—except for Emmie—she had either bought secondhand or had been given as a hand-me-down.

"Because you think someone broke in."

From his tone, she surmised that he still didn't believe her. "Yes, I think that someone broke in. That generator isn't mine."

"Someone broke in and brought you something rather than stealing something."

He was mocking her. She knew it sounded pretty stupid, but she didn't appreciate his pointing it out or using that tone with her. Her hand tightened around the neck of the flashlight. For a split second, she wished she was Emmie's age and had an excuse to act on her impulses. She would have loved to have hit this man and his mocking tone into the latter half of next week.

But she reined in herself and fell back on using logic and reason—even if he didn't have any. "You said you found the door unlocked."

"I did."

Well, that cinched it for her, if not for him.

"I always lock the door when I leave the house." She saw him look at her with doubt. She just knew he was going to say something again about people in rural areas being trusting. So she headed him off. "Times aren't what they used to be," she explained. "I trust my neighbors, but as you've just proven, people other than neighbors can come by. Those are the ones I lock my door against." And then she sighed, shaking her head as she began to scan the area with her flashlight. "Without much success, apparently," Georgie added under her breath, but audibly enough for Nick to overhear.

He was about to make a comment on what she'd just said when he saw her freeze. He saw nothing that would cause her to stop talking.

"What?"

She aimed her flashlight directly at what had caught her attention. She wasn't the world's best housekeeper, but she kept things neat, especially when she was going away.

"There's a newspaper by the window seat." Still aiming the flashlight on the paper, Georgie quickly crossed to the window seat.

Nick fell into step behind her. "So?"

She picked up the newspaper and, with the flashlight in one hand, looked at the date on the front page. "So, it's from last week." She dropped the newspaper back on the window seat.

He still didn't see what she was getting at. "Again, so?"

Did she have to hit him over the head with it? "I wasn't here last week."

That again. Nick shook his head, his skepticism all but shining like a beacon. "So you say."

She was tired of his not-so-veiled accusations. Tired of protesting and saying the same thing, over and over again.

"I can give you a list of the towns I've been in. I pretty much shadowed the circuit. I entered one if not more events in each town. People saw me. My daughter thinks I'm special, but even so, I haven't found a way to be in two places at the same time." And if that didn't make him shut up and finally go away, she didn't know what would.

The faintest hint of amusement lifted the corners of his mouth. "Would you want to be?"

What kind of a question was that? Was he deliberately trying to hassle her? Of course he was. Well, then, she just wouldn't let him, that's all.

Raising her chin, she gave him an answer she was fairly certain he couldn't argue with.

"Every mother wants to be in two places at once, if she's worth anything. She wants to be with her child and she wants to be doing whatever it is she needs to do to earn a living for that child." At least, that was the way she'd felt since the day Emmie was born and she'd fallen instantly and madly in love with the tiny baby. Taking her along with her on the rodeo circuit was the closest she could come to being with Emmie and still earn a living for them at the same time.

She had passion, he'd give her that. Passion that unfortunately drew him in. It took effort for him to mentally pull back. "Is that supposed to convince me that you're innocent?"

Maybe she *would* give in to her impulse and just smack him. It wasn't as if Sheffield didn't deserve it. "No, my innocence is supposed to convince you that I'm innocent."

Instead of commenting on her claim, Nick looked at her thoughtfully. She looked damn sincere. "How long do the events that you participate in last? Your portion of them," he elaborated.

She shrugged, thinking. "I don't know. Five, six minutes maybe." Although there were times, like when her horse had stumbled last year, when it had felt like an eternity—going by in slow motion. "Why?"

"Five, six minutes," he repeated. "So you wouldn't have to hang around all day if you didn't want to, would you? Just show up for your part of the contest and then you could leave."

She knew what he was getting at. Obviously he thought the events were all close by. Either that, or the man thought she had some kind of magical horse that flew her home and back. If she had a magical horse that could fly, she wouldn't have to be competing on the rodeo circuit in the first place.

But instead of telling him that, or what kind of an asinine blockhead she thought he was, she said something she knew he could understand. "I've got people to vouch for me."

She saw Sheffield raise a skeptical eyebrow. "Friends?"

"Yes, friends." Something she doubted that Sheffield had.

His expression didn't change. "Friends lie for friends."

There was no winning with this man. Or reasoning for that matter. Her frustration rose another notch. She struggled to keep her voice down in order not to wake Emmie.

"Are you determined to arrest me?"

He tried to sound impartial, even though right now, everything *did* point to her.

"I'm determined to make the threatening e-mails stop and have whoever has been sending them up on charges because, in case you didn't know, it's against the law to threaten a candidate for the presidency of the United States."

She resented his implication. That she was some hick who had no knowledge of the law. They weren't that far from San Antonio and even if she hadn't been to college, she'd been to the school of hard knocks and she'd graduated at the top of her class.

"Yes, I know that," she said between gritted teeth, "And again, *no* I didn't do it. Now someone, as you so cleverly pointed out by pulling up the Web thingy on my computer—"

"Web site," he supplied, interrupting her.

"Whatever," she said, struggling to rein in her temper. "Someone did and according to you, they did it from here. I know it wasn't me, so by process of elimination, it had to have been someone else. *Someone who broke in*," she emphasized. "I don't know who or why, but it *wasn't* me. I don't know how else to say it." She'd pretty much reached the end of her rope here. *"IT WASN'T ME,"* she enunciated the words close to his ear so that not even a single syllable was lost on him.

"There's a newspaper I didn't bring in on the window seat and a dinky generator I never saw before stashed under my card table. Someone's been here." Her eyes blazed as she looked up at him. "Now you can believe me or not, I really don't care. But I do intend to get to the bottom of this because my house has just been violated and I don't like it."

Marching away from him, she returned to the kitchen and reached for the wall phone.

Nick snapped to attention and quickly cut the distance between them until he was right next to her. "Who are you going to call?"

It had been over four years since she'd found herself answering to anyone. She'd been more or less on her own since then and it grated on her nerves to be bombarded with questions like this—and expected to answer them.

"Somebody who knows I don't lie," she bit off. Lifting the receiver, she began pressing the buttons before she even had the phone to her ear. "The sheriff. Hey, what are you doing?" she cried. The agent's hand had covered hers and he pushed the receiver back down on the hook.

"I can't let you do that," Nick told her simply.

"Why?" she demanded. In the front yard, when she'd threatened to call the sheriff on him, he'd told her to go right ahead. Why was he changing his mind now? "You said I could."

"There's a little matter of jurisdiction."

"This is outside of Esperanza. That puts it into the sheriff's jurisdiction," she retorted. "He's the sheriff for the entire county."

"The e-mails are threats against a United States Senator," he reminded her. "That makes it a federal case."

Incredibly frustrated and stymied, Georgie wanted to scream. "I bet you like making a federal case out of everything."

Nick didn't rise to the bait she'd dangled in front of him and made no comment.

Desperate, not sure what the man was going to do next but fairly certain she wouldn't like it, Georgie tried to appeal to his better nature—if he had one.

"Look, Sheffield, I need someone who knows me. Someone who can make you believe that I'm not lying. Someone who can make you understand that I never sent any of those e-mails." *Because I sure can't.*

He supposed there was no harm in throwing her a bone. And there could be a very slim chance that she was telling the truth.

"Okay, let's just say for the sake of argument, you're right," he told her. "You're innocent. You're not the one sending those e-mails." Nick paused, the import of his own words replaying themselves in his head. If what she was suggesting was true, then that shifted the focus. This could be about her, not the Senator.

Or, that could be what she wanted him to think.

Nick explored the first question. "Why would

someone set this up to make it look as if you were threatening the Senator's life?"

How many times did she have to say it? "I don't know." She uttered each word carefully so that maybe this time, it sank in. "If I did, believe me I would tell you."

His mind whirling, he hardly heard her. "Do you have enemies?"

She shrugged. She didn't like to think so. "I don't know. Everyone's got enemies, I suppose. But nobody I know wants to see me in prison. Not even Kathy Jenkins."

Nick's interest was immediately aroused. They had a name. "Kathy Jenkins?" he repeated, his manner coaxing her to continue.

"I beat her in the barrel racing events in the last three towns."

The surge of adrenaline subsided as suddenly as it had begun. Nick sincerely doubted that all this was about barrel racing.

He tried again. "Nobody has it in for you? Your ex-husband? A jilted boyfriend? Some girl whose boyfriend you stole?" With each question, he watched her face for a reaction. Instead, he saw a wall going up.

"You always think the worst of people?" she asked.

"It's my job."

"If my daughter wasn't sleeping in the other room, I'd tell you what you could do with your job." Blowing out a breath, she went down the list he'd just raised. "There's no ex-husband," she deliberately avoided his gaze, wanting to see neither pity nor judgment in his eyes, "there's no jilted boyfriend and the only thing I ever 'stole' wasn't a boyfriend. It was a twenty-five cent candy bar when I was six. My mother made me give it back and apologize. I worked off my 'offense' by straightening bottom shelves in the grocery store for Mr. Harris for a month."

He could almost see that. She probably looked a lot like her daughter at that age. "Sounds like a strict mother," he commented.

Georgie instantly went on the defensive. "She was a good mother."

Well, there was a sore point, he thought. He wondered why.

"Didn't mean to imply otherwise," he told her. Nick looked at her for a long moment, common sense wrestling with a budding gut feeling—or was that just temptation in another guise? "I'll look into it," he finally said.

It had been so long between comments, she wasn't sure what he was talking about. "Excuse me?"

"Your alibi."

She hated the way that sounded, as if a lie was immediately implied. She didn't have an "alibi," she had a life. But in this case, she supposed having an alibi was a good thing.

"Then you believe me?"

He'd always played things very close to the vest. It was better that way—for everyone. "Let's just say I'm trying to keep an open mind."

He didn't strike her as someone who normally kept an open mind. "I guess maybe Emmie's hitting you with the tire iron did some good."

"Don't push it," he advised. "I just don't want to be wrong."

"I wouldn't want you to be wrong either," she told him pointedly. The subject of logistics occurred to her. "Does this mean you're going to be staying here?"

He nodded slowly. It wasn't something he was happy about, but this was going to take at least a day, if not more.

"For now."

"I've got a guest room in the back." She jerked her thumb toward the rear of the house.

He knew that. He'd done a very thorough surveillance of the house when he'd first gotten here, thinking he'd find the perpetrator at home.

The room in question was full of boxes filled with all kinds of things, none of them new. "You're using it for storage."

"There's a bed in there," she volunteered. The boxes were piled on top and all around it. "You're welcomed to it."

He could just see her trying to wall him in. "Here's just fine."

Here? Did he mean to stretch out on the sofa? She supposed she could move Emmie and hope the little girl went on sleeping. Unlike her brother Ryder, who could sleep while being tossed around in the funnel of a twister, Emmie was easily roused.

Moving over to the sofa, she began to pick up her daughter.

As with the flashlight, Nick caught her wrist and stopped her. "What are you doing?"

She wished he would stop touching her. "Moving Emmie so that you can have the sofa."

"Leave her where she is," he instructed, releasing her wrist. "I don't want the sofa. I'll take the chair." He nodded toward it.

Toward the left of the sofa, the item under discussion was an overstuffed chair that had once belonged to her grandfather, the famous rodeo star she'd been named after and whose last name she'd taken when she began riding herself. George "Rattlesnake" Grady. He'd favored that chair for some fifteen years and it still retained his shape. She loved it dearly, but it was hardly comfortable enough for Sheffield to spend the night in.

Georgie eyed him dubiously. "You won't get much sleep in it."

"I don't intend to sleep."

Which meant that he intended to watch her, she thought, immediately suspicious. And that in turn put them back in two separate camps.

Still, he wasn't slapping handcuffs on her and shouting that she was under arrest. She supposed that she could deal with anything short of that.

And come the morning, she promised herself, after she deposited her winnings into the bank, she'd find a way to set Mr. Secret Service agent straight.

Once that happened, her life as Georgie Grady, rancher, could finally begin.

Chapter 6

"What?"

Georgie stared across the counter at the bank teller as if he were babbling gibberish.

It was just a little after nine in the morning and Georgie stood in the center window of the First Western Bank. Of the two banks housed in Esperanza, First Western was the older, more established one. That was why she'd originally chosen it. Safety and stability had always been exceedingly important to her.

Getting here this morning was a semi-victory on her part. A victory because that Secret Service agent who'd invaded her life hadn't wanted her to go into town. Semi because in order to leave the house at all, she'd had to accept that he was accompanying her. He'd told her in no uncertain terms that he wouldn't allow her to leave his line of sight for more than five minutes. Five minutes being the amount of time, according to the insufferable man, that a person should be able to take a shower and get dressed again. She hadn't bothered pointing out how ridiculous that was because she'd been in a hurry to get to the bank to put her money away.

Because she'd been in a hurry, Georgie had given in to him and even agreed to let him drive Emmie and her in his sedan. All she'd wanted to do was to get to the bank to make this final deposit.

And now all she wanted was not to throw up. Within the last minute, her stomach had twisted into a knot and then risen up into her throat.

If only she could do the last few minutes over again. Walk in, nod at the teller and have the man take her deposit slip with a smile, and not say what he'd just said.

She just couldn't have heard him correctly.

Javier Valdez looked at her over the tops of his small, rimless glasses. "I said I guess we're going to have to open an account for you."

That made absolutely no sense.

A feeling of impending doom tightened about her throat. She fought to ignore it.

"But I already have an account," Georgie reminded him. To back her up, she pushed forward the bankbook she'd brought with her, along with her deposit slip and the money she'd won during the last five months. "This one. Trudy Miles opened it for me the day before she retired," she remembered. "It was the same month that Emmie was born."

The month she'd realized that she wasn't a child anymore. Eighteen or not, she was a mother. A mother with responsibilities. Clay had given her the hundred dollars that she'd deposited that day. It was a gift for

Emmie, her brother had told her. He was giving her money because he "wasn't any good at buying stuff for babies." Georgie could remember tearing up as she'd made that first deposit.

Now tears threatened to come for a completely different reason.

Javier frowned. "But you closed that account," he told her gently. "Said you lost the bankbook so we had to match up your signature. Don't you remember?"

That was impossible. She hadn't been here in five months. She *hadn't*.

"You saw me?" she challenged. Behind her, she heard Sheffield shifting his weight. Probably getting ready to handcuff her and lead her off, she thought. With all her heart, she wished the man was somewhere else. Preferably in hell.

"Everybody saw you," Javier told her with a soft laugh. "That red hair of yours is hard to miss." He smiled at her. A widower, it was obvious that he was a little smitten with her. "Nobody else around here's got hair the color of a Texas sunset."

"But that's not possible," Georgie insisted.

Listening to the exchange between the Grady woman and the bank teller, Nick found himself thinking that the distress and anguish in her voice sounded genuine. She was probably an accomplished actress. Most con artists were and this was beginning to take on the shape of a con.

But still, he couldn't quite shake off the effect of her voice.

Moving forward so that he stood beside Georgie, Nick appraised the short, dark-haired teller. "Were you the one who closed the account for her?"

Javier's black eyes darted toward Georgie, as if to

silently ask if it was all right for him to answer the question. "Is he with you?"

Beads of sweat slid down her spine at the same time a chill took hold of her. Javier's voice echoed in her head. It took her a second to make sense of the question. She was doing her best to block the onslaught of some very terrifying thoughts.

"For now, unfortunately, yes," she reluctantly acknowledged.

Javier's eyes shifted back to the tall man beside Georgie. "No, I didn't. Mr. Welsh did."

"Can you get him over here?" Under no circumstances could that be mistaken for a request. It was a tersely worded command.

One that clearly made Javier nervous. Sheffield probably got a lot of that, Georgie thought. And he probably reveled in it. Right now, she didn't care what the Secret Service agent did as long as he got this mess untangled for her.

Clearing his throat, Javier shook his head. "No, I can't."

Georgie felt Sheffield take a half step closer. The very movement seemed intimidating to Javier. She saw the man's eyes widen.

"And why's that," Nick's eyes dipped down to the teller's name tag. "Javier?"

"Mr. Welsh is on vacation," Javier recited, never taking his eyes off the man beside Georgie. "His daughter's getting married in Colorado, so he and Mrs. Welsh went there."

Pretty convenient, Nick thought. "When did he leave?"

Javier looked like a man whose mind had gone blank. And then, mercifully, he recovered. Partially. "A few days ago."

"Can you get him on the phone?" Nick asked in the same no-nonsense monotone.

Was he actually going to help her? Georgie wondered. The thought made her feel a little better.

Javier opened and closed his mouth several times without actually saying anything intelligible. A squeak emerged. Flustered, he glanced over his shoulder at the small row of desks lined up against the wall.

"Mr. Collins?" Javier's voice cracked as he squeezed out the bank manager's name. "Could you come here, please?"

A tall, somewhat heavyset man in his thirties came over after pausing to close a folder on his desk. Crossing to the teller's window, Allen Collins offered Georgie a genial smile.

"Nice to see you again so soon, Georgie. Emmie," he nodded at the child. "Change your mind about closing your account?"

This was some awful nightmare. It had to be. "I didn't close my account. I haven't been here," she insisted. "I've been on the road. Winning this." She pushed the neatly banded pile of checks forward. "There's got to be some mistake." She silently pleaded with him to agree.

Nick's eyes shifted from the bank manager's face to Georgie's profile. The teller's statement dovetailed nicely to back up the fact that the Grady woman had been here all along, churning out poisonous e-mail. That was his intellectual take on the situation. His gut, however, said something else. Her eyes conveyed that her whole life had been turned upside down. It had him doubting the validity of his own theory.

"No, no mistake," Collins assured her. In the face of

her insistence, his expression seemed just a shade uneasy. Suddenly, he held up his right index finger, indicating that she needed to wait for a moment. The manager crossed back to his desk and the old-fashioned rectangular metal file box he kept there. Flipping through it, he found what he was looking for. Collins removed a single index card and brought it back with him to the window.

Placing the card on the counter, he turned it around so that she could see. "See, there's your signature, plain as day."

Georgie stared numbly at the card. The signature was dated last week. It matched the original one from five years ago down to the circle over the letter *i*.

Was she losing her mind? Or was someone playing a horrible joke on her?

All she could do was repeat what she knew to be true. "I didn't sign this."

"But that's your signature." At this point, the smile on the bank manager's face wore thin.

Georgie was afraid to look at Sheffield, afraid of what she'd see on his face. Smug triumph. What the bank manager was saying made it look as if she'd lied to Sheffield about her whereabouts. As if she'd been here all the time, conducting her life. Raiding her bank account and sending threatening e-mails to damn Joe Colton.

But it wasn't true. None of it.

Stubbornly, Georgie shook her head. "Someone must have forged it. I didn't sign the card, I didn't close the account." Her voice rose as she enunciated each word. "I *wasn't* here."

"Mama was with me, riding in the rodeo," Emmie piped up. The pint-sized defender added in a logical voice, "Somebody stole our money." And then she turned around to look at the man who'd come with them. "Are you going to help us get our money back?"

No way was this a four-year-old, Nick thought. She had to be one of those midgets—what was it they called themselves these days? Little people? She was one of them. And right now, this little person was putting him on the spot.

Rather than answer her directly—he had no idea how to have a conversation with someone too young to vote—Nick looked at the bank manager.

"You have surveillance cameras in this place?" he asked Collins.

The bank manager took offense. The smile on his face vanished without a telltale trace. "Just because we're a little off the beaten path doesn't mean that we're primitive."

Nick heard what he needed to hear. "I take that as a yes. Mind if I see the footage from the day Ms. Grady was supposed to have closed her account?"

Collins squared his shoulders. "I'm afraid that's highly irreg—"

Nick stopped him by taking out his badge and ID and holding them up in front of the man.

The man's small, brown eyes darted back and forth, reading the information over twice, before he finally raised them to look at his face. "Secret Service?" he asked uncomfortably.

Nick's own expression was impassive, giving nothing away. "Yes."

Collins and Javier both gazed uncertainly at Georgie. Collins found his tongue first. "This is a government matter?"

"It's complicated" was all Nick would say.

"No, it's not," Georgie cried, turning toward him. Her bank account had nothing to do with the government. "Someone's stolen my money." She thought of the e-mails, the ones she hadn't sent. Was there a connection? Had someone done all this to get back at her for something? Or was this a random attack? "And my identity."

"Georgie, you don't look so good," Javier observed. There was concern on his drawn face. "You want a glass of water or to sit down, maybe?"

"What I want," she replied, desperately trying to get a grip, "is my money."

This couldn't be happening. By her reckoning, with this last batch of winnings, she should have been up to a little more than three hundred thousand dollars. More than enough to buy her some time and some peace of mind before she decided what she wanted to do with the rest of her life. Instead, someone had wiped her out. All she had left were the winnings in her hand. Thank God for that.

And then, as if she wasn't already reeling from this unexpected turn of events as well as being accused of terrorism by computer, something else suddenly occurred to Georgie.

Oh, dear God, no.

Georgie struggled to keep her hands from shaking as she pulled her wallet out of her back pocket. Flipping it opened, she took out her credit cards. There were four in all. She clutched them for a moment, as if that could somehow keep them safe. Keep them hers.

Watching her, Nick frowned. Now what? "What are you doing?"

Georgie's breath grew shallow. She wasn't going to panic, she wasn't. She knew if she did, she'd scare

Emmie. As it was, she was scaring herself. But this thing was just mushrooming. Before answering, she turned the cards face down one by one.

Picking up the first one, she searched for a toll-free number. "I've got to make some phone calls," she told him, hoping against hope that she was wrong. The sickening, metallic taste in her mouth told her she probably wasn't.

The expression on the manager's face turned compassionate. "You're welcome to use the phone on my desk, Georgie."

She nodded, murmuring, "Thank you."

The manager beckoned her over to the far side of the bank, unlocking a swinging half door so that she and Emmie could enter.

Georgie felt as if she was moving in slow motion, trapped in a nightmare she couldn't wake up from. And all the while she kept telling herself that this couldn't be happening. She had been knocked down so many times before and had always managed to get up again. If the worst came to pass, she could do it again. But this time it would be harder. This time her daughter was old enough to understand what was happening.

Nick followed her, putting his hand out to stop the door as the manager began to close it after Georgie and her daughter had passed through.

"The tapes?" he prodded.

Embarrassed, the manager's face turned a light shade of red. "Yes, of course. Right this way." He led them to a small back room where all their monitors and tapes were kept.

Georgie was barely aware of Sheffield leaving. Very slowly, as if she'd just aged fifty years, she gripped the side arms and lowered herself into the manager's chair.

Taking a deep breath, she pulled the streamlined, black phone closer to her on the desk.

"It's gonna be all right, Mama," Emmie assured her quietly. She offered her mother a big, broad smile.

Georgie almost cried.

She looked into the small, perfect face. That was supposed to be her line. She was the one who was supposed to do the comforting, not be the one on the receiving end.

Doing her best to rally, she gave the little girl's hand a quick squeeze. "Of course it is, Emmie. I just have to make a few calls, get a few things straightened out, that's all."

Georgie hoped to God she sounded convincing.

"It was her." The manager repeated nervously as he entered the small, darkened room. Nick was directly behind him. "The tape'll prove it."

So he'd already said. But the more the manager echoed his statement, the less inclined Nick was to believe that Georgie had actually closed her account. Why go through this big act if she knew it was closed? For whose benefit?

The pieces just didn't fit together.

"Let's just see it" was all that Nick said in response.

He noted that the bank manager seemed to be growing more agitated. Because he'd made a mistake? Or because he was guilty of something? There was no way to tell—yet. This situation was getting messier by the minute.

"Right," Collins agreed, as if forcing himself to sound cheerful. Opening the deep drawer where surveillance tapes from the last month were kept, he rummaged around. "Somebody took them out of order," he complained. He read the dates marked on the side of the tapes under his breath. "Finally." He flashed a smile at Nick, then let it fade when all he got in response was a stony stare.

Plucking out of the drawer the tape in question, he held it up like a trophy. "Here it is," he declared with relief, as if the mere finding of the tape would somehow vindicate him.

Nick nodded toward the video player. "Play it," he instructed.

"Yes, of course." But Collins continued holding the tape in his hands in a manner that indicated he didn't know which end played. "Abby?" Collins turned toward the teller directly outside the small room where the video equipment was kept. "Would you play this for Mr. Sheffield?"

Abby entered dressed in a turquoise skirt so tight it resembled a tourniquet. Her eyes swept over Nick slowly, taking in every inch from head to toe. The appreciative smile was quick in coming.

She'd taken measure of him, Nick thought. As an expert on body language, he could tell she liked what she'd seen.

Abby took the tape from the manager, but her eyes remained on Nick. "It'll be my extreme pleasure," she purred.

Tape in hand, Abby sat down at the video recorder, taking care to sit slow enough to better show off the more compelling parts of her anatomy. Tucking her legs over to one side, she leaned forward and popped the tape into the machine. After glancing over her shoulder at Nick, she hit Play.

"Here we go," she announced.

The time stamp in the corner said it was nine o'clock, which was when the bank opened its doors. Nick had no desire to stand behind the brassy blonde and watch an entire day's worth of transactions.

"Fast forward it," he told her.

Again, she looked over her shoulder at him, her smile particularly seductive.

"Whatever you want," Abby said, her tone indicating that she was open to more than working the buttons on the machine.

Nick ignored her the way he did anything he didn't particularly care for. Focusing solely on the activity on the screen, he watched and waited. Customer after customer came and went across it, all of them resembling characters going through their paces in a keystone cops silent movie.

And then he saw her. Georgie. Tight jeans, work shirt, worn boots and all.

"Slow it down right there," he ordered. Abby complied. It was obvious she had no idea what he was looking for, nor did she want to know.

Nick caught his breath.

There, on the screen, with her telltale red braid hanging down to the small of her back, was Georgie Grady.

Chapter 7

"That's her," Collins said eagerly, needlessly pointing to the screen at the only bank customer on the monitor. There was relief in his voice as he added, "I told you she was here."

Nick ignored the man. He was too busy watching the woman, who was a dead ringer for Georgie, move up to the teller's window and place a briefcase on the counter between them.

"Keep going," he told Abby when she glanced up at him.

The teller on the tape disappeared for a moment. When he returned, he had an index card with him. The signature card, Nick assumed. Within moments of signing the card, the transaction was completed. The woman on the screen took back her briefcase, now filled with what he assumed were the proceeds from her account, and then hurriedly moved away. Nick watched the scene intently.

"Rewind," he instructed. When Abby did as he asked, he had her stop at the same place as before and watched the scene again. And then a third time.

Puzzled, Collins looked at him. "What is it you're looking for?"

Nick blew out a breath, still looking at the screen. "An explanation."

This time it was the teller who glanced up at him and asked a question. "For?"

"For starters, why 'Georgie' kept her head turned away from the camera the whole time." Was it just a coincidence, or was there a reason the woman on the screen had done that?

Something wasn't quite right and he couldn't put his finger on it. Yet. He told Abby to play the tape one more time.

"Most people don't even realize that there's a camera there," Collins told him, trying to be helpful. "Ms. Grady was probably lost in thought and just in a hurry to do whatever it was she wanted to do with all that money she withdrew."

"I know what I'd do," Abby commented. The smile on her lips was seductive as she gazed up at the tall, dark Secret Service Agent at her side.

"Uh-huh," Nick answered, lost in thought. It wasn't clear who the response was directed toward. "Play it again," he instructed.

Maybe he was making too much of this, Nick thought, watching the scene for the fifth time. Maybe he was looking for a zebra when there was a bucking horse right in front of him. After all, the bank manager was certain that the woman on the video tape was Georgie Grady and that did, after all, support his initial theory that the woman had been here all along, sending those threatening e-mails to the Senator that she'd denied having anything to do with it.

Here it was, all neatly gift wrapped for him with a bow on top and he was pushing it away, Nick up-braided himself.

All that was left to do was to arrest the woman and bring her back with him for prosecution.

So why was he hesitating?

Because his gut told him something wasn't right? Or because something a bit lower than his gut was muddying up his thinking?

No, damn it, he wasn't the type to let his personal feelings—when he even had them—to get in the way of his judgment. There *was* something wrong with what he was watching on the tape and he thought he finally had a bead on what it was.

A noise directly behind him had Nick quickly turning around, one hand on the hilt of the weapon he wore.

Georgie was in the doorway, her face ashen. Not because of the firearm. The woman had probably grown up around guns all of her life. No, there was a different reason for the lack of color in her face. One hand on the doorjamb, she looked as if she was struggling to stand up.

"You're on the surveillance tape," he told her, watch-ing her reaction.

She didn't seem to hear him. Or, if she heard, the words apparently didn't penetrate. She made no response to his statement one way or the other.

"There are charges on my credit cards," she told him. The words sounded as if she was being strangled.

"That's what they're for, to charge things with," he replied.

Some of the color returned to her cheeks. She continued to hold on to the doorjamb for support.

"Charges I didn't make," she snapped.

It was official. The unthinkable had happened. Something she had never dreamed of *ever* happening, not to her. She'd read about this in the newspaper. But now she was the victim.

Her identity had been stolen.

Her identity, her money and her life.

Both of their lives, she amended, looking down at her little girl.

"Somebody's stolen my identity." Every single card she owned had been taken and used, even the two she kept as emergency backups, the two she *never* used except for once a year just to keep them active.

The simple sentence got her all of Nick's attention. "Are you sure?"

Georgie felt a wave of hysteria rising. Last night, she'd been flush, sitting on top of three hundred thousand dollars. This morning she was all but broke and fiercely in debt. And about to be arrested. How could everything have gone so wrong so fast?

"Of course I'm sure," she retorted angrily. Did he think this was a game? Why would she do that? What would she gain by pretending that her identity had been stolen?

Georgie unfolded the piece of paper she'd used while speaking to the customer service representatives at the four different credit card companies.

"There's a whole list of charges from stores on the damned Internet. Stiletto heels, fancy clothes, fancier undergarments." She pointed to the name of an exclusive shop that had only recently launched online sales. "CDs by people I wouldn't listen to, DVDs of movies I wouldn't be caught dead watching—"

The mention of stiletto heels and Maid of Paradise bras and microscopic panties had Nick's mind booking passage on a ship he couldn't allow to leave the harbor. Still, for one unguarded moment, he couldn't help imagining what she would have looked like, wearing only those items.

"Planning on doing some entertaining?" he quipped.

Her eyes blazed at the question and even more when she thought of the unknown person who had done all this to her.

"Planning on a murder if I ever get my hands on the person who's responsible for all this," she retorted.

He looked at her for a long moment, playing the devil's advocate. "You still say it's not you."

Georgie squared her shoulders, as if that could somehow help her get the point across more forcefully. "With my dying breath," she told him fiercely. "Not that you believe me." The last sentence fairly sizzled with her anger.

That was just the problem, Nick thought. He was starting to believe her.

He glanced at the bank manager who still stood at the desk. The man was obviously taking in every word and trying—without success—to look as if he wasn't.

"Make me a copy of that section of the tape," Nick instructed.

Clearly feeling that he was off the hook, Collins snapped to attention, more than happy to comply. "Right away," he promised.

Nick heard the bank manager murmuring to Abby,

telling her to make the copy because she was the one running the tape.

That taken care of, Nick took hold of Georgie's elbow and led her out of the small, dark room. Emmie hurried to follow.

"Let's just say," he told Georgie evenly, "for now, that I'm not a hundred percent convinced that that's you on the surveillance tape."

"Of course, it's not me. That's what I've been trying to tell you all along." She shrugged out of his hold. Wanting to remain aloof, curiosity got the better of her. "What makes you think it isn't me?"

"You walk differently." That was what had bothered him while he was initially watching the tape.

Georgie stared at him. She wasn't aware of there being anything unique about her gait. "What?"

Nick elaborated. "The woman on the tape was in a hurry, but she still walked like she knew everyone was watching her. She minced and put a little wiggle in her step. You walk like you've got somewhere else to be and you cut through that distance like a ranch hand. There's nothing feminine about the way you move." Other than her body, he added silently. But that was neither here nor there and certainly not something he was about to admit to her.

She wasn't sure if she was clear about what was going on here. "Are you insulting me or finally coming to my rescue?"

He didn't view it as either and he didn't care for the tone she was using. "I'm making an observation. You want my help or not?"

In a perfect world, Georgie thought, she would have lifted her chin, told him what he could do with his help.

She could handle the situation by herself. But this wasn't a perfect world and without doing a single thing to bring about this awful chain of events, she knew she was in way over her head. Like it or not, she had no recourse but to accept his offer.

Still, the words had a bitter taste in her mouth and burned her tongue as she said them. "I want it."

Nick felt something suddenly clutch his leg. Startled, he looked down to see that the woman's daughter had all but wrapped herself around him.

Emmie smiled up at him gleefully. "I *knew* you weren't as bad as you looked."

He kept forgetting that she was there, a pint-sized recorder with ears, taking in everything and absorbing it rather than letting it go over her head like the average four-year-old.

"You sure she's only four?" he asked Georgie.

"I'm almost five," Emmie announced proudly as her mother gently removed her from the Secret Service agent's leg and then protectively kept her hand on her shoulder. "Mama said we had to come back because Uncle Clay wants to help celebrate my birthday."

"Uncle Clay," Nick repeated, raising his eyes from the child to look at Georgie. "Is that what you have her call your boyfriends?" he asked mildly, giving no indication that her answer, one way or the other, meant anything to him. " 'Uncle?' "

"No, that's what I have her call my older brother." Overwrought, and stressed near to the breaking point, not to mention that she hadn't had any sleep because she'd spent the night verbally sparring with Sheffield, she glared at him. "Don't you pay attention? I said I didn't have a boyfriend."

As he looked at her, Nick found it hard to believe she was single. She was far more than passably pretty. Then again Georgie Grady could also slice any man to bloody ribbons with that sharp tongue of hers and he was fairly certain, given half a chance, that she would run over anyone who got in her way.

"Got that tape for you," Collins called out, coming up behind Nick. He held the tape aloft as if it was the pot of gold at the end of the rainbow.

Georgie shifted uncomfortably. Sheffield had said that he thought the woman in the tape was an impostor, disguised to make people think it was her. What if he was only putting her on? What if he was just saying that to make her put down her guard?

"What are you going to do with that?" she asked Sheffield. "Use it at my trial?"

He'd never believed in putting all his cards on the table until the game was over. This was far from over. "Maybe, maybe not. Right now, I'm going to have it expressed back to Prosperino in California and have my tech support see if he can clean up the picture and magnify the image."

The image. She noted that he didn't refer to the person in question as her. Georgie supposed that it was a start. "Okay."

He was going to need a padded envelope and postage. "This place have a post office?" He tossed out the question to both Collins and Georgie.

"A post office, two banks, a city hall and a sheriff's department. Some people even think we're close to civilized," Georgie answered with a trace of resentment at the way he'd dismissed Esperanza. It was all right for her to feel hemmed in by the town once in a while because she lived here and for the most part, she loved it. But he had no right to look down his nose at it. Or her.

About to comment on her quip, he decided to keep it to himself. He hadn't actually meant what he'd said as an insult, just that Esperanza felt so damn rural to him. He was accustomed to places like Los Angeles and New York where you could find whatever it was you needed within a very small radius.

"Show me" was all he said.

"Fine, I will." Still numb and shaken, Georgie turned on her heel to lead the way out of the bank.

"*We* will, Mama. I know where the post office is, too," Emmie reminded her.

The one bright spot in her life, Georgie thought, taking Emmie's hand in hers. "Sorry," she apologized. "*We* will," she said, correcting herself. Emmie's smile was positively beatific.

"Can we do anything else for you?" Collins called out after Nick.

"I'll let you know," Nick tossed over his shoulder without slowing his pace.

"Who are you calling?" he asked Georgie some twenty-five minutes later.

They'd gone to the post office and he'd gotten the tape off, sending it by overnight express. Once it was on its way, he'd called his tech to alert him to its arrival. Georgie had been unusually quiet through it all and he'd begun to think that maybe the events of the last day had her in a state of shock.

But now, sitting in the passenger seat in the dark sedan he'd rented, Georgie pressed a single button on her cell phone before placing it against her ear. Instead of answering him, she held up her finger, indicating that he'd have to wait his turn. It didn't exactly make him very happy.

"Hi, it's me," she said as someone on the other end apparently picked up. Nick listened, trying to put things together from only half a conversation. "Last night. Look, can you come on up to the house? Something's happened. No, not to Emmie, she's fine." He saw her turn and look over her shoulder at the little girl in the car seat as if to reassure herself. "No, I'm not hurt. Why do you always have to think the worst? Okay, okay, maybe I was a trifle melodramatic, but I really do need to see you." She paused to listen to the person on the other end, then said, "Good. 'Bye." She closed her phone again and slipped it into her front pocket.

"Who were you talking to?" Nick asked again.

Had she called for reinforcements? Was he making a mistake after all, giving her the benefit of the doubt about this? At the very least, he didn't relish the fact that someone else would be nosing around at her house while he was there.

"My brother. One of my brothers," Georgie amended.

These days, she tended to forget about Ryder. She didn't like to dwell on her other brother because then she'd have to think about how Ryder was faring in prison and she didn't like doing that. It made her worry about him despite the fact that he'd been found guilty by a jury of his peers and he had committed the offense that had landed him there. She couldn't help it. He was still, after all, her brother and she could remember him in better days. Remember him with a great deal of affection. Ryder wasn't bad, just misguided. Like her, he missed their mother. And, unlike her, he'd resented their older brother when Clay had taken over as the head of the family.

Nick spared her a look. "You've got more than one?"

He was going to make another call to Steve when he got the chance. He wanted to find out as much as he could about this woman.

"Two," she told him. "Clay and Ryder. Both older." And they both had the tendency to treat her like a child. At times, Clay still did, but then, he was the oldest and saw himself as more of a patriarch than a brother. "I was talking to Clay."

"Where's Ryder?"

She shrugged, deliberately looking out the window. "He's not around right now."

Nick picked up on the odd note in her voice. "Where is he?"

"Not here" was all she said.

It was bad enough that the people in town knew that her brother was in prison. She didn't want Sheffield knowing it as well. He'd probably think of them as being white trash or something equally demeaning. For that matter, she didn't want him to know anything about her family. Someone like Sheffield, with his black suit and his dark aviator sunglasses, would look down on the fact that her mother, a former rodeo star herself, had had an affair with a married man. And that he was a Colton.

In an act of self-defense, she leaned forward and turned up the radio a shade. He'd fiddled with the dials on the way over until he'd located an oldies station. She had nothing against old rock and roll songs, but when she was tense—and she was now and would remain so until everything was squared away again—nothing calmed her down like the familiar. In this case, that meant country and western songs.

She switched the dial over to one of several country and western stations broadcasted in the area. Out of the corner of her eye, she saw Sheffield's shoulders stiffen. Georgie smiled to herself.

Deal with it, she ordered him silently.

Because the woman apparently didn't seem to want to talk about her other brother, he let the subject drop. If he needed to know the whereabouts of this Ryder, he would. For now, he blocked out the tale of a broken-hearted cowboy, singing his tale of woe to the only dependable force in his life, his horse.

Nick sighed. Damn but he hated country music.

A tall, dark-haired, rangy-looking man sat on the front steps of the ranch house. The moment they pulled up in the yard, the man stood up, dusting off his jeans. Nick judged him to be in his mid-twenties. The set-in tan testified to his earning a living by working outdoors.

There was something self-assured about the cowboy. This was a man who led, not followed. Nick was on his guard instantly.

"Uncle Clay," Emmie cried, squirming out of the car seat and leaping from the car. She sailed gleefully into the man's arms as the latter squatted down, arms spread, just as she reached him.

"Man but I've missed you. You must've grown a foot since I last saw you. How's my favorite girl?" he asked, rising and swinging her around.

"I'm fine," Emmie declared. "But Mama's got troubles," she added solemnly.

Holding his niece to him, Clay turned to look at the

stranger with his sister as they both got out of Nick's sedan.

The man wasn't her type, Clay judged. Georgie didn't like men in suits and sunglasses. Too soft. As for him, he didn't trust a man whose eyes he couldn't see when he was talking to him.

"Is that the trouble right there?" he asked Emmie, nodded his head toward the stranger.

Emmie twisted around to see who her uncle was referring to. She giggled and shook her head. It was obvious to Georgie, who came to reclaim her, that her daughter had changed her mind about the man. "No, that's Nick."

Clay looked at the stranger grimly, his deep espresso-colored eyes growing hard. "What's a Nick?" he asked.

Chapter 8

For the space of one moment, Georgie struggled with the very strong desire to just fling herself into Clay's arms and tell him what had happened, starting with Sheffield tackling her in the front yard. Clay would take care of everything for her, the way he used to. The way he had when their mother died.

But she wasn't that little girl anymore. Even back then, she'd had a tendency to resist Clay's protective ways because to be taken care of carried a price tag. It meant surrendering her independence, and independence meant everything in the world to her. Hers had been hard won and it was a trophy she would fight to retain to her dying breath.

So rather than throw herself into her brother's arms, she stood where she was, holding herself in check as she smiled and greeted him warmly.

"Hi, Clay."

"Hi, yourself." Clay nodded at her. His sister had never been the easiest woman to deal with. She only accepted help under loud protest. That was why he'd been surprised when she'd called, saying she needed to see him. This was more like her. "Nice to see you back, rodeo queen. You home for good now?"

Nick noted that Georgie seemed to bristle at the nickname. Or maybe it was the question and the unspoken implication behind it—that her brother didn't want her out there, competing—that had her stiffening.

The laugh that passed her lips was short and rueful. "I was going to be."

Clay's dark eyes slanted toward the man with his sister before he asked, "But?"

Georgie blew out a breath. She was still struggling to get a grip, to stop feeling as if she'd been physically and emotionally violated. "There've been some nasty developments."

Clay's frown deepened. Again he looked at the man who'd gotten out of the driver's side of a dark four-door sedan. His brother radar had gone up the second he saw that. "Like?" he asked.

She did her best to sound removed from what she was saying. The words came tumbling out with no preface, no preamble. "Somebody stole all my money, Clay. And broke into my place while I was gone. Whoever did was sending threatening e-mails to Joe Colton—on my computer."

At the mention of the Senator's name, Clay murmured an ambiguous sounding "Oh."

There was a world of meaning hidden behind the

single word, Nick thought. Something was going on here that he wasn't getting—and he didn't like it.

Never one to mince words, Clay figured he'd held his peace long enough. He nodded toward the stranger. "What's he got to do with it?"

"I work for the Senator," Nick told him before Georgie could say anything. "And I came to bring in the person sending those threatening e-mails."

Reading between the lines wasn't difficult. "It's not Georgie, if that's what you're thinking," Clay informed him. There wasn't so much as an inch of room left for an argument. That settled, Clay shifted his attention back to his sister. "Who stole your money?" he inquired.

It was obvious that whoever it was, the man or woman was going to be in a hell of a lot of trouble once Clay tracked him or her down. Clay did not take kindly to anyone messing with his family. And since he'd washed his hands of Ryder when his younger brother had been sent to prison for sneaking illegal aliens over the border, that left only Georgie—and Emmie.

"I don't know," Georgie answered, doing her best not to let the distress show in her voice. She glanced at Nick as she spoke. "But they think it's me. On both counts."

"You?" he retorted incredulously. "You been traipsing around, following that damn rodeo for the last five months, living out of your trailer like some gypsy." He looked over at the stranger to make sure he'd gotten all that. "Just when the hell were you supposed to have done all this?"

Georgie looked at Nick again. "You have the dates the e-mails were sent, right?"

The petite, incredibly feisty woman had succeeded in

doing what no one else had in recent memory. She'd made him feel foolish even though he was just doing his job.

"On every one of the e-mails," he replied without a shred of emotion.

"My sister doesn't have the time for that kind of stupid nonsense," Clay told him tersely. "I don't think she even knows how to send an e-mail. For the last five months she was too busy trying to win trophies."

"Prize money, Clay," Georgie corrected, annoyed.

How many times did she have to tell him she didn't care about the accolades, the glory part? There was a very practical reason why she'd done what she had. Because competing in rodeo events was all she knew. She'd been put on a horse before she could walk and both her grandfather and her mother had been rodeo legends in their time. Rodeoing was in her genes.

Besides, it was the fastest way she knew to make money. Hell, it was the *only* way she knew how to make money.

"I was trying to win prize money so that Emmie and I could stay put here and she could go to school like a regular little girl come the fall." She glanced down fondly at her daughter.

"I'm not a regular little girl," Emmie interjected with protest, wrinkling her nose with disdain. Fisting her hands, she dug them into her hips the way she'd seen her mother do countless times.

"I know that, sweetie," Georgie told her, kissing the top of her daughter's head, "but we don't want the other kids to hear that. They'll be jealous."

Emmie nodded, understanding. Georgie bit her tongue to not laugh.

"You could have done that without risking breaking

every bone in your body," Clay told her. He'd been after her to quit the moment she'd told him she was going to compete. A lot of things could happen to a woman on the road with only a kid. "I would have been happy to give you the money."

They'd been through all this before. More than once. "I don't want to take your money, Clay."

Clay threw up his hands in frustration. "A loan, then. Damn it all, Georgie, what's my money good for if I can't do what I want with it?" he demanded.

Georgie patted him on the shoulder, the way she used to when she'd tried to calm him down and keep his sun-tanned complexion from turning a bright red.

"I'm sure that you'll find something else to do with it, big brother," she answered. And then she eyed him squarely, her lighter tone changing. "I don't want to be beholden to anyone, Clay, not even you. I'm my own person. If I take money from you, that changes everything."

He didn't see how. Damn it all, Georgie could still frustrate him the way no other woman could. "I'm not buying you, Georgie. I'm not even renting you. I just want to help."

"You can help by coming to Emmie's birthday party next week," she told him brightly, winking at her daughter.

Finding an in, Emmie was quick to try to further her own agenda. "You can buy me a pony, Uncle Clay. I won't give it back."

Again he laughed, this time the sound was softer. "Nice to know one of the women in the family has some sense," Clay told the little girl with affection. His eyes shifted toward Nick and the warmth abruptly evaporated. Clay looked the man up and down. "You some kind of government man?" he inquired.

"He's a Secret Service agent," Emmie was quick to inform him, enunciating the occupation carefully so as not to get it wrong.

Clay's eyes swept over the other man again. He would have pegged him for a member of the FBI or CIA instead. "Oh. You're a long way from home, Secret Service agent. Aren't you supposed to be guarding the President or something?"

"During an election year, we're assigned to the presidential candidates," Nick explained patiently, even though it was against his nature to explain himself at all. But being a stranger and alone here, he began to think he needed all the support he could get. "And someone's been sending threatening letters from your sister's house to the Senator." How many times was he going to have to repeat that story before he could finally leave? he wondered in frustration.

"You got somebody house-sitting?" he asked his sister. Georgie shook her head. "Then someone broke in."

She rolled her eyes. Didn't any man ever listen? "I already told you that."

Clay made up his mind. "That does it. You're getting your things and staying with me, both of you." For his money, they didn't even have to bother to pack. He could send one of hands to do the packing for her. "I've got the bigger place, anyway."

"You've got the much bigger place," Georgie acknowledged, "But that's not the point."

He might have known she was going to argue about this. Nothing came easy when it came to Georgie. "And what is the point, Georgie? Besides the one on top of your head, of course?"

She ignored the dig. Clay was just being frustrated because he knew he couldn't win. "The point is my home is here and nobody is going to run me off it."

He could admire bravery—when it came to someone else, not his sister, not his niece. "You've got Emmie to think of," he pointed out. "What if whoever broke in decides to come back?"

"Then I'll apprehend them," Nick told him, wedging himself into the conversation.

Clay looked at him coldly, as if he'd forgotten about his existence. "And just how to do you intend to do that?"

"By staying here until I can get to the bottom of this," Nick told Georgie's brother. It was obvious that the answer was not to the other man's liking.

Indignation blazed in Clay's dark eyes. "You're not staying here," he informed Nick.

Okay, enough with the big protector, Georgie thought. She got in between the two men. "This is my place, Clay," she reminded him. "I get to say who stays and who goes. And if I want Sheffield to stay here, then he stays here. My decision, not yours."

Judging by the other man's expression, Nick wouldn't have been able to say who was more surprised by her statement, her brother or him. He was tempted to ask her just when he had become part of the home team instead of someone she wanted to get rid of, but he knew to leave well enough alone.

Because of the present complexity of the situation and the doubts that had arisen in his own mind as to her culpability, he had planned to remain here, at the apparent starting point of the e-mails, until this was all resolved—or until he managed to catch Georgie Grady in a glaring lie—he wasn't completely convinced of her innocence. But one way or the other, he intended to get some answers.

Clay sighed. "You always were pig-headed."

Georgie flashed a particularly wide smile for Clay's benefit. "Nice to know that you can count on some things staying the same, right?"

Clay didn't answer. He didn't like the idea of some D.C. government spook watching over his sister. After all, she was nothing to the man. Besides, what if the other man started getting ideas about Georgie? Ideas that had nothing to do with e-mails and everything to do with the fact that his sister was a damn pretty woman.

Clay slipped his hands into his front pockets, rocking back on his boot heels. "I can hang around for a while if you want," he offered.

"You've got a ranch to run," she answered. "A successful ranch," she added. They might have their differences and she resisted his taking charge of her life, but she was proud of her brother and what he had accomplished despite the odds against him. "And I'm a little old to be needing a babysitter."

Clay didn't bother to hide his scorn of Nick. He trusted the Secret Service agent about as far as he could throw him. Less. "I wasn't thinking of you just now."

Since Sheffield had said he was going to try to help her, Georgie felt the need to apologize for Clay's behavior. "You've got to excuse my brother. He's used to being in charge of everything, whether we wanted him to be or not."

Clay took instant umbrage. "You don't have to make excuses for me to a stranger."

The last thing Nick wanted was to be in the middle of a family fight. "I assure you, all I'm interested in is finding out who sent those e-mails."

"And in getting back Mama's money," Emmie reminded him. When he looked down at her, she continued, "Remember? You said that in the bank, that you were going to get back her money."

Even Clay had to laugh at Emmie's interjection. "Don't say anything around half-pint you don't want coming back to haunt you. She doesn't forget a thing. And I mean *nothing*."

Nick looked to Georgie for guidance. "Are most kids her age like that?"

"Most kids *any* age aren't like that," Georgie told him. Draping her arm over the girl's shoulders, she gave her a quick squeeze. "Emmie's one of a kind."

"Unique," Emmie declared, gazing up at her mother. It was obvious that she liked the sound of the word.

Clay ruffled his niece's hair. "That's right, half-pint. Unique." He paused for a moment to turn to his sister. His expression softened. "You sure I can't talk you into coming over to my place and staying there for a few days?"

"I'm sure." Maybe, if things got worse, she'd taken him up on his offer. But right now, she wanted to face this on her own. "You're within hollering range, big brother," she told him cheerfully. "I'll holler if I need you."

"Yeah, right." She was too proud. He didn't believe her for a minute. "When pigs fly."

Georgie grinned, amused. "Definite right after that, I promise."

Clay addressed Nick. "See that nothing happens to

either of them, Secret Service agent. I'm holding you personally responsible if it does." Not that there was much comfort in that, he thought.

"Don't worry, Mr. Grady," Nick assured him. "It won't."

Clay's expression darkened instantly. "The name's not Grady."

Confused, Nick shifted his eyes to Georgie before looking back at her older brother. "Your sister said she wasn't married, so I just assumed that Grady was the family name."

"It is," Clay told him, then added, "Our mother's family."

Taking pity on him, Georgie began to explain, "My grandfather was a rodeo star—"

"Like my grandma," Emmie piped up with pride. George "Rattlesnake" Grady had died before she was born, but her mother's stories had made the man seem vividly real to the little girl.

Clay doled out his words slowly. "Grady was their last name."

Georgie picked up the thread. "I took it as my stage name." Nick felt as if he was suddenly a spectator at a tennis match. "To keep the family tradition alive." That was apparently as much as she was willing to share at the moment. Turning on her heel, she faced her brother. It was obvious that she was dismissing him even though she'd been the one to ask him to come over to begin with. Calling on a woman's prerogative, she'd had a change of heart. "I'll call you if anything comes up."

Clay didn't look as if he believed her for a moment. "Yeah."

"I promise," Georgie repeated earnestly. "You'll be the first to know."

Emmie tugged on her shirt, her lower lip stuck out like a little perch. "Not me, Mama?"

She grinned. No matter how awful she felt, Emmie always managed to cheer her up, just by being there. "All right, Uncle Clay will be the second to know." She looked up at her brother. "Good enough?" she asked him.

Clay snorted. As if he had a say in this. It was like trying to win an argument with a rock. "Guess it'll have to be."

"Give your uncle a kiss, Emmie," Georgie urged, gently pushing the girl toward Clay. "One of your butterfly specials. That'll cheer him up."

Okay, he'd bite, Nick thought. "What's a butterfly special?"

Before Georgie could explain, Emmie turned toward him. "I'll show you," the little girl volunteered. She tugged on his jacket. "Well, c'mon. You've gotta bend down."

Feeling awkward, Nick did as the little girl instructed and bent down to her level. She leaned forward and he felt the slight brush of her small, rosebud lips against his cheek. And then there was something more. Just the slightest sensation. He realized that Emmie had turned her face slightly and she was fluttering her eyelashes against his skin, just above where she'd kissed him.

Something warm and nameless materialized within his chest and spread.

Giggling, Emmie danced away on tiptoes, moving toward her next target: Clay. "Your turn, Uncle Clay. Bend down."

He did and she repeated the brief performance. And

then, backing away from her uncle, again on tiptoes, Emmie steepled her small fingers in front of her mouth to hold back another pleased giggle. It escaped anyway. Her laughter was infectious as it filled the air.

"Now I'm good to go," Clay told her, straightening. The smile left his lips as he raised his head and regarded Nick one last time. "*You* call me if anything comes up," he ordered. "She probably won't." He nodded his head toward his sister.

"All right." It was neither a promise nor lip service. Calling the other man was something he would consider doing or not doing when and if the time came. "By the way," he began, remembering a lost thread of the conversation. He fell into step with the man as the latter headed toward his parked truck.

Georgie and Emmie stood where they were left, watching and, in Emmie's case, waving.

Clay didn't even bother turning around to look at the man addressing him. "Yeah?"

"What is your last name?" Nick asked. "Just for the record."

Clay didn't pause until he'd reached his truck. Then he turned and gave him one last long measuring glance. Clay laughed, shaking his head. There was very little humor in the sound. If Nick listened closely, he would have noted a touch of irony.

"You government types do like to keep your 'records' straight, don't you?" Clay mocked. "Okay, 'just for the record,' Sheffield, it's Colton. Clay Colton. Colton, in case you're wondering, was the name of the no-good, worthless excuse of a man who thought my mother was good enough to warm his sheets, and have his bastards, but wasn't good enough to marry."

With that, Clay got into his truck, leaving Nick to stare after him in stunned silence. The name Clay had just uttered echoed over and over again inside Nick's head.

Colton.

Chapter 9

Nick turned away from the road. Georgie and her daughter were on the steps of the front porch, about to enter the house. He addressed the back of her head.

"Why didn't you tell me your last name was Colton?"

His question stopped her for a moment, but then she continued walking. She didn't bother to turn around. "You never asked."

He followed her into the house. This wasn't some abstract conversation they were having, this had direct bearing on the reason he was down here and he meant to get to the bottom of it.

Had everything she'd told him up to now been a lie, after all?

"Don't give me that. Seems to me that only a guilty person would have kept that kind of information back."

Georgie kept going until she came to the kitchen. Although she knew the state of affairs within her refrigerator—empty—she opened it anyway, just to confirm that her mystery squatter hadn't left behind any food.

"How about a person who doesn't share things that are nobody else's business but their own?" She closed the refrigerator door a little harder than she needed to and squared her shoulders in an unconscious, defensive movement. Her eyes narrowed. "I don't see you telling me about your parents, or lack thereof."

She added the latter as she thought of her absentee father. The one she'd never met or even heard from—until just recently. For some reason, out of the blue, Graham Colton had materialized, saying he wanted to make amends for his past behavior. Had her mother been alive, she would have tried to find the good in the man, but her mother was gone. The time for mending fences was long gone. She was doing just fine without having the man in her life at this stage. And she intended to continue that way.

Nick set his jaw hard as he pointed out the obvious. "I'm not the one sending threatening e-mails to a United States Senator."

Georgie whirled around on her heel, her hands fisted at her waist to keep from taking a swing at this infuriating man.

"Well, funny you should say that because neither am I and the sooner you get that through your thick head, the sooner both of us will be happy and you can be on your way."

Gleaning what she needed to from her mother's words, Emmie turned her big green eyes up to the man in the black suit. "You're not gonna help my mama?"

Nick had never spent much time dealing with children. Consequently, he had no idea what to make of them and it had been so long since he'd even *had* a childhood. But he knew hurt when he saw it. He knew an accusatory tone when he heard it, and Emmie Grady—or Colton—was wielding both like a well-trained samurai swinging his sword.

Georgie draped her arm protectively over the little girl's slim shoulders. "He's gonna help mama by leaving, baby," she told her daughter. Looking at Nick, she said, "There's your hat, there's your car, what's your hurry?" uttering the ironic line to usher him along on his way. She might have known better.

"No hurry," he responded, then regarded Emmie, "And yes, I'm going to help your mama." Because, he added silently, this all somehow went together.

To his surprise, Emmie took his hand and began to pull him toward the living room, her small face a wreath of smiles. "I knew you would."

Georgie sighed. Maybe Emmie saw some good in him she was missing. At any rate, she seemed to be stuck with the man for a while. Yes, she'd told her brother that Sheffield could stay at her place, but that was just to restore her independence, her authority over herself in case Clay wanted to institute some form of martial law over her life. She'd silently hoped that Sheffield would leave once her brother did. No such luck, it seemed.

"I suppose you'll be wanting lunch."

"Eventually," Nick allowed. And then he realized what she was saying. He eyed her sharply. "Don't bother yourself. I'll go into town and grab something to eat. You do have a restaurant in Esperanza, right?"

She thought of the one where her mother had worked all those long hours after giving up her career on the rodeo circuit. The rodeo had been her mother's first love, but she had given it all up for them, for Clay, Ryder and her, to give them a stable home life. Georgie couldn't help wondering if her mother had ever regretted what she'd done.

She had a feeling she knew the answer.

"Yes, we have a restaurant in Esperanza, a damn decent one, too, but I've got to go back into town to get some food for Emmie and me. I might as well feed you, too," she told him.

Georgie was annoyed with herself for not tending to that, too, when she'd gone into town earlier. But discovering that she was flat broke had made her forget the basics. Like the importance of stocking her pantry and refrigerator.

It was time she got a grip on herself and started functioning like the independent woman she was, not like some scatterbrained woman she wasn't.

Grabbing the keys she'd left on the table, Georgie gestured toward her daughter. "C'mon, Emmie, we've got to go back into town."

Emmie surprised both her mother and Nick with her next words. "Can I stay with Nick, Mama?"

"That's Mr. Sheffield, honey," Georgie corrected. Emmie called the cowboys on the circuit by their first names, but that was different. Those were men who doted on her. This was an agent of the government. "And I'm sure he's got a whole bunch of things he wants to do that don't include babysitting a little girl."

Her request completely mystified Nick. "Why would you want to stay with me?"

"'Cause I've got questions to ask you," Emmie told him solemnly.

Had Emmie been older, he would have suspected a setup, with Georgie putting words into the child's mouth. But Emmie looked too young to be a shill, even for her mother. "Questions?"

Emmie nodded, her red curls bouncing like thin springs about her head. "Like how do those go on?" Before he could ask what she was referring to, Emmie pointed a small index finger at the handcuffs hanging off his belt. Usually hidden by his jacket, the garment had gotten stuck on them, exposing just enough steel to capture Emmie's attention.

Georgie took hold of Emmie's hand and began to lead her to the front door. "Careful what you wish for, honey. He just might show you," she murmured under her breath, but loud enough for both Emmie *and* Nick to hear.

It suddenly occurred to him that there was an advantage to having the little girl remain. Moving quickly, he shifted himself in front of mother and daughter before they could reach the front door. "She can stay."

Georgie looked up at him and read between the lines. The man was pretty transparent. "Don't worry, I'll be back. You don't need a hostage," she told him deliberately.

She took a step to get around him. He took one to keep in front of her. "If Emmie stays here, I'll be sure of it."

Did he think she was born yesterday? Or did he just think she was that stupid? "I'm not leaving my four-year-old daughter alone with a man I don't know."

"Five, Mama, I'm almost five," Emmie reminded her, holding up five splayed fingers.

Nick ignored the little girl. "Fair enough," he

allowed. He'd set about as many wheels in motion as he could right now. This could come under the heading of surveillance work. "I guess we're going grocery shopping then."

The only one who seemed happy about the arrangement was Emmie, who suddenly threaded her tiny fingers through Nick's while still holding on to her mother's hand. Positioned between them, she gleefully proclaimed, "Just like a real family."

It took everything Nick had not to yank his hand away.

The ache the words created within Georgie's chest was immeasurable.

I can't give you that now, Emmie. But maybe someday, she promised. *Maybe someday.*

"Careful, honey, or you're going to give Mr. Sheffield a heart attack," she said flippantly. "He'd probably got a wife and kids at home."

Never one to hold back, Emmie took her question to the source. "Do you?" Emmie pressed, twisting around to get a better look at Nick's face as he dropped back a step.

Reaching the truck, Georgie picked up her daughter and slipped her into the car seat, securing the belts. All the while Emmie craned her neck, watching Nick and waiting for an answer.

"No," he answered in a monotone. "I don't." Getting into the cab of the truck, he waited for Georgie to climb in on her side and give him the keys. There was no way he was allowing the woman to drive. There'd be no telling where they would wind up if he did.

The shopping expedition into town took a little less than two hours, start to finish.

At the checkout counter, after everything had been

tallied, Georgie reached for one of her credit cards, then remembered that she'd canceled them all. That left her dependent on cash until the companies issued her new cards and sent them.

Murmuring an apology, Georgie dug into her wallet for cash. Nick elbowed her out of the way and handed the checker a hundred dollar bill.

"That should cover it," he said.

The young woman behind the counter looked barely out of high school. She regarded the bill with suspicion as she held it up to the light, angling it as if she expected to see the word "counterfeit' written across the back.

So much for trust, Nick thought, mildly amused at another stereotype biting the dust. "It's real," he assured her.

The young blonde flushed. "We don't see many of these," she responded, handing him change with what could only be described as an inviting smile.

"You didn't have to pay for it," Georgie protested, pushing the cart out of the store.

"You don't have to cook for me," he countered, keeping step. Emmie had wound her fingers around his left hand again, all but skipping alongside him and her mother.

You'd think Emmie would have better judgment than that, Georgie thought. She was about to make a cryptic comment about cooking for him, then sighed. She had to think of Emmie and set a good example. So she nodded and said, "Fair enough, I guess."

He surprised her by loading the grocery bags into the truck, then picking up Emmie and depositing her into her car seat. Allowing him to buckle in Emmie, she still checked to see that the belts were secure.

"Would you like to redo them?" he asked.

"Just making sure she's secure. I don't expect you've had much experience with kids' car seats."

"A seat belt's a seat belt," he responded. "You want to drive?" he asked, holding out the keys.

She was about to snatch them away. The keys and the truck that went with them represented her independence. But then she shrugged. She didn't want to do what he expected her to do.

"You can drive," she told him, climbing into the passenger seat.

She missed the smile that curved the corners of his mouth just before he got in.

After he'd helped Georgie and Emmie bring in the grocery bags, it dawned on him. Power had been restored to the house, just as Georgie had foretold last night. That meant that he could get back to working on her computer in an effort to see if he had missed something the first time around, before the power from the portable generator had given out.

"I'm going to get back to working on your computer," he told her as he began to leave the kitchen. "Whoever stole your identity might have been using it to do their 'shopping' with your credit cards."

"What do you hope to find?" she asked. She couldn't begin to fathom using the machine as a tracking device, but then, she'd be the first to admit that she was naive in the ways of computers.

"I don't know yet," he admitted.

"Well, that's not very encouraging."

"Most clues turn up by accident," he told her, leaving the room.

"Definitely not encouraging," she murmured under

her breath. Pushing everything else out of her mind, she turned her attention to making lunch. Specifically, to making burritos. Mexican food always made her feel better and she really needed something to make her feel better.

Left to her own devices, Emmie decided that now would be as good a time as any for "Mr. Sheffield" to answer those questions buzzing in her head. Slipping out of the kitchen, she came bounding into her mother's bedroom.

"Hi," she declared cheerfully. Not standing on ceremony, or hanging back, she planted herself beside him at the card table.

Nick looked up. Lost in thought for a moment, he'd forgotten about the little girl.

"Hi," he murmured and, inadvertently, opened the door for her. The questions came, fast and furious, as to how his handcuffs worked. Why did he need them? Did he see many bad people? What did he do when he saw them? And on and on. There seemed to be no end in sight, her fertile mind coming up with question after question.

Emmie only stopped to draw breath when he chose to answer a question. She distracted him to the point that he eventually placed what he was doing on hold. He'd found what he was looking for, at least to some extent. Unearthing user history, he found a score of places that had been hit, all online stores. Unlike Georgie, whoever had used this computer had a log-on user name and password for each site. He was going to have to get Steve hooked up to the computer in order to ascertain them. He had a feeling that if he found the names, he'd find the person sending the threatening e-mails as well.

God, he hoped he wasn't being taken for a ride—by two redheads.

"Lunch is ready, you two." Standing in the doorway to her bedroom, Georgie repeated what she'd first called out from the kitchen, getting no response. It seemed that her daughter and her uninvited "guest" hadn't heard her so rather than call again, she decided to just fetch them and be done with it.

She hadn't expected to find them kneeling on the floor on opposite sides of her bed. Especially not Sheffield.

Georgie looked from her daughter to the man who had summarily invaded her life and turned everything within it upside down. She decided that she'd get a better answer from Emmie than from Sheffield.

"Just what in the name of all that's sacred are you doing, Emmie?" she asked, addressing the top of the little girl's head—it was all that was peeking out from the far side of her bed.

Emmie popped up, grinning and looking very pleased with herself. "Playing cops and robbers, Mama. I'm the cop."

Georgie turned to see the Secret Service agent on his knees, handcuffs securely on his wrists and an exceedingly sheepish look on his face. "I guess that must make you the robber." She didn't bother struggling to keep the amused expression from her face.

Silently declaring the game to be over, he rose to his feet. "Yeah." He thrust his bound hands before him and at Georgie. "Get these off me." The widening grin on her face did not fill him full of confidence.

"Not so fast," Georgie drawled. "I think I like having you handcuffed."

But Emmie was already making her way to her new playmate. "But he can't eat if he's handcuffed, Mama," she said, the soul of logic. Taking the key she'd placed in her pocket, Emmie inserted it into the lock and turned it.

Handcuffs unlocked, Nick quickly removed them from his wrists, still not entirely sure how he'd allowed himself to get "captured" in the first place.

"I know," Georgie agreed, "But he'd be a lot less trouble that way."

Rubbing his wrists, Nick temporarily deposited the handcuffs into his pocket. "You know the penalty for falsely imprisoning a Secret Service Agent?" he asked Georgie.

Georgie turned her face up to his innocently. "Peace and quiet?" she ventured.

He had no idea why, but he had this overwhelming urge to kiss the grin off her lips. Had to be all this fresh air, he theorized. It was obviously doing strange things to his head.

"Get a move on," Georgie ordered. He wasn't sure if it was aimed at him, or her daughter, or both. "The food's getting cold." She led the way back. Nick did his best to keep his eyes fixed on the back of Georgie's head rather than on the way her hips swayed in her tight jeans as she walked.

The rest of the day was spent less pleasantly, spinning his wheels, making very little headway, although Steve told him that he would do his best to hack into Georgie's computer and get past the encrypted passwords. Nightfall came before he knew it.

Emmie seemed to finally run out of energy and had to be carried off to bed, sound asleep. Something stirred within him as he watched Georgie carry her daughter to her room. For some reason, the extremely domestic scene got to him and started him thinking. Wondering about the road not taken.

And then he shook off those thoughts. He wasn't interested in that road, he reminded himself. He would have been bored within the first day.

But watching Georgie Grady/Colton now, he had to admit that there was something going on. It was the "what" that remained unidentified to him.

Careful, Nicky, he warned himself. *You don't want to be making any mistakes now.*

He was human and he'd been conned before. But never by anyone nearly so attractive. Never by anyone he'd felt so attracted to.

In her defense, Nick supposed that Georgie could actually be telling him the truth. That she was a victim in all this. He had Steve checking all that out for him, checking her out, to make sure she was who she said she was and had, as she claimed, not even been near a computer these last few months.

In the meantime, he thought cryptically, he was doing his own checking out. Up close and exceedingly personal. So personal, he could feel his blood stirring.

It had been a long time since he'd thought of himself as anything other than a law enforcement agent of one type or other. But Georgeann Grady made him remember that beneath the oaths he had taken and the extreme devotion to duty he felt, there beat the heart of a man.

A man who'd been far too long without the touch of a woman.

The power was on, but she seemed to prefer having the fire in the fireplace lit. He watched now as the light from the fireplace caressed the outline of Georgie's small, trim, jean-clad body. She moved about the rustic living room that could have easily come off the set of a Hollywood western. Except that it was genuine.

As genuine as she claimed to be?

Something inside him hoped so.

Not very professional of you, Nicky.

He wasn't supposed to be taking sides. His only interest in being here was to guarantee Senator Joe Colton's safety as the latter continued to make his bid for the presidency. Everything else was supposed to be secondary.

But, Nick had to silently admit, that was just a wee bit hard to remember right now.

Earlier, before she'd put her precocious handful of a daughter to bed, Georgie had fed his appetite by whipping up some kind of a delicious concoction out of the vegetables she'd pulled from her garden. Vegetables that, by all rights, should have been withered and dried. She'd mentioned that a friend came by on occasion to weed and tend the garden. Still, it surprised him that somehow she'd managed to make something mouth-watering out of very little.

Almost as mouth-watering as she looked to him right then.

Again, he was reminded of the appetite that hadn't been fed, hadn't been satisfied.

And wasn't going to be, Nick sternly told himself. At least, not now. Maybe when things took on a more definite shape and all the questions in his head were, once and for all, answered to his satisfaction, there would be time to explore this feeling. To explore this woman. But not now.

Damn it.

"I can turn the lights back up," Georgie said, breaking into his train of thought as she turned around to face him. If she noticed the way he was looking at her, she gave no indication. "But Emmie wanted to pretend that we were still roughing it. This way, she could pretend we were camping out. Emmie really likes to camp out."

"And you?" Nick asked, moving closer. "What do you like?"

The very breath stopped in Georgie's throat as she looked up at him.

And then, all sorts of things ricocheted in her head.

Things that didn't make sense.

Things that had to do with needs rather than the logical behavior she had been trying so hard to embrace for the last few hours.

"I think you've got a fair shot of guessing that one," she told him softly.

Chapter 10

Nick was acutely aware that he was crossing a line. A line he had never ventured over before in his adult life.

His action was reminiscent of the rebellious youth he'd been rather than the man he had carefully and painstakingly evolved into. The man would have never given in to the moment, to the temptation shimmering before him.

No matter how much he wanted to.

But it was the rebellious teen, who hadn't quite figured out how to harness himself, how to tame his impulses, who surfaced.

Nick cupped the sides of Georgie's face in his hands and brought his mouth down to hers as if he had no choice in the matter. And it was that needy soul, the one who had never connected with anyone after his mother's desertion, who silently cheered as sensations shot through him, causing him to deepen the kiss that was far from innocent.

My God, what's going on?

The shell-shocked question echoed in Georgie's brain before it showered down on her in shattered fragments. Before she embraced the wild feelings that had materialized out of nowhere. When Nick kissed her, she voluntarily fell headlong into it, losing herself. She could sooner stop breathing than pull back.

The ensuing rush was incredible.

It had been so long since she'd allowed a man to kiss her. The last few years, she'd lived her life almost exclusively in the world of men, but they were her friends, her mentors, her protectors. They looked out for her almost as if she were a beloved little sister. Once or twice, a new member had joined the circle and attempted to hit on her. But there was always someone to set the newcomer straight and he would obligingly back off.

As far as the men on the rodeo circuit were concerned, Georgie was family. Her boundaries were to be respected and not crossed.

And she had gone along, silently grateful for the protection, for being left alone on the complex romantic playing field.

She thought she was all right with that. She thought wrong.

This need that had sprung up from nowhere, exploding like a misstep taken in an active minefield, had to have had its origins somewhere, didn't it?

The more Nick kissed her, the more she wanted to be kissed. The more she realized how much she'd missed being kissed, being treated like a desirable woman rather than just a mother, just a sister, just a worthy competitor. There was nothing wrong with any of that, but it didn't begin to address the needs that had quietly been growing in the dark. Growing until they burst at the seams.

He should pull back.

He should get a grip and stop. *Now*, before he compounded the mistake.

But the feel of her soft body urgently pressing against his had set off all sorts of demands within him that were close to impossible to rein in.

He tried to talk himself out of it, using logic. It could all be just part of her plan to seduce him, to turn his head and make him oblivious to her guilt, to the con she wanted to put over on him.

God help him, he didn't care.

He'd sort it all out later. Right now, something far more important was going on. And besides, deep in his gut, he felt she was innocent. That was supposed to count for something, wasn't it? Gut feelings?

Or was he just trying to rationalize his behavior?

Breath short, pulse racing and adrenaline pumped up so high he thought he was about to plunge off the side of a cliff into a glass of water three hundred feet below, Nick still somehow managed to break contact and pull his head back.

Somehow managed to pull his lips away from hers. "Georgie—"

That's all he said. That's all he could say. Because she rose up on her toes, whispered a plea, "Don't ruin this," and sealed her mouth to his as she drove her fingers into his hair, anchoring herself to the sensation that thundered through her.

It was all he needed. The go-ahead signal. Had he been made of cardboard or metal, he could have called a stop to it. But he was flesh and blood and his flesh and blood called to hers.

As he tightened his arms around her, his mouth roamed Georgie's face, her neck, the soft skin that peered out from where the first button of her blouse pulled against its hole.

As he kissed her, his mouth doing wild, wonderful things to her system she'd never experienced, Georgie felt his fingers freeing the buttons on her blouse.

And then her blouse was hanging open, exposing her lacy bra and showing off her tanned, firm skin to its best advantage.

His lips anointed her skin.

With unsteady hands, Georgie began to undress him, first pushing the damn black jacket off his shoulders, down his arms, then setting siege to his shirt. She yanked the edges out of his waistband, but as she began to free the buttons, she felt herself being picked up into the air.

Startled, she looked at Nick, a silent question in her eyes.

"Your daughter might wake up," he told her, his voice husky with emotions that had yet to be spent.

Oh, God, Emmie. She'd forgotten about Emmie.

If she'd been thinking clearly, she would have been embarrassed that he was the one who thought of Emmie. After all, she was Emmie's mother. But Georgie was grateful that he knew Emmie could come out of her room at any time, looking for her. Her heart swelled and an incredible wave of tenderness washed over her. That one simple act made her see him in a completely different light.

Again she sealed her mouth to his, kissing him long

and hard. The only reason she broke contact was because he was depositing her on her bed.

And then he was helping her out of her jeans, pulling them down about her thighs and then her knees. His own knees felt almost weak as she raised her hips to help with the effort. Raised them so that they were closer to him.

Tossing the jeans aside on the floor, Nick reached for the soft, light blue bikini panties she still had on. Meanwhile, she had tangled her fingers in his belt, drawing it quickly through its loops. She didn't even wait to have it hit the floor before she yanked on the zipper.

The button that fastened the trousers in place went flying. Momentarily distracted, Nick glanced to see where it had landed.

Georgie pulled his face back down to hers. "I can sew," she told him just before she captured his mouth again.

She desperately wanted nothing to stop her. If she paused, if she thought, logic and her sense of self-preservation would get in the way and stop her.

And she didn't want to stop.

She wanted to dash up to the highest pinnacle, to feel that rush through her veins just a moment before it was all over. She needed to feel that more than she could possibly ever put into words.

With a mighty tug, Georgie freed him of both his trousers and the underwear beneath them, bringing both down around his surprisingly muscular thighs and then off his torso completely. They fell into the shadows, along with the button.

"Learn that on the circuit?" he asked, trying to hide the desire that throbbed through his veins beneath a glimmer of humor.

"No," she whispered, her breath lingering on his

face, "but I could hog-tie you in a minute eight if you want a demonstration of what I did learn on the circuit."

He framed her face with his hands, drawing the length of his naked body over hers. "Later."

"Okay."

It was the last thing she remembered saying before everything exploded within her. Before he made her feel beautiful. Before her skin went on fire as he branded her with his hands, his mouth, his tongue.

Georgie swallowed strangled cries as he made her climax and then continued, doing it again.

And again.

Until she thought she was just going to expire from exhaustion.

With her last ounce of available strength, Georgie wrapped her legs around Nick's torso, stirring up temptation he couldn't resist, couldn't ignore or back away from.

Balancing his weight across his hands as if he were coming down from a powerful push-up, Nick plunged into her. A moment later, he was employing a rhythm that was older than time, and as new as the next second.

At the end, she would have cried out if his mouth hadn't covered hers. She arched up as far as she could, trying to absorb every last fragment of sensation and hug it to her breast.

Then she realized that he had stopped moving.

When he rolled off her the next moment, she expected Nick to get up. To act as if all of this was no big deal. The way Jason had. Jason was her only frame of reference, the only other man she had slept with.

That Nick didn't automatically get up surprised her. That he slipped his arm around her and drew her closer to him surprised her even more.

Almost as much as it surprised him.

He wanted to hang on to the sensation, to the exquisite moment, knowing that once it faded, there would be anger.

His own directed at himself.

Because he had slipped off the path he'd laid out for himself—slipped off big time. But just for a moment longer, he wanted to pretend that there were no consequences, that he had done nothing wrong. He'd simply enjoyed another human being.

He felt her turning her head toward him. Felt her studying him for a long, silent moment. And then she asked, "Did I just compromise you, or did you just compromise me?"

The question took him aback. So much so that he raised himself up on his elbow in order to look at down her. "What?"

Georgie blew out a long breath. "What just happened here?"

He grinned. The temptation to say that they'd just stood in the path of a twister was hard to resist. Instead, he teased her. "You are Emmie's biological mother, right?"

Georgie frowned as she shook her head. "I'm not talking about the process. I *know* what happened here, but," she looked up at him. "What happened here?"

She couldn't word it any better than that. Because something *had* happened here. Something unsettling and overwhelming.

Nick shrugged, trying his best to regain ground, to appear nonchalant. But underneath, he was wondering the same thing. He did his best to define it. "I think we just had a moment."

She glanced at her wristwatch. "It was a hell of a lot

longer than just a moment. More like an hour," she corrected.

He laughed then. And laughing beside her felt almost as good as making love with her.

It had been a long time since he'd laughed. Longer than the last time he'd allowed himself to make love to a woman.

His laugh was deep and rich, making her feel inherently good. Inherently happy.

"That's a nice sound," she told him, unconsciously curling her body into his. "You should laugh more often."

He thought of the life he had been leading. There was satisfaction, but no humor. "Not much to laugh at in my line of work," he responded.

"Your line of work," she echoed thoughtfully. And then she smiled to herself at the irony. "You mean catching bad guys like me?"

He looked at her for a long moment. Again, his instincts told him she was innocent. But there was the evidence to consider. Her IP address and her computer were involved in this. Logically, that would mean that she was too. *And* she had hidden her last name from him. Because she was accustomed to using her stage name, or because it made her look guilty?

"Tell me about your father," he finally said.

He felt her stiffen slightly against him, and then he saw her force herself to relax. "Is this how you conduct your second wave of interrogation? Naked?"

Nick shifted, pulling her toward him. His hand gently rested on the swell of her hip. He felt himself being aroused again. Something else out of the ordinary, he thought. Usually, when he got to this part, he'd be sated and that would be that.

Not this time.

"It does have its advantages." Maybe it was the moment, or the aftermath of lovemaking, but he leveled with her. "My gut tells me you're innocent—"

She didn't bother suppressing the smile that rose to her lips. "Your 'gut,' or something else?"

"My gut," he assured her. "But I need to be convinced a little more." A wary expression came into her eyes. He could guess at what she was thinking. That he was coaxing her to make love with him again. "No, not like that. Answer my question. Tell me about your father."

"Nothing to tell." Rather than look at him, Georgie stared off into space, doing her best to divorce herself from her words. She'd convinced herself that it didn't matter, that the years when she'd wanted her father were in her past. She'd gotten over that. But a part of her still hurt, still smarted from being abandoned along with her brothers and mother. And she would never forgive him for turning his back on her mother.

"He came into my mother's life, turned her whole world upside down, gave her three babies and then left. He went back to his rich wife. I never knew him when I was growing up, although Clay said he came around for a little while." She set her jaw hard as she continued. "Now he's back, trying to make amends. Probably because his own kids can't stand him from what I hear." She told him with no little feeling, "I've got no use for him."

This didn't sound like the Joe Colton he knew. Joe Colton was an honorable man. He would have never had an affair, especially not one that extended over several years' time. But to be thorough, he had to ask. "What's your father's first name?"

"Graham." She knew where he was going with this. "Don't worry, Secret Service Agent Sheffield, it's not your precious Senator. Just somebody with the same last name."

He watched her face. Unless she was one hell of an accomplished actress, he thought, she was telling the truth. "But you're all related."

"Maybe. But I don't care," she added truthfully. "I care about my immediate family. My daughter and my brothers." Ryder might have taken a few wrong turns that had landed him in prison, but he was still her brother and she loved him. There were ties that went beyond logic. "I care about the men I ride the rodeo circuit with," she told him. "And that's it. Oh, and I care about who's been impersonating me." She could see that the addition surprised him. And then she said with feeling, "Because I'm going to strangle her."

He laughed softly at first, then realized that there was no humor in her eyes. "You sound as if you mean that."

"Of course I mean it." As she spoke, her indignation at what the other woman had done grew like a flash fire. "She stole something precious from me."

Her life savings. He could understand her anger. "The money—"

But Georgie waved her hand at that. The money represented security and was exceedingly important, but something was more important to her. "That's secondary. She stole my good name. I don't know about where you come from, Sheffield, but around here, your good name, your word, means something."

A woman of integrity, he thought, nodding. But then he supposed he could expect nothing less of her, just from what he'd learned in the last twenty-four hours.

Georgie cleared her throat, feeling somewhat awkward. She was still naked, still lying beside a naked man and without her passion, which was spent, or her anger, which was slowly settling down, she felt uncomfortably vulnerable even though she couldn't exactly explain why.

"Um, don't you think you should get up and go to your bed in the guest room?"

"Right. Sure." And then, giving in to impulse, Nick lightly brushed his lips against her bare shoulder. Something began to stir within him again. "In a minute—or so."

Damn, there it went again, that blaze that he seemed to be able to ignite within her. She should be sated, for heaven's sake, and yet, she wanted more. She wanted to take another wild ride before the night was over. What had come over her?

"Are you starting up again?" she asked, turning her body to his. And then she smiled before he could answer—because another part of his body had answered her question for him. The smile entered her eyes and seemed to simply glow everywhere. "I guess so."

Damn but she was beautiful, he thought. "Anybody ever tell you you talk too much?"

She seemed to roll his question over in her mind, her smile widening as she did so, pulling him in. "You wouldn't be the first."

"I didn't think so." But something inside of him, as he brought his mouth down to hers again, whispered that he wanted to be the last. And telling Georgie she talked too much had nothing to do with it.

Chapter 11

In order to keep his word and satisfy Emmie, who popped up like toast the next morning to remind him of his promise to "make everything right for Mama," Nick spent the first part of his morning at Georgie's computer, tracking down all the charges incurred on her credit cards. Just to play it safe, armed with the user names and passwords Steve had sent him, Nick decided to go back over the last five months.

One by one, he secured the information, then printed it out for her. When he had the charges in a rather overwhelming stack, he gave the pages to her and left it up to Georgie to decipher, separating the piles into charges she had run up and the ones that could be attributed to the "Georgie" doppelganger.

Having lived up to his part of the bargain, Nick got down to his real work. He decided that it might be advantageous to find out as much as he could about the man who had fathered Georgie and her brothers, the mysterious and, from what he'd gathered, self-centered Graham Colton.

It took some digging at first, but once he had some key pieces of information to work with, the rest came more easily.

An hour after he'd gotten started, hopping from screen to screen and from site to site, he found himself staring at the information the winding trail had brought him to. And discovering something he would have rather not found out.

Because what he'd found out unearthed another battery of questions and, more importantly, doubts.

Away from Georgie and the attraction he experienced whenever he was within ten feet of her, Nick felt uncertainty taking root again.

Had he been played?

Or was there some outside chance that she actually didn't know that her father, Graham Colton, was the Senator's younger brother? After all, not even he had known that the Senator had a younger brother, much less what his name was.

But then, Graham Colton wasn't *his* father. Wouldn't Georgie have connected the dots? Or was politics something she blocked out, the way so many other people did? After all, it wasn't as if Graham Colton had been a doting father. All the evidence he'd come across so far pointed to the fact that he'd been, probably still was, a womanizing, narcissistic, greedy scum. In Georgie's place, he wouldn't have wanted to have anything to do with the man either. But did not wanting contact mean ignorance of his family background?

He wasn't sure.

With a sigh, Nick stretched out his legs beneath the table, debating his next move. What he'd just found out wasn't something he could keep to himself.

But if he told Georgie, one of two things could happen. If she didn't know, this would be a hell of a shock for her. And if she did know and had lied to him, he wasn't certain how he'd deal with that particular scenario.

He supposed that he could hold off telling her. There was time enough to discover whether he'd made love with an innocent or a scheming witch. He'd just begun to entertain illusions, he didn't want to have to risk losing them already.

There was one person he did have to tell. The one person who deserved to be apprised of anything he found out as soon as possible.

Nick shifted in his chair, sitting up straight again as he took his cell phone out of his pocket. He pressed the single button that would connect him to the Senator's private cell.

Waiting, Nick counted off four rings before he heard the sound of a phone coming to life on the other end of the line. A dynamic, resonant voice said, "Hello?"

Even the man's voice inspired him with confidence, Nick thought. "Senator Colton, this is Nick Sheffield."

"Nick." Pleasure flooded the Senator's voice. "I was just wondering when I'd be hearing from you. I was beginning to get concerned that you decided to forget about the campaign and just settle in." There was almost a wistful note in his tone. "Awfully pretty country down there."

"If you like the rustic life," Nick responded, not quite able to get himself to agree to the Senator's assessment. He was just *not* the rural type. Nick was fairly certain that his voice gave him away on that count. "I'm calling because I found where the e-mails were coming from."

The Senator immediately heard what wasn't being said. "But not the person sending them?"

No doubt about it, Nick thought. The Senator was quick on the uptake. "Well, there seems to be some doubt about it," he told the man. "The woman whose computer was used to send the e-mails was out of town during the period of time we've blocked off."

"Is someone else in the family doing the sending, then?"

"I'm looking into that," Nick told the man. Uncomfortable with what he was about to say, he shifted in his seat. "Senator, there's something else."

"Go on."

There was no easy way to say this. Since the Senator didn't talk about his brother, Nick assumed that there was bad blood between them. Or hard feelings. The Senator was a successful, powerful, well-liked man. Maybe his brother, who hadn't seemed to have amounted to very much in his lifetime, was resentful of his success. "The woman's last name's Colton. Graham Colton's her father."

"It was Georgie's computer that was being used to send the e-mails?" Joe asked, surprised.

So much for catching the man off guard. But then, that was part of what he admired about the Senator. The man was as savvy as they came and literally seemed to be on top of everything. No one had ever managed to catch him sleeping.

"You know about her, sir?"

"Yes. And about her brothers, Clay and Ryder, as well. I know all about my brother's other family, Nick." Nick thought he heard a stifled sigh on the other end. "Proud woman, Mary Lynn. After Graham had deserted her, I tried to give her money but she refused to accept my help."

Nick wondered if the Senator had kept tabs on the family through the years. "She's dead, sir, according to the daughter."

"Yes, I know. Terrible shame. Graham loved her in his own way. Probably the one actual love of his life," he speculated. "Unfortunately, he loved his wife's money more." Nick heard the Senator sigh on the other end. "Don't waste your time with Georgie. She wouldn't have sent the letters or the e-mails. She's just like her mother, proud and filled to the brim with integrity."

He'd had no personal dealings with the young woman, but nonetheless, he had kept tabs on her. After all, she was family. It wasn't her fault that her father had turned out to be so shallow.

The Senator's tone changed. "Listen, since you're down there, I was wondering if you might do me a favor and look in on a Jewel Mayfair. She runs a branch of the Hopechest Ranch. A foundation that, as you know," he added quickly, "is near and dear to Meredith's heart. My wife's afraid that Jewel might not be quite up to all the challenges running something of that nature entails. Let me give you Jewel's number," Joe offered.

"That'll make it simpler," Nick commented, flipping over a piece of paper he pilfered from the printer.

As the Senator read off the phone number, followed by the address where the foundation was located, Nick quickly wrote down everything. "Got it," he told the Senator, then added, "I'll call her later this afternoon if that's all right with you."

"Of course. No real hurry. Just keep me in the loop," the Senator requested just before he terminated the call.

Slipping the cell phone back into his pocket, he looked up and realized that his wife had been standing in the doorway to his office, listening. He smiled at the woman who had won his heart so many years ago.

"I've got him looking in on Jewel."

Meredith strode in on those long legs of hers that he had always admired. Her legs had been the first thing to catch his attention. The trim, but curvy figure—a figure she still maintained—had been a very close second. "I heard."

Joe gave her a long, knowing look. "Now maybe you can stop worrying about her."

"Maybe."

He laughed then, seeing right through her. "Your problem, Meredith, is that your heart's just too big," he told her. "You can't keep worrying about the immediate world."

"Not the immediate world," she protested, even though she had always been a soft touch. "Just the part that's related to me."

Coming up behind him, she lightly feathered her long fingers along his forearm. He wore his sleeves folded up, a symbol of his getting down to work. She'd always loved the way that looked. Loved the way he just got better looking with age, keeping his physique muscular and fit by working out and riding whenever he got the opportunity. There were telltale sprinkles of gray in his dark brown hair, but they only succeeded in making him look more distinguished.

He'd get the female vote without even trying, she thought.

Joe turned around to face her. "You know, things might be a little easier for you if you told Jewel that you're her aunt."

But Meredith shook her head, her short, golden-brown bob swaying from side to side. "That would mean that I'd have to tell her that Patsy was my sister. I've gotten Jewel to like and trust me. If she knew that I was the sister of the crazy birth mother who stabbed her father to death on the day she was born because he'd stolen Jewel and given her to a doctor who promised to place her in a good home, she might look at me differently. She certainly wouldn't trust me anymore. I can't risk that. She's been through too much already. On top of not getting any closure from Patsy because Patsy was in a mental institution when she tracked her down, don't forget Jewel also lost her fiancé and her unborn baby in that car crash they were all in. That's more than any one person should have to put up with. I just barely got her out of that depression she'd spiraled down into."

He tucked his arms around her waist. "I'd say finding out that she had such a terrific aunt might just begin to make up for the rest of it. At the very least, that should help her start to heal."

She smiled up at him, stealing a moment as she wrapped her arms about his neck. "Think you're smart, don't you 'Dr.' Colton?" she teased.

There were times he wished he was just like everyone else, that he didn't feel as if he had a mission to fulfill, a cause to champion in order to pay society back for all the good fortune he'd had during his lifetime. That if he wanted to take some time with his wife, a score of responsibilities wouldn't get in his way.

Compromising, Joe stole a quick kiss. "Yes, I do. But

only because I hung out with this really terrific, smart woman. Some of that had to rub off."

She laughed softly. "That silver tongue of yours is definitely going to get you elected." With a reluctant sigh, she disengaged her arms from around his neck. "I'd better leave you to your work."

"Promise me you'll stop worrying," he said, running his forefinger down along the furrow that had formed just above her nose, smoothing it.

"I'll try," she told him, crossing her heart. Right after I call Clay and ask him to watch over Jewel, she added silently. That was what she should have done in the first place, Meredith decided.

Joe released her just as the phone on his desk began to ring. "That's all I can ask," he told her before turning his attention to the person on the other end of the line.

Instantly, he became Senator Colton again, getting back to the ground work for his campaign.

"I've got something," Georgie announced, waving a piece of paper over her head she walked quickly into her bedroom.

Nick was exactly where she'd left him, sitting at her computer. He tried not to type too forcefully on the keyboard because with each stroke, the card table would wobble precariously.

After a beat, he looked up from the screen on the monitor. "What?" he asked absently. Focusing, he realized that Georgie was holding one of the statements he'd printed out for her.

"I found a charge here that had to have been made in person. There's no online site for it. Baker's Jewels," she told him. When he watched her blankly, obviously waiting for more, she explained, "It's the name of a jewelry store in Esperanza."

Her one piece of good jewelry, a bracelet her mother had given her on her sixteenth birthday had come from there. She'd left that in the safety deposit box, along with the deed to the ranch and several pieces of her mother's jewelry that her mother's lover—Georgie couldn't bring herself to think of him as her father—had given her in what Georgie assumed was a moment of weakness. All the pieces of jewelry had been stolen from the safety deposit box. Something else she intended to get back along with her good name.

"I'm going there now. To the jewelry store," she added in case Nick didn't follow her. He had that faraway look in his eyes, as if pondering some deep problem. "You want to come along with me to make sure I don't make a break for it?"

She made the suggestion glibly, as if she really didn't want him along, but the truth of it was, she did. He'd awoken something within her last night, something she hadn't even realized was there. She wanted to prolong that feeling for as long as she could. Having him around did that for her.

Nick weighed his options. If he opted to go with her, it would seem as if he didn't trust her and she'd take offense. If he remained, there was a small chance she could bolt. He didn't want to be standing there with egg on his face even though the Senator had said he didn't believe she had a part in this.

Before he could say anything, his cell rang.

"Go ahead, answer it," she urged, waving her hand

at his pocket. "I've got to go round up Emmie anyway. I'll get back to you," she promised, already going out the doorway.

"Sheffield," Nick said the moment he had the phone to his ear.

"Nick, someone tried to break in last night."

He recognized the voice. Garrett Conrad, the Secret Service agent he'd left in charge while he was gone. Garrett was competent, but a little wet behind the ears.

"Garrett, I just talked to the Senator this morning. He didn't say anything about it to me."

"That's because he doesn't know yet," Garrett answered. "I wanted to tell you first and ask what you wanted me to do about it."

Damn, he was wasting his time here. He should have remained in Prosperino. "Give me the details," Nick ordered.

Garrett recited the events as he'd committed them to memory. "Whoever it was by-passed the security system somehow. Several of the surveillance cameras had black paint sprayed on their lens. The window to the downstairs library was broken. We found a gun nearby. He must have dropped it—and the credit card."

"He dropped a credit card *and* the gun?" Nick asked incredulously. Whoever had tried to break in was smart when it came to technology and seriously lacking when it came to common sense. "That's a little too pat, don't you think?"

Garrett paused, as if framing his answer. "Not every criminal belongs to MENSA."

This sounded more like the work of a high school drop-out. "What's the name on the card?"

There was noise on the other end, as if Garrett was

looking for the card. "Got it," he murmured under his breath, then read, "Georgeann Grady."

Okay, that cinched it, Nick thought. If he'd had any doubts, this erased it. Someone was definitely out to frame Georgie.

Was it a matter of someone trying to kill two birds with one stone? Or was this strictly about revenge with the focus entirely on bringing Georgie down any way they could?

"It couldn't have been her," Nick told his subordinate flatly. "Georgeann Grady has been here in Esperanza for the last two days."

"Maybe she's working with an accomplice?" Garrett suggested.

"An accomplice who is trying to implicate her?" he asked incredulously. "It doesn't make any sense. No, my guess is that someone is trying to frame her." Restless, Nick got up and began to pace. "The question is, is whoever's behind this trying to get the Senator, too, or is there some other connection we're missing?" He stopped by the window and looked out. Miles of flat land spread out before him. God, but the terrain was lonely. "Tell Steve I don't want him leaving his desk until he has a complete history on the woman. If she had so much as a schoolyard altercation in kindergarten, I want to know about it. Is that understood?"

"Understood." He could almost see Garrett snapping to attention. "I'll have him get back to you."

When he put away his phone, Nick felt the back of his neck prickling. As if he were being watched.

Glancing to the doorway, he saw Georgie. She held on to Emmie's hand. Antsy, Emmie all but danced from foot to foot.

"I had lots of 'altercations' in kindergarten," Georgie told him crisply. There wasn't even a hint of a smile on her face.

Emmie tugged harder on her hand. "What's a 'cation, Mama?"

"Altercation," Georgie corrected. "That's a fancy word for fighting."

Emmie's green eyes widened. "You punched someone out, Mama?" she asked, clearly fascinated.

Georgie wasn't ashamed of what she'd done. She'd been raised to stand up for herself. Her brothers had been proud of her. "Only when some nasty little kid called your grandmother or your mama a bad name."

"I'd altercation them too," Emmie told her solemnly, carefully enunciating the word.

It took effort not to laugh, but she didn't want to hurt her daughter's feelings. Emmie's heart was in the right place. Georgie gave her a little squeeze.

"I know you would, pumpkin. I know you would." All the while, she kept her eyes on Nick. "Why are you investigating me again?" She thought they were past this, especially after last night.

Or was she an idiot to believe that?

"Because somebody tried to make it look as if you attempted to break into the Senator's house in Prosperino. A gun and a credit card were conveniently left on the premises." He didn't want her to think he had any doubts about her innocence. "And because the laws of physics haven't been, to my knowledge, repealed in the last few days, you couldn't have been in two places at once."

"Mama rides really, really fast," Emmie offered helpfully.

Nick shook his head. "Not that fast. She would have had to have been in California and her bedroom at the same time last night."

Looking every inch like a miniature adult, Emmie nodded her head. "And she was there with you the whole time."

Startled, Nick exchanged looks with Georgie. It was Georgie who spoke first. "Emmie, how do you know where he was?"

"'Cause I went to see him in the guest room. He wasn't there. Then I went to your room and there he was. You were asleep. Was he keeping you safe, Mama?"

It was ironic that the little girl would choose those exact words.

"Yes, honey, he was keeping me safe," she told her seriously, then glanced up at Nick. "Okay, Emmie and I are off to Baker's Jewels."

He made a quick decision. "I'm coming, too," he told her.

A twinge of disappointment twisted inside of her. "Still don't trust me?"

"It's not you I don't trust," he answered, getting his suit jacket from the back of the chair and slipping it on. "I think I need to go on keeping you safe," he said, using Emmie's words. The little girl flashed him an approving grin.

His tone told Georgie that there was no way she was going to argue him out of it. She didn't bother wasting her breath.

"Okay, c'mon. Let's get going. The sooner we get to the bottom of this, the better."

"My thoughts exactly," he agreed.

Except that, she thought as she led him out of the house, once they got to the bottom of this, he'd be gone again.

She blocked out the thought as best she could. There was no point in dwelling on what she couldn't change.

Chapter 12

"Another day, another surveillance tape," Georgie quipped as they drove back from Baker's Jewels later that day.

She was referring to the surveillance tape on the seat between them. Nick had obtained it from Clyde Baker, the jewelry store owner. Clyde had come to the store to speak to them personally. Getting on in years and in progressively poorer health, he left the running of his store to his employees and his nephew, Thom.

Consequently, he had not been there on the day that "Georgie" was supposedly in to buy a very expensive diamond and ruby ring. But Thom had. However, Clyde's nephew didn't have much of a memory to draw on. To him, the woman on the surveillance tape and Georgie appeared to be one and the same, which he said as he viewed the tape.

Nick had said nothing in the store to contradict that assessment, only thanking Clyde for his cooperation and promising to return the tape "soon."

Georgie fidgeted. Nick had been quiet on the way back from town. Her exasperation got the better of her. "So now you think it's me again."

His mind elsewhere, it took him a second to focus on Georgie's accusation. He spared her a glance. "Did I say that?"

She blew out a breath, her irritation growing. "No, but you didn't *not* say that either."

"This time, two negatives don't make a positive," he told her. He'd been entertaining a new theory since they'd gotten back into the truck. At the moment, he tried to work the theory out in his head.

It took her a second to decipher his words. "So you don't think it's me." It was more of a question than a statement.

This time he looked at her for more than just a fraction of a second. "No."

She wanted more than that. She wanted something, an explanation, that would make her feel more secure. "Why not? Clyde's idiot nephew did."

Her question made him laugh softly. "You just said it yourself. His 'idiot' nephew. Obviously Thom is not a keen observer. The woman on the tape was made up to look like you, but if you watch the tape closely, you'll see the inconsistencies." The silence was pregnant. She waited for him to give an example, Nick thought. "For instance, the woman's taller than you."

"How can you tell?"

"Because on the tape, she's facing Thom over the counter and she's half a head shorter than he is. You're a whole head shorter." The corners of his mouth curved. "And you've got more curves than she does." He saw a blush rise up her cheeks and found it engagingly attractive.

"What's curves, Mama?" Emmie piped up from the confinement of her car seat in the back.

"We'll talk about that later, when you're older," Georgie promised quickly. "It'll make more sense to you then." She turned to look at Nick. "I guess this woman dressed up like me so she could get away with using my credit card."

"That's part of it," he agreed. "But I think it's more complicated than that. I think she's trying to ruin you."

Georgie snorted. That was a no-brainer, she thought. "Well, she's cleaned out my bank account and maxed out my credit cards. I'd say that she's doing more than just trying."

"Are we ruined, Mama?" Emmie asked, sounding clearly distressed.

"Not if I have anything to say about it."

Both Nick and Georgie said the same words at the same time. Hearing the other say it, they looked at one another in surprise.

Nick grinned. "Hell of an echo in here." And then he remembered Emmie was in the back, listening to everything. "Heck," he amended. "Heck of an echo in here."

Georgie laughed, appreciating the fact that Nick was trying to police his language around her daughter, although the words really had no effect on Emmie. She took solace in the fact that Nick seemed determined to come to her aid and track down this impostor. At this point, her independence didn't matter. She more than welcomed his help.

"Why would this woman be trying to ruin me?" Georgie asked.

"That's what I intend to find out," he told her. Reaching for his dark glasses, he slipped them on again. The sun seemed to bounce off everything, giving off a glare that made it hard to see. "There's an outside chance that she's got some kind of grudge against all the Coltons and you're just the first one on her hit list."

"What makes you say that?"

"Because of the e-mails to the Senator." From what he'd gathered, it had all started there. "If it was just you she was after, she would have picked someone closer to home—either that, or she would have sent threatening e-mails to the President himself. That would have gotten a really quick reaction. Instead, she picked another Colton, one who was out of state. There has to be a reason for that." He just hadn't figured it out yet, he added silently. But he would. And soon.

Georgie rolled his words over in her head. "Makes sense, I guess."

Of course, with this growing headache, it was hard to make sense of anything. Georgie absently rubbed her temples with her thumb and middle finger.

Nick caught the telltale movement out of the corner of his eye. "Headache?"

It had begun in her shoulders and moved along the circumference of her skull, from rear to front. The tension of all this had finally gotten to her.

"A big one," she acknowledged. "It's still in the forming stage."

He dug into his pocket and handed her a small bottle that contained an extra-strength, over-the-counter, pain killer. The bottle was half empty, testifying to the fact that he used the pills a great deal himself. "Here, take two of these."

"And call you in the morning?" she quipped, quoting the instructions doctors were said to give.

"Or sooner," he murmured meaningfully, unable to help himself. He kept his voice low enough for Emmie not to hear.

Georgie gave the bottle back to him, unopened. "Thanks, but I've got my own way of dealing with killer headaches. The minute we get back, I'm going out for a ride."

That would have been the *last* thing he would have done for a headache. "Won't all that jostling just make it worse?"

"Nope, clears out my head. I haven't been on a horse since I came back. Maybe I'm going through withdrawal," she kidded.

As she contemplated the ride, she began to feel better already. There was nothing like going off into the country, just her and her horse, to restore peace in her world. She'd even gone riding shortly before she gave birth to Emmie. It was in her blood. Riding for her was as natural as breathing.

Getting on the back of a horse wouldn't have been his first choice—or his twentieth—to clear his head, or any other part of him. That fact underscored that they were from two very different worlds.

He had to remember that.

"I'll only be gone for a little while," she promised Nick and her daughter, getting on the horse she'd quickly saddled.

The palomino, a three-year-old mare named Blue Belle, was the mount that she took with her when she traveled the rodeo circuit. She'd given the mare a couple of days to relax and graze, but now it was time to renew their bond and she was more than ready.

Seated in the saddle, Georgie was filled with the sense that she'd come home and that all was right with the world.

"C'mon, Belle, let's ride." It was what she said to the mare whenever they were in competition. With a toss of her head, Georgie kicked her heels into Belle's flanks and the palomino took off.

It didn't escape Nick's notice that Georgie had entrusted him with her daughter. He'd finally won her, he thought with a tinge of unexpected satisfaction.

He looked down at the little girl beside him. "Let's go inside, Emmie, and see if I can get some good shots off the tape."

The little redhead cocked her head and eyed him quizzically. "You're going to shoot it?"

Nick laughed. "No, I'm going to try to freeze the tape so that I can get a good picture of the woman who's pretending that she's your mother. Maybe someone around Esperanza will recognize her and tell me her name."

Emmie nodded. "Okay. I'll help you," she volunteered.

The little girl slipped her hand into his and then glanced over her shoulder to look at her mother one last time. It was then that Emmie froze for a second before she let out with a bloodcurdling scream. Because at that exact moment, just as Georgie, her horse going at a full gallop, was about to head for the winding path that led away from the ranch house that she suddenly slid off her mount.

The saddle came off with her and she landed on the ground, hitting her head hard.

There was less than half a second between when Nick turned to see why Emmie screamed and his breaking into a run. A sick feeling churned in his stomach.

Emmie was right beside him, pumping her small legs as quickly as she could. She had speed, he had length. They reached Georgie almost at the same time.

"Georgie!" he called even before he sank to his knees beside her.

"Mama! Mama!" Grabbing her mother's hand, Emmie shook it, trying to make her mother open her eyes.

The sick feeling inside Nick's stomach spread throughout his body. He placed his fingers against Georgie's throat. The pulse he located made his own heart leap. She was still alive.

Emmie looked at him with huge, frightened eyes. "She's not dead, right? She's not dead." It wasn't a question, it was a plea.

"No, she's not dead," he assured her, relief flooding through him.

Emmie began to cry. "Why won't she open her eyes?"

He had to calm down Emmie. The last thing he needed right now was to have a hysterical child on his hands. He wasn't equipped to handle that. "Your mother hit her head pretty hard. It knocked her out."

Emmie caught her lower lip between her teeth. It was an obvious effort to keep herself from crying. She was more adult than some adults he'd known. "Like in the cartoons?"

He had no idea what they were showing in cartoons

these days. The last cartoon he remembered was from a childhood that seemed as if it was light years away from now. He vaguely remembered that there'd been a coyote walking on thin air, falling into the chasm only when he looked down and realized that there was nothing beneath his feet.

"Not quite like in the cartoons," he told her. He rose to his feet with Georgie's unconscious body in his arms. Rather than running off, the horse she'd ridden stood like a sentry beside her mistress. He knew Georgie wouldn't want the palomino to wander off. Nick glanced at Emmie. Despite the accident, the horse seemed tame enough. "Emmie, do you think you can take the horse back to the stable?"

"Sure." The little girl obediently picked up the reins that were trailing along on the ground. Authoritatively, she said, "Let's go, Belle."

The animal trotted patiently beside her like an over-sized pet. Emmie quickly led the horse into the stable and closed the stall, then dashed across the yard to join Nick as he entered the house.

Nick placed Georgie's inert form on the sofa. Emmie dashed into the kitchen. Within a minute, she reappeared with a wet towel.

"Here," she held it out to Nick. "You put it on her head," she told him solemnly. "Mama says it makes her feel better sometimes."

"Let's hope this is one of those times," he replied as he spread the cloth on Georgie's forehead, praying that there wasn't any internal damage.

The second the cold cloth touched her skin, Georgie began to moan. And then her eyes fluttered open. They shifted from Nick to her daughter as she struggled to put her world back in order. Her head felt as if it was coming apart.

"Mama!" Emmie cried. "You're back!" Ecstatic, she threw her small arms around her mother's neck.

Nick was tempted to pull the little girl back, but he decided that both Emmie and Georgie needed this re-affirming moment. Any pain that might have been generated from Emmie's hug was more than balanced out by the warmth he knew the contact created.

"Don't cry, honey, I'm okay," Georgie comforted her daughter, slowly rubbing Emmie's back the way she used to when Emmie was a baby and needed soothing. Feeling as if she'd been trampled by a herd of horses, Georgie raised her eyes to Nick. "What happened?"

She didn't remember, Nick thought. Had there been damage? Should he be rushing her to the hospital instead of just standing here? Being grateful that she was alive? It occurred to him that he didn't even know if Esperanza *had* a hospital.

"You fell off your horse and hit your head," Nick told her.

Georgie just stared at him, certain that she couldn't have heard correctly. "No. I never fall off my horse. Not once in all those years of competition. Not since I was ten," she recalled with emphasis.

He sat down on the edge of the scarred coffee table. "You did today."

She started to shake her head, then stopped as arrows of pain shot through her. "That's not possible," she protested in a voice that was definitely having trouble remaining even.

Emmie lifted her head from Georgie's chest. "I saw you, Mama," she confirmed.

"Look, that was a pretty nasty spill. I'm going to take you to the hospital. You just wait—" Rising from the table, Nick didn't get a chance to finish.

"No, no hospital," she said, her voice growing stronger. "I don't want to go to any hospital." Georgie closed her eyes for a moment as a wave of pain washed over her. And then it began to recede. "I just want to find out what's going on here."

"You fell off your horse," Nick repeated. "The saddle came off," he elaborated. "You must have forgotten to tighten the cinch."

She gave him a look that told him she'd sooner forget to put her clothes on when she left the house than to forget to tighten her cinch. "The saddle came off?" she asked incredulously.

He nodded. "Slid right off like butter."

Upset, confused, Georgie tried to sit up and get off the sofa. The room began to spin and she lay back even before Nick gently pushed her back.

"Something's wrong," she protested. "That's a hand-tooled saddle. My grandfather gave it to my mother and she passed it on to me—"

"Then it's old," he pointed out. "Things wear out."

"Not this saddle. It's well made and it's always been lovingly taken care of. There's no reason that it should have come off Belle like that."

He knew she wasn't going to let the matter drop and he wanted her to get some rest. "I'll go check it out," he told her. He began to go, then doubled back. He didn't trust her. "But you have to promise to stay here." When she didn't say anything, he pressed the issue. "You have to promise."

Trapped, Georgie blew out a breath. Emmie had

climbed up onto the sofa and curled up on her as if she was part of the sofa. "Okay."

Nick still didn't trust her. He decided to enlist help. "Emmie, I'm making you a deputy Secret Service agent—"

"You can do that?" Emmie asked, her eyes widening again. For the first time since she'd seen her mother fall, a smile flitted along her rosebud lips.

"I can do that," he assured her. "Now, you watch your mother. And whatever you do, don't let her get up."

"Not even to go to the bathroom?" Emmie wanted to know.

"Not even then," he said, starting to leave the room.

"You're a hard man, Nick Sheffield," Georgie called after him. She winced as her voice echoed in her head.

"And don't you forget it," he tossed back over his shoulder. "I'm counting on you, Emmie," he told the little girl.

"Okay," she answered solemnly. Emmie had scrambled off the sofa and had assumed a rigid stance, carefully watching her mother for any movement.

Nick hurried outside and ran the length of the yard until he reach where the saddle was lying on the ground. About to pick it up and bring it into the house, he decided to examine it. At first glance, it appeared that Georgie was right. The saddle was in excellent condition, despite its age.

He was in foreign territory here, Nick thought, looking over the square skirt, lifting the heavily decorated fender. Unfamiliar with a saddle's construction, he had no idea what he was looking for.

And then, miraculously, he found it. Despite his ignorance, even he could identify a cut cinch when he saw one. He examined the offending length of leather. The cinch had been cut three quarters of the way through. It was torn the rest of the way.

Someone had tampered with her saddle, hoping for just this kind of a scenario. Were they out to kill her, or just to scare her? And if it was the latter, to what end?

Either way, it confirmed what he was thinking. That Georgie was the prime target. He had to make her understand that without frightening her.

Or maybe, he decided, a little fear might just do the trick. Otherwise, he had a feeling she would continue thumbing her nose and being damn reckless. It was apparently in her blood.

Georgie stared at him. What he was saying wasn't making any sense. "Cut?" He nodded. "You're sure?"

"I might not be able to lasso a steer or whatever it is you lasso around here," he told her. "But I know a cut cinch when I see one. Hey, hey, hey." She'd begun to get off the sofa again. Nick pushed her back down just as he had the first time. "Where do you think you're going?"

She didn't do helpless well. The dizziness had abated and she wanted to examine her saddle. She just couldn't believe someone would have actually done this on purpose. "I want to go see my saddle for myself."

Nick looked at her for a long moment. He'd never met someone quite like her. But right now, her stubbornness was loosing its appeal. "Why would I make that up?"

Frustration ate away at her. None of this made any sense. She felt as if she was trapped in some surreal story. "I don't know, why would you?"

"I wouldn't," he told her firmly. "Someone deliberately cut your cinch in a place you wouldn't immediately notice if you were in a hurry." And maybe there was something she hadn't realized, he thought. "If you'd fallen off your horse ten minutes later than you did, God only knows how long you would have laid there, unconscious."

No longer a sentry, Emmie was once again huddled against her, holding on as much to receive comfort as to give it. "You're scaring her," Georgie chided him.

"No need to be scared," he told her. "I'm not leaving your side until this thing gets resolved."

He had some time coming to him, time he hadn't used because there'd been no reason to use it. He wasn't the type who enjoyed flying off to some fashionably popular vacation site just to spend hours lying on a beach. He enjoyed working, being useful. Finding out who was after Georgie came under that heading.

Georgie didn't reply, but Emmie raised her head and smiled at him as if she thought he was the Angel Gabriel, sent down to protect them. It was reward enough.

Chapter 13

The silence within the house was so pervasive, it all but throbbed. Only the sound of his fingers hitting the keyboard interrupted the quiet.

Having gotten as much as he could from the computer tower in Georgie's bedroom, Nick was now working on the laptop he'd brought from Prosperino. At the moment, he used a popular software to enhance the strip of videotape he'd frozen. He attempted to isolate a decent close-up of the woman posing as Georgie in order to print a photograph. He intended to show that around town until he found someone who recognized her.

A faint noise behind him caught his attention and he was on his feet, his weapon drawn. And then he let out a breath as he saw what or rather who was responsible for the noise.

"Do you have duct tape lying around?" he asked Georgie.

She vaguely remembered seeing a round wheel of silver, but for the life of her, she couldn't recall just where. "Some place, I guess," she said with a shrug, then asked, "Why?"

"I figured I'd use it to tape you to your bed," he told her, sitting down again and turning his attention to the laptop.

He heard the smile in Georgie's voice, heard the slight rustle as she crossed to the sofa rather than back to her room as he'd hinted.

"I didn't know that Secret Service agents were allowed to be kinky."

"Nothing kinky about it," he said matter-of-factly, doing his best to concentrate. It wasn't easy with her in the room. Not when she was standing there, wearing an oversized T-shirt and what he imagined to be little else underneath. "I just want you resting."

"I'm fine," she assured him. She leaned against the sofa's overstuffed arm. "Headache's almost gone."

"If you're so fine, what are you doing up?" he asked. Rather than look at her, he glanced at his watch. "It's almost midnight."

She shrugged and the hem of her T-shirt rose dangerously high across her thighs. His thoughts went AWOL for a moment before he reined them in again. "I heard you typing."

Nick cleared his throat. It felt as dry as dust. "Sorry, I'll try to type softer."

"No, I'm sorry," she said with feeling, surprising him. "Sorry you have to put in all this extra time. Sorry you feel you need to stand guard."

In his estimation, there was no need to be sorry.

"Nothing I haven't done before." Nick assured her. And then he smiled as a distant memory floated through his mind. "This beats sitting in a car all night, making sure no one tampers with it."

"When did you do that?"

"When I first became a Secret Service agent, I got tapped to babysit the President's car the night before he flew in to tour Los Angeles," he explained. "Some sort of political fund-raiser," as he recalled. "It's kind of a rite of passage, testing the new agent to make sure he's got the stamina for boredom."

"You actually had to sit in his car all night?"

Nick nodded. "Right from the time it was certified as 'clean'—no bugs, no bombs, no surprises," he elaborated. "Everything was deemed in perfect running order. It was my job to see it stayed that way."

Georgie couldn't envision herself doing something like that. She needed to move around. "I would have gone crazy, having to sit still like that for that long," she confessed.

He'd felt the same way. "Point is," he told her, "I can stay awake for a long time and I don't mind 'guarding' you." He smiled at her, keeping his eyes on her face. "You're a lot prettier than the car was. Now go to bed." He tried to turn back to his work.

"I'm not tired," she protested. She remained leaning against the arm. "I've had too much resting as it is." Georgie decided to sit down on the sofa beside him and slid into place. She tugged the errant T-shirt down before it had a chance to ride up. "Do you mind having some company?" It was intended as a rhetorical question.

He had the uneasy feeling that one thing would lead

to another. The only way he would get anything done tonight was if she retreated and left the room.

"I'd rather you were in bed." He did his best to sound removed.

Her eyes caressed his face. "I'd rather you were there with me."

Did she have any idea how much he wanted her at this moment? He sincerely doubted it. And if he didn't get her to leave soon, he was going to act on his impulse. Still, he tried to verbally push her away by sounding flip. "I don't think you're in any shape for what that implies."

Sensing he was weakening—which was only fair because she was already there—Georgie feathered her fingertips through his hair. "You'd be surprised. I'm very resilient."

He grinned, thinking of the other night. "Not to mention incredibly flexible."

"With what I do—did," she corrected herself since rodeo competition was supposed to be in her past now, "for a living, I had to be."

He picked up on the correction. She meant to stick it out, he surmised. Good for her. "What are you going to do now?"

The future no longer looked nearly as certain as it had a little more than forty-eight hours ago. "I was going to settle down, give the rest of my life some thought. Maybe raise quarter horses." But a ranch like that required money, a good deal of it. Her voice took on a tinge of sarcasm. "But that was before my bank account suffered a crippling withdrawal—"

Nick cut in. "I'll find your money for you," he promised.

That he did so surprised him since he'd never been

one to give his word easily. He preferred coming through and having success speak for him instead of making promises ahead of time. That way, if he failed, his word wasn't compromised.

Georgie watched him for a long moment, her eyes searching his face for signs that he was just paying lip service. She didn't find any. "You're that confident?"

His mouth curved. "I'm that good."

Georgie laughed. "No shaky self-esteem problem found here."

He knew his abilities and that he usually did what he set out to do.

"Can't afford it," he said simply. "You've got to have confidence in yourself. In my line of work, you hesitate and you're not just risking your own life but the life of the person you're supposed to be guarding."

Which meant that he had to be alert twenty-four/seven. "Pretty nerve wracking way to earn a living if you ask me."

Nick inclined his head in silent agreement. "Almost as bad as galloping at break-neck speed, zigging and zagging between barrels," he commented drily.

Amused at the wording, she said, "The horse does the galloping."

He spread his hands wide, as if accepting the correction. "My mistake."

Curious, and far more relaxed than when she'd walked in, Georgie looked at what he worked on. Her mouth dropped open when she saw the blown up image he'd enhanced. Life-size, it was more startling. "My God, that almost does look like me."

"The nose is wrong," he pointed out. "Hers is sharp, yours is…perfect," he finally said for lack of a better word.

Every time she tried to shut things down inside, to

bar him access, he'd say or do some sweet little thing and throw everything off again. She might as well stop telling herself that she wasn't attracted to him because she was. And pretending that she didn't care if he stayed or left was a crock as well. She cared—even though she knew it was futile.

"You know," she told him, "for a closed-mouth person, you do say some very nice things."

He didn't quite see it that way. If anything, he was being abrupt. It was easier maintaining distance that way. "I skipped class the day they handed out silver tongues."

She thought of Jason, of how he'd gotten to her, saying things that made her lower her guard. Made her dream. "Silver tongues are highly overrated."

Nick read between the lines. "Oh? Did Emmie's father have a silver tongue?"

She stiffened and he knew he'd wandered out onto sensitive territory. But his curiosity, his need to know about her past, about the man she'd made love with, got the better of him. He told himself it was just to fill out her profile, but he knew he was lying.

Georgie sighed. Nick was going out of his way to protect her and her daughter when he clearly didn't have to. That meant she owed him. So, if he asked a question, the least she could do was answer it.

Forcing herself to relax, she said, "Yes, he did. Jason Prentiss." She gave him Emmie's father's name before Nick could ask. "I actually thought that what happened between us would last forever." God, had she ever been that naive? "Instead, it barely lasted the summer."

"Does he know?" Nick asked. When Georgie looked at him quizzically, he elaborated, "That Emmie is his?"

"He knows there's a child," she replied with a vague

shrug. "But as to sex or name, he didn't want to get 'that involved.'" She was quoting what Jason had said to her the evening she confessed that she was pregnant. "He wanted me to have an abortion. When I refused to sweep the baby out of my life, Jason quickly swept himself out of mine."

She paused for a moment before continuing. It had been a long while since she'd given Jason much thought. She'd had too much living to do to waste a moment thinking about the man she no longer loved, perhaps had never really loved.

"I don't know where he is these days and I really don't care. Looking back, he wasn't all that special." She was smarter now and could see through shallow posers like Jason. "But he did leave me with something wonderful, so I can't bring myself to hate him. Without Jason, I never would have gotten Emmie in my life." Her face was passionately animated as she said, "I can't begin to tell you what that little girl means to me."

"I think I can guess."

She grinned and laughed softly at herself. "That obvious, huh?" she asked, threading her fingers through her loose hair. As he watched, it seemed to him to shimmer like firelight.

"Only if you're conscious."

Nick studied her for a moment, thinking about the effect she'd had on him in such a very short time. He'd crossed lines because of her, stepped out of the boundaries that defined who and what he was. Moreover, he'd felt things he'd never felt before because of her. Things he didn't readily want to stop feeling anytime soon.

But he would have to, he reminded himself. Unless…

"Did you ever think about pulling up stakes, moving

away?" he asked quietly, watching Georgie's face for her reaction.

Her goal had always involved coming back here, amassing enough money to stay put and find a way to make a comfortable living in Esperanza.

"Where would I go?" She'd never even considered living anywhere else on a permanent basis. "This is home," she insisted. "I was born here. This has always been my home. This is where I belong." There'd never been any question of that in her mind. "Where would I go?" she repeated.

"Oh, I don't know." Yes he did, he knew exactly where he wanted her to go. "Washington."

"The state?" Why in heaven's name would she want to go live there? If anything, Montana or Wyoming would have been more in keeping with her way of life, not Washington.

"The city," he corrected. "D.C."

That would have been even stranger than the state. She certainly didn't belong back east. "I don't—"

He cut her off before she could say no. He wanted her to understand why he was asking. Wanted her to consider her answer before she gave it.

"If the Senator wins the election—" Nick was fairly certain that the man would win the nomination of his party "—he's going to D.C. and he'll need a protective detail with him at all times."

"And that would be you?" She already knew the answer, but hoped against hope that Nick would tell her something different. She didn't want a half a continent between them.

"I'd be one of them," he told her. He saw the look on her face and didn't have to hear what her response would be to his suggestion about moving to a large city. He already knew.

"I'm a small-town girl, Nick," she told him. "I always have been. I'd be lost in a place like Washington, D.C."

He shook his head, even as he slipped his hands about her face and then through her hair, framing her face. "Nothing small town about you, Georgeann Colton."

"Grady," she corrected softly. "I tend to think of myself as Georgie Grady. There's nothing about me that belongs to the Coltons."

He smiled and a sadness took root within him. "I tend to think of you as vibrant and exciting."

He saw laughter in her eyes and felt his pulse quicken. "That, too."

"Go back to bed, Georgie," he told her, dropping his hands. "Before I forget I'm not supposed to make love with you."

She had no desire to leave. All too soon, he'd be the one doing the leaving. She wanted to grasp as much happiness as she could in the limited amount of time she had left.

Georgie didn't get up. Instead, she feathered a kiss along his throat. "I won't break if you kiss me, Nick. I promise."

After years of holding himself in check, of controlling his every move, his resolve had frayed and reached its breaking point. He felt his pulse racing as her breath slid along his skin. "You're going to be my undoing, woman."

She laughed lightly, deliberately banishing any thoughts of all the tomorrows that loomed ahead of her. Tomorrows when this man would be gone, fulfilling his destiny and living the rest of his life without her. For now, he was here and that was all she was going to focus on. Because the rest of it was too difficult to think about.

"Everybody's got a job to do," she murmured, again, kissing his throat.

He needed no more coaxing than that. Lifting her into his arms the way he had the night before, Nick carried her to her bedroom. This time he paused not just to close the door as he had last time, but to lock it as well—just in case Emmie decided to pay her mother another unannounced nocturnal visit.

He made love with Georgie softly, gently, and for half the night, until exhaustion claimed them both and they fell asleep in each other's arms.

On his very first job, Nick had schooled himself to sleep with one eye open. Any noise that was out of place was guaranteed to wake him.

As it did this time.

Instantly alert, he sat up, listening. Someone was trying to turn the doorknob and come in. Was it Emmie? He didn't think so. She would have called out for her mother when she couldn't open the door.

Whoever was on the other side of the door released the doorknob and retreated.

Someone was in the house.

Faster than the blink of an eye, Nick was up and pulling on his pants. He zipped them up as he crossed to the door, flipping the lock he'd secured earlier. Nick yanked the door open just in time to see a shadowy figure fleeing to the living room.

Nick broke into a run.

The intruder had too much of a head start on him.

Nick barely managed to get within reaching distance. Lunging, he caught the person—a woman he now realized—by the hair.

Without a backward glance, she continued running and made it to the front door.

The forward motion when he grabbed for her hair threw him off balance because, instead of bringing the woman down, Nick found himself holding on to a wig. A red wig. It was fashioned like Georgie's hair, with a thick, long, red braid.

It was too dark for him to make out any of her features, except that she appeared to be a blonde. His gut told him that the intruder was the woman caught on the tapes from both the bank and the jewelry store.

The lights suddenly came on, robbing the shadows of their space.

But the intruder was gone.

"What's going on?" Georgie cried, her hand still on the light switch on the wall. At seeing the wig he had in his hand, a sick feeling bubbled in her stomach. She heard herself ask, "What's that?" as she nodded at his hand.

He looked at it in disgust. "I seem to have scalped your impersonator."

Georgie felt both violated and mad as hell. It was bad enough to have someone break in when she was away, but to have an intruder invade her home, her sanctuary while she was sleeping in it, made it so much worse.

"She was here?" Georgie asked hoarsely.

He nodded. "Obviously she didn't know that you'd gotten back." Georgie crossed the room and headed straight for the coffee table, where she kept one of the two phones in the house. "What are you doing?" he asked as Georgie picked up the phone receiver and began to dial.

She didn't answer until she finished dialing. It was the middle of the night, but she knew the call would automatically be transferred to Jericho Yates's home. Jericho was the county sheriff and someone she'd known for a long time.

"No offense, Nick, but I'd feel a whole lot better if we brought the sheriff in on this." She saw he was about to protest her decision, but she wasn't going to be talked out of it. She had her daughter to consider. Georgie's voice picked up speed. "You can't stay here indefinitely and watch over us and if anything happened to Emmie because of this crazy woman—"

He wanted to argue with her because he preferred to keep this contained. But his conscience wouldn't allow it. Georgie was right, he wasn't going to be here in Esperanza indefinitely. He had a life, a career, waiting for him back in California. And she would go on living here. Georgie deserved to live without fear haunting her every move.

Stepping away, he waved at the phone. "Go ahead. Tell the sheriff to come," he told her. "Just don't mention anything about the e-mails."

The phone was still ringing on the other end. She covered the mouthpiece. "Why not?"

"Because that falls under my jurisdiction," he reminded her.

She didn't see how he could separate one issue from the other, but she didn't protest. She just wanted this impostor, this creature who'd taken her money, her name, her life, caught and punished.

A deep, sleepy voice came on on the other end. "Yates."

"Sheriff, this is Georgie Grady. Someone just tried to break into my house. Could you please come by first thing in the morning?"

"I'll do better than that, Georgie," the sheriff told her. "I'll be there in half an hour."

Chapter 14

True to his word, Sheriff Jericho Yates was standing in her doorway within twenty minutes.

Georgie had had only enough time to throw on clothes. Nick had gotten dressed and then done something on his computer that she hadn't had time to look at yet, but Nick had looked pleased with the outcome. He was in the process of printing whatever it was he'd come up with when the Sheriff had rung her doorbell. She'd flown to answer it.

Georgie didn't recognize the man standing next to the sheriff. The latter wore the uniform of a deputy and was a little shorter than Jericho. But then, at six feet three inches most people were a little shorter than Jericho. And, she'd come to know, a hell of a lot more cheerful than the serious thirty-five-year old.

Tall, broad-shouldered and lean-hipped, Jericho

Yates was a wall of solid muscle. Wearing his dark blond hair long and some facial stubble, he looked more like Hollywood's version of an old-fashioned lawman out of the 1800s. But the thing about Jericho was that, despite the fact that he hardly ever smiled and never used twenty words when three would do, he inspired confidence in the people he dealt with and protected. People felt safe when he was around, even though his territory stretched out beyond Esperanza to include the entire county.

Jericho's hazel eyes swept over her as he nodded a greeting. When his eyes shifted to look at Nick, they hardened just a touch. Strangers were subjected to close scrutiny.

Now, with the house lit up and the sheriff and his deputy, not to mention Nick all standing around her, Georgie felt a little foolish about the momentary attack of anxiety that had caused her to call the sheriff.

"I really didn't mean for you to come out to the ranch in the middle of the night, Sheriff."

Jericho's expression never changed, but she had the definite impression that he was looking right into her head.

"You wouldn't have called if you didn't. You would have waited until morning." Again, his eyes shifted over toward Nick.

The Secret Service agent had never felt himself being dissected and measured so quickly before, even when he'd originally applied for his present position. Leaning forward, one hand on Georgie's shoulder in an unspoken gesture signifying protection, he extended his hand to the sheriff. "I'm Nick Sheffield."

The deputy, who clearly was trying to emulate his boss, asked, "You a friend of hers, Nick Sheffield?"

"In a manner of speaking," Nick said, busy with his own process of measuring and dissecting. The sheriff was coming from a position of confident strength. He got the impression that the deputy had yet to achieve that for himself.

She felt tension in the air, or maybe that was just her. Clearing her throat, Georgie decided to get the introductions out of the way.

"Nick, this is Sheriff Jericho Yates. And—" Her voice trailed off as she realized something. "I'm sorry," she told the deputy, "I don't know who you are."

Maybe it was her, but she felt like there'd been an influx of a great many new faces in Esperanza since she'd left. The town was clearly growing. Until this moment, she hadn't realized how much she liked being able to recognize everyone she passed on the street until that ability was lost to her.

Jericho came to her rescue. "This is my new deputy, Adam Rawlings." He was still breaking in the man, but all things considered, Rawlings was coming along nicely. The deputy, he noted out of the corner of his eye, flashed a guileless smile at Georgie and then her "friend." "Anything missing?" Jericho asked as he walked into the house. He scanned the area and it didn't look as if anything had been disturbed.

This most recent break-in was the legendary straw that had broken the camel's back. Words just came pouring out. "The money out of my bank account. My mother's jewelry. My—"

Jericho stopped her, appearing slightly puzzled as he tried to make sense out of what she'd just said. "You emptied your bank account and then brought the money home?"

Frustrated, Georgie backtracked. "No, *she* emptied my bank account—*and* my safety deposit box and she was probably the one who's responsible for maxing out all of my credit cards."

Jericho held his hand up. "Slow down, Georgie," he instructed. When she stopped talking, he asked, "'She?'"

Georgie's head bobbed up and down. "The woman who's passing herself off as me. Right down to the wig." The second she mentioned the wig, she moved over to the coffee table where Nick had deposited the disguise. She held it up for the sheriff to see.

"She broke into the house at about three-thirty," Nick estimated. "I woke up when I heard her trying the doorknob—"

"To the house?" Jericho asked.

"No, to the bedroom. The door was locked." Jericho said nothing, but his silence spoke volumes. "I tried to get her but she had too much of a head start on me. She escaped."

"But one of you managed to scalp her," Adam added wryly, humor twisting his mouth. Jericho shot him a reproving look before turning his attention back to Nick.

He nodded toward the wig. "We're going to have to take that in as evidence."

Nick would have been disappointed if the man hadn't suggested that.

"You might want to run it for DNA," he encouraged. The Sheriff merely looked at him as if he'd suggested taking the wig dancing. "One of her own hairs might have gotten stuck in the wig."

"Watch a lot of TV, do you?" There wasn't even a single hint of amusement in the sheriff's voice.

"I was a cop in L.A.," Nick countered. They didn't

have the finest lab in the country, but at least they had access to it.

"That would explain it," Jericho murmured under his breath. "We don't have a forensic lab here. That'll have to go to San Antonio for processing. Might be six months before we hear anything. Maybe more. In the meantime—" he turned toward Georgie "—you know anyone who would want to do you harm?"

"Not off the circuit. And not really on either," she amended quickly. "Just knocked out of the running. But I've given up rodeoing." There, she'd said it out loud and made it public with someone who was in contact with most of Esperanza. The sheriff wasn't a talker, but word would get around. Not like lightning, more like the widening ripples in the lake after a rock was tossed in. "It's time I settled down. Emmie's going to be in kindergarten in the fall."

Jericho nodded. "Got a plastic bag we could use?" he wanted to know, then nodded toward the evidence that was back on the coffee table. "For the wig."

"Sure. I'll go get it." Georgie turned on her heel and went to the kitchen to find a plastic bag for the sheriff. So far, she was lucking out. Emmie was still asleep, but that was subject to change and she wanted these official-looking men out of her house before the little girl was up.

Nick stepped forward. He took the photograph he'd just printed out before Jericho and his man had arrived. He handed it over to the sheriff now. "You might want to pass around this photograph, see if anyone knows her."

Jericho took the snapshot from him and examined it for a long moment. It was of a young blond woman. "You had time to take her picture?"

"That's off a surveillance tape. She was using one of Georgie's credit cards to buy herself a diamond ring. When I pulled off her wig just now, I saw she had blond hair, so I changed the clip around, gave her blond hair," Nick told him.

Jericho studied the photograph, then raised his eyes to Nick's face. He had as many questions about him as he had about the woman in the photo. "Who the hell did you say you were?"

They both knew he hadn't identified himself beyond his name. "Just a concerned friend who wants to see Georgie reunited with her money."

"Right."

It was obvious by his tone that Jericho didn't believe him for a second, but for the time being, his skepticism didn't matter. They had to find this woman.

"Mind if I take a look, Sheriff?" Adam asked, nodding at the photograph.

"Help yourself." Jericho handed over the photograph, then waited for some kind of comment. "Recognize her?" he prodded.

Wide shoulders rose up and down in a noncommittal shrug. He had the photograph back to the sheriff. "Looks a lot like Miss Grady."

"That's the whole point," Jericho told his deputy patiently.

"Yeah, I guess it is," Adam agreed sheepishly.

It struck Nick that as far as deputies went, this one wasn't the sharpest knife in the drawer.

Georgie returned with a plastic bag. It still had the faint smell of the apples she'd just emptied out about it. Jericho nodded at her, then deposited the wig inside the bag, tucking in the long braid. It was a tight fit.

Jericho paused to ask her a few more questions, then seemed satisfied for the time being.

"We'll be back," he promised her, slipping the photograph that Nick had created into the front pocket of his shirt.

Georgie walked the two men to the door. "Thank you for coming so fast."

Opening the door, Jericho paused one last time. He glanced at his deputy. "I could leave Rawlings here to watch the house," he offered.

"That won't be necessary," she assured the sheriff quickly. She glanced over at the man who had shared her bed. "I've got Nick."

Again, there was no indication what he thought of her answer. "And that worked out pretty good for you, didn't it?" He was clearly referring to the fact that the intruder had broken in and gotten as far as she had with this "Nick" in attendance.

A wave of defensiveness rose within her. Her green eyes slanted toward Nick. "Overall, yes," she informed the sheriff quietly.

"Suit yourself," Jericho told her. "I'll be in touch," he repeated, tipping his hat to her, then nodding at Nick.

"Want some coffee?" she asked as soon as she had closed the door and the sheriff and deputy were on their way.

Nick glanced at his watch. It was barely five o'clock. "Why don't you go back to bed?" he suggested gently.

Georgie shook her head. There was no way she could go back to sleep.

"Too keyed up. Dawn's almost here anyway." She sighed. How had everything fallen apart like this? *Was* there someone out to get her? The very thought was guaranteed to keep her awake nights. "Might as well get ready for it."

Being with her this short time had made him a student of the inflections in her voice. He recognized that tone. She was too anxious to sleep.

"Then I'll take that coffee," he told her, following her into the kitchen. "As long as you hold back on the asphalt."

She laughed. "I'll see what I can do."

He couldn't talk Georgie out of coming with him, although God knew he'd tried. Knowing that the sheriff could only devote a small amount of time to finding the woman in the photograph, he'd printed up more than a hundred and got to work questioning people.

It was a day later and his showing the photograph around to the various shops, restaurants and bars in Esperanza had finally paid off.

The affable bartender/owner at Joe's Bar & Grill recognized the blonde.

He rubbed a cloth over the permanently scarred and stained counter as if it was second nature to him. "That looks just like the little girl who came to me looking for a job a while ago." He took a second look in the sparse light. It was the middle of the day outside, but inside the bar it was on the cusp of midnight. "I didn't have an opening, but I had her fill out an application anyway, in case one came up."

"You still have that application?" Nick had asked.

"Well, sure. Somewhere." The answer was meant to end the conversation, not tear it wide open.

"Would you mind getting it?" Nick asked. When the bartender remained where he was, massaging the counter, Nick took out a fifty and placed it in the path of the man's towel. He stopped rubbing.

Favoring his left foot, the bartender lumbered into the back to an overcrowded, small storage room. Nick followed with Georgie shadowing his every step. He would have felt a great deal better leaving her home but Georgie refused to be left.

It took the bartender a few minutes and several curses before he came across the application. The paper was stuck in a manila folder that had an altercation with a bottle of beer. Consequently, some of the writing was gone. But just enough still visible for Nick to piece together an address. He hurriedly wrote it down on the pad he carried with him.

"Okay," Georgie declared the second he handed the folder back to the bartender, "what are we waiting for? Let's go."

"I'll take you home," he told her.

"You will not," she informed him in no uncertain terms. "Whose life did she steal? Whose house was she squatting in?" Georgie demanded as they walked back out into the sunlight. "Mine, not yours. Mine," she repeated. "There's no way you're going to confront this Rebecca Totten without me," she told him.

He had a feeling that she meant that. That even if he brought her home, she'd follow him. She got a good look at the address as well. And because they'd left Emmie with Clay early this morning, there was no stopping Georgie from doing just that.

He could stand here and argue with her, but that would waste time. She was more stubborn than a legendary mule, even if she was a hell of a lot prettier.

"If you think that I'm going to let you—"

Nick threw up his hands, not wanting to listen to any more of her tirade. "Okay," he declared, knowing he was going to regret this, "You can come."

"Damn straight I can come," she shot back, striding to where they had parked his car. "Woman steals my money, taking food out of my child's mouth, not to mention my good name, there's no way I'm not going to take care of business," she informed him hotly. Reaching the vehicle, she waited for him to unlock the door.

Nick hit the proper button on his key ring. The car made a piercing noise and all four of the locks popped open.

"You know, you can put it down," Nick told her just as she got in on the passenger side.

"Put what down?" she asked, confused.

He rounded the trunk and then got in on the driver's side, slamming the door a little louder than he'd intended. "That chip on your shoulder."

"Just drive," she told him.

He backed out of the space, then put his car in gear. They drove down the main thoroughfare. "We don't know if this Rebecca is really the one we're looking for," he pointed out.

Rebecca was the one. She could *feel* it in her bones. But to forestall another argument, she told him, "Don't worry, Nick, I promise I won't punch her out until we have proof."

"Why doesn't that comfort me?" Nick shook his head as he took a right turn on the next corner. Georgie Grady was one of a kind, all right.

There was no answer when he knocked. After a second time, he took out his cell phone.

"Who are you calling?" she asked.

"A friend of mine to see if we can get a search warrant."

"That's going to take time," she complained.

"Yes, it is. You have any better ideas?" It was a rhetorical question. He didn't expect an answer. Waiting for his friend to pick up the phone on the other end of the line, Nick turned around to look at Georgie.

"Oh, look, she left the door open," Georgie announced glibly, turning the knob and walking in.

The door had been locked less than two minutes ago. An answering machine kicked in on the other end of his call. Nick cut it off, shutting the phone. "How did you learn to do that?" he asked.

"A girl picks things up along the way" was all she said. He had no need to know that Ryder had taught her how to pick a lock, or that Ryder was currently serving time in prison.

Once inside the small apartment, Nick pulled on a pair of rubber gloves before he started to methodically go through Rebecca Totten's things.

Impressed by the gloves, Georgie smiled. "You certainly come prepared," she commented.

"Saves time," was all he said.

Since she didn't want to leave any incriminating fingerprints here herself, Georgie put on a pair of work gloves she had stuffed into her back pocket and undertook her own search.

Because of the size of the apartment—little more than a studio—the search went quickly. There was nothing hidden in the bureau drawers, or, it appeared, the closet. Nothing in the tiny pantry either.

But the apartment came with a Murphy bed and when he pulled it down, Nick hit the jackpot. The unimaginative woman had succumbed to a cliché and hidden incriminating evidence under her mattress.

"Well, she's obviously not a professional," he murmured, letting the bed, now unmade, pop back up into the wall. He held the folder he'd extricated.

Georgie, on her knees examining the contents of pots that were stacked inside the stove, looked up excitedly. "You found something?"

The question wasn't even out of her mouth before she hurried over to join him in the tiny area designated as the "bedroom."

The folder contained several photographs of Georgie and a couple of the Senator. There were also a few receipts stuffed into the folder, including one for the wig *and* one for the ring from the jewelry store that had captured her on tape.

Nick almost found it amusing. What did the woman intend to do, use the receipts for tax purposes when she filed her 1040? Would she identify them as items bought in order to commit identity theft?

Or were the receipts intended for someone else to act as proof of what she was doing?

"We got her, don't we?" Georgie asked excitedly, clutching the large book she'd been going through in hopes of shaking loose evidence that might have been stored inside.

"Looks like," he agreed. "Right down to her crooked little feet."

Georgie closed her eyes, exhaling a deep sigh of relief. She tucked the folder into an oversized book that was on the coffee table in order to keep the photographs from bending. "Oh, God, it's over. The nightmare's really over."

That was when she heard it.

The sound of a gun being cocked.

Georgie turned around slowly to find herself looking at a young, petite blond woman who looked like her only in so far as they were both roughly the same age and had the same complexion.

"Not yet," Rebecca Totten told her. She held a gun directly at them. "You know, if you two stand just like that, one in front of the other, I can kill both of you using just one bullet. I like being frugal," she said, an unnerving smile curving her mouth. And then she sighed. "I really wasn't counting on this. You weren't supposed to figure out who I was," she said, seeming clearly put out. "But then, that's what makes life interesting, isn't it? All the twists and turns that you can't predict."

She looked at Georgie, her quirky smile deepening. "Bet you never predicted it would end like this. And, for what it's worth, I am sorry. But you are going to have to die. You know that, right?"

Even as she asked the question, the blonde raised her hand and took careful aim. Her hand began to tremble. Uttering a curse, she took hold of her right hand with her left, intending to steady it so that her aim was true.

Chapter 15

The moment she saw the gun, adrenaline surged through Georgie at the speed of light. Operating purely on instinct, she launched the book she held at Rebecca's arm to deflect the shot.

At the same moment, Nick threw his body in front of Georgie to keep her from being hit by the bullet. Seeing the book hit the woman, he dived for Rebecca, bringing her down. Grabbing her right arm, he forced it up so that the gun barrel was aimed at the ceiling as he tried to disarm her.

"No, no," the blonde cried wildly, frightened as she struggled for possession of the weapon.

Georgie scrambled to her feet, searching for something to use as a weapon or to knock Rebecca out. There was nothing readily available.

The sound registered belatedly.

A single, deafening shot going off.

For a split second, Georgie froze. She'd been around the sound of guns all her life, but this time, it was surreal.

A sick feeling twisted the pit of her stomach as she swung back around. Nick was on the floor, on his knees. There was blood all over him.

"Nick!" she screamed, fear all but gutting her.

Darkness swirled around her, threatening to swallow her whole. She fought to keep it at bay. It took a long, life-draining moment before she realized that Nick hadn't been hurt. That the blood that covered his signature black suit wasn't his, but belonged to the woman he now held in his arms.

"I'm all right. Call for an ambulance," he ordered Georgie. And then he looked at Rebecca. He could all but see the life force ebbing away from her. The woman was dying. He needed to know the answer before she was gone. "Rebecca, did someone put you up to this?"

The blonde's eyes were unfocused, staring off at something that was beyond his shoulder. Fear and bewilderment etched themselves into her pale, young features.

"It…wasn't…supposed to be…like…this…"

They were the last words she uttered.

Watching, holding her breath, Georgie squeezed the cell phone in her hand. "Is she…?"

The word didn't need to be said out loud. Nick nodded, then gently slipped his hand over Rebecca's eyes, closing them. Very carefully, he lowered the body onto the floor and then got up. Everything else was left just as it was, including the gun they had wrestled over, the gun that had been twisted so that it fired into her chest instead of his.

He'd literally dodged a bullet that time, he thought cynically, relieved to still be standing.

"You're not hurt, are you?" she cried. Not waiting for an answer, she pulled back the sides of his suit jacket, anxiously looking for holes.

He'd seen enough death to be rendered numb to it, but this one had shaken him. The young woman's life force had all but slipped through his fingers.

Glancing down at himself, he looked for a telltale hole that might have been the source of at least part of the blood flow. He knew that some victims of gunshot wounds didn't even feel the bullet entering and his entire body had numbed and tensed.

But there was no hole, no wound. All the blood belonged to Rebecca.

"No," he murmured almost distantly. "But this is going to generate one hell of a cleaning bill."

"Shut up," Georgie cried, throwing her arms around him and just holding him, grateful beyond words that he was still alive.

Nick looked over Georgie's shoulder at the body on the floor.

What a waste, he thought. What a useless waste. Rebecca Totten looked to be in her twenties, if that old. Ten minutes ago, she had her whole life ahead of her, and now, now there was nothing.

Very gently, he extricated himself from Georgie's hold. "Call the sheriff, Georgie," he instructed woodenly.

Stepping back, still holding the cell phone in her hand, Georgie did as she was told. Less than a minute later, the other end was being picked up. "Yates," a deep voice announced.

Her pulse still pounding, not to mention her head, Georgie drew in a long cleansing breath, then began talking.

Jericho and his deputy had been less than a mile away when the call came in. They were there, at the studio apartment, in under five minutes. The sheriff quickly took in the scene, his hazel eyes sweeping from one end of the studio apartment to the other, coming to rest on the woman on the floor.

"Dead?" he asked Nick. The latter nodded. Jericho squatted over the body without touching her, slowly absorbing everything. "How did she happen to get that way?" His even, low tone gave no clue as to what he was thinking.

"Self-defense," Nick replied.

Jericho rose, shifting his penetrating look to the Secret Service Agent. "We'll get back to that," he promised mildly. "Secure the scene, Rawlings," he told his deputy.

"Yes, sir," Adam murmured.

A thorough search of the small studio apartment yielded the final damning evidence. Under a pile of clothes in the back of the walk-in closet was an old gym bag. It was crammed full of money. Nearly three hundred thousand dollars.

Georgie's money.

Nick took a quick inventory of the amount after Jericho handed it over to him. "Looks like you're going to be getting that horse ranch after all," Nick commented.

"That's evidence for now," Jericho warned. "But there's no reason it won't be available to you soon," he added, his voice softening slightly.

The elation Georgie felt at actually recovering her life's savings was tempered in the next heartbeat by not just the pall of death, but the haunting realization that Nick would be leaving. The threat against the Senator was over.

She couldn't bear the idea of there being half a continent between them, be it California or Washington, D.C., and yet, pride kept her from asking him to stay. Especially because she wasn't sure of his answer. He'd seemed too focused on advancing his career when they talked last night.

And if she asked him to stay and he said no, it would drive a stake through her heart.

"Call the doc," Jericho said to his deputy. "Tell him we have a body for him." It was far from a usual occurrence. When Rawlings made no move to comply, Jericho paused to glare at him. The deputy looked pale. "You all right, Adam?"

Adam blew out a breath. Unable to draw his eyes away from the prone body when he first walked in, now he avoided looking at the dead woman.

"No," Rawlings said in a low voice. And then, because the single word begged for a follow-up, he explained, "I've never seen a dead body before."

Jericho nodded, understanding. "Not exactly a common sight around Esperanza. At least, not like that. Folks around here tend to die of natural causes, not from lead poisoning." Rawlings went to summon the doctor the department had on retainer. Jericho turned his attention to Nick and the next step in procedure. "I'm going to need a statement." Jericho's words took in Georgie as well. "From both of you.

"No problem," Nick replied. He wasn't aware that

he slipped his arm protectively around Georgie, but Jericho was. He noted, too, that she made no effort to shrug the arm away.

It was another two hours before Nick and Georgie were finally back in his car, driving to her ranch. But first they needed to stop by her brother's place to pick up her daughter.

The air was pregnant with the smell of impending rain. The silence between them grew oppressive.

Nick broke the silence first.

"Come with me," he said without any preamble. He spared her a glance before turning back to the monotonous road that stretched out before him. "Pack your things, pack up Emmie and come with me." The two sentences probably qualified as the most impulsive thing he'd ever said.

She could feel her heart aching already. But this wasn't just about her, or even just about them. There was Emmie to think of. Emmie, who deserved the best she could give her. Emmie, who deserved the chances she never had. "I can't."

"Why not?" Even as he formed the question, he knew the answer. But if he talked fast enough, maybe it wouldn't come. "By your own admission, you've been going from place to place at a moment's notice. Here today, someplace else tomorrow, living inside a rattling tin can on wheels." He looked at her again. God help him, he didn't want to stop looking at her. Ever. She was like a fever in his blood. He struggled to be rational. "I can offer you something a lot better than that."

Georgie clenched her hands in her lap, as if that could

somehow ground her. "I know, and I'm tempted. Oh, God, Nick, you have no idea how much I'm tempted—"

If she felt that way, what was the problem? "Then come."

"I can't," she repeated, her voice threatening to break.

He could feel his patience unraveling. It seemed so damn simple from the outside. *Could* be so damn simple. "For God's sake, why not?"

How did she make him understand when even her own heart was rebelling against her? "Because ever since I had Emmie, this was the plan. To make enough money to finally give her a home, something secure. Something my brothers and I didn't have, no matter how hard my mother tried. Money buys you security."

His hands tightened on the wheel as he struggled to understand and to be gracious. "So if I hadn't found that gym bag in the back of Rebecca's closet, I would have had a better chance of your coming with me."

She still wouldn't have left. Because this was Emmie's home. This were where their roots were and roots were oh so important to both of them.

"Don't," she begged. "Please don't." She blinked back tears. "You could stay here."

He saw no prospects for work in a place like Esperanza. "And do what?"

"Love me."

He felt his heart twist in his chest. "Not that that isn't a tempting proposition, but I need to be able to provide for you," he pointed out.

"No, you don't," she protested quickly. "I've got enough money to last us for a while. And then there's the ranch."

He wasn't cowboy material and they both knew it.

And no way would he live off her earnings. "That's not how it works," he told her.

A ragged sigh escaped her lips. Turning her head so that he wouldn't see her tears, Georgie looked out the side window. "I know."

The first thing Nick did when he arrived back in California was report to the Senator, who was still at his Prosperino estate. He found the man in his den, going over the latest draft to his next speech.

Joe Colton seemed delighted to see his chief Secret Service agent back.

Nick closed the door behind him. "It's over, sir."

Joe immediately thought of the threatening e-mails. The flow, according to his people, had ceased just before Nick had left for Texas. "You caught the man?"

"Woman," Nick corrected. "Turned out to be a twenty-one-year-old ex-waitress from Reno. Rebecca Totten."

The name meant nothing to the Senator. "Tell me, did she say what she had against me?"

Nick shook his head. "She didn't say much of anything."

Very quickly, Nick ran through the events, giving the Senator as succinct a version of the last five days as he could. He left out certain details, all of which had to do with Georgie. In his opinion, they neither added nor subtracted from the narrative.

Joe looked pleased at how things had been resolved, although he made it clear that he regretted that the young woman paid for her misdeeds with her life.

"Great job, Nick. I really appreciate your going the extra mile on this. Or extra several thousand miles as the case may be." Joe flashed the smile he was so famous for, the one that was from the heart and guileless and had won him such a huge following. He settled back in his chair. "Tell me, how's my niece doing?" he asked, noting that any reference to her was conspicuously missing.

Nick's voice was clipped as he said, "I managed to recover her money, so she can get on with her life, setting up a ranch to breed quarter horses."

Joe's smile widened. "From what I hear, that sort of thing is in her blood. Her older brother, Clay, has a ranch around there, too."

"I met him," Nick volunteered cautiously, wondering if this was going somewhere or if it was just harmless conversation.

Joe nodded. From where he stood, the head of his Secret Service detail seemed preoccupied. "Something wrong, Nick?"

"Jet lag," Nick told him a little too quickly.

"Uh-huh." Joe eyed him knowingly—or was that just his imagination? Nick wondered. "Why don't you take some time off to deal with that?" the Senator suggested. "You've more than earned it."

Time off was the *last* thing he needed. He needed to fill up his days with routines, not have them empty so that he could spend his time thinking.

"If it's all the same to you, sir," Nick said, "I'd rather just get right back into it. I've been away from the job too long."

Joe laughed, shaking his head. "Seems to me, you've been on it all this time."

Nick shrugged. "It's what I'm paid to do," he replied. "If there's nothing else—"

"Not right now," Joe answered.

With a nod, Nick took his leave. The moment he walked away from the Senator's den, he threw himself into his work. The first order of business was to get a complete update from the agent he'd left in charge about what had been going on in his absence.

And all the while, as he worked, reviewing schedules, planning for contingencies, Nick struggled to block out any and all extraneous thoughts. Extraneous thoughts that involved a woman with flaming red hair and eyes the color of a field of four-leaf clovers.

It was a losing battle.

Nick knew when he was licked. After two days of trying to get the upper hand and place his life back on the course it had been on these last few years, he was forced, for his own sanity, to surrender.

The first step was to tell the Senator that he needed to resign.

"Do you mind if I come in?" he asked the Senator, popping his head into Joe's office.

In the midst of packing up for yet another fund-raiser, this one taking place in Phoenix the next afternoon, Joe stopped what he was doing and beckoned Nick into his study.

"Come on in," he urged. Noting the serious expression on the Secret Service agent's face, Joe wondered if any more e-mails had surfaced. "What's on your mind?"

Tip-toeing around a subject had never been Nick's way. "Your niece, sir."

For a split second, Joe looked mildly surprised. And then he smiled. "Took you a while, didn't it?"

He'd thought he'd hidden his feelings rather well.

The Senator's question caught him off guard. "Excuse me, Senator?"

Joe laughed. "Don't play dumb with me, Nick. It doesn't suit you." Pausing to pour two fingers of Napoleon brandy for both himself and his, he felt, about-to-be-ex-head of Secret Service, Joe held out one glass to Nick. "I could see it when you came back to report to me."

Accepting the glass, Nick looked at him, puzzled. "See what?"

"That you didn't belong here anymore," Joe answered simply. "You belong back there, with her."

Nick paused to take a sip. The amber liquid warmed a path down to his gut. "I don't think I 'belong' anywhere," he confessed. "Esperanza is a one-horse town."

"It's a little bigger than that," Joe assured him. He'd kept tabs on its progress, as he did on everything that interested him. "And it's growing all the time. Man of your capabilities and talents can find a lot of opportunities there—or make your own. Heading a security firm comes to mind," he commented just before he took a sip of the brandy himself. "Seems to me that you've already found the most important thing."

He'd always admired and respected the Senator and enjoyed being privy to the man's insight whenever he could. He was going to miss that, he thought. "What's that?"

"The love of a good woman."

Joe looked at the framed photograph that stood on his desk. It was of Meredith and him taken on one of their all-too-brief vacations. He couldn't recall the location, only that something had caught her fancy and she'd been laughing when her image was captured, forever freezing the moment. Looking at the photograph now, he could almost hear her laughter. Warm like sunshine, he thought.

"Trust me, Nick, everything else is a distant second." Placing his glass of brandy on his desk, Joe put out his hand. "Much as I hate to lose you—and I do—this is the best reason in the world for you to leave."

"I'll stay until my replacement's trained," Nick promised, but Joe shook his head.

"Don't even give it another thought. Just go, get the girl," Joe encouraged.

"All right, then," Nick said, more than ready to do just that. "I need to ask a favor, sir."

Joe smiled at him warmly. "If it's in my power, it's yours."

Georgie couldn't sleep. Sighing, she surrendered to the haunting insomnia. That made two nights in a row now that she'd tossed and turned, exhausted and too keyed up to sleep.

By all rights, she thought angrily, she should be sleeping like a baby. Her name had been cleared, her money and her jewelry had been restored. Even the credit card companies had been convinced to cover their losses, restoring her credit along with her good credit standing. All of that had been Nick's doing and it meant that she could get on with her life unimpeded.

But despite all that, her life felt as if it was stuck in a tar pit and she couldn't move forward. Couldn't move because her heart was no longer a functioning part of her anatomy. It was two or three thousand miles away.

Where the hell was Prosperino, California, anyway? she wondered impatiently.

A sound she couldn't quite identify nudged its way into her consciousness.

What *was* that? Thunder?

No, this was constant, she realized, sitting up. Thunder rolled and then lightning flashed. This just continued. Besides, the weather forecast called for clear skies for the next day or so.

The only place it was raining was in her heart, she thought.

The unidentified noise sounded as if it was getting closer.

Georgie kicked off the sheet she'd had covering her. Leaving the shelter of her bed, she grabbed her robe and went to the front door. Might as well satisfy her curiosity if she couldn't satisfy anything else.

Her hand was on the doorknob, about to open the door in order to see what she could see. The knock startled her, causing a stifled gasp to escape.

Who the hell would be out this early, paying her a call? There was a chain on her door, fallout from her experience with that woman posing as her. She left it in place and cautiously opened the door a crack.

Her mouth dropped open. Fumbling with the chain, she yanked the door open.

"Nick?"

He smiled at her sheepishly. "It's me," he confirmed. The last word was muffled as Georgie framed his face with her hands and kissed him hard and long.

If this was a dream, she wanted to get the most out of it before it faded, she thought, her head spinning.

But it didn't fade.

And from her experience, dreams did *not* kiss like that.

Breathless, she dropped her hands to her sides and

took a step back, still half expecting him to vanish. After two sleepless nights, she was a perfect candidate for hallucinations.

He was still here, clutching flowers whose heads were bent.

"What are you doing here?" she cried, squeezing the question out.

"I came back," was his simple reply. And then he added, "To give you these." He thrust the bouquet of slightly wilting daisies into her hands. It was a pathetic offering, but when a man proposed and had no ring, he needed to bring something. Flowers were all he could think of and she'd mentioned liking daisies. "I had the pilot set the helicopter down in a field so I could pick them for you." He shrugged, embarrassed at the offering. "It was all I could find. They don't have twenty-four-hour flower shops."

She grinned, blinking back tears. He was here, he was really here. It didn't matter for how long, what mattered was that he was here. She pressed her lips together, feeling positively giddy, her thoughts making no sense. That was the only explanation for her saying, "Maybe you could open one."

"Mama?"

The sleepy voice belonged to Emmie who was standing in the living room, rubbing her eyes. When she focused them, the grin that came over her face threatened to split it in two.

"Nick!" she cried happily. The next moment, she broke into a run and launched herself into his arms.

Dropping to his knees, he scooped her up, love, unbidden, flooding through his veins.

"Mr. Sheffield," Georgie corrected her daughter, sniffing to keep the tears back.

"How about Daddy?" Nick suggested.

Stunned, Georgie looked at him. She *was* hallucinating, she thought. She had to be. But still the mirage remained where it was.

"What?"

"These are for you," he was saying to Emmie, taking out a very small, kid-sized pair of handcuffs. He'd obtained a pair and meant to mail them to her. Bringing them in person seemed like a better idea. "I got a junior set just for you."

But Georgie was still stuck on his last statement. "Nick, what are you saying?" Georgie demanded. "Why are you telling her to call you Daddy?"

"Because I want you—both of you," he clarified, looking at Emmie first, then Georgie, "to marry me."

"Yes!" Emmie cried before her mother could say anything, tightening her hold around his neck.

Georgie looked at him, dazed. She'd had time to think. Time to regret. As much as she felt her life was here, life without Nick was barren. The first two days had hardly moved. She had no reason to believe the days after would be any better.

"Do you really mean it?" she asked him, stunned and overjoyed at the same time.

"If I don't, that helicopter pilot who flew me here is going to be really ticked off. He wanted to take off at dawn, not in the middle of the night." But once the Senator had made the proper calls to facilitate the trip, Nick had been too eager to wait a minute longer.

Georgie pressed her lips together, her head whirling as she tried to make plans. "It's going to take me a little while to settle up," she calculated, "put the ranch up for sale—"

Nick interrupted her. "But then where will we live?" he wanted to know. "More important, where would the horses live?"

Georgie came to a screeching halt, completely confused. What was he saying to her? "What?"

Nick grinned, spelling it out for her. "I'm staying here. With you. God knows there's got to be something I can do besides shield people with my body."

She remembered he'd done just that in Rebecca's apartment. This time, Georgie didn't bother wiping away her tears. She kissed this man who had captured her heart long and hard, with all her soul. "Don't be too hasty, I like being shielded."

"Then it's yes?" he asked, not bothering to hide how important her answer was to him.

"Say yes, Mama," Emmie urged. "Say yes!"

"Yes," Georgie declared, laughing and crying at the same time. And then she regained a little control over herself. "I love you, Nick Sheffield," she told him with feeling.

She made his heart swell, he thought, and she always would. "I love you, too, Georgie," he told her. And then he dropped a kiss on Emmie's head. "Both of you."

With a cry of joy, Georgie wrapped her arms around his neck just as Emmie wrapped herself around both of their lower torsos, hugging them for all she was worth.

Nick lowered his mouth to Georgie's. The kiss was long and emotional and promised to bind them together for the rest of their natural lives.

Epilogue

The rain came down, sliding along the surface of the headstones like tears heavy with grief.

Because of the inclement weather, the cemetery was empty, except for the one lone figure who stood before a grave site that had only the simplest of markers to designate where the woman known as Rebecca Totten was buried.

Rebecca had no family, no people who came forward to claim her. No one who came to see her simple wooden casket as it was lowered into the ground. An anonymous envelope containing cash had been sent to the morgue. The note inside, printed on a generic laser printer, said the money was to be used for her burial. It was the only thing that had kept her from meeting eternity in the county's potter's field.

"They're going to pay for this, Rebecca. I swear to

you, they're going to pay for this. Every last one of those Coltons is going to wish they were never born before I'm finished with them. And I'm going to get that Sheffield guy, too. He should be lying here, not you. Not you." The last words ended in a sob he barely suppressed.

The rain began to fall harder, lashing down on the slicker he wore over his deputy's uniform.

He was alone in his grief. And now, without Rebecca, he was alone in the world.

Because of *them*.

How could everything go so wrong so quickly? He'd finally met someone he could care about, someone he *did* care about for the first time in his life, and they were set to make a life together. The plan had been perfect. They were going to start fresh, both of them, a whole new life together, funded by that little shrew's money. Taking it from her hadn't troubled his conscience in the slightest. If anything, it was poetic justice.

Georgie Grady was a Colton. She *owed* him. They all did. But instead of he and Rebecca living happily ever after, now he was going to have to live unhappily ever after without her. All because of that bitch and that man she had staying with her.

Well, they were going to pay. They all were. Pay for his growing up without a father, pay for his growing old without Rebecca. Someway, somehow, he was going to get them all. Especially the Senator. Because it was his fault at bottom.

Adam swore it in his heart.

It gave him a reason to live.

* * * * *

RANCHER'S REDEMPTION

BY
BETH CORNELISON

Beth Cornelison started writing stories as a child when she penned a tale about the adventures of her cat, Ajax. A Georgia native, she received a bachelor's degree in public relations from the University of Georgia. After working in public relations for a little more than a year, she moved with her husband to Louisiana, where she decided to pursue her love of writing fiction.

Since that first time, Beth has written many more stories of adventure and romantic suspense and has won numerous honours for her work, including the coveted Golden Heart award in romantic suspense from Romance Writers of America. She is active on the board of directors for the North Louisiana Storytellers and Authors of Romance (NOLA STARS) and loves reading, travelling, Snoopy and spending downtime with her family.

She writes from her home in Louisiana, where she lives with her husband, one son and two cats who think they are people. Beth loves to hear from her readers. You can write to her at PO Box 52505, Shreveport, LA 71135-2505, USA, or visit her website at www. bethcornelison.com.

To my family – you mean everything to me.

Thank you to my critique partner, Diana Duncan,
for her input and encouragement.

Thank you to Heath at Cooper Veterinary Clinic
for answering my questions about equine diseases.

Thank you to Brenda Mott for her help answering
ranching questions.

Thank you to Wally Lind and the crime scene writers
listserve for answering CSI questions.

Thank you to Marie Ferrarella, Justine Davis, Caridad
Piñeiro, Carla Cassidy and Linda Conrad, who
collaborated on THE COLTONS: FAMILY FIRST,
for making this series such fun to work on!

And thank you to Patience Smith and the rest
of the editors who worked on this continuity for
the opportunity to write Clay and Tamara's story.

Chapter 1

He had a trespasser.

Clay Colton narrowed a wary gaze on the unfamiliar blue sedan parked under a stand of mesquite trees. This corner of the Bar None, Clay's horse ranch, was as flat as a beer left out in the Texas sun, and he'd spotted the car from half a mile away.

He tapped his dusty white Stetson back from his forehead and wiped his sweaty brow. Finding a strange sedan on his property didn't sit well with him—especially in light of the recent trouble his sister, Georgie, had endured. He still got sick chills thinking how a woman had broken into his sister's home, stolen from her, passed herself off as Georgie.

A shiver crawled up Clay's spine despite the scorching June heat. Esperanza, Texas, his home for all his twenty-six years, had always been a safe place, no real crime to mention. He clicked his tongue and gave his workhorse, Crockett, a little kick. His mount trotted forward, and as he neared the car, Clay saw that the Ford Taurus had crashed into one of the mesquites, crumpling the front fender. A fresh sense of alarm tripped through him.

"Hello? Anyone there?" Clay swung down from Crockett and cautiously approached the car. Visions of an injured, bleeding driver flashed through his mind and bumped his blood pressure higher. "Is anyone there?"

He peered into the driver's side window. Empty. The car had been abandoned.

Removing his hat, Clay raked sweaty black hair away from his eyes and circled to the back of the sedan. The trunk was ajar, and he glimpsed a white shopping bag inside. Using one finger to nudge open the trunk, Clay checked inside the bag.

His breath caught.

The bag was full of cash.

Intuition, combined with fresh memories of Georgie's recent brush with identity theft, tickled the nape of Clay's neck, making the fine hairs stand up. A wrecked and abandoned sedan with a bag of money meant trouble, no matter how you added it up. He stepped back and pulled his cell phone from the clip on his belt. He dialed his friend Sheriff Jericho Yates's number from memory.

"Jericho, it's Clay. I'm out on the southwest corner of my land near the ravine, and I've come across an abandoned Taurus. The car hit a mesquite and banged up the front end, but I don't see any sign of the driver."

Sheriff Yates grunted. "You don't see anyone around? Maybe the driver tried to walk out for help."

Clay scanned the area again, squinting against the bright June sun from under the rim of his Stetson. "Naw. Don't see anybody. But it gets better. There's a bag of money in the trunk. A lot of money. Large bundles of bills. Could be as much as a hundred grand."

He heard Jericho whistle his awe then sigh. "Listen, Clay. Don't touch anything. Until I determine otherwise, you should consider the car and everything around it a crime scene."

"Got it."

"Read me the license plate."

Clay rattled the numbers off.

Through the phone, Clay heard the squeak of Jericho's office chair. "Thanks. I'll run a check on this plate, then I'll be right out."

Clay thanked the sheriff and snapped his cell phone closed.

Gritting his teeth, he gave the abandoned sedan another once-over. This was the last thing his family needed. After returning his cell to his hip, Clay climbed back on Crockett and headed toward his original destination—the broken section of fence at the Black Creek ravine. Regardless of where the car and money came from and what the sheriff determined had happened to the driver, Clay had work to do, and the business of ranching waited for nothing.

Several minutes later, the rumble of car engines drew Clay's attention. He looked up from the barbed wire he'd strung and spotted Jericho's cruiser and a deputy's patrol car headed toward the abandoned Taurus. He laid his wire cutters down and shucked his work gloves. Grabbing a fence post for leverage, he climbed out of the steep ravine and strode across the hard, dry earth to meet the sheriff.

Even after all these years, it felt odd to call Jericho "sheriff." Growing up together, he and Jericho had spent hours fishing and hanging around the local rodeo stables where Clay worked whatever odd jobs he could get. Though they'd never spoken much about it, Clay and Jericho had shared another bond—single-parent homes. Jericho's mother had left his family when he was seven.

Though Clay had known of his father, Graham Colton, the man had been an absentee father throughout Clay's childhood. When his mother died, Clay had finished raising his brother and sister while working odd jobs on neighboring ranches. The success both Jericho and Clay had achieved as adults was a testament to their hard work and rugged determination.

Jericho met Clay halfway and extended a hand in greeting. "Clay."

Shaking his friend's hand, Clay nodded a hello. "Afternoon, Hoss. So what did you learn about the car?"

Jericho swiped a hand through his hair and sighed. "It's a rental from a little outfit up the road. Reported stolen a few days ago."

Clay arched a thick eyebrow. "Stolen?" He scowled. "Guess it figures. So now what?"

Jericho squinted in the bright sun and glanced toward the stolen Taurus where one of his deputies was already marking off the area with yellow police tape. "Chances are that money didn't come from someone's mattress. Heaven only knows what we could be dealing with here. I'll call in a crime scene team to do a thorough investigation. Probably San Antonio. They'd be closest."

A crime scene team.

The words resounded in Clay's ears like a gong, and he stiffened. *Tamara.*

He worked to hide the shot of pain that swept over him as bittersweet memories swamped his brain.

Clay had two regrets in life. The first was his failure with Ryder—the brother he'd helped raise, the brother who'd gone astray and ended up in prison.

His second was his failed marriage. Five years ago, his highschool sweetheart had walked away from their three-year marriage to follow her dream of becoming a crime scene investigator. Clay blamed himself for her leaving. If he'd been more sensitive to her needs, if he could have made her happier, if he could have found a way to—

"Clay? Did ya hear me?" Jericho's question jolted Clay from his thoughts.

"Sorry. What?"

"I asked if you'd altered anything on or around the car before you called me. Say opening a door or moving debris?"

Clay shook his head. "I nudged the trunk open. One finger, on the edge of the trunk hood. Didn't touch anything else."

Jericho jerked a nod. "Good. I'll let the CSI team know. Be sure to tell your men this area is off-limits until we finish our investigation."

"Right." Removing his Stetson, Clay raked his fingers through his unkempt hair. "Guess I'm just on edge considering what Georgie's been through with that Totten woman."

"Understandable. But there's no reason at this point to think there's any connection."

"Yates." The deputy who'd arrived with Jericho approached them.

The sheriff turned to his officer and hitched his chin toward Clay. "Rawlings, this is Clay Colton. Clay, my new deputy, Adam Rawlings."

"Hey." Clay nodded to the neatly groomed deputy and shook his hand.

"Sorry to interrupt, Sheriff, but I found something. Thought you should take a look."

Jericho faced Clay, but before he could speak, Clay waved a hand. "Go ahead. I need to get back to work, too."

Pulling his worn gloves from his back pocket, Clay strode back toward the ravine where his fence had been damaged and got busy stringing wire again. He had a large section to repair before he went back to the house, and all the usual chores of a thriving ranch to finish before he called it a day. Unfortunately, though fixing the damaged fence was hot, hard work, it didn't require any particular mental concentration. So Clay's thoughts drifted—to the one person he'd spent the past five years trying to get out of his head.

His ex-wife.

If he knew Tamara, not only had she achieved her dream of working in investigative law enforcement, but she was likely working for a large city department by now, moving up the ranks with her skill, gritty determination and sharp mind. Once Tamara set her sights on a goal, little could stand in her way of reaching it.

Except a misguided husband, who'd foolishly thought that ranching would be enough to fill her life and make her happy.

A prick of guilt twisted in Clay's gut.

Why had he thought that his own satisfaction with their marriage and the challenge of getting the Bar None up and running would be enough for Tamara? Ranching had been his dream, not hers.

Why hadn't he listened, truly heard her, when she spoke of her hopes for leaving Esperanza and her dream of working in law enforcement? Because of the newlywed happiness in other aspects of their relationship, he'd too easily dismissed signs of her discontent and her restless yearning to achieve her own professional dreams. Soon even the honeymoon stars in her eyes dimmed, and her unhappiness began eroding their marriage.

He'd ignored the warning signs until the night they'd argued over the right course of treatment for a sick stud, and he'd returned from the quarantine stable to find her packing her bags. His heartache over having to put down his best breeding stallion paled beside the pain of seeing his wife in tears, pulling the plug on their life together.

Renewed frustration burned in Clay's chest. Failure of any kind didn't sit well with him, but failure in his personal life was especially hard to accept. His broken marriage was a blemish in his past that marred even the success of the Bar None. His single-minded dedication to building the ranch was what had blinded him to the deterioration of his relationship with Tamara. Until it was too late.

He gave the barbed wire a vicious tug. His grip slipped, and the razor-sharp barb pierced his glove.

"Damn it!" he growled and flung off his glove to suck the blood beading on the pad of his thumb.

Stringing wire might not take much mental power, but letting his mind rehash the painful dissolution of his marriage didn't serve any purpose. Tamara was gone, and no amount of regret or second-guessing could change that. Besides, he was married to his ranch now. Keeping the Bar None running smoothly was a labor of love that took all his energy, all his time. He'd scraped and saved, sweated and toiled to build the Bar None from nothing but a boy's youthful dream.

But today the sense of accomplishment and pride that normally filled him when he surveyed his land or closed his financial books at the end of the day was overshadowed by the reminder of what could have been.

Clay squinted up at the blazing Texas sun, which was far lower in the sky than he'd realized. How long had he been out here?

Flipping his wrist, he checked his watch. Two hours.

Crockett snorted and tossed his mane.

"Yeah, I know, boy. Almost done. I'm ready to get back to the stables and get something to drink, too."

Like Jack Daniel's. Something to help take the edge off. Revived memories of Tamara left him off balance and had picked the scab from a wound he'd thought was healed.

He snipped the wire he'd secured on the last post and started gathering his tools.

"Clay?"

At first he thought he'd imagined the soft feminine voice, an illusion conjured by thoughts of his ex-wife. But the voice called his name again.

He shielded his eyes from the sun's bright glare as he angled his gaze toward the top of the ravine. A slim, golden-haired beauty strode across the parched land and stopped at the edge of the rise. "Clay, can I talk to you?"

Clay's mouth went dry, and his heart did a Texas two-step. "Tamara?"

Chapter 2

Clay climbed the side of the ravine in three long strides and jerked his Stetson from his head. "What are you doing here, Tamara?"

His ex-wife raised her chin a notch and flashed a stiff smile. "I know I'm probably the last person you want to talk to today, but…I have questions I have to ask. About the crime scene."

An odd déjà vu washed over him as he stared at her. She looked just as beautiful as the woman he'd married, fought with, made love to, and yet…she'd changed, too. Her cheeks and jaw were thinner, more angular. She'd grown her hair longer, the honey-blond shade sporting fewer highlights from the sun, and a hint of makeup shaded her blue eyes and sculpted cheek-bones—a vanity she'd never bothered with when she worked beside him on the ranch.

He stood there, so absorbed by the shock of her presence and her beauty that it took a moment for her comment to sink in.

She had questions about the crime scene. Not questions about how he'd been, about their divorce, about the five years that had

passed since they'd last seen each other, sitting at opposite ends
of a table like two strangers in her lawyer's office.

He blinked. Scowled. "You're here with the CSI team from
San Antonio."

The instant the words left his mouth, Clay kicked himself
mentally. *Brilliant deduction, Captain Obvious.*

Tamara gave him a patient grin, apparently knowing she'd surprised him and cutting him some slack. If she were rattled by
their meeting, she didn't show it. But *she'd* had time to prepare.

"I've been with the department in San Antonio since I finished
my forensics training. Jericho—" She paused and lifted a hand.
"That is, *Sheriff Yates*—called us out to sweep the scene. I need
to ask you a few things. This a good time?"

Clay drew a deep breath, swiped perspiration from his forehead
with his arm and jammed his hat back on his head. "Sure. Shoot."

Tamara pulled a small notepad from the pocket of her black
jeans and wet her lips.

Clay's gaze gravitated to her mouth and froze on the hint of
moisture shimmering in the sunlight. Heat that had nothing to
do with the summer day flashed through his blood.

A picture of Tamara from high school flickered in his mind's
eye. Sitting on a corral fence rail at the rodeo where his mother
had been riding. Her silky hair tucked behind her ears. Her blue
eyes shining at him. Pure joy glowing in her face. He'd captured
her cheeks between his hands and leaned in to steal his first kiss
from her. She'd been startled at first. But soon after, her smile
had widened, and she'd returned his kiss in kind. The first of
thousands of sultry kisses they'd shared.

Yet now, gawking at her mouth like a schoolboy, he felt as
awkward and uncertain as he had that day at the rodeo. But she
wouldn't welcome a kiss today the way she had back then. He'd
lost the right to kiss Tamara years ago.

Warmth flared in her eyes before she averted her gaze and
cleared her throat. "When was the last time you were out on this
corner of the ranch?"

Clay shook himself from the unproductive nostalgia and focused on her question. "Earlier this week. Maybe Monday. I ride the perimeter to check fences and survey the property every few days. You know that."

She stopped scribbling on her pad and gave him a penetrating glance. "Assume I know nothing and answer the questions as honestly and completely as you can."

Gritting his teeth, he crossed his arms over his chest. "Yes, *ma'am.*"

"Have you disturbed anything on the scene from the way you found it?"

He shifted his weight and cocked his head, studying the pink flush of heat on her cheeks. She never could take much sun on her porcelain skin without burning. "I opened the car's trunk. One finger on the edge of the hood. I already told Jericho all of this." He hesitated. "You want to wear my hat until you finish out here? Your face is starting to burn."

She snapped a startled blue gaze up to meet his. "I— No. I'll be fine." She furrowed her brow as she studied her notes, clearly ruffled by his offer. "Um… You didn't touch the car otherwise?"

"No."

After several more minutes of her rapid-fire questions, he turned and strolled over to where Crockett waited patiently. Flipping open the saddle pouch across Crockett's hind quarters, Clay dug out the small tube of sunscreen he carried with him but rarely used.

Tamara followed him over to Crockett and reached up to stroke the gelding's nose. "Hey, Davy Crockett. How ya doin', boy?"

Crockett snuffled and bumped Tamara's hand as if he remembered her.

Still patting his horse, she asked, "Do you have any knowledge of who might have left the car here?"

"No." Clay uncapped the sunscreen and squeezed a dab on his thumb.

She consulted her notes again. "Do you have any idea where the money came from?"

"No, I don't." He stepped closer to Tamara, close enough to smell the delicate herbal scent of her shampoo, and she raised her gaze.

"When did you first find the—"

He reached for her, smearing the dab of sunscreen on her nose.

She caught her breath and stumbled back a step. "What are you doing?"

"Sunscreen. You're burning."

She grunted and gave him a perturbed glower. "Clay, I don't—"

He reached toward her again, and she backed away another step. With a resigned sigh, she rubbed the dab of cream over her nose and cheeks, then wiped her fingers on her jeans. "There! Okay? Now I have a job to do. Will you please just answer the questions?"

He tucked the sunscreen back in his saddle pouch. "Is all this really necessary? I've already told Jericho everything I know."

Her shoulders sagged with impatience and a hint of chagrin. "I wouldn't be here if it weren't necessary."

She may have been referring to her job duties, but the underlying truth of her statement hit him like a slap in the face. Nothing had changed. Tamara wanted no part of him and his lifestyle.

He braced his hands on his hips and kicked a clod of dirt. "You've made that pretty clear."

Tamara closed her eyes and released a slow breath. "Clay…"

"Forget it. Just ask your questions, Officer Colton." He glanced at her name badge and another jab stabbed his gut. "Sorry, Officer *Brown.* You went back to your maiden name, huh?"

"Clay…" She studied her notepad as if it held the secrets of the universe, and the silence between them reverberated with a hundred unspoken words and years of regret.

Finally Clay took his work gloves from his back pocket and slapped them on his leg. "Well, I'll let you get back to your job." He turned and stuffed the gloves in his saddle pouch.

Tamara didn't move. Didn't speak.

Clay took a sip of water from his canteen. Hesitated. "I'm

happy for you, Tamara. Glad to see you've accomplished what you wanted."

When she glanced up at last, suspicious moisture glinted in her eyes. But she quickly schooled her face and sucked in a deep breath.

"I—" She stopped herself. Glanced away. Flipped her notepad closed. "I'd better get back to work."

As she started back across the dry field toward the abandoned Taurus, Clay watched her long-legged strides, the graceful sway of her hips, the shimmer of sunlight on her golden hair. His chest tightened with an emotion he dared not name. Admitting he'd missed his ex-wife served no purpose, helped no one.

Giving Crockett a pat on the neck, he grabbed the reins and planted a foot in a stirrup. And hesitated.

He angled his gaze toward the scene where Jericho and his deputy stood while Tamara's team combed the area. Tamara pulled her hair back into a rubber band then tugged on a pair of latex gloves. Curiosity got the better of Clay.

He gave the gelding's neck another stroke. "Sorry, Crockett. I think I'll wait a bit before heading back to the stables."

Shoving his Stetson more firmly in place, Clay headed over to the stand of mesquite trees to watch his ex-wife work.

Tamara took out an evidence bag and tried to steady her breathing. She'd known returning to the Bar None and seeing Clay again would be difficult. But nothing had prepared her for the impact his espresso-brown eyes still had on her.

While working in Clay's stables early in their marriage, she'd been kicked by a mare that was spooked by a wasp. The powerful jolt of that mare's hoof had nothing on the punch in the gut when she'd met the seductive lure of Clay's bedroom eyes today. How could she have forgotten the way his dark gaze made her go weak in the knees?

Nothing about Clay had changed, from his mussed, raven hair that always seemed in need of a trim to the muscular body he'd earned riding horses and doing the hard work ranching required. He still wore the same dusty, white Stetson she'd given him their first Christmas together, and he radiated a strength and confidence that hummed with sex appeal.

She pressed a hand to her stomach, hoping to calm the buzz of bees swarming inside her. When she drew a deep breath for composure, she smelled the sunscreen he'd smeared on her nose, and a fresh ripple of nervous energy sluiced over her. A full day in the sun couldn't have burned her more than the heat of his touch when he'd dabbed the cream on her. She had far too many memories of his callused hands working their magic on her not to be affected by even such casual contact.

Her heart contracted with longing. No one had ever held such a powerful sway over her senses as Clay had. Not one of the men she'd dated since her divorce from Clay could hold a candle to the fiery attraction she felt for her first love. Her cowboy lover. The man she'd thought she'd grow old with.

Tamara sighed. She had to focus, get a grip. Emotion had no place in crime scene investigation, and she had work to do. She stepped over to where the team photographer was clicking shots of the Taurus's trunk. "You finished up front, Pete?"

"Yep. All yours. Do your thing."

Tamara pulled out her notepad and circled to the front of the stolen sedan. She noted a small scrape on the side panel and called it to Pete's attention.

"Saw it. Got it," the photographer called back to her.

Tamara moved on. She scoured the ground, the hood, the windshield, the roof and the driver's side before she opened the car door to case the interior with the same careful scrutiny. Any scratch, stain, dent, hair or foreign object had the potential of being the clue that cracked the case. Nothing was overlooked or dismissed.

As she collected a sample of fibers from the carpet, she heard a familiar bass voice and glanced toward the perimeter of the scene where Jericho Yates and his deputy stood observing.

Clay had joined his friend and was watching her work with a

keen, unnerving gaze. Tamara's pulse scrambled, and she jerked her attention back to the carpet fibers. Sheriff Yates made another quiet comment, and Clay answered, his deep timbre as smooth and rich as dark chocolate. Tamara remembered the sound of Clay's low voice stroking her as he murmured sexy promises while they made love. Just the silky bass thrum could turn her insides to mush.

Her hand shook as she bagged the fibers and moved on to pluck an auburn hair from the passenger's seat. She huffed her frustration with herself. She had to regain control, forget Clay was watching her and get back to business. She closed her eyes and steeled her nerves, steadying her hands and forcing thoughts of Clay from her mind.

"What you got?" said Eric Forsyth, her superior in the CSI lab, as he bent at the waist to peer through the open driver's door.

Tamara bagged the hair and labeled it. "Not much. I've never seen such a clean car. It's odd."

Eric shrugged. "Not surprising. It's a rental car. A company typically washes and vacuums the cars after every customer."

"That's not what I mean. I'm not finding fingerprints or stray threads. No footprints or tire tracks around the car. Not much of anything."

Eric scrubbed a hand over his jaw. "What's more, anything we do find is gonna be hard to pin to whatever happened here. God knows how many people have been in this car in the past month." He motioned to the bag in her hand. "That hair could belong to a schoolteacher from Dallas who rented the car two weeks ago."

Tamara sighed. "Exactly why it doesn't feel right. Even with the rental agency's regular maintenance, we should be finding at least traces of evidence. I think someone wiped the scene."

"You're sure?" Her boss adjusted his wire-rimmed glasses.

"The evidence—or lack of evidence—seems to point that way." She frowned. "Which tells me something bad happened here. Something someone doesn't want anyone to know about."

"Wouldn't be the first time. Well, keep looking. Maybe whoever wiped the scene missed something."

Tamara nodded. "Got it."

Clay tensed as the lanky man with glasses who'd been speaking with Tamara walked up to Jericho and shrugged. "My team isn't getting much for you to build a case on, Sheriff. In fact, our professional opinion is the scene has been wiped clean."

Jericho furrowed his brow and stroked his mustache. "Nothing?"

Clay turned his attention back to Tamara as he listened to the exchange between the crime scene investigator and the sheriff.

"Well, we found a partial print on the trunk. A hair on the front seat. A scratch on the front fender—but it looks old. There's already a little rust formed."

"No signs of foul play or a struggle?" Jericho asked.

"Not yet. But we're still looking."

Clay watched Tamara comb the Taurus with a calm, methodical gaze. She moved like a cat, her movements graceful, strong and certain as she inched through the interior, pausing long enough to bag tiny bits of God-knows-what and securing the evidence. Her professionalism and confidence as she processed the scene was awe-inspiring.

He remembered her awkwardness during her first weeks on the ranch as she learned to use the equipment and handle the horses. Though she soon picked up the finer points of ranching— he didn't know of much Tamara couldn't do once she set her mind to it—she'd never had the passion for the daily workings of the Bar None that he'd hoped.

Today, as she scoured the stolen car, her love for her job was obvious. She had been flustered when she questioned him, but seeing her again after five years had thrown *him,* too. Despite the awkwardness, she'd rallied and fired her questions at him like a pro.

"I did an initial survey of the area and didn't find much either," Rawlings said.

"Have you found anything that'd tell us what happened to the driver? Tracks of a second car for a getaway? Footprints leaving the scene? The fact that the money is still here bothers me." Jericho shook his head. "Who'd leave that much money behind unprotected?"

The crime scene investigator with the wire-rimmed glasses gave Clay a wary look then glanced to Jericho. "Good point. And, no. No footprints or tire tracks."

"It's been too dry," Clay volunteered. "Only rain we've had in weeks was a couple nights ago. A squall passed through. Hard and short. Any surface impressions that might have been left in the dust would have been washed away."

"I'm sorry, who are you?" the investigator asked, sending Clay a skeptical frown.

Clay offered his hand, choosing to ignore the man's churlish tone. "Clay Colton. You're on my ranch. I found the car. Reported it."

The man shook his hand. "Eric Forsyth. San Antonio CSI. I believe you already met my assistant, Tamara Brown?"

"Yep. Met, married and divorced." He gave the man a level stare. "She's my ex."

Forsyth arched an eyebrow. "Oh? She failed to mention that."

Clay quickly squashed the disappointment that plucked him. Apparently she'd cut him cleanly out of her new life. Setting his jaw, he angled his gaze to watch Tamara again. She was giving the driver's door a thorough go over, her jeans hugging her fanny as she squatted to study the contents of the map pocket. "She had no reason to mention it. It has no bearing on anything related to this case."

"We'll see about that." Forsyth turned to the sheriff, effectively dismissing Clay.

Clay ground his teeth and did his best to ignore the affront.

"Colton is right," Sheriff Yates said. "About the dry weather and the brief rain on Tuesday night. Whatever slight impressions might have been around before that storm were almost certainly lost to the rain."

Forsyth crossed his arms over his chest and grunted. "Yeah. There's a puddle of water in the trunk with the money. If the hood of the trunk was ajar, we can assume it's rainwater that leaked in."

"Which helps establish a time frame. If the car sat out here in the rain, we're looking at events that happened before Tuesday night." Jericho rubbed his jaw as he thought. "The car was reported missing Wednesday morning when the first shift arrived at the rental place and checked the inventory."

"I'll call the rental agency and ask them to send copies of the images from their security cameras for Tuesday. Maybe the theft was caught on tape," Deputy Rawlings said.

"Good thinking," Jericho said.

"You oughta talk to my neighbor, Samuel Hawkins, too." Clay crossed his arms over his chest as he spoke to Rawlings. "He came out here Tuesday evening to investigate a commotion he'd heard and found one of his longhorns tangled in that fence I was working on."

"Could the commotion have been something besides the steer?" Rawlings asked.

Clay shrugged. "You'll have to ask him."

"Why didn't your neighbor see the car when he was out here?" Forsyth asked.

"It gets mighty dark out here at night." Clay poked his thumbs in his back pockets and shifted his attention from his ex-wife's sultry curves and confident investigative technique to Eric Forsyth.

"The moon would have been behind the clouds, making it even blacker. He was on the lower side of that ravine—" Clay hitched his chin toward the steep drop-off a few hundred yards away "—with his hands full, tending an injured and agitated longhorn. Not surprising he didn't notice anything."

The crime scene investigator narrowed his eyes on Clay, but before he could reply, Tamara called out.

"Eric! Sheriff! I found something."

Clay whipped his gaze back to his ex. She lay on her back studying the underside of the driver's door.

Jericho, Rawlings and Forsyth all trotted closer to the abandoned vehicle. Clay hesitated only a moment before ducking under the crime scene tape and following.

"What do you have?" Forsyth asked, squatting beside Tamara.

"Hand me a swab." She extended her hand and wiggled her fingers.

Forsyth fished a clean cotton swab from the toolbox-like kit on the ground a few feet away and handed it to Tamara. With meticulous focus on her task, Tamara swiped a spot on the door. After rolling out from under the door and sitting up, she held the swab up to the sunlight and squinted closely at the sample she'd gathered.

"That's what I thought," she murmured, then tipped her head back to meet the expectant gazes of the men circled around her. "Our first sign of foul play, gentlemen. This is blood."

Chapter 3

After bagging the blood sample and wrapping up her sweep of the abandoned car and surrounding area, Tamara collected her equipment and prepared to leave for San Antonio. She was eager to start processing and analyzing the evidence she'd collected.

Blood.

Sure, a past driver could have gotten a bloody nose, and the rental company might have missed this drop during their routine cleanup. But coupled with the curious circumstances surrounding the scene—the money, the indications that the car had been wiped clean, the fact the sedan had been stolen—Tamara's bets were on the blood pointing to a violent confrontation involving the missing driver. That was the theory she would be trying to prove or disprove back at her lab.

She had ridden over from San Antonio with Pete, and the team's photographer was loading the last of his equipment into his SUV. Time to go.

But not before she took care of one last item.

She marched across the hard Texas dirt to where Clay stood beyond the yellow crime scene tape talking to Sheriff Yates.

"All finished, Sheriff. We'll let you know as soon as our test results come in."

Clay's gaze stroked her like a physical touch as she offered her hand to Jericho.

The sheriff clasped her hand in a firm grip. "It was good to see you again, Tamara. Take care and thanks for your help."

She pivoted on her heel to face Clay. Her stomach somersaulted when she met his dark brown eyes. Fighting to keep her arm from shaking, she stuck her hand out. "Clay, thank you for your help."

She was fortunate she'd finished speaking by the time he wrapped his long fingers around hers, because the moment he grasped her hand, her voice fled. A tornado of emotions sucked the air from her lungs, and heady sensations churned through her.

"No problem." The intimacy in his tone, the fire that lit his eyes sparked a heated flush over her skin. "If there's anything else I can do to help, don't hesitate to ask."

Was there any hidden meaning behind that offer, or had she imagined the intimate warmth in his tone? Fighting for oxygen, she tried to pull her hand back. But Clay refused to release her. He squeezed her fingers, his hot gaze scorching her, and he stroked the tender skin at her wrist with his thumb. "It was good to see you, Tee."

Her heart leaped when he used his pet name for her.

She nodded her head stiffly. "You, too."

"You're as beautiful as ever." The soft, deep rumble of his voice vibrated in her chest and stirred an ache she'd thought time had put to rest.

"Thank you," she rasped. This time when she tugged her hand, he let her fingers slip from his grasp.

Tamara curled her tingling hand into a fist and wrapped her other hand around it, as if nursing a wound. But her scars were internal, and seeing Clay today had only resurrected the pain she'd worked five years to move beyond.

Spinning away, she hurried to the SUV where Pete was waiting. She climbed into the passenger seat and angled the air-conditioning vents to blow directly on her face. If the summer sun weren't enough to induce heatstroke, the fiery look in Clay's eyes and the warmth of his sultry tone could surely cause spontaneous combustion.

"You okay?" Pete asked as they pulled away.

Not trusting her voice, Tamara nodded. She leaned her head back on the headrest and closed her eyes. The image of Clay's square jaw, straight nose, stubbled cheeks and thick eyebrows flashed in her mind. Her ex was pure testosterone. All male. Grit and determination.

Suddenly Tamara was blindsided by a need to see for herself what Clay had accomplished at the ranch, to revisit the haunts of her married days. She clutched the photographer's arm as he started to turn toward the highway. "Wait, Pete. Let's not go yet. I want to drive through the ranch. See the property, the house, the stables."

"What's up? You thinking Colton might be hiding something?"

She jerked a startled glance to Pete. "Heavens, no! Clay's as honest and forthright as a Boy Scout. He had nothing to do with that money or car."

"And you know this because…" He drew out the last syllable, inviting her explanation.

"I was married to him."

A startled laugh erupted from Pete. "Excuse me?"

"Before I came to San Antonio, I lived here. With Clay." Tamara tucked her hands under her legs and stared straight ahead. "We were high-school sweethearts and got married just hours after he signed the deed to this ranch."

Pete frowned. "Does Eric know? Are you objective enough to work this case?"

"I'm fine. There's no conflict of interest, because Clay's not involved. We can prove that easily enough if you're worried. And Eric knows…now. I heard Clay tell him."

"I suppose you know Sheriff Yates, too, if you lived out here for a while."

She bobbed her head, grinned. "I had a crush on Jericho for a while in tenth grade. Before I started dating Clay. Jericho's a good man. Salt of the earth."

Pete drummed his fingers on the steering wheel. "So what is it you want me to do here?" He waved a finger toward the windshield.

"Go left. I want to see how things have changed…or not. For old times' sake."

Pete complied, and Tamara sat back in the front seat, holding her breath as familiar landscape and outbuildings came into view. They drove past a corral where three magnificent stallions grazed. The horses looked up, tossing their manes as the SUV rolled by. As Tamara admired the striking males, melancholy twanged her heartstrings.

Lone Star had been a beautiful animal, too. After years of feeding and grooming the stud, Tamara had bonded with the best stallion in Clay's breeding operation. She'd been heartsick when she learned he'd contracted strangles, a bacterial disease that affects the lymph nodes, and devastated when Clay had chosen to put the horse to sleep rather than treat him for the illness. She still couldn't understand how her ex-husband could have been so clinical and emotionless about his decision, especially when she'd begged him to save the horse she'd grown to love.

"Quinn thinks putting him down is our best option," Clay had said.

"Quinn? It's not his decision! He's our *horse!"*

"He's the vet, Tee. His professional opinion counts—"

"More than mine? I'm your wife! What about what I want, what I think is best?"

"Ranching is a business, Tamara. I have to do what is best for the ranch."

"But why can't we even try—"

"My decision is made. Quinn knows what he's doing."

Tamara squeezed her eyes shut as revived pain shot through

her chest. Resentment for the veterinarian who'd held more sway over Clay than all her pleading churned with a bitter edge in her gut. Quinn Logan may have been Clay's friend, but Tamara had no respect for the man's medical choices. Every rancher she'd spoken to after Lone Star was put down told her strangles had a vaccine, could be treated with antibiotics.

Why hadn't Quinn taken measures to prevent the illness in the stud? And why had the vet dismissed the option of treating the animal's illness so quickly? Was he trying to cover his ass? Prevent a malpractice suit? The whole scenario seemed highly suspicious to Tamara, yet Clay had sided with Quinn.

The crunch of gravel beneath the SUV's tires told Tamara they'd reached the main drive to the ranch house. She peeked out in time to see them pass the barn where Lone Star had been quarantined—and put down. A sharp ache sliced through her, and she swallowed hard to force down the knot of sorrow and bitterness that rose in her throat.

What was it about this ranch that brought all her emotions to the surface, left her feeling raw and exposed? In San Antonio, in her lab, at a crime scene, she'd become a pro at suppressing her emotions and keeping a professional distance in her job. Yet a few hours in Esperanza had her dredging up old hurts, recalling the passion she'd once shared with Clay and longing for the early days in her marriage when life had seemed so golden.

"Nice place. How many acres does Colton have?" Pete asked, pulling her from her thoughts. His gaze swept over Clay's spread.

"He started with thirty acres. I'd guess he's up to about three hundred acres now." Tamara glanced through the open door of the building where Clay still parked his 1978 Ford pickup.

Still runs. Why should I get rid of it?

A grin ghosted across her lips. Practical, frugal Clay. He still had no use for waste.

Yet, for all his prudence, Clay *had* gotten rid of his wife.

Her smile dimmed.

After three years, their marriage had been damaged. The

incident with Lone Star had just been the final straw. For months, Tamara had felt herself suffocating, her dreams of working in criminal investigation withering on the vine. When they married, she'd put her aspirations on the back burner to help Clay get his new ranch on its feet. But the longer she'd stayed at the Bar None, the dimmer her hope of fulfilling her life's goals grew.

She'd awakened every morning to a sense of spinning her wheels, going nowhere. At night, she'd tumbled into bed, sore and tired to the bone from the arduous labor involved in running a ranch. Even her happy-new-bride glow had tarnished as, time and again, she'd taken second place in Clay's life to his land and his horses. Like the night he and Quinn ignored her opinion and put down the stallion she'd loved.

"Wow. That house is huge!" Pete sent her a wide-eyed glance.

She angled her gaze to the ranch house, a two-story wood-frame structure with a wide front porch and a warmth that had welcomed her home for three years.

She hummed her acknowledgment. "The previous owner had a big family and needed all four bedrooms. Clay and I kinda rattled around in all the extra space. We used the spare rooms for storage mostly."

Fresh pain squeezed her heart. She and Clay had planned to fill the bedrooms with their own children, had dreamed of outgrowing the house as their family multiplied.

Pete slowed to take a long look at the Bar None homestead. "Sweet digs. And you gave it up for a tiny apartment in the city?"

She gave him a withering glance. "We got divorced. Remember?"

"Ever miss the wide-open land and smell of horse manure? Or does the glamour of big-city life and crime solving fill the void?" His tone was teasing, but Pete's jibe touched a nerve.

Tamara scowled. "I've seen enough. Let's go."

The realization that she missed a lot of things about the Bar None caught her by surprise. The night she'd left Clay, she couldn't get away from the ranch fast enough.

But she missed the fresh air, the solitude, the animals…and Clay.

She huffed and shook her head. Fine. She admitted it. She missed her ex.

That didn't mean she was ready to run back to him and beg for a second chance. Nothing had changed between them. He was still a dedicated rancher, and she had her life, her work, her dreams that pointed her in a different direction.

As they bounced down the gravel driveway toward the old farm-to-market road into Esperanza proper, Tamara noticed the foals in the fields, the abundant supply of hay in the barn, the fleet of farm equipment, the full stables. Signs of prosperity and success.

Clay had his dream. His ranch was thriving. Bittersweet pride swelled in her chest. As happy as she was for Clay, she wondered if he ever regretted the costs of building the ranch. Did he ever miss the early days, miss their marriage? Miss *her?*

Chances were, she'd never know.

Clay climbed into the saddle and turned Crockett toward the main stable.

Thanks to finding the stolen car, he was well behind schedule for the day.

He didn't know what bothered him more, the evidence that a violent crime had taken place on his property or the reappearance of his ex-wife in his life. One could mean trouble for the ranch, the other could stir up past events better left alone. As a kid, Clay had learned the hard way what happened when you poked a hornet's nest. The summer after first grade, he'd spent two weeks recovering from that foolish bit of boyhood curiosity. His divorce from Tamara was still too fresh in his memory to dwell on the could-have-beens.

Still, he sighed. Having Tamara at the ranch again had felt natural. As if five years and countless lonely nights didn't stand between them.

He gave Crockett a pat on the neck. "You sure seemed glad

to see her. Bet you thought she had some of those sweet treats she used to spoil you with, didn't you?"

Clay sat straighter in the saddle and rolled his stiff shoulders. The simple joy that had filtered across Tamara's face when she'd recognized Crockett and patted the bay gelding made his breath lodge in his throat. Tamara's love of animals had been one of the reasons he fell for her, one of the reasons he'd believed she'd be happy on the ranch.

One of the reasons she ended up heartbroken. One of the reasons they'd fought the night she left. What would she think if she knew how much it had hurt him to have Quinn put down his prize stallion?

Clay shook his head and scoffed. There he went poking that hornet's nest again.

As they crested the rise at the north end of the main pasture, Crockett saw the shady barn where his evening hay and cool water waited. The bay picked up his pace.

Clay was just as eager to get a cold shower and a hot meal. But before he could call it a day, he had animals to feed and groom, stalls to clean, and financial reports to review. Hired hands helped with the daily chores and a part-time housekeeper cooked for him three nights a week, but ranching still filled every waking hour. Many times those hours extended late into the night if a horse got sick or a mare was ready to foal. Clay couldn't complain, though. Ranching was his life, his passion.

He thought again of the blood Tamara had found on the stolen Taurus and the huge sum of unclaimed money. A chill skated down his spine. Whatever seedy events had happened under the mesquites by the Black Creek ravine, Clay would make damn sure the ripples couldn't touch his ranch. Since Tamara had left him, the Bar None was all he had.

Tamara carefully transferred the partial fingerprint they'd lifted from the trunk to a slide and sent the image to the main computer for analysis. She wasn't holding her breath for a match, but she'd been surprised by what her tests had revealed in the past.

Forensics was a science. Her tests revealed facts and scientific data that had to be reviewed objectively. No amount of hoping the print would lead them to a suspect would change what the computer analysis told her was the cold truth.

Never mind that the crime scene was on Clay's land. Still, the notion that a heinous crime could have happened so close to where her ex slept at night made the fine hair on her neck stand up.

Tamara clicked a few computer keys. The hard drive whirred softly as the program searched local and state police databases for a match on the print. The familiar hum was comforting. Her lab was a safe haven of sorts. She was in her element here, where her logical mind could have free rein and her tender heart was never at risk of being broken. Statistics, patterns and chemical elements provided basic certainties with no room for emotional entanglement. At day's end, she could set a case aside like shedding a pair of latex gloves. No fuss, no muss. No heartache if things didn't work out as you'd hoped.

Not like her years of working the ranch with Clay, where a foal might be stillborn or a case of colic could be fatal or a prize stud could be put down in the name of business.

Tamara rocked back in the desk chair and propped her feet on the drawer. She watched the computer screen click through images, making mathematical analyses, comparing patterns and probabilities.

Numbers. Safe, unemotional numbers.

Tee, I have a business to run. Even if we could save Lone Star, the treatment would be expensive. He's contagious, and I can't afford for any other horses to get sick.

Her breath caught, and she slammed her feet back to the floor as she sat up.

For Clay, ranching had been about the numbers.

Her heart performed a tuck and roll. Maybe she and her ex-husband weren't so different after all. Was it possible Clay relied on the numbers, based his decisions on business models because they provided a distance, a safety net for the difficult decisions when a beloved horse was at stake? Was he trying to protect himself from the pain of loss inherent to the business of horse ranching?

Didn't she purposely refuse to think of the evidence she gathered in terms of the people who were involved, the lives taken, and the families shattered by the crimes?

Her computer beeped, telling her its work was done and calling her out of her musings. Rattled by her new insights about Clay's attitude toward ranching, her hand shook as she rolled the mouse to review the results lighting the screen.

Shoes scuffed on the floor behind her, and Eric stepped up to review the fingerprint analysis over her shoulder.

"You get a match?"

Tamara scanned the report. "No. The print's not in the state database."

Her boss sighed and rocked back on his heels. "Got anything on the carpet fibers?"

She spun the chair to face him and folded her arms over her chest. "Yeah. The color is called *basic beige.* It's an inexpensive brand sold by most do-it-yourself home stores and used widely by the construction company that built three-fourths of the new homes in Esperanza in the past twenty years. No help there."

Eric skewed his lips to the side as he thought. "How many homes could have been built in a podunk town the size of Esperanza?"

She grunted her offense. "Hey, I grew up in Esperanza, remember?"

"And you told me you couldn't get out of that two-horse town fast enough, if I remember correctly."

He was right. In high school, she'd been itching to shake the dust of Esperanza from her feet and head to New York or Chicago. But once she'd married Clay, she'd revised her plans for a while. She'd have been happy living in Esperanza with Clay until her golden years, if only…

She squelched the thought before it fully formed.

"I'll have you know, Esperanza had a boom of new houses in the early '90s. Surrounding towns did, too. The guy made a mint building small, affordable homes for the families who wanted the rural life and to be within easy driving distance of San Antonio."

Eric raised a hand. "Okay, so more than five houses with this carpet?"

"Way more. Try ninety to a hundred, if you count the surrounding towns and do-it-yourselfers." Tamara turned back to the computer and clicked a few keys. "I also found nothing on the red hair from the passenger seat. DNA breakdown for it and the blood from the driver's door won't be ready for a while yet. A batch of samples from the Walters case got in before us."

Tamara frowned. "I can't help but think we missed something. I was careful, and I double-checked everything, but…where's all the evidence? The scene was just too clean."

"You can always go back out to Esperanza and take another look. Head down to impound and check the car again. Maybe without your ex-husband watching your every move, you'll find something you didn't notice before."

Tamara snapped her gaze up to Eric's. "Clay didn't— I wasn't—"

"Save your breath. I saw how you looked at each other." Eric headed for the laboratory door. "Just don't let your feelings for your ex get in the way of this case."

She squared her shoulders, pricked by the implication that she still cared for Clay, that she was less than professional in her approach to her job.

Her boss turned when he reached the door. "Go back to Esperanza tomorrow and widen the search grid. I'll sweep the Taurus again and take Pete with me, so be sure to have one of the department cameras with you when you go."

"Right." Tamara swallowed hard. Being close to Clay and her old home had been hard enough the first time.

Maybe she could do her search without alerting Sheriff Yates or Clay. If she found anything significant, she'd call Jericho. If

she were lucky, she wouldn't have to face Clay at all. She hoped
not anyway. Her heart stung badly enough from their unexpected
encounter today.

The next morning, Tamara drove across the drought-parched
pasture at the far end of the Bar None and headed for the
mesquite trees near the Black Creek ravine. After parking her
Accord, Tamara climbed out and lifted a hand to shield her eyes
from the bright sun. She swept her gaze around the field. What
had she missed? The department's camera in hand, she headed
toward the stand of trees where the Taurus had been found. From
there she could fan out, searching in a methodical way, dividing
the land with a grid and going section by section.

After two hours of the tedious work, with little to show for
her efforts, Tamara had reached the edge of the Black Creek
ravine. She thought of Clay, striding up from the ravine yesterday when she'd sought him out for questioning. With his dark
good looks, cool control and muscled body, he personified the
rugged, larger-than-life attitude that made Texas famous.

The trill of her cell phone roused her from her wandering
thoughts.

She checked her caller ID and pressed the answer button.
"Hi, Eric. What's up?"

"You still in Esperanza?"

"Yeah. Why?" She nudged a rock with her toe then moved on,
her gaze sweeping slowly left to right and back again.

"Just wondering how much longer you think you'll be."

"Well, it stays daylight until almost 9:00 p.m., so I'd say I have
eight or nine more workable hours." She lifted a corner of her
mouth, picturing her boss's face.

"The scary thing is, I'm not so sure you're kidding." Eric
groaned. "Don't get me wrong. I love your work ethic. But I don't
need you running yourself down, wearing yourself out. I need
you mentally and physically sharp."

"I just don't want to leave until I'm sure I've covered every-thing this time. I should be finished in a couple hours."

"Well, you got anything yet?"

She sighed. "Nothing that looks promising."

When she finished the call with Eric, Tamara snapped her phone closed and cast an encompassing gaze around the area. Had she made the search grid large enough this time? Was she overlooking something?

As she walked the grid, she flipped her phone open again, and using her thumb, she punched in Pete's number in the photo lab. 5-5-5-3-0—

Suddenly the earth gave way beneath her.

Tamara gasped. Her phone flew from her hand as her arms windmilled and she scrambled to catch herself. The cave-in sucked her down, and she landed with a jarring thud. Terror welled in her throat as gritty dust filled her lungs and scratched her eyes. Raising an arm to protect her head, she winced as dirt and rock pelted her.

When the world stopped shifting, Tamara lifted her head, shook the loose dirt from her. She coughed out dust, and her chest spasmed. Searing pain arced through her torso, stealing her breath. She lay still for a moment, letting the fire in her ribs subside and collecting her wits.

Grit abraded her watering eyes. Blinking hard to clear her vision, she moved slowly, checking herself one limb at a time for broken bones. Every movement made her chest throb. She grimaced. Cracked ribs. Maybe worse.

Adrenaline pulsed through her. Hands shaking, she tried to calm herself without breathing deeply, which would only fill her lungs with more grit. As the dust settled and she could draw clearer air, the putrid smell of rotting flesh assailed her. She wrinkled her nose and squinted in the dim light. How far had she fallen? The sinkhole she'd landed in seemed to be six or seven feet deep. Like a grave.

She shuddered and quickly shoved aside the chilling thought.

Stay calm. Think. Clay and his ranch hands were too far away to hear her call for help. Her cell phone was—

She groped in the darkness, digging with her fingers through the soil and rock.

Fresh streaks of hot pain sliced through her when she moved. Tamara bit down on her lip and rode out the throbbing waves and ensuing nausea. Climbing out of this hole and driving to Clay's house was going to hurt like hell, but what choice did she have?

Holding her ribs, she shifted to her knees. A moan rumbled from her throat, and she gritted her teeth in agony. Before she tried pushing to her feet, she ran her hand over the dirt one more time, searching for her cell phone. She stretched as far as she could and found nothing but hot, crumbled earth. She crawled forward a bit, deeper into the shadows, and again shifted her fingers through the dusty debris.

Her hand bumped up against something large and heavy. When she tentatively brushed her hand along the object, she found it soft, like fabric. Or clothing.

Foreboding rippled through her.

She fished in her pocket for her keys, where she kept a small light on the fob to help her find the ignition switch at night. The bright LED light illuminated a tiny portion of the sinkhole. Holding her breath, she held the light toward the object.

And screamed.

Lying face down, mere inches from where she'd landed, was a man's dead and decaying body.

Chapter 4

Tamara struggled to regain her composure, find her professional detachment. She'd seen enough corpses through her job to stomach the grisly sight and even tolerate the smell to an extent. But the shock of finding the body so unexpectedly, the eerie shadows her key-ring light cast, having nearly fallen on top of the dead man…

She swallowed the sour taste that rose in her throat. Clenching her teeth to endure the sharp pain, she pulled herself to her feet. Her fingers scrabbled for purchase to climb out of the pit. By using the toes of her shoes to dig footholds, she managed to pull herself out of the sinkhole, one excruciating inch at a time.

Overwhelmed by the pain, the stench of death, the horror of what had happened to her, she braced on shaky hands and knees and retched—which sent fresh paroxysms of pain through her chest. The unforgiving Texas sun beat down on her and made her head swoon. Common sense warned her she had to get to her car, had to get out of the heat, had to get help for her injuries.

She had to report finding the dead man.

She shuddered.

A body.

The driver of the stolen car? Maybe. But if so, who put him down in that hole?

After struggling to her car, holding her aching ribs as still as possible, Tamara drove slowly toward the ranch's main house. The idea of facing Clay again hurt almost as much as the jarring bumps and jolts of the uneven pasture and pothole-riddled driveway.

She blasted her horn as she approached the house. Within moments, two irritated ranch hands stalked toward her car, shouting for her to quit honking. Others looked on, clearly curious about what she wanted. She scanned the approaching ranch workers, looking for the one man she wanted most to see and yet dreaded facing.

Finally she spotted Clay, hurrying through the front door of the white house and crossing the wide porch. A familiar beagle rose from his nap on the porch and romped across the yard at Clay's feet.

Tears of relief pricked her eyes, and she blinked rapidly to force them down. She swore to be strong in front of Clay if it killed her. Gaze fixed on her ex-husband, she waved off the ranch hands when they opened her door and offered her help.

The moment Clay realized who was behind the wheel of the Accord, his gait faltered for a second. His irritated scowl morphed into a look of shock then concern. He sprinted the remaining distance to her driver's side door.

Pushing aside one of his workers, he squatted in the *V* of the open car door. "Tamara, what's wrong? Why—"

"I fell…into a sinkhole. Out by the ravine." She closed her eyes and waited out a new wash of pain.

Clay mumbled a curse. "How bad are you hurt? Can you walk?"

Before she could answer, he shoved to his feet and leaned in to check her. Taking her chin in his fingers, he swept her face with his gaze, then touched a scrape on her temple.

Wincing, she grabbed his wrist to stop his ministrations. "I found a body."

Clay's thick eyebrows dipped, his dark eyes homing in on hers. "A body? Where?"

"In the pit. A man. He's been dead at least a couple days, judging from the stink."

Clay stiffened at the news, barely brushing her chest, but the contact sent a fiery spasm through her. She gasped and gritted her teeth.

"Where are you hurt?" he demanded, snatching his hands away from her.

A prick of self-consciousness filtered through her haze of discomfort. She must look frightful, scratched, bleeding and covered in grime. And after baking in the heat for hours, wallowing in a dirt pit, then dragging herself to her car, she had to be ripe.

By contrast, even breathing shallowly as she was to avoid pain, the aroma of sunshine and leather clung to Clay and filled her nose. Her heart gave a hard thump. So many precious memories were tied to his seductive scent. Memories that now left her emotionally raw.

"I…may have cracked…a rib or two. I can hardly…breathe. It hurts…every time I move—"

"Can you walk or should I carry you inside?"

Just getting to her car had hurt like hell. She was tempted to let him carry her, but she hated to seem needy. "I can walk."

"Hobo, get back," he told the beagle, who stuck his nose inside the car to greet the ranch's visitor.

Tamara smiled through her pain at the sight of the mutt, her old friend. She held her fingers out for him to sniff and scratched his head. "Hi, boy."

Clay placed a hand under her elbow to steady her as she rose slowly, stiffly from the car. New aches from the tumble into the pit assaulted her. Muscles cramped, joints ached, scrapes throbbed.

She hobbled a few steps and couldn't stop the groan that escaped her dry lips.

"That's it," Clay said and carefully lifted her into his arms.

She clutched the shirt at his shoulder when pain ripped though her chest. "No, Clay, I—I'm okay." She stopped to suck air in through her teeth. "Really. L-let me down."

He scoffed. "You can barely stand, much less walk."

"But if I move slowly, I can—"

"Don't argue." His penetrating espresso gaze silenced her.

Cradling her ribs, she rested her cheek on the soft cotton of his shirt. Being this close to him again stole her breath. Feeling the power of his arms around her, hearing the thud of his heart left her a bit dizzy. With Hobo barking excitedly at his feet, he strode with smooth quick steps, mindful not to jostle her, and soon had her in the blissful air-conditioning of his house.

He bypassed the living and dining rooms, heading straight down the long hall, through the kitchen and into the family room at the back of the house.

"Marie!" Clay called as he settled her on a cool leather couch.

A Mexican woman came out of the laundry room and appeared in the kitchen. "*Sí*, Mr. Clay?"

"I need the hydrogen peroxide and a damp cloth."

Tamara met the woman's startled expression and gave her a strained smile.

The woman pressed a hand to her cheek and hurried closer. "Oh, my! What happened?"

"I fell in some kind of sinkhole…out in the south pasture." She opted to leave out the detail about the dead body until the sheriff had a chance to investigate.

Clay made quick introductions between Tamara and his housekeeper. If the woman found it odd that Clay's ex-wife had been hanging around one of his pastures, she hid it well.

Tamara winced as she tried to find a more comfortable position.

Marie waved a hand toward her. "Mr. Clay, she needs to see a doctor. She's hurting."

Clay unclipped his cell phone and started dialing. "I know. I'm calling Doc Mason right now."

The older woman shook her head. "But Doc Mason is not here. He went on vacation, I heard."

Clay scowled and closed his phone. "Vacation? Doc never takes vacation. It's hard enough to get him to take off a day to go fishing."

Marie shrugged then hurried toward the hall bathroom.

"Clay, we have to call Jericho…about the body I found," she whispered so Marie wouldn't overhear.

"I will. First I need to make sure *you're* okay. If Doc is out of town, I'll have to call an ambulance, but the nearest one could still take almost an hour to get you to a hospital."

He stroked his stubbled cheeks, and the scrape of his callused palms on the bristles slid over her like a lover's caress. She knew so well the sandpapery scratch of his unshaven chin against her skin, gently abrading her during lovemaking. The sensation was tantalizing, thrilling.

Tamara took a deep breath to clear the erotic memories from her head and was rewarded with a sharp stab from her battered ribs.

Her grunt of discomfort darkened Clay's concerned stare to the shade of midnight. "Try not to move."

She quirked a grin. "Ya think?"

Her attempt at levity bounced off his tense jaw and stress-tightened muscles. He began to pace.

When Marie returned with the cloth and antiseptic, she sat on the edge of the couch and began dabbing the scrapes on Tamara's face. "Call the clinic," she said. "There is a doctor filling in for Doc Mason, I think."

Clay's eyebrows lifted, and hope lit his eyes.

His housekeeper nodded. "That's what I heard at Miss Sue's. Everyone was as surprised as you."

The mention of the local diner brought a smile to Tamara's face. "Gossip central. Is the pecan pie there still as good as it used to be?"

Clay gave Tamara a worried frown, as if her interest in the best pie in Texas were a sign of head injury. Flipping open his cell, he punched redial. His concern for her both touched her and chafed her independence. In their marriage, Clay's take-charge, assume-all-responsibility mode of operation had always been a mixed blessing.

Once arrangements had been made to meet the doctor on call at the Esperanza clinic and Clay had her settled in his pickup, Tamara shifted her attention once more to what she felt was a more pressing issue.

The dead man on Clay's property.

She borrowed Clay's phone as he drove her to town and called Sheriff Yates.

After Jericho assured her he'd start an immediate recovery and investigation of the body, she inquired what he'd learned about the money.

"Nothing yet. The serial numbers didn't turn anything up," Jericho said. "None of the banks in the area have a record of a withdrawal of that size or any other unusual activity. I'm checking the rest of the state now, but so far that money's proving a dead end."

The truck hit a bump, and she inhaled sharply.

Clay winced. "Sorry. No way to miss 'em all on this road."

"Tamara, is something wrong?" Jericho asked.

"Did I mention *how* I found the body?" She explained about her fall and that Clay was taking her to the medical clinic in town.

"Ouch. Broken ribs are a bear. Sorry 'bout that." She heard another voice in the background, heard Jericho reply. "Well, we're headed out to the Bar None now. I'll keep you posted."

"For the time being, you'll have to reach me on Clay's cell." She gritted her teeth as they lurched over another pothole. "But if you find my cell at the scene, I'd appreciate getting it back."

"Sure thing. Take care, Tamara."

When they reached Doc Mason's clinic in Esperanza, Clay helped her out of his truck and into the wheelchair a nurse brought out. He parked the wheelchair in the waiting room and walked up to the desk to check her in.

Tamara was grousing to herself about take-charge Clay's

latest crusade when the clinic door opened and a familiar blond-haired man walked in from the street. He slipped off his sunglasses and headed straight for the front desk.

"Billy? Billy Akers?" Tamara asked.

Her longtime family friend and former neighbor turned, and when he spotted Tamara, his face lit with an effusive grin. "Well, I'll be! Tamara the Brat! How are you?"

She smiled at his use of the nickname he and her older brother had given her growing up. Billy, who still had the build of a linebacker from his high-school days, hurried over to her and bent to give her a hug.

Tamara held up a hand to stop him. "Oh, uh...don't squeeze." She winced and pointed to her midriff. "Possibly broken ribs."

Scrunching his freckled nose, Billy made an appropriately sympathetic face. "Yikes. What happened?"

She waved his question off. "Long story. Gosh, it's good to see you. It's been years. How are your parents?"

Billy's face fell. "Well...not so good. Mama's been diagnosed with ALS...Lou Gehrig's disease."

"Oh, no!" Grief for the woman who'd been like a second mother to her and her brother plucked Tamara's heart.

"Seeing her suffering has been hard. Especially on Dad."

Tamara took Billy's hand in hers and squeezed it. "I can imagine. Oh, Billy, please give her my best. Tell her I'll be praying for her."

"I will." He hitched a thumb toward the front desk. "In fact, I'm here to refill one of her prescriptions." When he spotted Clay at the counter, a speculative gleam sparked in Billy's eyes. "Are you here with Clay? Does this mean you two are—" He wagged a finger from Clay to Tamara.

She shook her head. "No, nothing like that."

When she saw her denial hadn't satisfied his curiosity, she tried to work out the simplest explanation that would stave off the rumormongers. "I was on his property when I fell, and his house was the closest help."

"Why were you on his property? I thought you lived in San Antonio now."

"I do. I—" She sighed, then gave him a watered-down version of the truth. Knowing this town, word had probably already spread about the Taurus being found at the Bar None. "So I was looking around his south pasture and…*boom,* fell in a sinkhole. Thus the possibly broken ribs."

A bit of the color leeched from Billy's face. "You fell in a *hole?*"

She flashed a chagrined smile. "Klutzy me."

Clay strolled over and stuck out his hand toward Billy. "How ya doing, Akers?"

Billy shook hands with Clay. "I'm…uh, fine. You?"

"Good." Her ex shifted his gaze to her. "They're ready for you."

Billy excused himself, promising to give her regards to his parents and offering well wishes for Tamara's speedy recovery.

As Clay rolled her to the exam room, Tamara grinned. "That's a small town for you. Can't go anywhere without running into a neighbor or a lady from church or your parents' bowling partners."

"Which is why we always drove away from town for our dates in high school."

"Dates? You mean when we went parking." She wished she could recall the words as soon as she said them. No point reminding Clay of the car windows they'd steamed…or the first time they'd made love.

"Yeah. That's what I meant." His voice had a thick seductive rasp that told her those memories still affected him. Her pulse stuttered. Maybe he hadn't totally wiped her from his life after all.

Doc Mason's nurse, Ellen Hamilton, stuck her head into the hall from an exam room a couple doors down. "Right in here, Ms. Brown." After Clay wheeled Tamara into the exam room, the petite gray-haired woman laid out a sheet and a paper gown. "Would you like help changing out of your clothes, honey?"

Tamara tried to push herself out of the wheelchair and fiery needles stabbed her chest. She muffled a moan. Instantly Clay tucked his arms under hers, lifting her and helping her to the exam table.

Tamara glanced to the nurse. "Yeah. I think I'll need help."

"Fine." Ellen turned to Clay, her expression patient.

Unmindful of the nurse's stare, Clay took Tamara's foot in his hand and unlaced her shoe. After sliding it from her foot, he moved to the next shoe.

Tamara was so stunned at his presumptuousness that she could only gawk. When he gave her foot a soft rub, her breath snagged in a hiss of surprise.

Foot massages after a full day tending the ranch had been one of Tamara's greatest pleasures when they were married, a relaxation treat that often led to full body contact, clothes shed, lusty appetites sated.

Clay's eyes locked with hers, and he grimaced. "Sorry. I was trying to be gentle."

She started to tell him the gasp hadn't been one of pain, but the nurse cleared her throat.

"I meant that *I'd* help her change." Now her expression was challenging. She lifted a sculpted eyebrow and tipped her head toward the door.

Her ex-husband wasn't stupid and wasn't easily cowed. He straightened his spine and set his jaw in a manner that Tamara knew well. He had no intention of backing down.

Tamara almost laughed at the standoff, until she realized that Clay thought he still had a right to be in the exam room with her, that it was natural for him to help her change into the hospital gown. A warm swirl of nostalgia flowed through Tamara followed closely by a shot of irritation.

Clay had lost any claim to such marital intimacies when he signed their divorce papers without blinking, without so much as a tremble of his hand. She, on the other hand, had been shaking so badly she barely recognized the signature she'd scratched as hers.

And now he wanted those privileges of familiarity back? She didn't know whether to laugh or cry.

"Would you please step outside, Mr. Colton?" Ellen Hamilton asked.

A muscle in Clay's jaw twitched. He raised his chin, his eyes determined.

"Clay." His name squeezed past the lump of regret that clogged her throat.

He snapped his rich coffee gaze to hers, and the stubborn glint faded, replaced by a wounded expression, a chagrined acceptance that plucked at her heart. He hid it well. Someone who didn't know Clay and his take-no-prisoners attitude, his stubborn cowboy pride, would have missed it. But Clay had been her husband, half the blood and breath that made her whole. An ache wholly unrelated to her injuries pulsed through her chest.

He ducked his chin in a quick jerky nod of understanding and concession that broke Tamara's heart. "I'll be in the waiting room when you're ready to go."

He left without a backward glance, and the room seemed infinitely colder and more lifeless with him gone.

A moment later, a lean man in his late forties with thinning dark hair stepped into the room and shook Tamara's hand. "Ms. Brown, I'm Frank O'Neal, Dr. Mason's fill-in. I hear you took a nasty tumble."

"You heard right."

The doctor flashed a polite smile. "Well, let's see about getting you all fixed up."

Over the next hour, Dr. O'Neal X-rayed and examined Tamara from head to heel. He taped her ribs, gave her injections for pain and to relax her cramping muscles, all of which made it far easier for her to move unassisted. While the X-rays developed, she redressed by herself, though the process wore her out.

She sat in the exam room alone, remembering Clay's earlier hurt expression, when the sound of raised voices filtered through the door left cracked open.

Concerned that something was wrong, Tamara strained to hear the exchange between Ellen Hamilton and Dr. O'Neal.

"How long…—azine…missing…" Dr. O'Neal groused.

"I don't know." The nurse who'd stood up to Clay sounded shaken.

"…your job to…any idea…hell we could catch if…missing?"

"…well aware…accounting of…narcotic. Doc Mason always…himself."

"Have any…—peared before?"

The nurse's answer was too quiet for Tamara to make out.

The scuff of hard-soled shoes drew closer then hesitated just outside the exam-room door. Tamara looked up, and through the narrow opening, she met the doctor's shaken gaze. The man's brow furrowed, and he rubbed a hand over the nearly bald spot on his head. Appearing agitated, he glanced away for a moment before schooling his expression and entering the exam room.

He plunked two bottles of pills on the exam table and gave Tamara a tight grin. "I want you to take one of these every four to six hours when you need them for pain. The other is a muscle relaxant. Since people react differently to this medicine, it'd be wise for you to have someone stay with you while you recuperate."

She studied the bottle of pills. "I occasionally get migraines. These won't trigger a headache, will they?"

He shook his head. "Shouldn't. This is one of the best pain meds on the market. However some people report getting sleepy, some get loopy, some feel a little dizzy."

Clearly the man didn't want to acknowledge that she'd overheard his heated discussion with his nurse. Tamara took the hint and dismissed the issue.

Dr. O'Neal shoved his hands in his lab coat's pockets. "Do you have a roommate?"

"No. I live alone in San Antonio."

A knock sounded on the door before it was opened. Clay peered into the room. "Ms. Hamilton said to come back, that you were ready to go?"

The doctor nodded. "I was just telling Ms. Brown that the prescription I've given her for pain could make her sleepy or one of several other side effects. She needs to get plenty of rest and to have someone with her for the next couple days until she knows how her body reacts to the meds."

Clay nodded. "She can stay with me."

Tamara shot him a startled glance. "No, Clay, I couldn't… I—"

"I could admit you to the hospital for observation if you'd rather." Dr. O'Neal gave her a teasing grin, but also arched an eyebrow, telling her the threat wasn't idle.

"No, I—"

"Good. Make sure she takes it easy," Dr. O'Neal said with a nod to Clay. "And I'd like to check in with you again in a couple days to see how you're doing."

Holding his Stetson, Clay fiddled with the brim. "When do you expect Doc Mason back?"

The doctor glanced up from scribbling a note on Tamara's chart. "Not sure. He didn't give us a time frame. Just said he needed to get away for a while."

Clay cocked his head. "Well, good for the Doc. He's sure earned a vacation. Can't say I remember the last time he took off longer than an afternoon to fish."

The nurse bustled in with Tamara's X-rays and clipped them on the light board.

Dr. O'Neal stepped over to study the images. "Well, I don't see any fractures. All in all, I'd say you were quite lucky to walk away from a fall like that with no more than bruised ribs and some superficial lacerations. If you take it easy over the next few days, limit your activity and take your muscle relaxants, you should make a full recovery in a couple weeks."

Tamara thanked the doctor, paid the bill, and soon she and Clay were headed back to the ranch.

Staring at her hands as they drove, she considered Clay's invitation to recover at the Bar None. He hadn't so much asked her as declared that was how it would be. Did he really want her there? Or was he motivated by guilt and responsibility because she'd fallen on his property? Either way, sharing the same roof with Clay, even if just for a few days, would be awkward at best.

"Clay, I—" When his dark brown eyes met hers, her argument drowned in their fathomless depths. She fought the mule-kick loss of breath. "I…think I'll be fine at my place in San Antonio. I appreciate the offer, but—"

His brow lowered. "You have someone in the city who can stay with you?"

"Well, no."

"You heard the doctor. You need rest and someone to keep tabs on you."

"I know, but—"

Clay's cell trilled, cutting her off.

"Hello? Hey, Jericho." Clay glanced at Tamara. "Yeah, she's with me. We're headed home from Doc Mason's clinic. Why?" When he frowned, Tamara's pulse kicked up. She didn't need more bad news.

"Maybe. Let me ask her." Clay held the phone against his chest. "Feel up to a short side trip by the south field? Jericho is out there with Deputy Rawlings, and they haven't found the body you saw. They need you to show them where it is."

The injection she'd gotten for pain at the doctor's office was already making her drowsy, but she had a duty to her job and to the deceased man's family. She stroked a hand over her taped ribs. "Sure. I can manage."

Ten minutes later, she and Clay were standing with Jericho and Deputy Rawlings beside the sinkhole. The sheriff shook his head. "We've been down with searchlights. Turns out this hole is an offshoot cave from the old tunnel Clay and I used to play in when we were kids."

"A tunnel? For what?" Tamara asked.

Clay shrugged. "Don't know what it used to be, but the tunnel's been there for decades. When I bought the ranch, I put barbed wire across the entrance of the tunnel so none of my horses would wander in there and get stuck."

"The point is, ma'am," Rawlings said, narrowing a look at Tamara that suggested he thought she'd lost her mind. "Sheriff and I have been all up and down the passages of the tunnel, and there's no body in there."

All three men turned toward her. She bristled. "I saw the body myself! I touched it, not more than four hours ago!"

She shuddered at the memory.

The sheriff looked skeptical. "Did you hit your head when you went down?"

"There *was* a body, Jericho!" Nausea swirled in her gut. Did they think she was lying? Or hallucinating?

"I'm sure you were in shock," Jericho said. "Maybe—"

"No maybes, Jericho." His shoulders squared and stiff, Clay took a step closer to her side. "If Tamara says there was a body, there was a body."

Her protest stuck in her throat. She turned to Clay, wide-eyed, her mind reeling, her heart full. They'd been on opposite sides of so many issues in the final months of their marriage, she'd grown used to butting heads with this stubborn man. Having him back up her story, believe her on something as important as this, touched her deeply, warmed her soul.

Suspicion furrowed tiny creases at the corner of Clay's eyes. "The only real questions here are who moved the body…and why."

Chapter 5

Tamara limped across Clay's family room and eased her throbbing body onto one of the leather sofas. Fatigue bore to her bones. The painkiller dulled the ache, but her muscles were stiff and sudden movement sliced rippling pain through her abdomen. As the prescription kicked in, her body begged for rest and her eyes screamed for sleep. But restless thoughts zinged through her brain.

Where was the dead man she'd found in the tunnel? Was it possible she'd imagined the body, as Rawlings had suggested?

She shook her head to clear the medicated haze. *No!* Her hands had touched cloth. She had smelled decaying flesh. She had seen the partially buried corpse.

Someone had moved the dead man. But who?

Her CSI team would vindicate her. Even now they were searching the tunnel, looking for hairs, blood or tissue to substantiate her claim and try to identify the victim. With luck they'd also find footprints or drag marks showing the body had been moved.

Clay carried two glasses from the large farm-style kitchen and set one on the wagon-wheel coffee table in front of her. "Marie says she made a fruit salad to go with dinner, but you can have some now if you're hungry."

"No, thanks." Tamara sipped her drink. Sweet tea with lemon, just the way she liked it. Clay had remembered.

She closed her eyes and battled the swell of bittersweet emotion the simple kindness stirred. Though stress and the effect of the painkiller had her on edge, she couldn't allow herself to lose it.

Of course he'd remember her favorite drink. They'd been intimately connected since high school, mind, body and soul. He'd have to be thickheaded to forget such a basic preference. Clay was anything but stupid. His slow gait and laid-back manner belied the razor-sharp mind that clicked behind those dark eyes.

"You should go to bed. You've had a rough day." Clay sat on the opposite couch.

"Not until I hear back from my team." She huffed her frustration. "I should be out there. This was my case."

Clay arched an eyebrow and shot her a skeptical look. "You're in no condition to work."

"I know but—" She balled her fists and sighed, trying find the words to express how the waiting killed her, how she hated starting something she couldn't finish, how the need for answers kept her mind in turmoil.

"But it's hard to rest up here when your heart and mind are down at that tunnel with your team," Clay finished for her matter-of-factly.

She blinked, her stomach flip-flopping. "Yeah. Exactly. How did you know?"

He shrugged and took a long swallow of his iced tea. "It's hard for me to delegate, too. I have to be hands-on with anything that matters."

She curled up her mouth. "I remember. It's called being a control freak."

His brow creased. "I'm not a control freak."

"Are you kidding me?" she sputtered. "Control freak is putting it mildly. You're hyperresponsible and a workaholic, too. You're talking to your ex-wife. I *know* you."

"Maybe. But people can change."

Tamara leaned back against the sofa. "Have you?"

He stared down at his boots for a moment before he spoke. "I see the world differently now. I understand what matters, what doesn't." He glanced at her. "That's what changes. A person's beliefs. And beliefs, convictions are what drive decisions."

So what mattered to Clay now? Where did his convictions lie? The questions begged answers, but they stuck in her throat.

Asking would imply that she still cared, still wanted to know what made this man tick. She couldn't risk putting any more of herself on the line than necessary. Being in these familiar surroundings, around so many people and places that evoked heartbreaking memories was difficult enough.

Instead, she flipped open Clay's cell phone, which he'd given her to babysit until she found or replaced hers. No messages. She closed the phone and sighed.

"They'll call when they know something." Clay pushed away from his couch and crossed to the one where she sat. He took the phone from her. "Go lie down. I'll wake you if there's news."

"I'm too antsy to sleep." A giant yawn escaped, calling her on the lie.

"Tee, you're dead on your feet, all banged up, and under doctor's orders to rest. Don't be stubborn." He took her hand and pulled her gently to her feet.

Her head spun. From Clay's touch or the dizzying effect of her pain medicine? She closed her eyes and held on to Clay's shoulders until the light-headedness passed. When she looked up, she met his concerned gaze.

"Tee, you all right?"

"Yeah, it's just the drugs. I see now why Dr. O'Neal advised me to have someone around. This stuff packs a punch." She blinked her dry, scratchy eyes.

"You can nap upstairs as long as you want. If you need

anything, use the intercom and Marie or I will get it. Don't attempt the stairs on your own while you're still under the influence, so to speak. Okay?"

She heard Clay, but his words seemed to travel through water. Her head felt stuffed with cotton, and her eyelids drooped. "Yeah, I promise. No stairs. I…" She stifled another yawn. "I could just sleep on the couch here. I don't need—"

"Don't be silly. You can have my bed."

"Your—" Clay swept her into his arms before she could protest, before her dulled reflexes could respond.

"There's junk piled on the guest bed. Mine's the only one made up right now." Clay's strong arms anchored her close as he started for the stairs in the main hallway.

Clay's bed? Her heart pattered, and a spurt of adrenaline briefly cleared the haze muddling her mind. *Their* bed, he meant. The one they'd bought with the proceeds of his first horse auction. The bed where they'd slept for three years, nursed illnesses, and made love countless times.

Was he trying to make this convalescence harder on her?

She struggled to organize her thoughts as the painkiller numbed her mind. "Clay, wait. I don't think this is a good idea."

"Marie changed the sheets this morning." He climbed the stairs smoothly, without breaking his pace or sounding even a tad winded, despite her added weight.

"No, that's not what—"

He ducked into the first room on the right and lowered her onto the handmade quilt that covered the mattress.

Stretching out on the soft bed, Tamara almost groaned in pleasure. Encroaching sleep suddenly seemed more appealing. The effort to lift her leaden arms seemed daunting, but she was still wearing the dirt-, sweat- and blood-smeared clothes she'd had on when she fell in the sinkhole. No, not a sinkhole. A tunnel.

There was a body. Wasn't there? Her muzzy brain tripped over images and tangled emotions.

"I need to…get out of these…clothes." She plucked awkwardly at the buttons of her blouse. The task seemed almost too taxing as her eyes slid closed.

Clay slid her shoes from her feet and rubbed her tired arches. At the doctor's office... No, he was soothing her feet now. Tamara did moan this time as Clay's strong, talented fingers worked the ache from her heels, her toes...

Bliss.

After stripping off her shoes and socks, Clay massaged Tamara's foot. The bruises on her arms and the scrapes on her face were a chilling reminder of how lucky she'd been not to have been hurt far worse.

He was relieved to see her color returning. When he'd driven her to the doctor's office, her face had been frighteningly pale, evidence of her pain. Pain he'd have gladly endured for her if he could have. Frustration and helplessness haunted him.

A shudder started deep in his bones, working outward until his whole body was shaking. When she fell, she could have broken her neck, could have broken a rib and punctured a lung. He could have lost her.

Clay exhaled a slow sigh. Tamara was already lost to him. He'd given up any claim to her the day he let her walk away from their marriage.

He stroked the side of his ex-wife's face, and she angled her head to rest her cheek against his hand. Her brown eyelashes drifted down and fanned her ivory skin like dark lace on silk.

"Thank you, Clay...for being there today," she murmured sleepily.

"No problem, sweetheart."

So he'd driven her to the clinic. Big deal. But where had he been five years ago when she needed him? Why had she thought she'd be happier without him? The failure of their marriage gnawed at his gut. He couldn't change the past, couldn't change the mistakes he'd made or the hurt he'd caused no matter how much he wanted to.

Her wan complexion, the harsh red scrapes on her chin and the shadows under her eyes made her appear fragile. Vulnerable. His Tee would hate to be called either. But as he watched her drift into a drug-induced sleep, his protective instincts surged.

Drawing a ragged breath, Clay withdrew his hand from her cheek, and she whimpered a protest. He surveyed the stained and torn shirt and jeans she was wearing. The least he could do while she slept was wash the blood from her clothes.

"I'm gonna help you get out of these dirty things, okay, Tee?" She opened her eyes and nodded.

He slid open the top button of her blouse, while she fumbled to unfasten the bottom one. Working his way down, careful not to bump her bruised ribs, he parted her shirt, and the stark white tape binding her ribs came into view. Clay frowned. He'd had injured ribs before when he was thrown from a horse at a rodeo in high school. Hurt like fire.

He'd do everything possible to make Tamara comfortable and her recovery easier. Knowing she was wounded on his property chafed at his sense of duty all the more. The law might say he was no longer her husband, but he couldn't so easily dismiss his obligation to take care of her.

Tamara tugged on her blouse then winced.

"Careful," he whispered. He eased her elbows from the sleeves, admiring the muscle tone in her slim arms. After discarding the soiled shirt, he turned his attention to her bra. The scrappy lace didn't keep many secrets about what lay beneath. Not that he didn't have images of Tamara's rose-tipped breasts burned in his memory.

Still, Clay hesitated. Heat prickled his skin as erotic memories flashed in his mind.

He'd undressed this woman hundreds of times. He knew every inch of her skin, the exact curve of her waist and hips, the feel of her legs wrapped around him.

But he wasn't her husband anymore.

"Now the jeans." Clay unfastened the fly and tugged on the legs to slide them over her hips while she pushed from the waist.

An enticing hum of pleasure rumbled from her throat as the restrictive denim glided from her legs, and Clay had to bite back his own moan. Tamara's legs were every bit as long and shapely as he remembered.

Blood pulsed south as his gaze skimmed up those sexy legs and paused at the pale pink bikini panties. Panties that matched her lacy bra.

"This, too," she mumbled, sliding the bra's straps from her shoulders. "The underwire is poking me. It hurts."

Air snagged in Clay's lungs as he wedged a hand behind her back to unhook her lingerie, drawing him dangerously close to the nearly naked woman on the bed. Desire vibrated in every muscle and heated his blood. When she pulled the unhooked bra away and dropped it at his feet, he almost choked on the groan that rose in his throat.

Her nipples beaded when bared to the cool, air-conditioned bedroom, tempting him to draw them into his mouth and bathe them with his tongue.

Tamara draped an arm around his neck and nuzzled his cheek. "You smell good. Like sunshine."

Clay swallowed hard, keeping a tight rein on his self-control by reminding himself that she was injured and under the influence of medications. He had too much respect for her to take advantage of her condition.

Her fingers tangled in the hair at his nape, and she pressed a warm kiss to his jawline. "You need a haircut," she murmured. "Maybe I could do it later."

Clay gritted his teeth and pulled away from her tantalizing touch. He thought about past trims—Tamara's fingers combing through his hair and massaging his scalp, the glide of cool steel scissors against his neck, and his wife's long legs straddling him as she snipped his bangs. By the time she'd finished, his every nerve ending would be lit like a firecracker and he'd be ready to explode.

No way in hell could he endure that exquisite torture now and keep his sanity.

When she moved her lips to the shell of his ear, he sucked in a sharp breath and backed out of her reach. His self-control was hanging by a thread, ready to snap.

"I'll get you a T-shirt," he rasped and rose from the bed, his own jeans uncomfortably tight. Clay rummaged through his dresser and pulled out a blue cotton shirt for her to sleep in. With the back of his hand, he wiped a cold sweat from his brow and turned back toward the bed.

If he were a gentleman, he supposed, he'd avert his gaze or close his eyes.

But he wasn't feeling especially gentlemanly at the moment. Besides, this was Tamara. His Tee.

Even five years after their divorce he still felt territorial toward her. She'd given her virginity to *him.* Since high school, *he'd* been her husband, her lover, her protector.

So as he walked back to the bed, he drank in the sight of her. Her golden hair spread across his pillow, and he knew tonight it would still hold her honeysuckle scent. He drank in the expanse of silky skin and the graceful curves of her legs. He gazed hungrily at the hollow of her throat, where she loved to get gentle nips.

In his mind, he raked his hands over the swell of her breasts and teased the budded tips with his thumbs. He remembered how kisses at the small of her back would make her sigh and had to grit his teeth to squelch the need that pumped through his veins to hear that breathy moan again. He let his imagination linger at the *V* of her legs where the pink bikini panties hid a place he'd explored well with his hands and his mouth before claiming her in the most intimate way.

Tamara stirred, her hand stroking down her arm as goose bumps prickled her skin.

Clay shook himself from his erotic daydreams. Wary not to hurt her ribs, he helped pull the T-shirt over her head and smooth it into place. Then, taking an afghan from a chair in the corner of the room, he covered her and stepped back.

A bittersweet ache blossomed in his chest. At the same time, she looked both delicate and strong. Innocent and sexy. Familiar and changed. She looked beautiful.

He didn't question the impulse to kiss her forehead before he left her to nap. It felt right. Just as having Tamara in his home, in his bed, in his life again felt right somehow.

Clay chided himself as he closed the door to his room.

You're being a sentimental fool. She left you once, and when she's healed, she'll leave again.

Believing anything else would only set himself up for heartache.

Tamara woke when a quiet rap sounded on the bedroom door.

She opened her eyes a slit and needed a second or two to remember where she was. Clay's bedroom.

When she glanced down to check her watch, she noticed her dishabille. Her eyebrows snapped together. She didn't remember changing clothes. She didn't remember much, in fact, after Clay picked her up and carried her.

Clay?

Adrenaline spiked through her as the possibilities unfolded in her brain. Snapshot images of holding him, kissing him, making love to him flashed in her brain. But were they real memories or wisps of a steamy dream?

"Tamara?" The door opened a crack, and Clay moved halfway into the room.

She bolted upright, and a shattering pain streaked through her chest.

"Oh!" Sinking back to the bed, she clutched her ribs and grimaced as the throbbing made black spots swim before her eyes.

Clay hurried to the side of the bed. "Whoa! Take it easy. The doc said to stay still, move slowly until those muscles heal."

"I know," she wheezed. "I just— You startled me."

"Sorry." Clay pushed hair back from her face, and the light brush of his fingers against her cheek made her forget her pain.

"How long was I asleep? And more important, who…undressed me?"

One black eyebrow lifted, and the corner of his mouth twitched. "You don't remember?"

His amusement didn't bode well for her. She closed her eyes. "Oh, no. What'd I do? What'd I say? And remember, I was under the influence of painkillers. You can't hold me to anything."

His hand squeezed hers. "Don't panic. I helped you change, but…nothing happened."

She peeked up at him and saw heat flickering in his eyes.

"Not that I wasn't mighty tempted." His wicked grin made her toes curl.

While she calmed the jangling inside her, she glanced down at the soft T-shirt she was wearing and fingered the hem. Clay's T-shirts had always been her favorite sleepwear. She inhaled the clean, outdoorsy scent that clung to the shirt and smiled. "And my clothes?"

"In the dryer. Not quite good as new, but at least clean again. You're welcome to wear any of my shirts you want, too."

Tamara nodded. "Thanks."

Clay rubbed his hands down the legs of his jeans. "So…I would have let you finish your nap, but…I promised I'd wake you when I had news."

She perked up. "Did my team find something in the tunnel?"

Lips tight, he gave her a jerky nod. "Blood. No report yet on whether it matches the blood from the Taurus."

"No, there wouldn't be so soon. The analysis takes hours at best. Days sometimes." She chewed her bottom lip as she let this information sink in. "So there was a body. I didn't imagine it."

When Clay frowned, she held up her hand to forestall his comment.

"I only mean this vindicates me. That Rawlings guy, Jericho's new deputy, wasn't convinced I hadn't hallucinated the whole thing. Jericho seemed skeptical, too."

If Tamara says there was a body, there was a body.

Clay's voluntary and definitive support spun through her again, warming her.

She cleared the sudden thickness from her throat. "Did they find anything else? Anything that might tell us who took the body?"

"Like a signed confession?" He flashed a crooked grin.

She chortled. "If only it were that easy."

Clay shook his head. "Jericho didn't mention anything else… Oh, yeah—except your cell. They found your phone in the hole. Still works. Needs a good cleaning but you should be able to salvage it. Meantime, you can use mine to call your team, if you want."

"Yeah, I think I will."

When Clay rose from the edge of the bed, she paused and caught his gaze. "Wait, I… I wanted to thank you."

He cocked his head. "For?"

"Standing by me today, believing me when the evidence didn't support me. Your faith in me…meant a lot." The piercing quality of his dark stare stole her breath, held her captive for a few staggering beats of her heart.

He said nothing for several seconds, and she tried to interpret the flicker of emotion that sparked in his eyes. When he wanted, Clay could play his feelings so close to his chest, even she had a hard time reading him.

"You had no reason to lie," he said finally and turned for the door.

She knew this tactic of his well. Minimizing an issue that could stir deeper emotions. Glossing over anything that might delve into his softer side. Heaven forbid the tough cowboy, the born leader, Mr. Responsibility-of-the-world-on-his-shoulders let his guard down.

As Clay left the room and closed the door, disappointment plucked at Tamara, and a years-old ache snuck out of hiding to nip at her again. He hadn't dismissed her gratitude…exactly. But he had avoided the meaning behind what he'd done, the importance of it to her. How many times in their marriage had Clay done much the same thing? When she'd raised a concern, Clay had all but patted her on the head and told her not to worry.

Over the years, in subtle ways, she'd gotten a message that had ultimately undermined her happiness and broken her marriage: she wasn't important. Her opinions hadn't mattered. Her wishes had been ignored. Her feelings had been minimized. She'd never felt an equal partner in their marriage, much less in the running of the Bar None.

Of course, Clay was far too kind and considerate to have done any of it on purpose. In fact, when she'd called him on it once, he'd been truly stunned by the suggestion that he was dismissing or undervaluing her. But intentional or not, the distance between them grew until she even doubted whether Clay really loved her.

The night her pleas to try to save Lone Star rather than put him down were ignored, she'd had enough. She'd left Clay to pursue her dreams, build a life for herself where what she wanted mattered.

Clay hadn't changed. She'd be crazy to make the same mistakes again and to lose herself once more in Clay's overpowering shadow.

The soft pad of footsteps on the stairs pulled Clay from his perusal of the Bar None's business records. He looked up from his desk just as Tamara walked into the office.

"What are you doing up?" he said with a mock severity. "You're under doctor's orders to get bed rest, young lady."

Tamara wrapped a lock of her long hair around her finger and sent him a coy grin. He felt his gut somersault like a schoolboy's.

"I'm supposed to rest, but Dr. O'Neal never said it had to be in a bed. I can rest downstairs. Maybe on a sofa in the family room? I was bored up there by myself."

He quirked a grin and pushed back from his desk. "All right. Can I get you anything?"

"I'll take you up on the offer to use your phone. I want to call my lab."

He unclipped his cell from his belt and handed it to her.

Keeping her back straight and a hand on her sore ribs, Tamara sat on the edge of a chair by his desk and punched in a number.

"CSI lab," a male voice answered, loud enough for Clay to hear.

Wincing, Tamara held the phone away from her ear. "Eric? It's me. What'd you come up with in that tunnel? Clay heard you found blood?"

"Geez, Tamara, are you all right? Sheriff Yates said you'd fallen through the ceiling of the tunnel, got banged up pretty bad." Her boss's voice carried so well, she might as well have had him on speaker.

"Yeah, I fell, but I'll be fine in a couple days. Bruised a few ribs. Nothing major."

"Bruised ribs is nothing major?"

She rolled her eyes, even as she shifted stiffly on the chair. "Don't worry. I'll be back to work in a day or two."

Clay rocked forward in his seat, prepared to interrupt with his protest, when her boss steamed, "Oooh, no, you won't! You're injured. As of right now you are on medical leave for a minimum of one week."

"What?" Tamara gasped, and her gaze darted to Clay's as if seeking confirmation she'd heard correctly.

He crossed his arms over his chest and leaned back in his chair, a satisfied smile on his lips.

"Don't let me see you in here until you are able to give me one hundred percent. I need you healed and in top form. At least one week. Paid leave, of course, but I don't want you to push yourself. If you need more time to get well, take it. Understood?"

"Yes," she groused. A crease lined her brow as she exhaled. "Can you at least tell me where the case stands? What did you find at the tunnel?"

Clay perked his ears. The investigation of what happened out on the south pasture might not involve him directly, but if something illegal, something tragic had happened on his land, he wanted to know about it. This case had already gotten Tamara injured, and he needed facts if he was going to protect her from any further harm.

"Look, you don't…" Her boss hesitated.

"Eric, talk to me." Tamara lowered her head to her fingertips and massaged her temple. "This is my case. I did the initial investigation. I have a right to know."

A heavy sigh rattled from the phone. "Well, we don't have any final results back, of course, but…initial tests show the samples from the car door and the tunnel are the same blood type. The body you saw was most likely the source of the blood in the car. We'll know for sure when the DNA report comes back on the blood and hair."

Tamara's head came up. "Hair?"

"We recovered a few hairs with roots from the scene today."

"What else?" Excitement filled her voice.

"Not much. There were impressions where footprints might have been but they'd been obliterated. Deliberately. Someone is literally covering his tracks."

"Interesting." Tamara chewed her bottom lip as she thought. Passion for her job shined in her blue eyes. He could almost see the wheels of her analytical mind clicking, and pride swelled in his chest. Along with regret. No wonder she hadn't been happy in their marriage. Clearly she was in her element on the crime scene team, dissecting evidence and putting the pieces of scientific data together to see a bigger picture.

"If someone moved the body, could be because they know we're onto them," Tamara said.

Clay sat forward in his chair as his pulse kicked into high gear. He didn't like the new twist on this case.

"Yeah. Could be. And cornered animals are always the most dangerous, so be careful," Eric replied, echoing Clay's thoughts.

As Tamara finished her conversation with her boss, Clay curled his fingers into his palm and stewed over whether news of the investigation could have traveled so fast or if someone could have been watching the crime scene when Tamara had been out there, alone. An uneasy chill slithered down his spine.

The possibility that someone could know of Tamara's involvement in the investigation and could be looking to silence her shook him to the core. Clay gritted his teeth and balled his fists even tighter. Anyone looking to hurt his ex-wife would have to come through him first.

Chapter 6

The next evening after dinner, Clay found Tamara in the family room, stretched out on one of the long leather couches with multiple pillows stacked behind her. She'd found a pair of his drawstring running shorts and put them on, cinched to fit her slim waist, with another one of his old T-shirts.

As she was reading one of his magazines, she stroked one bare foot down her opposite leg, calling his attention to the sleek curve of her calf and her trim ankle. The action struck him as so provocative, his body tightened in a heartbeat. Of course, since he'd helped her change out of her bloody clothes yesterday, visions of her nude body and her lacy undergarments had taunted him to the point that she could sneeze and he'd find it arousing.

While he stood at the entry to the family room, his body humming, Tamara laid the magazine on her lap and reached down to rub her heel. With a hiss of pain, she sank back into the pillows and grimaced. "Dang it."

Shoving away from the door frame where he'd propped his shoulder, Clay strode forward. "You need another pill for the pain?"

She raised a startled gaze to him. "Considering how the last one knocked me out, I'm not going to take more until I'm ready for bed." She tipped her head. "You're back early. Are you done in the stables already?"

Nodding, he moved around the antique wagon-wheel coffee table and lifted her feet into his lap as he joined her on the couch. "Many hands make light work and all that jazz. I really don't need as many guys as I have working for me now, but I can't bring myself to let anyone go. They have families to feed."

She raised her eyebrows. "And you can afford all those salaries?"

He shrugged. "The past couple years have been good. My new stallions are bringing in top stud fees, and last year I sold some property I wasn't using, which brought in some extra cash. So, yeah. I can afford the salaries for now."

"Good. I'm really happy for you. I'm thrilled to see the Bar None doing well. No one deserves it more than you." She grinned, and the warmth of her smile soaked all the way to his bones.

He wasn't the sort of man who needed anyone's approval to feed his self-esteem, but Tamara's opinion was different. She'd been there from the beginning, when he'd learned ranching during high school. She'd labored beside him from the day he'd inked the deed to the day she walked out of their marriage. She knew how long he'd dreamed of building his own ranch, knew how hard he'd worked to achieve his success. And shared in the pain of what his success had cost him.

Guilt plucked at him, and he quickly shoved the reminders of his failed marriage aside.

Wrapping his fingers around her bare foot, he squeezed her toes and rubbed her heel between his palms. "Your feet are freezing. You want a pair of socks?"

"Mmm, no. Just keep doing that. It feels great." She tipped her head back, arching her neck. A purr of satisfaction rumbled from her throat and ricocheted through him. Heat blasted through his veins, and the tight coil of sexual tension he'd fought all day vibrated, ready to spring.

"You have magic hands, Clay Colton," she said, her tone husky. "I've missed your foot massages." She met his gaze through her fringe of brown lashes, and he recognized the spark of desire that warmed her eyes.

In the past, his foot massages had often been foreplay to more tantalizing moments, and the sights, sounds and sensations of those encounters washed over him in living color. With a breathy sigh, his ex shifted on the couch and offered him her other foot, the movement nudging the already straining fly of his jeans. His gaze traveled up her long legs and stopped at her chest, where his T-shirt clung to her breasts and delineated her peaked nipples. She wasn't wearing a bra. Understandable, in light of her sore ribs. Yet knowing that tidbit made a shudder ripple through him. More fodder for his overactive fantasy life concerning his former wife.

Clay swallowed a moan. He'd known full well what he was doing when he sat down on the couch with her and initiated the foot rub. He'd been playing with fire, testing Tamara. Would she welcome his touch or push him away?

"You know what I'd like?" Tamara wound a wisp of her long gold hair around a finger, a look of pure satisfaction on her face.

"What's that, Tee?" Forcing aside his sensual thoughts, he focused his attention on her request. From the moment he'd first laid eyes on her in junior high, he'd do anything in his power to give Tamara whatever she wanted, whatever made her happy. Even if it meant sacrificing his own happiness. Their divorce was proof of that.

"I was thinking…maybe tomorrow—"

The trill of the house phone interrupted her.

Clay shook his head. "Ignore it. Finish your sentence."

"No. It'll keep." She pulled her feet from his lap. "Answer it. That could be Jericho with important information."

Sighing, Clay shoved off the sofa and retrieved the cordless phone from the kitchen counter. "H'lo?"

"Hi, Clay. It's Jewel."

Guilt kicked him in the shin, and he cringed internally. He'd been meaning for days to call and check up on Jewel Mayfair, the manager at Hopechest Ranch, a home for troubled teens.

Months ago, following the tragic death of her fiancé and unborn child in a car accident, Jewel had moved to Esperanza. His aunt Meredith had been concerned about her niece and asked Clay to keep tabs on Jewel, whom she knew was still hurting and vulnerable. Clay had dutifully taken his distant relative under his wing, but the chaos of the past few days had sidetracked him.

"Hi, Jewel. Is everything all right?" He cradled the phone on his shoulder as he strolled back into the family room. This time he sat on the couch opposite Tamara. A guy could only withstand temptation for so long.

"Oh, we're fine," Jewel said. "I just wanted to bring some of the girls over tomorrow to ride the horses again…if it was okay for you."

Clay raked a hand through his hair, mentally reviewing his agenda for the next day. "I don't see why not. About ten? Before it gets too hot?"

"Sounds great. Thanks, Clay. You're a dear."

As he disconnected and set the phone on the wagon-wheel coffee table, Tamara's expression was curious.

Clay propped his elbows on his thighs and steepled his fingers. "You remember meeting my uncle Joe and aunt Meredith out in California?"

Tamara nodded. "The senator and his wife."

"Right."

"His campaign for the White House has been big news lately."

Clay arched an eyebrow, surprised that Tamara had been keeping up with his family, even if Joe's political career was national news. Nodding toward the phone, he added, "That was Meredith's niece, Jewel. I don't think you ever met her."

Tamara scrunched her nose in thought. "Doesn't ring a bell."

"Well, Jewel recently opened a branch of the Hopechest Ranch here in Esperanza, and she brings the kids over now and then to ride the horses."

"And they're coming tomorrow, I take it?"

He grinned. "That's one of the reasons I fell for you, darlin'. You're sharp."

She smirked. "I can eavesdrop with the best of them."

Clay sat back on the couch, and for a moment, a comfortable quiet fell between them. Tamara was the first to break the silence. "Tell me about the rest of your family. Is Georgie still on the rodeo circuit?"

"For now, although I think she'd like to settle down, give Emmie a more permanent home."

Tamara frowned. "Emmie?"

Clay exhaled slowly and rubbed a hand over the day's growth of stubble on his jaw. "Oh, man. That's right. Georgie didn't tell us she was pregnant until after you left."

Tamara's eyes widened. "Georgie has a daughter?"

Unable to hide his pride when he thought of his niece, Clay smiled broadly. "She's four and a half and is the spitting image of her mother. Precocious. A tomboy like Georgie. And she'll talk your ear off."

"And she has her uncle Clay wrapped around her little finger?" Tamara flashed him a knowing grin.

He spread his hands. "Guilty as charged."

"So then…is Georgie married?"

Clay's gut roiled thinking of the city slicker who'd gotten his sister pregnant then abandoned her. "Naw. The guy left her. But Georgie's a great mom and has a new guy in her life."

Tamara smiled. "A cowboy from the rodeo circuit, no doubt."

"Actually, no." Clay chuckled and dropped his bomb. "A Secret Service agent."

"What?" Tamara sat up too fast and pressed a hand to her ribs. Wincing, she settled back against the pillows. "How did she meet a Secret Service agent?"

Clay summarized the events of the past few weeks, including the break-in at Georgie's house, her brush with identity theft and being framed for threatening Joe Colton and his campaign. He explained the danger Georgie had been in, and how Agent Nick Sheffield had helped clear her name.

Tamara gave a low whistle. "Thank God she's all right. So do I get to meet this hero agent and Georgie's daughter while I'm in town?"

He turned up a palm. "I don't see why not. I'm sure Georgie'd love to catch up with you."

"I'd like that." Tamara's smile faded, and she hesitated. "And Ryder? What do you hear from him?"

Mention of his incarcerated brother sent a jolt of self-censure through Clay. He surged to his feet and stalked toward the fireplace. Keeping his gaze fixed on the Texas flag over his mantel so Tamara couldn't read the guilt in his expression, he said, "I haven't had any contact with Ryder in years."

"Wh-why not?"

Tamara's incredulous tone only deepened Clay's remorse. His broken relationship with his younger brother was difficult enough without Tamara judging him for his decision.

Clay clenched his teeth, and every muscle tensed. "Ryder left me no choice. He wouldn't listen to me, refused to turn his life around. I did *everything* to get through to him and nothing worked. You know how Ryder was in high school. All the trouble he got into, the scrapes with the law. Defacing public property. Stealing cars to joyride with his friends."

"But he was a good kid deep down. He was just rebellious and—"

Clay slapped a hand on the mantel in frustration. "And his rebellion finally landed him in jail!"

Tamara gasped.

Clay hazarded a glance over his shoulder and met Tamara's stricken expression. Turning away, Clay shoved his hands in his pockets, though the roil of emotions in his gut made him restless.

"He was caught transporting illegals over the border from Mexico. He's serving time."

"Oh, no! Oh, Ryder. How awful."

Acid swirled in Clay's stomach, crept up his throat with the sour taste of failure. "I tried to talk to him at his sentencing, but it was like talking to a stone wall. He wouldn't even look at me. I told him then that I'd had enough."

"Enough?" Tamara repeated hoarsely. "What are you saying? It was your choice to break ties with him?"

Memories of that last day scrolled through Clay's mind. His brother's pale, stony expression. The nauseating scent of floor cleaner that hung in the courtroom. The cold bite of the over-air-conditioned room.

A chill washed over Clay, sending a tremor though him.

When a warm hand touched his arm, he jolted. He turned with a jerk to find Tamara standing behind him, her face wan and confused.

"Clay, tell me you didn't abandon Ryder when he went to jail."

Her stricken expression and strangled tone knotted his chest with grief and frustration. "I'd done everything I knew to do! Ryder wouldn't listen. He was bent on self-destruction, and damn everyone and everything else. He left me no choice! For his own good—and for mine—I had to wash my hands of him."

Tamara's eyes grew round in dismay. "He's still your brother! Doesn't that count for anything?"

"Apparently not." Clay fisted his hands in his pockets, trying to rein in his runaway emotions. "Georgie tried writing to him, but he never replied. He's never responded to any attempt to communicate with him."

Tamara spread her arms. Her blue eyes blazed with condemnation. "So that's it? You just cut him out of your life like some cancer?"

Clay swiped a hand through his hair and clenched his teeth, struggling to keep his temper in check. "What do you want me to say, Tamara? This isn't the way I wanted things to turn out. God knows I tried to save my brother, but I—"

"Gave up." Her clipped tone sliced through him.

He narrowed a sharp gaze on her, stunned by her bitterness. Denials formed on his tongue then died when a nagging voice in his head echoed her accusation.

She stepped closer, one arm holding her ribs, her piercing blue gaze locked on his. "Shouldn't surprise me you'd walk away from your brother. It wouldn't be the first time you threw in the towel."

He stiffened. "What does that mean?"

"You gave up on Lone Star, too."

Clay groaned. "Good God, Tamara, that was completely different! He was incurably sick and hurting. And *contagious*. He'd never recover enough to breed again, so he'd lost his value as a stud."

"So his life was nothing more than a ledger balance to you?"

Clay huffed and rubbed the back of his neck. "Money was a factor, but not the only consideration. If you'd listened to Quinn that night instead of becoming irrational and—"

"Irrational?" Her voice leaped an octave higher. She poked Clay in the chest with a finger, her face flaming. "Just what is so *rational* about cutting someone you love out of your life because they become inconvenient? I loved that horse, but you wouldn't even consider trying to save him. Strangles is easily curable. I asked around. You gave up on him too soon!"

"Tamara, listen to me—"

"No, *you* listen. Growing up, my family had no money. My family was all I had to count on. Family is important. Sure, life can be hard. Relationships are hard, but you don't give up on the people you love without a fight!"

Clay grew still, staring at the color in his ex-wife's cheeks, the tears blooming in her eyes. "Are we still talking about the horse? Or even about Ryder?"

Tamara drew a shaky breath. "What if we aren't?"

He inhaled slowly, struggling to calm the riot jangling inside him. "You're the one who walked away, Tamara. I didn't cut you out of my life."

"But you didn't do anything to stop me. You didn't say a word. You didn't so much as flinch when you signed the divorce papers. I could only assume that meant you didn't care." She motioned to the Texas flag on the wall and the antique lanterns on his mantel. "And where are the lithographs and dried flower arrangements I bought for the mantel? The curtains I made for the kitchen? Don't think I haven't noticed that you removed every trace that I ever lived here or helped decorate this house. The evidence says you *did* cut me out of your life." She ducked her head and swiped a tear that dripped from her lashes.

"Tamara…" He sighed, afraid if he spoke his voice would betray the heartache that had a stranglehold on his throat.

"Over the years," she whispered, her voice cracking, "I told myself you were just in shock. Maybe you did care, but you didn't know what to do or say. That our divorce hurt you as much as it hurt me."

The pain in her voice flayed Clay's heart. A bone-deep tremor wrenched him. "Tee, don't do this…"

"But after hearing how you walked away from Ryder when he needed his big brother the most, maybe I was wrong."

Her words landed a sucker punch. He couldn't breathe. Couldn't think. His body and brain buzzed numbly. He shuffled back a step then turned. "I… I have things to tend to in the stable."

His gait stiff, he stalked toward the back door.

One hand on the doorknob, he paused and jammed his Stetson on his head. Glancing back at her, he rasped, "I know that I failed Ryder, failed you, failed in our marriage. I have to live with that truth every day. But don't for a minute think that I didn't care."

With that, he stepped outside and closed the door.

Tamara fought to calm the ragged breaths that triggered waves of pain in her chest. But the ache in her soul cut far deeper than the injury to her ribs. Clay's parting shot reverberated through her, rattling the defenses around her heart.

His words echoed with a guilt and pain she'd never imagined Clay harbored. The idea that Clay bore the same scars she did from their divorce shook her to the core.

Had it just been easier to leave the ranch, believing Clay hadn't cared? Had her own heartache blinded her to signs he wanted her to stay, wanted to make the marriage work? Signs that he had loved her?

In a criminal investigation, her team had to consider *all* the data. Especially the pieces not immediately visible to the naked eye. Looking at the big picture was essential in order to see where each bit of evidence fit in the greater whole. That she could have been so tunnel-visioned concerning something as important as her marriage galled her. Further proof that emotions skewed her judgment.

At work she appreciated the clinical nature of her scientific analyses and regimen. She considered the elimination of an emotional factor a blessing. Facts were safe. Science didn't break your heart or steal your hope. But data and analysis couldn't fill the empty spaces in your soul on lonely winter nights and didn't bring the joy of sharing life's simple pleasures.

Tamara dashed moisture from her cheek with her hand then, finding a napkin on the kitchen table, she blew her nose.

Her job might be safe, but did she want to be as cold and clinical in her personal life as she had to be on the job? Wasn't that exactly what she found so unfathomable about Clay's dealings with Ryder, with his sick stallions, with their divorce? Life wasn't a crime lab where emotions could be taken out of the equation. Relationships weren't sterile bits of evidence to be dispassionately dissected.

I know that I failed Ryder, failed you, failed in our marriage. I have to live with that truth every day.

Her heart gave a painful throb. She should have known her world-on-his-shoulders ex would assume full responsibility for the dissolution of their marriage, that he'd take the blame for his brother's poor choices.

Gathering her composure, Tamara jammed her feet into the shoes she'd left beside the couch and headed outside to find Clay. She regretted losing her temper with him and the hurtful things she'd said. She couldn't let Clay go on thinking their divorce, or Ryder's incarceration, was his fault.

When she stepped out on the back stoop, the sweet scent of alfalfa hay from the stables greeted her, and a chorus of crickets and frogs sang their nighttime melody. The sounds and smells of the countryside in summer carved a hollow ache in her soul.

As a teenager, she'd dreamed of leaving Esperanza as quickly as possible. The confines and isolation of her hometown had felt claustrophobic and limiting. After living in San Antonio for five years, she found that she missed much about small-town life. If she'd been so wrong about Esperanza, what else had she misjudged in her youth?

She strolled slowly to the main stable, careful not to jar her ribs and giving Clay an extra moment or two to himself. They both needed a few minutes to cool off and think.

In the yellow glow of the stable's bare lightbulb, she spotted Clay, leaning against the gate to one of the stalls. Still, quiet, his head bowed, he was the image of a man in pain. Her heart broke and bled for him.

How had they come to this? Clay had been her whole world at one time, her knight on a white horse—or rather her cowboy in a white Stetson. Knowing how they'd grown apart, let petty grievances come between them, left a stark, cold emptiness deep inside her.

As she approached the stable, Hobo, the beagle mix, trotted out to meet her with a wagging tail and a baying bark. Hobo had been Clay's dog when they married, but the mutt's cold nose and sloppy dog kisses had burrowed deep into her affections from the day she'd met the friendly beagle. Leaving Hobo behind when they divorced had been almost as hard as leaving Clay.

Tamara smiled as Hobo wiggled and yipped at her feet. "Hi, boy. How are you?"

Her voice alerted Clay to her arrival. Jerking up his head, he grabbed a curry comb from the nearest shelf and started grooming his gelding, Crockett. Tamara pretended not to notice his haste to cover his pensive brooding.

Hobo planted his paws on Tamara's leg and nuzzled her hand, lapping at her with his warm tongue. The enthusiastic greeting from her old friend, as if five years hadn't elapsed since he'd last seen her, touched something already raw and vulnerable inside her. The tears she'd just gotten under control pricked her eyes again.

"Good boy, Hobo." She bent at the waist to pat the dog, but her ribs protested the movement with a sharp stab. "Ooo!"

Clay glanced over just as she grabbed her side and winced. He crossed the stable in quick strides and pulled the dog away. "Settle down, Hobo. You're going to hurt her."

"No, he's okay. I just tried to pat him and bending down didn't work."

"Oh." Clay met her gaze with a tender warmth that arrowed to her heart. He stooped to scoop Hobo into his arms. "How 'bout this?"

While Clay held the squirming beagle, Tamara leaned in to get canine kisses and rub his floppy ears. As she hugged Hobo, the emotion that tightened her throat came as much from Clay's sweet gesture as her reunion with her old pet. His thoughtfulness didn't surprise her. His consideration and kindness had been at the core of why she'd fallen in love with him.

So how could a man with such a magnanimous spirit *not* have understood that his take-charge manner and solo decision making in their marriage had left her feeling trivialized and unimportant?

"I think the mutt missed you," he said as Hobo wiggled and licked her hands.

"I missed him, too," she replied around the lump in her throat. She swallowed hard and tried to shove down the tears that burned her sinuses. Being so weepy wasn't like her. But, heck, she'd had a couple of highly stressful days, and the pain meds had weakened her defenses. Coupled with the barrage of bittersweet memories that had surrounded her since returning to the Bar None, no wonder she'd become a leaky faucet. With a fortifying breath, she gave the beagle a final pat and stepped back. "Thank you, Clay."

He lowered the dog to the ground and shrugged. "No problem."

When Clay turned to go back into the stable, Tamara caught his arm. "Wait. I came out to say…I'm sorry."

His brow creased, and warm, dark eyes bore into hers. "Don't be. Most of what you said was right. I've made a lot of mistakes." He faced her more fully and nudged his Stetson back. "But I… I'm not as coldhearted as you seem to think. I feel the loss of my brother every day, and I regret my failure with him more than you could know."

"Clay." She pressed a hand to his cheek and moved closer. "Stop blaming yourself for the way Ryder turned out. He made his own choices and has to live with the consequences. You did your best in an untenable position and can't be held liable for your brother's mistakes."

Clay shook his head. "I didn't do enough to save him from the path he was on when I could. If I'd been harsher with him or kept closer tabs on what he was doing—"

"He'd only have rebelled more. Ryder had to learn from his own mistakes, find his own path. You and your mom gave him solid roots, and someday, when he's ready to turn his life around, that foundation will still be there."

He sighed and glanced away. "Maybe."

Frustration clawed at her, but she wouldn't argue the point with him anymore. Not tonight. She had more important things on her mind he needed to hear.

"You can't assume all the fault for our divorce either, Clay. I can't stand the thought that you've blamed yourself for five years."

A muscle in his jaw twitched as he clenched his teeth and

narrowed a trouble gaze on her. "If I'd been the husband you needed, you wouldn't have left."

Her breath snagged in her lungs. "Don't you ever get tired of carrying the weight of the world on your shoulders? A marriage takes two people." She hesitated, knowing she needed to say more. "And…I was wrong to accuse you of cutting me out of your life. You had every right to get rid of my décor from the house. It's your home, and if you didn't like the things I chose—"

"Tee…" Clay sank his fingers into her hair and cradled the base of her skull. Light from the stable glinted in his midnight eyes. "I liked what you added to the house just fine. But after a while, I couldn't take seeing reminders of you, reminders of how I'd let you down. It hurt less to erase you from the house…just as I had to make a clean break from Ryder."

His thumb stroked the sensitive spot behind her ear, and Tamara's head swam dizzily. "You never said anything, never let me know how you felt. During our divorce, you always seemed so distant, so stoic. Why didn't you tell me how you felt?"

His gaze dipped to her lips, and he pitched his voice soft and low. "Would it have made a difference?"

She scowled. "Of course it would have."

He shook his head. "My feelings for you couldn't have solved any of our differences. You had a dream that didn't include ranching. I knew that even when we got married, but I'd convinced myself I could make you happy anyway. Problem was, getting the Bar None up and running filled every hour of my day. That didn't leave much time for you, for your needs. When you were ready to pursue your dream, it would have been selfish of me to hold you back."

She caught her bottom lip with her teeth and sighed. "I just wish—"

"Shh." He pressed a finger to her mouth, and his touch sparked a shimmering heat that spun through her. "No more regrets tonight, okay?"

Tamara threaded her fingers through the raven hair curling at his collar and studied the play of moonlight across his stubble-dusted jaw. The truths she'd learned about Clay tonight, her new insights regarding the pain he'd hidden from her tangled around her heart. "Forgive me, Clay. I never wanted to hurt you. I never meant—"

He silenced her with the soft crush of his lips. His kiss wiped all thoughts of past mistakes and old hurts from her mind. The world shrank to her and Clay. She forgot that she no longer belonged in Clay's arms. All that mattered was the gentle persuasion of his mouth, the sweet sensations that made her head swim and her knees weak. He brushed a callused palm down her cheek, and she leaned into his caress.

You're home.

The words filtered through her mind, but some spoilsport part of her brain rejected the idea with a cold dash of reality. The biting chill of truth washed through her and seeped to the bone.

Inhaling sharply, she backed from his grasp and turned away.

"Is it your ribs? Did I hurt you?" Concern softened his tone and added sting to her sobering awareness.

A sinking feeling settled in her gut.

My feelings for you couldn't have solved any of our differences.

Clay was right. The problems that had ended their marriage still stood between them. Nothing had changed. No amount of wishful thinking could erase the past five years.

Clay swept her hair from her face and brushed his knuckles along her cheek. "Tee, what's wrong?"

"I can't… We can't…let that happen again." She cast a sorrowful glance to him. "I'll be leaving in a couple of days and…" She dropped her gaze and stepped away. "Let's not complicate things. This is hard enough for me without…" Her voice cracked, and she hurried into the stable without finishing the thought.

Kissing Clay might be paradise, but Clay wasn't her home anymore. She'd signed away the right to hold him, to kiss him, the day they divorced.

Chapter 7

Clay followed Tamara as she moved from one stall to the next, visiting each horse, asking about every one and stroking the animals' necks.

She had always had a soft spot for the animals on the ranch, a trait that could be a mixed blessing. The night Lone Star had been put down, Tamara's tender heart had been a curse. She'd been deaf to his and Quinn's attempts to explain why euthanasia had been the kindest thing they could do for the suffering stallion. The normally treatable strangles had become systemic, progressed to fatal bastard strangles. Antibiotics wouldn't have saved him.

He thought he'd explained this to Tamara, but her lingering bitterness made him wonder how much of the truth she really understood. That night, she'd been inconsolable. Her reaction made doing the right thing so much harder. He'd hated to see Tamara's pain. With the loss of his best stud, the livelihood of his ranch at stake and his wife an emotional wreck, Clay had held on to his composure the only way he knew how.

Distance. Denial. Corralling his emotions.

When Tamara had walked out and he'd been left alone in the echoing silence of the house, he'd wallowed for one miserable night in pain, tears and drinking. But by the light of day, he'd had to put on a brave face and soldier through for the ranch hands who depended on him for jobs and the animals who had to be cared for—no matter how rotten his life became.

In the weeks that followed, even when he'd thought bankruptcy was inevitable, he'd learned what really mattered to him. *Tamara.*

Only the realization had come too late. Her leaving had sucked the soul from his life, and all his efforts to save his ranch seemed pointless if he couldn't share it with the woman he loved.

But failure in one area of his life didn't excuse failure in another. Clay had survived Tamara's leaving by burying himself in the business of ranching. He'd been determined that his ranch would not only survive but would thrive. He poured every ounce of his energy into the Bar None, and the ranch's current success bore witness to endless hours of hard work, innovative cost-cutting measures, and his bullheaded pride.

"She looks ready to pop, poor girl. When is she due?"

Tamara's question yanked him from his musing. He replayed the question in his head, mentally catching up. He glanced at the mare in question and scratched his chin. "Um, a matter of days. We're keeping a close eye on her. There were problems with her last delivery."

Concern flickered in Tamara's eyes.

He waved off her worries. "Nothing serious. We're just being cautious."

Tamara nodded and turned back to the mare. "So what's her name?"

"Doesn't have one. You're the one who insisted on naming all the animals. The men and I just call her the roan mare."

Tamara rolled her eyes then tipped her head. "She looks like a Lucy to me."

Clay chuckled and shook his head. "Then Lucy it is."

Judging by her reaction to Hobo and the horses tonight, her tenderheartedness hadn't changed.

Neither had his response to Tamara's kiss. Clay's gaze drifted to his ex's lush mouth, and a renewed kick of desire flashed through him.

She still had the power to set his whole body on fire with the simple touch of her lips. Clay's blood heated thinking about the kiss they'd shared.

Let's not complicate things.

Weren't things already complicated? A dead body and stolen car had been found on his property. His ex-wife was recovering in his home from a nasty fall. And after just two days with Tamara, his feelings about his brother, his divorce, his plans for the ranch were all tangled and turned upside down. He was questioning everything he thought he knew about his life and what he wanted for the future.

Not complicate things? He grunted.

That particular horse had already escaped the barn.

Tamara's initial response to their kiss indicated that she still had feelings for him. She had been as deeply affected as he had. Of course, sex had never been their problem. They'd always had a fiery passion for each other and a magical rapport in bed.

Tamara gave the mare's nose another pat. "Hang in there, Lucy. You're in good hands." She turned from the last stall and cast her gaze around the stable as if checking for any horse she'd missed.

He propped an arm on the door of an empty stall. "I think that's everybody."

"Where's Trouble? Do you still have her?"

"Trouble?"

"The kitten I rescued from the Handleys' dog."

"Oh, the barn cat." He chuckled. "I didn't realize you'd named her. I call her Cat."

"Cat? How imaginative." His ex wrinkled her nose and looked

so adorable he wished he could pull her into his arms for a bear hug. But even if her ribs had been in any condition to endure such affection, Tamara had made her wishes clear.

Let's not complicate things.

Clay pushed away from the stall with a shrug. "Come on. She's probably out by the truck. I've been finding paw prints on my windshield every morning."

Sure enough, they found the calico curled in the bed of his truck on a horse blanket. While Tamara cooed over the cat, Clay studied the shimmer of pale moonlight in her hay-colored hair, the dusting of freckles that danced across her nose. He'd kissed every one of those freckles when they'd been married and...

With a huff, he kicked the gravel at his toe. Enough living in the past. Tamara's presence at the ranch was an anomaly. The minute her ribs healed, she'd be gone again. Reviving old memories would only prolong the ache when she left.

Trouble stood and stretched, butting her head against Tamara's hand. She laughed and obliged the cat, scratching her behind the ear and stroking her glossy coat while murmuring sweet nothings to the purring feline.

Clay watched, fascinated. "She never begs for attention like that from me."

Tamara glanced at him. "Do you ever give her unsolicited pats?"

No. He opened his mouth to answer, but Tamara's knowing expression stopped him in his tracks.

"Maybe she knows not to expect anything from you," Tamara said softly.

So he didn't lavish the barn cat with affection. So what? That didn't mean he was cold and unfeeling as she'd accused him earlier that evening. He simply knew better than to grow attached to ranch animals. Ranching was a business, and emotions played no part in sound business decisions.

Yet as Tamara stared at him this muggy June evening, a hurt he'd seen often toward the end of their marriage shadowed her eyes. His pulse stumbled.

I don't feel like I matter to you anymore—if I ever really did. I feel you pulling away and don't understand why. What changed?

Echoes of their last argument rang in his head, and remorse bit him hard. Had his wife left because she felt unloved? He'd always questioned how she could accuse him of not caring about her.

He looked at Trouble, eating up the loving attention Tamara offered, and frowned. The cat's affection for him or lack thereof had never mattered to Clay. The cat merely served a function on the ranch—catching mice in the barn. Period. But did Trouble's dismissal of him serve as an allegory for a bigger picture?

Like the cat, had Tamara sensed something lacking from him in the final weeks of their marriage? Had he given her a message he hadn't intended, something that told her he didn't care?

Tamara clicked her tongue then laughed when Trouble flopped on her side and batted at Tamara's long hair.

Watching his ex-wife play with the barn cat, Clay dusted off the defensive assurances he'd used after the divorce to soothe his conscience. She was the one who'd broadcasted her unhappiness like a beacon. She'd made clear her wish to follow her dream of a career in criminal investigation. Her restlessness had been obvious in every way. Yet she'd accused him of pulling away. The irony and unfairness of her accusations had chafed. Now her claims gave him pause.

Sensing her disquiet and longing for her own career, had he anticipated her leaving him and withdrawn, held back his heart in self-defense? Had he unwittingly set in motion a self-fulfilling prophecy that led to his divorce?

The possibilities took root in his brain and grew. Clay's hands became sweaty, and his heart beat double time. He raked his hand through his hair, knocking off his hat. He sank down on the tailgate of his truck while his thoughts roiled and his gut pitched.

He'd always had a nagging sense that he was to blame for Tamara's unhappiness. But he'd never been able to pinpoint where he'd gone astray or exactly how he'd let her down.

"Clay, what's wrong?" Tamara moved up beside him and placed a hand on his forearm. Her brow puckered in concern.

"I… Nothing. I just…" He scooped up his Stetson and absently fingered the rim.

Trouble followed Tamara over to the tailgate and rubbed against Clay. He lifted a shaky hand and stroked the cat from head to tail. Encouraged by the attention, Trouble climbed into his lap and butted his hand again.

"See?" Tamara said. "She was just waiting for you to show a little interest."

The good-natured jibe reverberated through Clay, and he held his breath.

Looking back at the events five years ago, he couldn't shake the notion that he'd set in motion a vicious circle. The more he'd withdrawn from Tamara to protect his heart from her inevitable leaving, the unhappier and more unloved she'd felt, precipitating her departure and their divorce.

He expelled his pent-up breath in a whoosh and braced an arm on the truck bed.

Lifting a stunned gaze to Tamara, he rasped, "Did I really withdraw from you in those last months of our marriage? Did I make you think you weren't loved?"

Tamara's face paled. "What makes you say that?"

"That's what you told me the night you left. You said you thought I'd been pulling away, that you felt like you didn't matter."

Tamara shook her head and turned away. "Let's not rehash that argument and stir up hard feelings again tonight. I said I was sorry for what I said earlier and—"

He placed a hand on each shoulder and gently turned her around. "Forget what we said earlier this evening. I'm asking about what I did in the months before you left that made you think I didn't care."

Tamara ducked her head and sighed. "Please, Clay. I don't want to open old wounds again. Can't we just let bygones be bygones?"

"Not if I did something to hurt you." He put a finger under

her chin and made her look at him. Tears filled her blue eyes and clawed at his heart. "Tee, you have to know I'd never consciously do anything to cause you pain. I didn't contest the divorce, because I didn't want to hold you back from following your dream, having the career you wanted."

"I know that. Now. But back then…I was confused." She pulled away, rubbing her arms as if chilled. "I was trying to figure out how to balance my need for a career with my marriage, and all I really knew was the longer I stayed at the ranch, the more I felt I was losing myself in your shadow."

"Tamara, I'm sorry if I—"

She spun back toward him and pressed a hand to his lips. "Don't. There's enough blame for both of us."

He captured her hand and kissed the fingers she held over his mouth. Her eyes darkened to the color of the sky at the first daylight. Finally she slipped her hand from his and stepped back.

"We were so young when we got married, Clay. Maybe if we'd waited…" She shook her head. "Well, we'll never really know. Speculation and second-guessing solve nothing." She took another step back. "Good night, Clay."

With that, she turned and hurried toward the house. He watched her retreat until she disappeared inside the back door, then he tipped his head back to stare at the moon.

Trouble meowed and wound through his legs, purring.

With a grunt, Clay crouched to scratch the cat's head. Second-guessing might not solve anything, but Clay knew tonight there'd be no escaping the regrets and doubt-demons his new insights had created.

Chapter 8

The next morning, Tamara, with the help of her pain medication, slept in for the first time in many months. After a bite of breakfast, she returned to the guest bedroom Marie had prepared for her to read an action-adventure novel she found on Clay's bookshelf. After a few chapters, she heard a car horn toot, followed by slamming doors and the chattering of young voices. Parting the window's miniblinds, she peered down at the driveway where an SUV had parked. Clay greeted the blond-haired woman who climbed from the driver's side with a hug and a peck on the cheek.

Stepping back from the window, she scowled. She hadn't even considered the possibility that Clay could have a new woman in his life. Did she really think Clay would spend the rest of his life alone? He had so much to offer a woman, so many warm and wonderful traits.

But last night, he'd kissed *her*.

Kiss or not, what claim did she have on him now? She'd chosen to leave Clay years ago, and she refused to second-guess that decision. As she'd told Clay last night, regret served no purpose.

Still, curiosity got the better of her, and she headed downstairs to meet the ranch's guests. With the good night's sleep under her belt and a couple of Advil in her system, she felt considerably better. Her general aches were all but gone, and her rib pain was manageable as long as she didn't move too fast or jar her midriff.

Tamara stepped out on the wide front porch. The day's heat and humidity slammed into her like walking into a brick wall. And it was only ten-thirty. Welcome to summer in Texas.

Clay looked over as she crossed the yard, and his sexy grin made her insides quiver.

"Speak of the devil." Clay slid an arm loosely around Tamara's waist and motioned to the woman with him. "Tamara, this is Aunt Meredith's niece, Jewel Mayfair. She runs the new Esperanza branch of Hopechest Ranch."

As she shook hands with Jewel, Tamara remembered the call Clay had taken last night regarding the plan to bring several girls from Hopechest Ranch over to ride horses. The bubble of jealousy popped. Jewel was family. A distant connection through marriage, but family nonetheless and no competition for Clay's affections.

Get real. In order to be jealous, you'd have to still consider yourself in a relationship with your ex.

Admitting she still had feelings for Clay would start her down a slippery slope. Definitely not where she needed to go if she wanted to survive the next few days of recuperation with her heart intact.

While they exchanged the customary courtesies, Tamara took stock of Clay's relative. Jewel was lovely, with short, wavy hair and beautiful brown eyes. Tall for a woman, especially in her fashionable cowboy boots, Jewel Mayfair had enviable curves in her slim figure. Yet for all her elegant beauty, dark smudges under her eyes and fine lines of fatigue in her face hinted that she hadn't slept well or was under a great deal of stress.

Understandable. Running Hopechest Ranch and acting as

mother to numerous teenage girls had to have more than its share of pressures and long nights.

Clay lowered his voice and whispered to Tamara. "You sure you feel up to being on your feet?"

The tickle of his breath in her ear sent a delicious and distracting shiver down her spine.

She met the dark concern in his eyes and smiled. "I'm much better this morning. Thanks."

His gaze lingered as if he deciding whether to chide her and send her back into the house.

"Really," she said, stroking a hand down his recently shaved cheek.

Mistake.

Touching him stirred all those old memories of greeting him in the morning with a kiss and savoring the scent of fresh hay that clung to him following his morning chores. A crackling energy zinged through her and made her knees weak.

The fire that danced in his eyes told her he sensed the same electricity humming between them.

She caught her breath. She was treading into dangerous territory. The kiss they'd shared last night was proof of how easily she could slide back into her role as Clay's lover, forgetting the obstacles and hurt between them. Still, all the sexual heat in the world couldn't save their marriage five years ago. Indulging that physical attraction now could only cause more pain in the long run.

Because she couldn't give her body over to Clay without involving her heart.

Jewel cleared her throat, jerking Tamara and Clay from whatever spell had held them the past several seconds. When Tamara glanced back at their visitor, Jewel wore a knowing grin.

Clay shifted his feet awkwardly. "Well, I'll, uh…" He rubbed his hands down the seat of his jeans and stepped back. "I'll leave you two ladies to talk. I gotta finish saddling up a few horses for the girls. I know they're eager to start their ride."

"Thanks, Clay." Jewel gave him a little wave as he strode back toward the barn. Turning to Tamara, she said, "Care to join me at the riding ring? I love to see the girls' faces when they get up on a horse for the first time. They're always so excited."

"Sure." She fell in step with Jewel.

"I was sorry to hear about your fall." Jewel gave her a worried glance. "You seem to be getting around pretty well considering…"

"A full night's sleep did me wonders. I can't remember the last time I had more than five hours."

"Me either." Jewel gave her a forced grin, but her eyes seemed troubled.

Sensing she'd touched on a sore subject, Tamara shifted gears. "So how long have you been bringing kids out to the Bar None?"

Brightening a bit, Jewel shrugged. "Pretty much since we opened a few months ago. Clay's been a godsend with all his support. I can call him night or day if I need something, and he's always willing to lend a hand. And there wouldn't be a Hopechest Ranch in Esperanza if Clay hadn't sold us a piece of the Bar None to build on."

Tamara snapped a glance toward Jewel. "He did?"

"He didn't tell you?"

Tamara shook her head. "Not that he had any reason to tell me. Since our divorce, we don't discuss Bar None business. In fact, before a couple days ago, I hadn't seen Clay in five years."

That news seemed to surprise Jewel. "I'm sorry. I thought… well, I assumed really that…because of the way you two looked at each other just now that…"

Heat climbed Tamara's throat and stung her cheeks. "That what?"

"That maybe you were getting back together…or at least were still close," Jewel ventured hesitantly. "It's just you two seemed so…" she waved a hand as she searched for the right word "…connected."

Tamara opened her mouth to deny Jewel's assumption, but her voice stuck in her throat. What *was* going on between her and Clay? And if his friends were picking up on a shared undercurrent, what signal was Clay receiving from her that she didn't intend?

Already disconcerted by that thought, Tamara glanced toward the riding ring in time to see Clay shake hands with a tall man in his early forties. The man's thick brown hair fell in his eyes and shone with auburn highlights in the morning sun. Her steps faltered. Quinn Logan.

Jewel stopped and gave Tamara a frown. "I'm sorry. Have I said too much?"

Tamara forced a grin and shook her head. "No. It's not you. I just…well, I've sorta seen a ghost from my past."

Jewel turned and scanned the riding corral. "You mean the guy talking to Clay?"

"Yeah." She inhaled as deeply as her sore ribs would allow and blew it out slowly.

"I remember seeing him out here before when I brought the girls, but I was never introduced. Who is he?"

"Clay's good friend, Quinn Logan. He's Clay's veterinarian."

Tipping her head, Jewel arched an eyebrow and gave Quinn an appraising scrutiny. "And quite the good-looking vet at that, huh?"

Tamara wrinkled her nose and resumed walking toward the corral. "I suppose…"

"I hear a *but* at the end of that sentence. Why? Is he married?"

"Widowed. His wife died right before I moved away from Esperanza. I don't think he's remarried. Although I guess *I* wouldn't have heard if he had."

Jewel frowned. "Why not? You said he was a good friend."

"Of Clay's. More like my old nemesis."

Jewel's puzzled look spoke for her.

Scowling, Tamara shook her head. "Sorry. That sounded melodramatic. It's not as bad as that, but Quinn was a major factor in the events that finally killed my marriage."

Jewel gave Tamara a look that said Tamara's comment intrigued her but she was too polite to press for details. They'd reached the split-rail fence that circled the corral, and Jewel walked over to a young Mexican woman who was watching the activity in the ring. "Let me know if you get too hot, Ana. I brought plenty of bottled water, and I'm sure Clay wouldn't mind you going inside if you needed to get out of the sun."

Tamara noticed the young woman's rounded belly when she turned to smile at Jewel. "I'm fine. Stop worrying, Miss Jewel. Baby and I love the sunshine and fresh air."

Jewel laughed. "If you can call the smell of horse manure fresh air…"

Tamara joined Jewel at the rail and propped her arms on the top beam. "If you spend much time around horses, eventually you don't notice the smell."

"Tamara, this is Ana Morales. She's staying with us at Hopechest Ranch until her baby is born."

Tamara greeted the young mother who'd been blessed with all the best features of her Mexican heritage. Her black hair was thick and glossy, and her olive complexion and dark eyes had a healthy glow.

"When are you due?" Tamara asked.

Ana flashed a shy smile. "Three months." She glanced away and slid a protective hand over her stomach. "If you don't mind, Miss Jewel, think I'll go see the other horses."

Tamara gave Jewel a puzzled look as Ana headed toward the stables. "Was it something I said?"

Jewel shook her head and placed a hand lightly on Tamara's arm. "No, no. It's not you. Ana's a sweet young lady, really bright and well-spoken, but she's also very private. She doesn't like to talk about herself."

"So I scared her off by asking about her due date," Tamara said.

Jewel opened her mouth as if to deny it, then shrugged. "Maybe. Please, don't take it personally. She's going through a rough patch, being away from her family, and feels the need to keep to herself more than the younger girls." Jewel paused and gave a self-conscious grin. "Although I've been keeping to myself out at the Hopechest Ranch myself, so I don't have room to talk. I've been in town for several months, and I still haven't met many folks."

Tamara noticed Jewel's gaze stray back to Quinn but kept her own focus on Clay as he tightened the stirrups for one of the girls. "If you want to meet people in Esperanza, you need to go to Miss Sue's diner. Not only do they have the best food in town, it's where everyone who is anyone goes to see and be seen."

Jewel's face warmed, and she nodded. "Oh, yes. I've been to Miss Sue's. I was told as soon as I got to Esperanza that her pecan pie was heaven on a plate."

"Heaven on a plate. That's about right!" Tamara laughed then grabbed her ribs. "Oh, ow! Note to self—laughing hurts."

Jewel winced and muffled a chuckle. When her new friend's attention fixed on Quinn again, something inside Tamara nudged her to explain her cool attitude toward the vet. "I don't want to leave you with the wrong impression about Quinn. I—" Dropping her gaze, Tamara kicked a clod of dirt with the toe of her shoe. "Right before we divorced, we had to put one of Clay's best stallions to sleep." Her heart ached as the memories stirred again. She explained to Jewel in general terms how she and Clay had argued over the best course of action and how Quinn had influenced Clay's decision for euthanasia, despite viable treatment options. "I didn't like the way Quinn handled the whole situation, and I let him know it. When I questioned him about his recommendation, all he'd say was euthanasia was 'for the best.' His evasiveness made me think he was hiding something."

Jewel furrowed her brow. "Like what?"

Tamara sent Quinn a dark look. "I don't know. Maybe he missed signs of the disease in earlier examinations and was afraid we'd sue for malpractice. Or…there's a vaccine for strangles, the disease that Lone Star contracted. So maybe he'd been negligent about vaccinating Clay's horses."

She faced Jewel and shook her head in consternation. Maybe she shouldn't be unloading her frustrations on someone she'd just met, but Jewel held her gaze with an earnest interest and caring. Tamara had felt an immediate connection with Clay's relative, and when Jewel nodded her head for her to continue,

Tamara continued venting. "And why couldn't they have treated Lone Star with antibiotics? Everyone I talked to in town said most horses recover from strangles with the right treatment. Anyway, the whole incident just seemed fishy. And I'm not the only one who thought so. I had people calling me for weeks afterward asking what had happened and second-guessing Quinn's actions."

Jewel's gaze moved to something behind Tamara, and she schooled her expression. With her eyes, she signaled Tamara to brace herself and turn around.

Tamara's gut clenched. She pivoted on her heel.

"Hello, Tamara." Quinn stood behind her with his thumbs hooked in his pockets. He gave her a quick smile that was polite but lacking any warmth. Beneath the scar that ran down his cheek, courtesy of a feisty stallion, his jaw was tense.

"Quinn." Tamara twitched the corner of her mouth, the best smile she could manage with the swirl of resentment and painful memories that churned through her. She dutifully made the introductions between Jewel and the veterinarian without any flourish, and they shook hands.

"What brings you out to the Bar None today?" Jewel asked, picking up the conversation when Tamara and Quinn lapsed into an awkward silence. "None of Clay's horses are sick, I hope."

"No, ma'am. Nothing like that." Quinn's mood brightened when he answered Jewel. "I stable my stallion here." He hitched his head toward a black horse still waiting to be saddled. "That's Noches. I come by a lot to check on him and visit with Clay."

Jewel flashed a smile and nodded. "He's a beautiful animal."

"Before I leave, I plan to check on one of Clay's mares that's about to foal. But first, I promised Clay I'd help him with all those pretty young ladies you brought. Not that we expect trouble." He raised a hand to reassure Jewel. "But it's best to have plenty of hands around when you're dealing with inexperienced riders."

"Well, I appreciate your donating your time to the girls. They love coming out here to see the horses."

"My pleasure." Quinn smiled at Jewel then shifted his attention back to Tamara. His grin faded. "Well, I better be getting back to work. Good to see you, Tamara."

"You, too," she lied, the civility sour in her throat.

As Quinn strode away, Jewel gave a low whistle. "Wow. For June, it sure feels frosty out here."

A twist of compunction tightened Tamara's chest. "I know it's petty of me. I don't like the bad blood between us. But that night was so painful for me…for all of us. There were lots of hard feelings, and bitter words and accusations that can never be erased. I'm as much to blame as he is for the rift in our friendship—and we did used to be friends, just like he and Clay still are. But some things are hard to get past."

"I understand." The sadness that flickered in Jewel's eyes echoed her words, and for the second time, Tamara wondered about the troubled shadows in Jewel's gaze. "Have you talked to Clay recently about what happened that night, why he went with Quinn's recommendation? Maybe now, with some distance from the situation, he could better explain his perspective."

Tamara grunted and cast Jewel a quick side glance. "As a matter of fact, the topic came up last night in a…" she searched for the right word "…heated, no…*emotional* discussion we had. It was the first time Clay and I had talked about some of the issues that led to our divorce and…well, it was a painful conversation with lots of hot buttons."

Tucking a wisp of hair behind her ear, Jewel faced Tamara and leaned against the fence. "I guess I was thinking that with the time you two have had since the divorce, that now might be a good chance to resolve some of those touchy issues. It's obvious you still care about each other."

"I don't know." Tamara's lungs constricted at the thought of hashing out all the old grievances with Clay. He'd tried to discuss some of their problems last night, and she'd bolted like a skittish colt. She wasn't prepared to face those resurrected memories.

Jewel's warm smile encouraged confidences, and again

Tamara felt a kinship and connection to her new friend. "What good would it do to open old wounds?"

"You might find the peace you need to have closure. Or you might be able to put the hurt and resentment aside and repair an old friendship." Jewel sent a meaningful glance toward Quinn.

Tamara stared into the riding ring without really seeing. Rather than Jewel's charges on horseback circling the corral, her vision was filled with reruns of last night's emotional exchange with Clay. He'd given her an opening to explain why she'd left, and she'd dodged the issue like a coward.

"Or...I could just be horning in where my advice isn't wanted." Jewel's comment pulled Tamara back to the present.

With a contrite grin, Jewel shrugged. "Sorry. Hazard of the profession. I spend most of every day counseling and advising the girls at Hopechest Ranch. Sometimes it's hard to turn the psychological training off and mind my own business."

"No, don't apologize. You're right, and you've given me a lot to think about."

As if she weren't already spending every waking hour thinking about Clay—the mistakes they'd made in their marriage, the passion they'd shared in bed, and the cherished traditions they'd created on holidays and special occasions.

The missed opportunities to save their relationship.

She watched Clay lead a younger girl's horse around the perimeter of the corral, coaxing the first-time rider with warm encouragement and sunny smiles, and Tamara's heart split open. She wanted to reclaim all the things she and Clay had once shared. She wanted a second chance to make their relationship work.

But could they overcome the obstacles that had torn them apart the first time? They'd both changed. Their lives were on divergent paths. How could they possibly make it work? And more important, was a second chance even what Clay wanted?

Chapter 9

Later that morning, as Jewel and the girls from Hopechest Ranch loaded back into their SUV to leave, a blue pickup rolled up Clay's driveway, kicking up a plume of dust.

"Well, we sure are popular today," Clay said under his breath to Tamara, who stood beside him on the front porch, waving goodbye to Jewel and her charges.

"It's Dr. O'Neal. Since when do doctors make house calls?" Tamara cast Clay a curious glance. "Did you call him?"

He shook his head and walked down the steps to greet the doctor.

"So how's the patient doing?" Dr. O'Neal gave Tamara a measuring scrutiny. "I take it you're feeling better if you're on your feet."

She bobbed her head. "Much." Tipping her head, she asked, "Did we miss an appointment or is this a courtesy call?"

"I was passing right by here on the way into the office, so I thought I'd save you a trip into town for a follow-up exam."

"That was thoughtful. But…" Tamara turned her attention to

Clay. "I was just about to talk my ex into taking me to Miss Sue's for lunch."

Clay cocked an eyebrow. First he'd heard. Not that he wouldn't make the time if lunch at Miss Sue's was what Tamara wanted. He conducted a mental inventory of his to-do list. With a bit of rescheduling and delegating, he could free up the afternoon.

"We could have stopped by the clinic after we ate." Tamara's gaze returned to the doctor. "Assuming a follow-up is really necessary. I feel much stronger. My ribs don't hurt nearly as much. Well…unless I cough or laugh or move suddenly."

Dr. O'Neal nodded. "That's good." He paused then angled his head in query. "Are you still taking the painkillers I gave you? Used as directed the drug is perfectly safe but…" His face grew somber. "They can become addictive if you rely on them too long."

Tamara smiled politely. "I've switched to the over-the-counter stuff to control what aches and pains remain."

The doctor raised a palm and grinned. "Then it seems my work here is done." He offered his hand to Clay.

"Any word from Doc Mason?" Clay asked as they shook hands.

The doctor's smile faded, his brow puckering, and he seemed at a loss for words for a moment. "Last I heard, Doc had decided to extend his vacation. He's really taken by the Arizona climate and scenery. In fact, he mentioned retiring there."

Clay exchanged a startled glance with Tamara.

"He's talking about retiring? That doesn't sound like the Doc Mason I know." Clay scratched his jaw. "The man's a ball of energy, and his medical practice, his patients are his life. Why would he leave his friends and home to retire in Arizona?"

Dr. O'Neal scrubbed a hand over the thinning patch of his short-cropped hair and cleared his throat. "I don't have an answer for that, but that's what the Doc's message said." He backed toward his truck. "Well, good to see you're feeling better, Ms. Brown. I'd better be off."

Clay frowned and sent Tamara another curious look as the fill-in doctor beat a hasty retreat. As Dr. O'Neal's pickup crunched down the gravel driveway, Clay climbed the porch steps and tipped his head. "Miss Sue's, huh?"

She grinned. "Please? If you can afford the time away. I've got a powerful hankering for pecan pie. And I'd love to see Becky French and the folks in town."

He slid a hand down her cheek and tweaked her chin. "All right. Anything for you, love. Just let me get my keys, and I'll meet you at my truck."

Clay strolled inside, and as he passed the hall mirror he noticed the sappy grin he wore. He sighed and snatched his keys from the kitchen counter. In the two days Tamara had been with him, he'd gotten lulled into a sense that her presence meant a return to a familiar status quo. Falling back into old habits had been far too easy, and seeing her in his home made five years of her absence melt like snow in Austin.

If she was feeling well enough go into town, if she only needed over-the-counter medicine for the ache in her ribs, she'd be leaving the Bar None again. Soon.

He pressed his hat farther down on his head and strode out to his truck, trying not to dwell on the unrest that swirled in him at the thought of Tamara's imminent departure.

He'd known her stay at the ranch was temporary. He just hadn't been prepared for the mixed emotions she'd awakened in him.

When she'd left five years ago, he'd managed to suppress his pain and shut down his feelings by pouring his energies into the ranch. This time he wasn't sure any amount of avoidance or diversions could heal the inevitable heartache. He now recognized what he'd denied before. For all their differences and difficulties, Tamara meant more to him than anyone or anything—including his ranch.

Tamara gazed out the window of Clay's truck as they rolled down Main Street into Esperanza. Details she had understandably missed on their trip to Doc Mason's clinic, now caught her eye and raised endless questions.

"Is June Yardly still the librarian?" she asked Clay as they passed the small library.

"Nope. She retired a couple years back."

"Yates Feed and Supply is still in business." She smiled. "When did that mini-mart open? Has it hurt business for the local merchants?"

Clay shrugged. "Not that I've heard. Town folk are loyal to their own."

He found an empty parking spot in front of the sheriff's office and cut the engine.

When she'd called her lab in San Antonio earlier that morning, Eric had been evasive, saying that while she was on medical leave, she needn't worry about the current cases. Tamara considered stopping in the sheriff's office to see what new information Jericho had on the investigation. But she caught a whiff of the inviting aromas that spilled out of Miss Sue's across the street, and her stomach growled. The visit to Jericho's office would wait.

Clay escorted her across the street with a proprietary hand at the small of her back. Just as he had on numerous occasions in the past. But those days were gone. And by this afternoon, she needed to be gone from Esperanza as well. She had no excuse for prolonging her departure. A wistful longing pricked Tamara. How was it that in high school she couldn't wait to get out of this small town? Now being in Esperanza and seeing all the familiar faces felt like a homecoming.

When Clay opened the door for Tamara, the clank of an old cow bell heralded their arrival. She preceded him into the diner, redolent with tempting aromas of fresh-brewed coffee and home-baked bread and bustling with lunchtime traffic. She sat at the only free table. After shaking hands with an elderly man she didn't recognize, Clay folded his long legs under the wooden table and set his Stetson on the chair beside him.

Tamara glanced at the other diners, many of whom sent curious stares her way. "I think I know who will be the center of the gossip in town this afternoon." She grinned and leaned closer to Clay as if sharing a juicy secret. "Did you hear about Clay Colton? He was at Miss Sue's today with his ex-wife. Bold as brass. I hear she's been staying out at his place since Thursday! What do you suppose that means?"

She flashed him a playful smile that elicited a lopsided grin in return. He wrapped his hand around hers, and heat curled inside her.

"We could really get the rumor mill buzzing if you were to kiss me right now." He tipped his head, and a challenging glint sparked in his eyes.

A flutter of longing flapped in her chest. Kissing Clay again had immense appeal, but she didn't dare confound things between them. Her emotions were already tangled.

Becky French's arrival at their table with glasses of ice water spared Tamara from responding. "Why, Clay Colton. What are you doing in here in the middle of the day? Don't normally see you in here until supper time."

A resident of Esperanza for all of her sixty-plus years, Becky French had always reminded Tamara of Mrs. Santa Claus. Short, plump and gray-haired, Becky had a bubbly personality and lively blue eyes that cinched the comparison. Seeing the dear older woman was as much a treat for Tamara as the long-anticipated pie.

Clay smiled at the diner's owner and shrugged. "Tamara had a craving for your pecan pie. Who am I to deny a beautiful woman such a basic request?"

Becky's head swiveled toward Tamara, and recognition lit her eyes. "My goodness, Tamara! I'd heard you were in town."

As Becky stepped around the corner of the scarred wooden table to wrap her in a hug, Tamara braced for the painful squeeze. But Becky hesitated then frowned. "Wait a minute, Billy Akers said somethin' about you breaking your ribs? Are you all right?"

"Just bruised, not broken. But I'll take a rain check on that hug today. Okay?"

Becky nodded and stepped back with a smile. "My gracious, it's good to see you!"

Tamara felt more than saw the gazes of other customers turn toward her and Clay. By nightfall, every citizen of Esperanza would know the divorced Coltons were having lunch together at Miss Sue's.

Becky took their lunch order, promising to save Tamara a large serving of pecan pie, and hustled off to the kitchen. Tamara studied the familiar décor. Little had changed since the days when Clay's mother had run the diner. Even the curtain across the front plate-glass window was the same. Mismatched wooden tables filled the tile floor, and framed bits of the town's memorabilia hung on the walls. Though old, the diner had passed from one set of loving hands to another through the years and remained tidily kept and filled with homey charm. Nostalgia tugged her heart as she remembered evenings she'd spent at Miss Sue's, first with her own family and later with Clay during high school.

"Uncle Clay!" The delighted squeal from a little girl at the front door cut into Tamara's memories. The red-headed pixie hurtled herself into Clay's arms and hugged his neck. "I didn't know you'd be here!"

Clay's face lit with a warm grin. "Hey, pipsqueak. How's my favorite cowgirl?"

"Fine as frog's hair!" The little girl's green eyes danced with joy and mischief.

Clay laughed. "Where did you hear that expression?"

She shrugged. "One of Mama's rodeo friends."

The spitfire glanced at Tamara and blinked curiously. Tamara didn't need to see the child's mother entering the diner to recognize Georgie Colton's daughter. The girl was, as Clay'd told her, the image of Clay's sister.

"You must be Emmie," Tamara said with a broad smile.

Dressed in a Western snap-front shirt, jeans and boots, the girl nodded. "How'd you know?"

"Because you look just like your mom."

Emmie rolled her eyes. "Everybody says that!"

Clay tweaked the girl's nose. "Because it's true."

Georgie reached the table with a handsome black-haired man at her side. "Emmie, I've asked you not to—" She stopped abruptly and gasped. "Tamara?"

"Georgie!" Tamara pushed to her feet and ignored the pain as she hugged her former sister-in-law. After a round of introductions, during which Tamara met Nick Sheffield, the new man in Georgie's life, and Clay summarized the events that had brought Tamara back to town, Georgie pulled extra chairs up to their table so she, Nick and Emmie could join her brother for lunch.

"How long will you be in town?" Nick asked Tamara.

"Not long. I'm feeling stronger already, and I really need to get back to work."

Clay grunted. "Your boss put you on medical leave. Remember?"

"But I—" Tamara snapped her mouth shut and swallowed her protest. Nick and Georgie exchanged a look, and in deference to their audience, she changed the topic. "Clay tells me you ran into a little trouble recently yourself."

Georgie shivered. "Yeah. I'm so glad that nightmare is over."

Nick wrapped a protective arm around Georgie. "The important thing is you and Emmie are safe now, and the woman responsible was stopped."

"Amen to that." Clay raised his ice water in salute.

"Have you seen any old friends since you got in town?" Georgie asked and flipped her long red braid to her back. "I mean besides Jericho." She flicked her hand in dismissal. "That was business and doesn't count."

Tamara propped her elbows on the table and knit her brow in thought. "Well, Quinn was out at the ranch earlier, although we didn't say much more than hello." She met Clay's gaze across the table, and his expression said he knew the grudge Tamara still carried toward his good friend.

"Logan? The vet?" Nick asked.

Remembering that the former Secret Service man was new to Esperanza, Tamara nodded confirmation.

"Quinn Logan," Georgie said and clucked her tongue. "I just don't understand why he is still single. Maybe I could introduce him to—"

"Little sister, the last thing Quinn needs is another well-meaning woman trying to fix him up. Give it a rest, okay?"

"I just—"

Clay made a slashing motion across his throat to forestall Georgie's protest.

"Oh, I saw Billy Akers when I was at Doc Mason's clinic to get checked after my fall." Tamara chuckled. "Man-oh-man, my brother and Billy used to give me such a hard time when I'd beg to tag along with them."

Georgie grinned then her smile dimmed. "I heard his mom was real sick. Did he say how she was doing?"

Tamara sobered and nodded. "He said it's ALS. She's not doing well." She glanced at Clay. "Before I leave town, I want to stop by and give Mrs. Akers my best. She's such a dear lady, like a second mother to me. It's been far too long since I visited her."

Clay nodded. "Just say when. I'll take you."

"Wait, I thought Doc Mason was out of town." Georgie tipped her head. "Who treated you when you went to the clinic?"

"His fill-in, Dr. O'Neal."

Becky French arrived at the table with Tamara and Clay's orders. "Frank O'Neal? Nice fella. Needs a little more meat on his bones if you ask me. He came in here for lunch a few days ago and ate a salad and unsweetened tea." Becky harrumphed. "No wonder he's skin and bones." She slid Clay's hamburger and Tamara's tuna melt onto the table. "I think he's planning to buy into Doc Mason's practice when the good doctor retires."

Georgie chuckled. "*If* he retires. Doc Mason loves his work more than anyone I've ever met!"

Clay frowned. "Which is why this sudden vacation he's on seems odd to me. Dr. O'Neal stopped by the Bar None this morning to check on Tamara and said Doc Mason has extended his trip. He likes Arizona so much he's thinking of retiring there."

"I've been to Arizona! Haven't I, Mom?" Emmie chirped. "With the rodeo."

"Righty-o, honey."

The diner owner shook her head. "Staying in Arizona? That's crazy. The people in Esperanza are family to Doc. Why would he retire someplace he doesn't know anyone?"

Clay shrugged, and Tamara recognized the worry that darkened his eyes. The old doctor's absence really bothered Clay, and she was itching to discuss his suspicions when they had more privacy.

"Speaking of family—" A smile lit Becky's face, and she pulled a white envelope from her apron pocket. "You haven't seen my sweet grandbabies! I just got a new set of pictures from my youngest son, Tamara. Have a look."

Tamara took the stack of photos the diner's owner handed her and, while Becky took Georgie, Nick and Emmie's orders, she flipped through the series of smiling-baby shots. Maternal longing tugged deep inside Tamara as she studied the photos.

If she and Clay hadn't divorced, would they have a child by now? Would their baby have had Clay's brown eyes or her blue ones? She shook her head and set the fruitless thoughts aside.

"Can I have a milkshake?" Emmie asked. "I promise to eat my whole lunch."

Georgie ruffled her daughter's short hair. "All right. But for dessert. Deal?"

Emmie beamed. "Deal!"

Becky laughed. "Enjoy this age. They're not always so agreeable. When they become teenagers…" The older woman threw up her hands and rolled her eyes. "Take T. J. Ward, for example. Macy's got her hands full with that one. Jericho got called outta here the other night because T.J. was stopped out on the county highway driving eighty miles per hour. Drag racing the Horner boy, I think. Macy, the poor dear, has had such trouble with him. The boy's been so rebellious lately, and it just keeps getting worse."

Shaking her head in dismay, Becky headed back to the

kitchen with Georgie, Nick and Emmie's orders. Clay traced the grain of the wood in their table with the handle of his fork and shook his head. "I know what Macy's going through. Ryder was the same way after Mom died. Let's hope she figures out how to get through to T.J." He heaved a sigh and stabbed at his hash browns. "My lack of parenting skills landed Ryder in prison."

"Clay—" Tamara began before Georgie sputtered.

"What! Back up there, big brother. Your lack of parenting skills? It was Ryder's lack of self-discipline and good judgment that landed him in jail. You did all you could."

"And it wasn't enough or our brother wouldn't be in prison." He waved his fork in dismissal. "Forget I said anything. Let's not ruin our lunch by discussing my failures."

Georgie leaned across the table and grabbed her brother's wrist as he tried to eat a pickle spear. "I'll drop it if you get one thing straight. You gave Ryder and me the best foundation you could after Mom died. No one worked harder or coulda been more dedicated. I turned out okay thanks to your guidance, so keep that in mind before you start calling your efforts a failure."

Tamara held her breath while Clay locked silent stares with his sister. When he dropped his gaze, he said calmly, "Your sleeve is in my ketchup."

Georgie jerked her arm back with a gasp, checking the damage.

"Oh, well. It'll wash," Emmie said, patting her mother's back. Tamara hid a grin behind her napkin as she wiped her mouth.

"Did you tell Clay about Meredith's trip out here yet?" Nick asked.

Clay cocked his head. "Aunt Meredith's coming to town?"

Georgie nodded and swiped one of Clay's pickles. "On Friday. Mostly she's coming to check up on Jewel, I think, but I was hoping we could all get together for a meal. You have plans for this weekend?"

Clay glanced to Tamara and raised his eyebrows in query, as if consulting her.

She waved a hand. "Don't look at me. I'll be back in San Antonio by then."

"Aww," Emmie whined.

"Why the rush to get back?" Clay asked. "Your boss has you on medical leave, and I know Meredith would love to see you." He cocked his head toward Emmie. "You wouldn't want to disappoint my niece, would you?" Emmie beamed and gave a smug nod. To Georgie, Clay said, "Why don't y'all come out to the Bar None. I'll smoke some brisket and ask Marie to make a big bowl of potato salad. Y'all can bring a dish, and we'll have a family barbecue."

"Yeah!" Emmie's eyes danced, and she squirmed on her chair. "Can we, Mom?"

Georgie cast an inquiring glance to Nick, who gave a nod. "Sounds like a plan. Tamara, please stay for the barbecue. It's only a couple extra days, and it's been too long since we had a chance to catch up."

Her gaze moved from Georgie's expectant look to Emmie's eager face, before meeting Clay's piercing dark eyes. "I…guess so."

While Emmie cheered, Tamara's lunch did somersaults in her stomach. As much as she appreciated the invitation to join the Coltons' barbecue, she was no longer a part of the family and pretending only made it harder to leave.

Clay leaned close to his niece and whispered something that made the girl giggle and his own eyes light with affection. His love for Georgie's daughter was heartrending.

A wistful longing gripped Tamara by the throat. Why couldn't Clay have loved her with the same devotion and obvious joy that he had for his family and his ranch? If she had another chance to make her marriage work, if she tried harder to show Clay…

Tamara cut the thought off, unfinished.

She had a new life, a new career, a new appreciation of who she was and what she could accomplish when she dedicated herself to a goal. She'd worked hard to get where she was in the CSI department. How could she give that up to come back to the Bar None? Her dreams had taken her away from Esperanza, but had her dreams changed? She'd taken for granted her home, friends, family when she lived here, and she wanted those things again. But did she have the same courage to follow *that* dream as she'd had when she pursued her career years ago? Was it worth the risk of getting hurt again?

Tamara sighed and mentally chided herself. An invitation to a barbecue hardly translated to Clay wanting a second chance or meant that his feelings for her had changed.

Becky French returned to the table with food for Georgie's family and a large slice of pecan pie for Tamara. She gave Becky an appreciative smile then stared at the sumptuous dessert with a heavy heart.

Her return to the Bar None, this treasured glimpse at how the Colton family was doing since she'd last seen them, the precious moments she'd spent with Clay were drawing to a close. Suddenly Miss Sue's pecan pie didn't seem nearly as sweet or satisfying as spending time alone with Clay.

Chapter 10

As they left Miss Sue's diner after lunch, Clay's thoughts returned to the startling news of Doc Mason's plans to retire out of state. Clay had known the man his whole life and had never heard the doctor mention living anywhere besides Esperanza. Doc Mason loved the small town and its citizens. This new twist on his vacation sounded odd.

As he cranked his truck's engine, he glanced across the front seat where Tamara was leaning her head against the headrest and had closed her eyes. "Tee, are you all right?"

"Mm. Just sleepy. My full stomach plus the warm truck are a double whammy." She yawned to punctuate the sentiment.

He lifted a lopsided grin and tucked a wisp of her hair behind her ear.

Her eyes flew open at his touch, and she turned a bright gaze to him.

"Do you feel up to making a stop on the way home?"

She shrugged. "What'd you have in mind?"

He shifted gears but didn't back out of the parking spot yet. "I'd like to stop by Doc Mason's clinic and talk to his nurse. Maybe Mrs. Hamilton knows something more about the reasons behind his changed plans."

Her brow furrowed. "This thing with Doc Mason really bothers you, doesn't it?"

He gritted his teeth and glanced away for a moment. Opening up about the depths of his concern and his disappointment that Doc Mason could be leaving town for good needled him awkwardly.

But this was Tamara. Sharing his worries with her felt natural, felt right. Despite the five intervening years since their divorce.

"I've told you how Doc Mason used to take me fishing as a kid, right?" He glanced at her, and she nodded. "Well, he did other stuff for us, too. Maybe because we didn't have a dad around, maybe just because he's a nice man. But I… I always looked to him as something of a father figure—even now that I know Graham Colton is my real dad."

Tamara's eyes softened, and her expression warmed. "I suspected as much."

Encouraged by her response, Clay added, "In fact, Doc Mason has always been more like a father to me than Graham Colton ever could be. Doc was there when we needed him as kids, and he's still a good friend. What I'm hearing about his retirement plans just doesn't add up."

His ex-wife sent him a poignant smile. "So let's go see what his nurse knows."

Clay turned the truck engine off, and they walked the short distance to Doc Mason's clinic.

Ellen Hamilton was behind the reception desk when they entered the waiting room, and she greeted them with a cheery smile. "What brings you two in today? I thought Dr. O'Neal checked on Ms. Brown this morning."

"He did," Tamara said, "and I appreciate the personal attention."

Clay slid his hands in his pockets and rocked back on the heels of his boots. "We're here on another matter. I have some questions about Doc Mason's vacation and his new retirement plans."

The welcome in Ellen Hamilton's face morphed into wariness. "What questions?"

"Well, for starters, exactly what did he say when he called?"

Ellen picked up a pen and tapped it on the appointment pad. "I wouldn't know. I didn't take the call."

"Who did?" Tamara asked.

Ellen divided a nervous glance between them as she hesitated. "Our...answering service."

"Someone in town?" Clay studied Ellen's telltale fidgeting. Why did their questions make the nurse so edgy?

"No. We use a professional answering service based out of San Antonio. The message was included in a morning e-mail with a report on all calls taken."

Clay removed his Stetson and raked his hair back from his eyes before replacing his hat. "What exactly did the e-mail say?"

Scowling, Ellen stood and stepped away from the reception desk. "Perhaps I should get Dr. O'Neal if you have more questions."

Clay narrowed a curious gaze on the nurse as she backed toward the patient rooms. "Is there a problem?"

"Wait here." Ellen disappeared down the hall for a moment during which Clay exchanged a puzzled glance with Tamara.

"What do you think?"

She twisted her lips in thought. "I smell a rat. She seems awfully nervous."

"You think they're lying?"

"Not necessarily. But maybe we aren't getting the whole truth either."

A frowning Dr. O'Neal appeared from the hallway. "What's going on here, Colton? Why are you giving my nurse a hard time?"

Clay lifted his eyebrows, startled by the doctor's assessment. He cast a quick glance to Ellen as she returned to the front desk. "We're just looking for a few answers about Doc Mason's sudden change of plans."

"How do you know the change is sudden?" Dr. O'Neal crossed his arms over his chest and glared back at Clay. "Maybe he's been considering retirement privately for some time. What business is it of yours what he does anyway?"

The doctor's combative attitude set off warning bells, but Clay kept his reply calm. "He's my friend and has been for years. I'm worried about him."

"No need to be. The man's on vacation. No harm in that, is there?"

From the corner of his eye, Clay noticed Tamara shift her body to a more defensive position as the conversation took a decidedly hostile tone. But Clay kept his gaze narrowed on Dr. O'Neal.

"Where did he go? Did he leave the name of the hotel where he'd be staying or a number where he could be reached?"

"Of course." Ellen pulled a sheet of paper from the top drawer and waved it. She smiled smugly as if she'd just won a point in an argument. "Right here."

As she stashed the sheet back into the drawer, Clay moved forward and stuck a hand on the edge of the drawer to keep her from closing it. "Mind if I have a look?" He snatched up the paper before she could answer and quickly scanned it. The sheet was a blank piece of stationery from a resort called the Desert Palms, Inc.

Ellen snatched the sheet back. "You can't do that! If Doc Mason had wanted you to know where he was, he'd have told you!"

Dr. O'Neal stepped closer. The thin, balding man puffed up as if ready for battle. "I have to ask you to go now. We're quite busy and don't have time for any more of your questions."

Clay sent a meaningful glance to the empty waiting room but didn't comment. "Fine. But if Doc Mason calls again, please let him know I want to speak with him. He knows both my cell and home number."

Dr. O'Neal shifted his feet and jerked a nod. "I will."

Clay touched the brim of his hat and gave Ellen a tight smile. "Ma'am."

Tamara preceded him out of the office and sighed as the clinic door swooshed closed behind them. "Wow. They sure were acting weird. I have to wonder why they would be antsy about us asking such basic questions. We weren't accusing them of anything."

"I'm wondering the same thing. Hey, you have a pen with you?"

"Uh, probably." Tamara dug in her purse and came up with a ballpoint pen.

"Thanks." He uncapped the pen with his teeth and scribbled a number on his hand.

Tamara tipped her head, and her inquiring expression asking what he'd written.

He turned his hand to show her. "The number for the resort where Doc Mason is staying. I plan to call him myself and see what's going on."

She nodded and gave him a coy smile. "Good thinking. I was wondering if you got a long enough peek at that paper to get any valuable information."

They headed down the sidewalk toward his car in companionable silence. Clay started to drape a possessive arm around Tamara's shoulders as they walked but stopped himself.

Tamara wasn't his anymore.

The past several days had felt so comfortably familiar, so natural, he had to remind himself the divorce wasn't some terrible nightmare he'd woken up from three days ago when Tamara returned. Her presence was temporary.

We can't let that happen again. I'll be leaving in a couple of days....

A pang of disappointment shot through him, and he tucked his hands in his pockets with a sigh. He both treasured and damned the circumstances that had brought Tamara back into his life. For the past five years, he'd managed some semblance of a normal life by numbing himself against the pain of his failures, locking away reminders of what he'd lost. But having Tamara back at the ranch these past few days had brightened his life like sunrise after a dark night, refreshed his spirits like a cool breeze on a stifling day. He'd begun to *feel* again. Joy and pain. Hope and regret. A whole tangle of emotions he'd shoved down and denied for the past five years.

Let's not complicate things.

Clay curled his fingers around the keys in his pocket and squeezed his fist until the metal bit into his palm.

"If they'd been at a crime scene I was working," Tamara said, her nose scrunched in thought, "and I'd gotten answers like that, coupled with the jittery, defensive behavior they exhibited, I'd have them at the top of my suspect list."

"But they're not suspects in a crime. So why so touchy?"

"Beats me." She bit her bottom lip and sent him a side glance as they strolled past storefronts on Main Street. "My lab should have some results back on the blood sample they found in the tunnel. I'd like to stop at the sheriff's office long enough to see if Jericho has any new information."

He nodded. "Good idea."

When Clay and Tamara walked into the sheriff's office, Jericho's deputy, Adam Rawlings, looked up from a large sandwich. Mouth full of the bite he'd just taken, he mumbled, "Can I help you?"

Before Clay could answer, Tamara stepped forward and took the lead. "Is Jericho in? We were hoping he had the results back from my lab on the blood found at the tunnel."

Clay cocked his head and studied the taut, all-business stance Tamara had assumed. A measure of pride tickled inside him at seeing his ex-wife in professional mode. She'd always been competent and unintimidated in business matters, but he detected a new level of self-assurance and assertiveness that he'd never known her to have before. His teenage bride had grown up a lot in the five years they'd been apart.

Deputy Rawlings bobbed his head as he chewed. "He's in. And I think he just took a call from the CSI lab this morning."

The scuff of shoes heralded Jericho's arrival from a back

room. When he noticed his visitors, the sheriff's face brightened. "Hey there. What brings you two to town?"

Clay shook his friend's hand. "The quest for pecan pie originally."

Tamara quirked a smile and gave Jericho a peck on the cheek. "Now that Miss Sue's has satisfied my pie craving, I wanted to check with you about the results of the blood analysis my lab ran. Do you have that data?"

Jericho's expression grew more somber, and he hitched his head toward his desk. "Came in earlier. I've got it over here." As he crossed the floor to his desk, he gave Tamara a measuring glance. "You appear to be feeling better. Those ribs all healed up?"

"Not entirely, but I'm making progress." Tamara lowered herself carefully into a chair in front of Jericho's desk. She sat on the edge of the seat, keeping her back straight, and pressed a hand to her side when Jericho ducked his head to dig out a file from his desk drawer.

Clay frowned. Was the long trip out wearing on her? If so, why hadn't she said anything?

"You can look over the specifics if you want, but the long and short of it is, we got a match. The blood in the tunnel, presumably from the body you saw, is an exact match to the blood from the door of the stolen Taurus." Jericho slid the file folder across his desk to Tamara.

"And what have you learned about the car?"

Jericho stroked a hand over his mustache and sighed. "Dead end there. The surveillance camera at the rental agency has been on the fritz for about three weeks. There is no security tape of the night the Taurus was stolen."

"What about the money? Any leads on where it came from?" Clay asked.

"Nope," Rawlings called across the room from his desk. Clay turned on his heel to face the new deputy, who wiped his mouth on a napkin before continuing. "I called every bank within a hundred miles. No one withdrew a lump sum of one hundred thousand dollars in the past two months. A few random large withdrawals—" He waved a hand in dismissal. "Fifty K here, thirty-five K there, but recent history on those accounts didn't show the withdrawals to be unusual. Big business accounts. Nothing that'd send up a red flag anyway. Same with deposits. Nothing suspicious happening. I've sent word out on a broader scope around the country, but nothing's come back yet."

"So another dead end?" Tamara pressed her mouth in a hard line of discontent.

Jericho's frustration etched creases around his mouth and eyes. He rocked back in his chair, and the springs squeaked. "That's about the size of it right now. Wish I could tell you more. I don't like the idea of an unsolved car theft and a possible murder—with a missing body—any more than you do."

Clay's gut pitched as the words *missing body* struck a raw nerve. The body had turned up shortly after Doc Mason left on his vacation. The idea sifted through his brain and chilled him to the marrow.

Clay folded his arms over his chest and lowered his brow. "Jericho, are you aware that Doc Mason is out of town?"

"Yeah, I heard something about that at Miss Sue's earlier this week. Why?"

"Tamara and I were just at the clinic, and they've had a message that Doc Mason is extending his vacation and may retire in Arizona. But no one has actually talked to Doc and…well, something about his absence just doesn't sit right with me. He's not the sort to leave town for long periods. This town is his life, his home. He never wanted to leave. So why now? What changed?"

Jericho rocked forward again and propped his arms on his desk. "I have to admit, I hadn't given Doc Mason's trip any real thought, what with everything else that's been on my plate, but…now that you mention it, it does seem out of character."

"Honestly, the timing of his absence, what with this body

being found…" Clay blew out a breath through pursed lips, not even wanting to vocalize the rest of that horrible thought.

Tamara gasped. "Oh, God, you don't think…?"

"Rawlings," Jericho interrupted, "get out to Doc Mason's house and have a look around. I want to know if there's any sign of foul play or clues where he might be."

"Yes, sir." Rawlings shoved back from his desk and headed out.

Clay glanced at the number written on his hand. One way to put his mind at rest.

He stepped forward and placed a hand on the receiver of Jericho's phone. "Can I make a toll-free call? We might be able to settle at least one question with a call to the resort where Doc's supposed to be staying."

Jericho nodded. "Be my guest."

Clay dialed the number, and when the line at the other end rang, he punched the speaker button on Jericho's phone.

"Desert Palms Rehabilitation Center. How may I direct your call?"

Clay frowned. "I was under the impression Desert Palms was a vacation resort. I'm looking for someone, last name Mason, who said he'd be there."

"A patient?"

"Well, I…don't know." Clay rubbed his jaw, unsettled by this new twist regarding Doc's whereabouts. "He's supposed to be on vacation. But he's a doctor so maybe he was there for a seminar or something?"

"No, sir. We don't have seminars, and there is no doctor on staff named Mason. Privacy laws prevent me from giving out patient information."

"Ma'am," Jericho said, leaning toward the phone to be heard better, "this is Sheriff Jericho Yates in Esperanza, Texas. We can issue a subpoena for patient records if needed, but right now we just need to confirm that Doc Mason is, in fact, at Desert Palms. He's the subject of a missing persons search and possibly connected to a murder investigation."

"Murder?" the operator gasped.

"I can verify my credentials with your supervisor and local authorities if you wish, but if you'd just check your records to see if Doc Mason is there, you could clear up a lot of issues in our investigation without digging into the red tape."

"Sir, I—" The woman hesitated. Sighed. "We had a Dr. John Mason scheduled to check in here a couple weeks ago, but…he never arrived."

Ice streaked through Clay's veins. "Did he call to cancel the reservation?"

"No, sir. He just never showed up. We never heard from him, and no request was made for a return on the deposit for the room. That's all I can tell you."

Tamara's and Jericho's faces reflected the same worry that was churning through Clay.

"Thank you for your cooperation, ma'am." Jericho gave the woman his contact information and badge number to file regarding the inquiry and disconnected the call.

A pregnant silence filled the room. No one moved until Bea Hooper stormed through the office door from outside.

"Sheriff, if you don't do something about Walter Sims's dogs, I swear I will! They got into my garbage again last night, and they bark at all hours! How many times do I have to complain before somebody does something?"

Jericho's shoulders drooped, and he rubbed the back of his neck. "Clay, Tamara, I'll keep you posted if I hear anything new. For now, let's keep this between us. Agreed?"

Clay nodded. "Got it." He spared Mrs. Hooper a quick glance before sending Jericho a last sympathetic look. "Good luck."

The corner of Jericho's mouth twitched, but he composed himself as the irate woman stomped up to his desk. Clay led Tamara outside, and they strolled in silence back to the truck. Once inside with the doors closed and the air-conditioning cranked full blast, Tamara voiced what Clay was thinking. "We need some of Doc's DNA to determine whether the body I found was his. Should we call Jericho back and ask him to have Rawlings collect a sample from Doc's house?"

"No need," he replied. "I know where we might get a sample of his blood."

Chapter 11

Tamara frowned as she gaped at Clay. "You know where to get Doc Mason's blood?"

He nodded. "Doc and I went fishing Memorial Day weekend, and while he was cleaning a fish with my knife, his grip slipped, and he cut his hand."

"And you didn't clean the blood off the knife?" she asked in a tone that said she was more surprised by the possibility that he'd neglected to clean up than she was asking about the viability of a sample.

"We wiped it off some, but it's a fishing knife, Tee. A little more dirt wasn't going to make a difference. We were more concerned about disinfecting Doc's cut and finding a clean wrap for it until he could get to his office to sew up the gash. I hadn't given the knife any more thought until just now. But there's probably still enough of his blood on the blade for your tests."

She nodded. "Okay. We can take it to my lab today and get tests started."

Clay squeezed the steering wheel, reluctant to consider that his friend could be dead. "Tamara, you saw that body. Do you think it could have been Doc? Could you tell anything about the person's age or hair color or anything?"

With an apologetic glance, she shook her head. "Not really. I was so stunned to realize what I was looking at, what I had touched… It was too dark to see any detail, and the body was mostly covered by dirt from the cave-in. I didn't look closely. I know I should have, but I was shaken up, hurting… I wasn't thinking professionally at the time."

"Understandable, considering the circumstances." Clay tipped his head from side to side, stretching the kinks knotting his neck.

"Clay?" Tamara paused, her gaze steady on him and concern dimpling her forehead. "Did you know… Did you even suspect that Doc Mason had a drug addiction?"

"We don't *know* that he does." Clay took a slow breath and reined the defensiveness in his tone before continuing. "Let's not jump to any conclusions until we get all the facts."

"He made a reservation and paid a deposit to go to a drug rehab center in Arizona. That's not a vacation. He was trying to break an addiction. What other reasonable explanation could there be?"

Frustration balled inside Clay's chest. He smacked the steering wheel with his palm. "I should have known, should have seen it."

Tamara gave an incredulous laugh. "Don't you go assuming the blame for this, too! Why would you know? How often did you see Doc?"

"Not all that often. But I just went fishing with him a few weeks ago."

"How did he seem then?"

He sighed. "I got the feeling he wasn't himself, wasn't feeling well that day, but…I didn't say anything." Clay thought back, re-membering details about the last time he'd seen Doc. "His hands were shaking when he cleaned that fish. That's probably why he cut himself. But a drug addiction? Doc Mason?" He shook his head. "It doesn't make sense. Doc would never—"

He exhaled a sharp breath. Denials didn't change the fact that Doc *had* made that reservation at the drug rehabilitation center.

Tamara turned toward the window and leaned her head back on the seat. The outing had taken a toll on her. She needed to get off her feet, needed rest.

"Do you know if Doc has any enemies? Anyone who would want to ruin his reputation or…hurt him?" She angled her head to look at him again.

"Enemies? Doc Mason is one of the kindest men I know. He never met a stranger, would never hurt a fly. He was a healer, and he loved people. All people." He cut a side glance to Tamara. "So, no. I can't imagine anyone wanting to hurt Doc in any way."

"I know you love him like a father, Clay, but I need you to think about the question as objectively as possible. Did he mention trouble with any of his patients the day you went fishing?"

Clay pinched the bridge of his nose, trying to recall what he'd talked to Doc about on their fishing trip. "No. The man doesn't have any enemies that I know of."

Clay slowed the truck to make the turn at the Bar None. As he bounced down the gravel driveway, he noticed Tamara clutching her side and squeezing her eyes shut.

"How easily…can you find…that knife?" she asked between pothole jolts.

"Real easy. It's in my tackle box."

"Get it, put it in a plastic zip-top bag, and let's take it to my lab. The sooner we know if the body I saw was Doc, the sooner you can put your mind at ease."

Clay's need for answers about Doc Mason battled his concern for Tamara. As eager as he was to get the DNA tests started, his ex-wife needed rest more than she needed to make a trip to San Antonio. "Why don't you come in and take a nap first. We can bring the knife to your lab tonight or first thing tomorrow."

Tamara blinked her surprise. "Tomorrow? I thought you were chomping at the bit to get answers."

"I am. But you need to rest. I saw you holding your side. I know you're hurting."

Her expression softened. "Maybe a little, but the case is more important. I'll have another Advil and be fine."

When he shook his head, she pressed a hand to his cheek and smiled. The cool touch of her hand sent a cascade of sensation over his skin. His breath snagged.

"I'll be fine, Clay. Right now, what we need is answers. Get the knife. Okay?"

The gentle request in Tamara's cerulean gaze burrowed to his heart. How could she not know he'd always been eager to do her bidding? The few times he'd had to tell her *no* had devastated him. Especially the night Quinn had put Lone Star to sleep. Clay could still see Tamara's tears, hear her pleas, feel the anguish that had rolled off her like a smothering flood.

Shoving those memories down, he wrapped his hand around hers. "All right. But if I get any hint you're taxing yourself, we come straight back here so you can rest. Deal?"

"Deal. You're sweet for worrying about me." She brought his fingers to her lips, and the soft caress of her mouth, her breath, slammed into him like a fist to the gut.

He gritted his teeth and fought down the urge to grab her and kiss her the way his body and his heart wanted. Deep, hot, soulful embraces. The way he had kissed her, here in this truck, so many times before. Knowing she wasn't his to kiss anymore ripped through him with a gnawing ache.

He swallowed hard to clear the bitter disappointment from his throat. His muscles taut with frustration, he backed away and opened the truck door. "I'll be right back."

As he stalked to the barn to find his tackle box, the sultry summer day seemed to mimic the need humming in his body. Thick humidity clogged the air in the same way heated desire made his blood run heavy in his veins. A dragonfly buzzed past him, its wings fluttering in the rapid tempo of his runaway pulse.

Clay took off his Stetson and, with his forearm, swiped the

perspiration beading on his brow. Sex, as good as it had been with Tamara, hadn't been enough to save his marriage. Sex with his ex-wife would only cause complications and mixed emotions neither of them were prepared to deal with right now.

Doc Mason was missing, possibly dead.

He had to put thoughts of Tamara's sweet touch and sensual body out of his head and concentrate on finding out what had happened to Doc.

Taking his fishing gear from a shelf in the barn, Clay found the knife and carefully held the grip with two fingers. Smears of blood still stained the blade near the handle.

His gut twisted. Who could have known the bloody knife had been a harbinger of the blood that would later be spilled on his property? Had Doc been murdered less than a mile from Clay's house?

Clay sighed and headed for the kitchen to find a plastic bag. He didn't know what had happened to Esperanza's doctor, but he owed it to his lifelong friend to find out.

The chill from the over-air-conditioned forensics lab nipped Tamara's bare arms as she meticulously swabbed a sample of blood from the fishing knife's jagged blade. Having a personal stake in the results made her job feel strangely different. The emotions she typically locked away in the lab crowded around her and set her on edge.

Or maybe it was just having Clay hovering behind her, watching her work, that made her hands shake. She sensed his gaze on her, had the image of his dark, bedroom eyes in her head as she transferred the blood onto a slide.

Earlier in his truck when she'd kissed his fingers, the fire in his eyes had scorched a path through her. His desire to devour her on the spot had been all too clear. A rebellious part of her soul had wanted the same. Desperately.

Yet something had stopped Clay. He'd walked away without

so much as a kiss. The voice of reason or memories of old hurts had cooled the heat of the moment and doused his passion.

While the wild part of her that wanted to make love to Clay with careless abandon stung from the rejection, her practical side sighed with relief. Making love to Clay could only lead to more pain, reviving more memories of what could have been. She'd wallowed in enough regrets the past few days. Being back in her lab, in the environment where she had to be clinically detached, helped her steel her nerves and push away the maudlin moment.

After she'd prepped the blood sample, she stripped off her latex gloves and rubbed the chill bumps on her arms. She usually wore a lab coat, but had left hers in her apartment the morning she'd gone to the Bar None to make a second search of the area where the stolen car had been found. She hadn't been back to her apartment since.

She jotted a few notes in the case file and rubbed her temple.

As long as she was back in San Antonio, maybe she should stay at her own place. For good. When she remembered the barbecue Clay was planning for his family on Saturday, her heart sank. She didn't want to miss the opportunity to visit with the rest of the Colton clan. But was that wise?

Spending any more time with Clay, renewing attachments to him and his family, the animals at the Bar None and her friends in Esperanza taunted her like a carrot dangling just out of reach. That wasn't her life anymore. She'd made her choice five years ago, and she wouldn't look back.

She had a satisfying job and… Tamara frowned. What else? She had her job and…nothing. No boyfriend. No family nearby. Few friends outside of the forensics department. Not even a pet.

She'd left Clay to pursue her dream of a career in forensic science, and since then she'd buried herself in her job. Her work *was* her whole life.

Her lungs seized. Her ears buzzed. Her pen clattered to the table. Knees shaking, she eased onto the stool beside her.

She'd sacrificed her marriage for her career because she'd felt incomplete, she'd felt lost and smothered at the ranch. She'd pursued one dream, but sacrificed the home and family and love that nourished her soul.

No wonder the time she'd spent at the ranch was such a welcome change. No wonder seeing the animals and smelling the hay and breathing the country air brought such a rush of relief and pleasure.

"Now what do you do?"

Clay's question cut into her whirling thoughts, and it took a moment for her to realize he meant the next step in the DNA analysis, not what she wanted to do about her lonely life.

Flustered, she smoothed an unsteady hand over her hair and tightened her ponytail. "I, uh… I'll be right back."

"Tee, what's wrong?"

With Clay's worried gaze following her, Tamara scurried out of the lab and down the hall to the ladies' room. Bending over the sink, she splashed cool water on her flushed cheeks. She sucked in a calming breath and dried her face with a wad of paper towels.

Raising her eyes to the cracked mirror above the sink, she stared at the pale woman reflected there.

Her life was still out of balance. She'd been living a clinical, emotionless life, centered around her career. She'd neglected her empty ache because acknowledging what was missing brought back memories of the man she'd loved and given up.

With a humorless laugh, she shook her head. "Now what do you do?"

She had no answer. She couldn't change the past, and now she and Clay had too much hurt, too many barriers, too much distance between them to move forward. Didn't they? Her head gave a painful throb, the first sign of a potential migraine. She shoved her troubling new revelations aside, hoping to forestall a stress-induced headache.

Upon returning to the lab, she finished the notes she'd been making in the case file and mustered the courage to face Clay's curious scrutiny. "The analysis takes a while and can be pretty tedious. You could…go out for coffee or a snack, find someplace more comfortable than our lab to wait. I'll call your cell when I'm finished."

Clay crossed his arms over his chest. Angling his head, he studied her with a narrowed gaze before answering. "Am I in your way?"

Tamara blinked. "Well…no."

He glanced to Jan Howard, one of the technicians working near them. "Ma'am, am I interfering with your job?"

The female tech gave Clay a lustful grin. "Heck, no. I've enjoyed having such handsome company this afternoon. Your presence has made comparing fingerprints way less boring. Besides, I'm off in ten minutes, and then I'll be out of *your* way." With a wiggle of her eyebrows, she continued working.

He jerked a nod to Tamara. "In that case, I'll stay and wait with you."

Tamara drew her brow into a *V,* making a mental note to kill her coworker. Working with Clay watching her every move—especially after her upsetting revelation and with a burgeoning migraine—was nerve-racking to say the least. "But wouldn't you rather find a coffee shop or browse through a bookstore?"

His gaze was unflinching. "No. I want to be here."

Covering a sigh, she shrugged. "Okay. Have it your way." Tamara rolled her shoulders to loosen the kinks and moved to the next step in the analysis.

Her stomach flip-flopped. After Jan left for the day, she would be spending several hours in her lab—alone with Clay.

"So now we wait for the computer to do its thing before we go on to the next step." Tamara rolled her chair back from the desk where she'd been working for an hour and rubbed her eyes. Whatever had upset her before, she'd shaken it off and dived into her work with dedicated professionalism.

Clay had watched in fascination as Tamara proficiently manipulated the blood sample, mixed chemical solutions and operated high-tech equipment with finesse. She seemed so at home in the lab, so energized and skilled, that Clay could only marvel at how far she'd come from the early days when she'd learned the ropes at the ranch. The crime lab was where she belonged, not mucking horse stalls.

His chest squeezed with regret. Any doubt he'd had about whether he'd made the right choice by standing aside to let her follow her dream vanished. Any faint hope he'd had that spending a few days with him at the ranch might make Tamara consider reconciling flickered out.

Clay frowned. At what point had *he* begun thinking in terms of a reconciliation? False expectations were dangerous, and he'd do well to keep his wishes in check. The raw ache gnawing at him as he watched her now proved that point.

After what seemed like endless waiting, Clay stood and stretched his sore back. If his muscles were this stiff, he could only imagine how badly Tamara's ribs must hurt. For the past hour she'd kept one arm curled around her abdomen, and he'd seen her wince several times when she likely thought he wasn't looking.

Concern for her well-being frayed his patience with the tedious process. The clock in the corner of the computer screen read 10:04 p.m., so she'd been on her feet or hunched over a computer better than half a day. And that was after spending the morning about town in Esperanza.

Something had to give. She was driving herself to exhaustion, and his private thoughts were making him stir-crazy.

Clay cracked a knuckle and looked around for an excuse to convince her to take a break. "Can I get you anything from the vending machine? I'm ready for some midnight munchies."

She shook her head. "No food in the lab. Sorry. Our break room is down the hall and around the corner. Be warned—the coffee is toxic," she said without looking up from the computer monitor. "Stick to a soda from the machine."

"You're not coming? I thought you said we had to wait on the computer."

She tipped her head from side to side and massaged her neck.

"I'm going to catch up on some backlogged work while I wait. You can go on without me."

Clay braced a hands on his hips and gritted his teeth. "Like hell."

His profanity caught her attention. She glanced up with a bleary-eyed gaze. Lines of fatigue and pain creased the corners of her eyes and mouth. "What?"

He stepped over to her chair and wrapped his hand around her upper arm. "You're done for the day. I'm taking you home."

"I'm not finished." Tamara tried to shrug away from his grip but he held fast, careful not to hurt her in the process.

"Someone else from your lab can take over and call us with the results."

"If we're going to expedite the results, I need to—"

"Then we won't expedite the results. Your health is more important than getting some tests back a few hours faster. Hand this off, so you can get off your feet. You look ready to drop."

She hesitated, holding his gaze, clearly weighing her options and taking stock of her fatigue. "Let me finish one more thing, and I'll leave the rest for Eric to pick up in the morning."

He narrowed a skeptical gaze on her. "How much longer?"

She turned up a hand. "Twenty minutes. Half hour max."

He huffed his resignation and released her arm. "Twenty minutes. No more."

Tamara opened a file and scribbled notes as she clicked through several computer screens, documenting her progress. Clay reclaimed his seat on the stool behind her, watching the clock. Twenty minutes to the second, and they'd be outta there.

After a few minutes on the computer, Tamara called her boss to brief him. Eric promised to pick up the analysis first thing in the morning, then he read her the riot act for disobeying his order to stay away from the lab until she'd fully recovered.

Clay lifted a corner of his mouth. He liked Eric more all the time.

Tamara groaned as she hung up the phone. Then, scrubbing her hands over her face, she turned her chair to face him. "Okay, I'm ready to go."

Gathering his Stetson from the worktable behind him, Clay handed Tamara her purse and hustled her out of the lab. In the elevator, Tamara slumped against the wall and closed her eyes. "We missed dinner."

"I offered to take you out to get something," Clay countered.

She peeked up at him. "I know. Thanks. But I couldn't leave in the middle of things." Eyes drooping, she said through a yawn, "You could have gone without me."

"Where's the fun in that?"

She smiled and laid a hand on his cheek. "You must be starved."

"I'll live. Drive-throughs are still open."

The elevator opened, and he followed her outside into the humid night air.

"You have a preference where we stop?" he asked as they started down the concrete steps. He realized that she was lagging behind and turned to find her.

"Anything you want is—"

She stumbled down a step. Her hand flailed for something to grab.

His heart lurched, and he rushed forward. As she pitched off balance, he caught her around the waist. Tamara landed against him with enough force to knock the breath from him. She gave a small cry of pain that wrenched his gut.

He dragged air back into his lungs. "Tamara, are you okay?"

She clutched his arms, steadying herself and catching her breath. The scampering beat of her heart against his chest matched the galloping thud of his own.

Tipping her head back, she peered up at him with wide eyes. "Yeah, I—I don't know what happened. I just got so dizzy for a minute, and—"

"Because you've pushed too hard today."

She ducked her chin to rest her forehead against his shoulder. "I am awfully tired."

Clay scowled in self-censure. "I should have insisted on taking you home at the first sign you were wearing out."

"Stop blaming yourself. You're not my keeper." She sighed. "Maybe I should skip dinner and go straight home. Will you take me to my apartment?"

Her request plucked a twinge of disappointment in him. He shouldn't be surprised that she'd call her apartment *home* or that she'd want to go to her own place instead of back to the ranch. But hearing her call someplace besides the Bar None *home* stung.

Clay pushed aside his hurt in order to concentrate on what was best for Tamara. Tonight, however, what she needed was the Bar None.

He cradled her face and tipped her head back to meet her gaze. "I'll take you back to the ranch with me. You're exhausted, and I want to make sure you rest like you're supposed to tomorrow."

"Clay…" Her expression reflected her disagreement but also her reluctance to argue the point. She pushed against his chest, but he wasn't ready to let her go.

Instead he raked a hand through her hair, freeing the soft strands from the cloth band she'd worn as she worked. He finger-combed the silky tresses to fan over her shoulders and frame her face. The golden highlights shimmered in the Texas moonlight, and her eyes were sparkling sapphires.

His heart swelled to overflowing. Why had he ever let her go? Only after she'd disappeared from his life did he realize how much she meant to him. And now it was too late. She had a new life, a new career that made her happier than he ever had.

He rubbed his knuckles along her jaw and sighed. "You were amazing today. Criminal investigation suits you, and you're good at what you do. I'm glad you were able to make your dream a reality."

She blinked, apparently startled by his compliment. "I— Thank you, Clay."

"It's all the more obvious to me today after watching you work that this is where you belong. I guess things do have a way of working out for the best, huh?"

Moisture filled her eyes, and her expression darkened. If he hadn't known better, he'd have said his assessment had disappointed her.

Or was that just wishful thinking on his part? He'd give anything to hear her disagree, to hear her say she wanted to come back to the ranch—back to him—for good. But he couldn't ask her to give up her dreams for him. Her head bobbed in a small nod. "I guess they do."

One second stretched into the next and still he held her close, already hating the emptiness to come when he let her out of his arms. His Tee was so strong, so lovely, even with fatigue shadowing her eyes. She'd become even more confident, more poised, more beautiful as a woman than she'd been when she first captured his attention in high school.

Remorse twisted a knot in his chest. He couldn't undermine her newfound independence. This time around *he* had to be strong enough to walk away from *her.* But he would take one last memory. He may have seen the truth about her new life, but at that moment, nothing in heaven or earth could stop him from kissing the woman who still owned his heart.

With a gentle hand at her nape, he drew her close and lowered his mouth to hers. Her startled gasp melted into a contented sigh as she relaxed against him. The brush of her lips on his fired every nerve ending and shot sparks through his blood. He teased the seam of her mouth with his tongue, and she opened to him willingly.

She tasted as sweet as the honeysuckle nectar he'd sipped as a kid. As sweet as he remembered. Clay angled his head to deepen the kiss and savor her more fully.

Her hands slid to his back and curled into his shirt. When a raspy moan rose in his throat, she answered with her own mewl of pleasure. The seductive purr reverberated inside him until his whole body vibrated with desire, coiled tight and ready to spring.

Clay surrendered to the ebb and flow of her kiss. The bittersweet memories that raced through his mind of other times that he'd held Tee, kissed her, made love to her rocked him to his marrow. But none compared to the power and depth of the sensations and emotions Tamara's kiss stirred in him tonight.

The combination of sensual heat and his cold regrets made a strange cocktail. For the moment, Clay tried to ignore the acid bite in his gut that knowing he'd lost Tamara stirred. He focused instead on the caress of her fingers as she kneaded his shoulders then ran her hands through his hair, knocking his hat onto the steps.

She gasped unsteady breaths as he trailed kisses along her jaw to nuzzle the place behind her ear that always sent her over the edge. She whimpered her pleasure when he flicked his tongue over that sensitive spot, and he nearly came undone himself.

A car horn blasted down the block, and Clay tensed. He yanked himself back from the brink. This wasn't the right time. Wasn't the right place.

With a few more tender kisses to his cheek and chin, Tamara also backed away. She buried her face in his chest, trembling despite the warm evening air. "We should go."

"Yeah." Clay gritted his teeth and struggled to regain his composure. This small taste of Tamara wasn't nearly enough.

But already he'd taken more than he should.

Let's not complicate things.

Too late. His feelings for his ex-wife were nothing if not complicated. He was torn, aching inside. As desperately as he wanted her, he wasn't what she needed. The ranch wasn't where she belonged. He'd never put his desires ahead of what was best for Tamara. Just as he hadn't when they divorced. Now, after seeing Tamara in the forensics lab, he knew with a greater certainty that their divorce, however painful, had been the best gift he could give her. He pressed a kiss to the top of her head, inhaling the delicate floral scent of her shampoo. "I can bring the truck around for you if you—"

"No." She laced their fingers and squeezed his hand. "I'm okay now. I'll walk."

Keeping his hand in hers, ready to steady her if needed, Clay led her down the stairs toward the parking lot. His own legs felt a tad rubbery still, thanks to her potent kiss, but he'd be damned if he'd show her any sign of weakness. His failure today had already cost her too much. No matter what she said, he'd been wrong to let her stay in the lab so long when he knew she was hurting and exhausted.

As they neared his truck, his thoughts returned to the reason they'd been in the lab to start with. Doc Mason's disappearance. The possibility his friend had been murdered.

"So how far in the DNA analysis did you get? How soon will we hear whether the blood in the tunnel is a match with Doc's?"

She squeezed his hand and shrugged. "Not far enough to make me happy. When we hear results is gonna depend on Eric. He said he'd try to expedite it, but we also have a local caseload."

Clay nodded. "I know. I appreciate your department pushing this through. It's just not knowing what might have happened to Doc…"

Tamara stopped and clasped his hand between hers. "Clay…"

He met the dark look in her eyes with a tremor of apprehension. "What?"

"I know what Doc Mason means to you, but my gut tells me you should prepare for the worst."

Chapter 12

Thanks to a full day of ranch duties, Clay didn't see Tamara the next day until after he'd given the horses an early dinner and finished his evening rounds, securing the stables. He checked on Lucy, the pregnant mare, before heading in for his own supper, but she still showed no evidence that she was ready to foal.

He rubbed the stubble on his jaw and scowled. Quinn had told him if the foal didn't come by the weekend, they'd need to induce labor or consider a C-section.

As he entered the house, the enticing aroma of popcorn greeted him. Following his nose, he found Tamara curled on one of the couches in the family room with a large bowl on her lap. As welcoming as the scent of food was, having Tamara waiting for him gave him greater pleasure.

"That sure smells good. I'm famished." He hung his hat by the door and sauntered closer to snitch a piece of the buttery treat. His gaze drank in the warm glow in Tamara's cheeks and the sparkle in her eyes. More than food, he was hungry for her.

She patted the sofa cushion beside her. "Join me. Marie brought a DVD with her she thought I'd like. I was just about to start watching."

Clay tugged at his sweaty shirt. "I need a shower. Can you wait about ten minutes?"

"Sure. While you clean up, I'll reheat the stew Marie left." Tamara pushed carefully off the couch and padded barefooted into the kitchen. "Marie is great. Where did you find her?"

Desire flared hotter as he appreciated the way the running shorts she wore hugged her fanny and left her long legs bare. He schooled his thoughts. What had she asked?

"Oh, uh…her husband is one of my hands. Their only son just left for college so between empty-nest syndrome and tuition bills to pay, she was thrilled to have someone new to look after. Her cooking alone is worth every penny."

Clay's stomach growled, and he grabbed another handful of popcorn before taking the steps two at a time. Upstairs, he hurriedly stripped out of his dirty work clothes, eager not to waste a single moment that he could spend cuddling with Tamara. Chick flick. Thriller. Horror. The movie didn't matter to him as long as he could hold Tamara the way he used to, feel her smooth legs stroke his, smell her shampoo as she tucked her head under his chin, savor the warmth of her body. He might not get another chance to hold her, and he intended to enjoy every moment tonight.

In the shower, as the steam and pounding spray massaged his tired muscles, he conjured images from past showers. Memories of Tamara's sleek body, glistening with soapy bubbles as she rose on her toes to kiss him, pumped heated need through his blood.

Since their kiss on the steps outside the CSI lab, Clay's thoughts had lingered dangerously close to various scintillating memories involving his ex. Even the grueling manual labor he'd done today, hoping to push the erotic images from his head, had been no use. His body hummed like a live wire, and no amount of hammering or shoveling had helped.

In record time, he was showered, shaved and loping down the stairs to join the beautiful woman sharing his home.

Tamara glanced up when she heard Clay bound down the stairs. So did the cat on her lap. She stroked Trouble's back, enjoying the soothing purr that rumbled from the cat's throat.

Clay stopped in the entry to the family room, and his contented smile morphed into a confused frown when he spotted Trouble. "What's the cat doing in the house?"

Tamara ignored the gruffness of the question and lifted a sassy grin. "Getting a good head pat, right now, I'd say."

Clay arched an eyebrow, silently calling Tamara a wiseacre. "Okay, *why* is the *barn cat* in the house? She's bound to have fleas."

Tamara continued scratching Trouble behind the ear. "Maybe. But I got lonely after Marie left and...well, I guess I should have asked first, but I didn't think you'd mind."

Clay opened his mouth then shut it again. He crossed the room and sat on the edge of the sofa next to Tamara. He gave Trouble a perfunctory stroke. "I don't mind in principle, but she should be treated for fleas before you make this a habit."

Tamara met Clay's eyes and held her breath. *A habit* implied she'd be at the ranch enough in the future to establish a routine. Did he mean he wanted her to stay?

As if sensing she'd read something into his statement, Clay backpedaled. "I mean, if you were going to be here or if you wanted to—" He sighed. "Hell, Tee. We need to quit dancing around what's on both of our minds."

Tamara's curled her fingers into the cat's fur, her pulse keeping time with the old railroad clock on Clay's mantel.

He turned to face her more fully. "Having you here has been great. And I think it's pretty plain we still have feelings for each other, but..."

He shook his head. *But.*

The one word was a pinprick to any fantasy she'd harbored concerning the future.

"But we're still divorced, still haven't settled the issues that led to our breakup, still have separate lives, different goals, demanding jobs?" she finished for him.

His eyes darkened to the color of midnight, and a muscle in his jaw ticked. "Pretty much."

His agreement snuffed her last glimmer of hope that this time, with hindsight to guide them, they could make a fresh start, have a second chance. Disappointment and grief even deeper than she'd known when she'd first left him years ago sliced through her.

Forcing a note of cheer into her voice, she gave him a tight smile. "Well, at least we've had a chance to clear up a couple misconceptions and renew our friendship. Maybe this time we could keep in touch?"

He took a while to answer, but finally shrugged. "Yeah, maybe. For tonight, let's just enjoy each other's company and not let regrets or recriminations spoil this chance to just…*be*."

Just be? He made it sound so easy. As if she could turn off the rush of bittersweet memories that surrounded her, stem the tide of affection and desire that washed over her whenever he was near.

But one thing was clear. Her feelings for Clay and her nagging questions about whether they could have a second chance to make their marriage work didn't matter. Just as he'd been able to dismiss her and what she wanted when they were married, with his declaration that their time together was almost up and reconciliation was off the table, he'd shut out her opinion once again.

Nothing had changed. She'd been telling herself that since she arrived, but she'd let a few kisses and tender moments fool her into thinking she mattered to Clay, that they had a chance…

She scooted the cat from her lap and dusted Trouble's hair from her shirt and shorts. "I'll fix your stew, if you'll start the movie."

Oh, Lord… She prayed Clay hadn't heard the wobble in her voice. She had to be strong, not let him know how badly the idea of leaving the ranch again hurt.

She drew on the detachment she'd learned in the CSI lab and shoved the tears in her throat back down. *Just be.* For tonight she'd do her damnedest to simply savor Clay's company and accept the evening as a gift. A stolen moment with a man whose part in her life she cherished but who'd moved on.

On her way back from the kitchen with Clay's dinner, she gave Trouble one last pat then let her out the back door.

Clay ate his stew from a tray as the movie, an action-adventure with a romantic subplot, started. Tamara tried to lose herself in the storyline, but the scent of soap from Clay's shower and the clink of his spoon as he ate kept her hyperaware of his presence. Of every move he made. And if she weren't already more attracted to her sexy cowboy than her heart could stand, Clay's nothing-will-come-of-this stance taunted her like a penniless kid in a candy store. The kisses they'd shared had had her secretly dreaming of making love to her ex. At times, when Clay looked at her with desire blazing in his eyes, she'd hoped their mutual attraction was the first step to a reconciliation. Likewise, their compatibility as they searched for answers concerning Doc Mason's disappearance had her believing they could work through their personal differences with the same cooperation.

She'd deluded herself.

With the remote, Clay paused the movie long enough to take his dish to the sink. When he returned, he sat on the sofa where Tamara had her feet tucked under her and a throw around her shoulders. Stretching his legs out on the couch, he nudged her shoulder, guiding her to lean back against his chest.

Her heart pounded, and the emotions she'd barely managed to quash resurfaced.

What was he doing? Cuddling on the couch was his idea of just being?

"Clay…" A thousand questions and protests tangled with the part of her that wanted to burrow against his body and shut the rest of the world out.

"Hmm?" He rearranged the throw to cover them both.

She hesitated.

"Did you get enough to eat?" she said instead of the words of longing on her tongue.

How can you say we have no future one minute then hold me like this the next?

"Yeah. Thanks." He kissed her temple then used the remote to restart the movie.

As he gently wrapped his arms around her, nestling her head under his chin, Tamara relaxed against him. Safe. Warm. Wishing she could stay there forever.

Again two words filtered through her head. *You're home.*

Tears pricked her eyes. If only Clay felt the same way.

Chapter 13

The next morning Tamara woke to the early stages of a migraine headache. Though she didn't get them often, when her migraines struck, they were debilitating. By noon she was curled up in bed, the room dark, and one of the painkillers Dr. O'Neal prescribed in her system, lulling her into a restless sleep. Marie and Clay checked on her a few times, but she had no appetite and even soft voices hammered her head.

The day was a wash. Wasted.

The morning after that, feeling significantly better but a bit like she had a hangover, she mourned the precious time with Clay she'd lost. Eager to make up for the day she'd spent in bed, Tamara rose early and met Clay downstairs as he came in from feeding the horses and making his morning rounds.

Concern shadowed his eyes when he spotted her at the kitchen table sipping her coffee. "Headache gone?"

"Mostly. Tylenol should be enough to handle the last dregs today. So what'd I miss while I was wiped out yesterday?"

"Well, Lucy dropped her foal."

She sat straighter in her chair. "Are they okay?"

"They're both fine, thanks to Quinn. Things got hairy for a while when the foal got stuck, but Quinn worked a miracle to bring Linus into the world safely."

She exhaled deeply. "Thank goodness."

Relief that the horses were all right swirled with disappointment that she'd missed the arrival and grudging gratitude that Quinn had been on hand to help. She took another sip of coffee before something Clay said registered. "Linus?"

"You named the mother Lucy, so I figured Linus was appropriate. You know, Peanuts?"

"Yeah, I… You *named* the foal." Her heart swelled, and she gaped at Clay in wonder and joy. What had changed with Mr. The-Animals-Aren't-Pets?

Clay hesitated. "Yeah. Sorry, did you want to do that?"

"No, that's not… Look who's turned over a new leaf!" She chuckled and jabbed him playfully in the arm.

Grinning sheepishly, he ducked his head and rubbed the back of his neck. "Well, since his mom had a name, I figured…" He shrugged, minimizing what he'd done.

But Tamara couldn't write off this change in Clay's attitude so easily. Naming a new foal was a small thing, but it pointed toward a willingness to make changes. The hope that had died two nights before flickered to life again, tumbling her thoughts and perceptions about her ex once again.

Before she could question him more about the birth or other ranch business, the house phone rang, and Clay snatched it up on the second ring. "Bar None. This is Clay."

His eyes flicked to her, his brow creasing. "Yeah, she's right here. Who's calling?"

Worried over Clay's frown, she held out her hand for the phone.

"It's your lab. The results are in on the blood sample from the knife."

Adrenaline spiked her pulse as she raised the receiver to her ear. "Hey, what'd you learn? What do the tests say?"

Clay held her gaze with a dark, uneasy scrutiny. A muscle in his jaw twitched as he gritted his teeth, a sure sign he was as apprehensive about the results as she was.

"Let's see…" Eric cleared his throat, and she heard rustling papers. Her nerves jangled while he scanned the report. "Ah, here we go. Looks like the two blood samples are a match."

Clay obviously read the heart-wrenching truth in her expression. Doc Mason, a man who'd been like a father to him, was dead.

Covering his mouth with a hand, he squeezed his eyes shut and bit out a curse word. He turned his back to Tamara, and his shoulders slumped.

Tamara fought down her own grief, wanting to stay strong for Clay, needing her professional detachment as her boss continued, "The root hair they found in the tunnel is excluded though. So we may have identified the body, but we still don't know who put the guy in the tunnel. Want me to call this in to the sheriff? What's his name? Yates?"

She drew a slow breath. "No, I'll let him know." Keeping an eye on Clay, who'd braced his arms on the kitchen counter and hung his head, Tamara finished up with Eric then disconnected. Her heart ached for Clay, who'd already lost so many people in his life he cared about. His mother, Ryder…his wife.

Tamara squared her shoulders.

No. He hadn't lost her.

They might not be married any longer, but she cared deeply about him. Tamara swore she'd be there for him as he grieved for Doc Mason. Without speaking, she returned the phone to its cradle and wrapped her arms around Clay from behind. She laid her head on his bent back and heard the steady thud of his heart.

A heart she knew was breaking.

He turned to draw her into a tight hug, heaving deep breaths as he battled his emotions. His eyes were dry, but pain ravaged his face. "Who could do this? Why would someone want him dead?"

She rubbed his back, at a loss for words. "I don't know, sweetheart."

"Someone moved his body." Clay's body tensed, and his voice quivered with anger. "Someone faked calls to his answering service, lied about him being in Arizona and retiring."

"It would seem."

He leaned back and narrowed a keen gaze on her. "And that money. That doesn't make any sense. Who would leave that kind of money behind? What was the money for?"

Tamara shook her head. She wished she had answers for Clay. "Jericho is a good lawman. He'll get to the bottom of this."

"Things like this don't happen in Esperanza. Who could have—" Clay stopped, and his gaze shifted away as if a thought had occurred to him.

"What?"

"Dr. O'Neal. He's not from Esperanza. He's taken over Doc Mason's practice and was acting nervous when we were there asking about Doc."

Tamara stiffened as a memory from the day she'd injured her ribs tickled her brain. "Clay, I didn't say anything before because, honestly, I didn't think it meant anything and—"

"Tell me." He dark eyes lasered into her.

"The day you took me to get my ribs X-rayed, I overheard an argument between Dr. O'Neal and his nurse. I was waiting for my prescriptions and, well, I heard raised voices in the corridor behind the exam rooms."

Clay stepped back but kept a hand on each of her elbows. "What did they say?"

She shook her head slowly, trying to remember. "I only heard bits and pieces, but I remember him saying something about accounting for narcotics. I think something was missing. I thought he was fussing at her for sloppy paperwork, because he said something about it being her job." Her gaze snapped to Clay's. "She said Doc Mason always did whatever it was himself. Keep the records of narcotics in the office maybe? I know I heard 'missing' and 'narcotics.'"

Clay's jaw tightened.

"Do you think this was about drugs? Could Doc have caught someone stealing drugs and been murdered for trying to stop them?"

Clay flinched at the word *murder.* The shadow of grief, temporarily pushed aside as they reasoned out the mysteries surrounding Doc's death, returned with vengeance.

"We need to tell Jericho all this," he rasped.

She nodded. "In a minute." Stroking his cheek, she hugged him closer, not caring about the lingering soreness in her ribs. Only Clay mattered.

When he pulled away a moment later, he raked his fingers through his raven hair and grimaced. "We don't even have his body to bury. Doc took care of people his whole life, and we can't give him a decent burial."

"We'll find him, Clay. I swear we will. And we'll find the person responsible for his death, too. I know Jericho won't rest until the culprit is caught." She paused and caught his hand in hers. "And neither will I."

Conviction and tenderness flared in his dark brown eyes. He gave a jerky nod then lifted the phone again. He punched in a number, and when Jericho answered, he put the sheriff on speaker. "Tamara's here with me. She just heard from her lab."

"And?" She heard the squeak of Jericho's chair and pictured him leaning forward, stroking his mustache and bracing for the news she had.

"The DNA from the blood on Clay's fishing knife, Doc Mason's blood, matched the sample my team recovered in the tunnel where I saw the body." She filled him in on the other details Eric had about the unmatched root hair, then waited for Jericho's response.

His sigh whispered over the phone. "Well, damn. Doc was a good man. He'll be missed."

She told him about the argument she'd overheard between Dr. O'Neal and his nurse as well. "I don't know if it has anything to do with Doc's death, but all that money…well, I thought it was an angle you might want to explore."

"You bet. I'll leave no stone unturned," Jericho promised.

"So where do we go from here? How do we catch the bastard who murdered him?" Clay asked.

"Whoa," Jericho said. "Slow down, partner. We don't *know* that he was murdered. We don't have any hard evidence that points to murder."

Clay slammed his palm on the kitchen counter. "Sure as hell looks that way to me!"

"But Jericho and I have to work from the facts," Tamara said. "Not appearances, not speculation or hearsay." She swallowed hard, knowing how difficult all the unknowns had to be for Clay.

"Clay, you know I'm doing everything I can to solve this case. What I need from the two of you is time. As before, I'm asking you not to tell anyone what we know." Jericho's tone made clear the request was more an order. "If word gets around that Doc is dead and his body's missing, we could tip off whoever's responsible and give him more lead time to cover his tracks."

"Or…" Clay crossed his arms over his chest as he leaned a hip against the counter. "Knowledge that we're onto him might make him panic. Flush him out. Make him careless. If he makes a mistake, maybe we'll finally have something to catch him with."

Tamara chewed her bottom lip, deferring to Jericho. This aspect of the investigation was out of her jurisdiction. Esperanza's sheriff had to make the call.

"Clay, I understand your frustration, but we're going to do things my way for now, especially for the next few days until the funeral is over. Rumors spread like wildfire when the whole town's gathered in one place like that."

Tamara knitted her brow. "But we don't have the body and—" She stopped when it clicked that Jericho wasn't talking about Doc's funeral. Icy dread balled in her gut. "Jericho, what funeral do you mean? Who died?"

"You hadn't heard? Geez, I'm sorry. I figured as close as

you'd been to her someone would have called…" He sighed and pitched his voice lower, softer. "Honey, Tess Akers died. The funeral's Thursday."

Tamara gasped, shock and grief kicking her hard. Tears flooded her eyes, and she met Clay's gaze. His arms opened, and without giving it a second thought, she stepped into his embrace. They held each other, leaned on each other, grieved with each other for long silent moments. In a span of minutes, they'd both lost someone near and dear to their hearts.

Sharing the ache of loss with each other seemed as natural as breathing. She couldn't think of anywhere she'd rather be, no one who could understand and comfort her the way Clay did. For years he'd been her lover, her best friend, her confidante. They had a bond no divorce document could sever. That truth didn't escape her.

As she wept quietly in Clay's arms, she grieved for their marriage as well. When she'd left Clay, confused and hurting, lost and alone, she'd walked away from her soul mate.

The entire town of Esperanza turned out for Tess Akers's funeral. The woman who'd taught home economics at the high school and Sunday school at the Baptist church, who'd chaired the town's rodeo festival for years and been a regular at Miss Sue's diner for Saturday lunch, had touched many lives. But none more than Tamara's.

While Clay and Quinn Logan talked with Jack Akers, Tamara strolled through the Akerses' house, telling herself she *wasn't* avoiding Quinn. Nursing her years-old grudge seemed petty in light of Jack and Billy Akers's loss.

Still, she wasn't up to the awkwardness of making idle chatter with Quinn today.

She glanced at pictures of the woman who'd opened her home when Tamara had tagged along with Billy and her older brother after school. Mrs. Akers had been a mentor and friend to her in high school after Tamara's mother died, and she'd encouraged

Tamara to follow her dreams of a career in forensic science after she'd married Clay.

Tamara's chest squeezed. She hated that she'd neglected to come by and visit Mrs. Akers as she'd sworn she would when she heard how ill the woman had become. But she'd been too preoccupied with Doc Mason's disappearance, too wrapped up in her feelings for Clay, too confident that there'd be time later for visiting....

"That one was always my favorite of her."

She hadn't noticed Billy Akers's approach until he spoke. His blond hair was a mess, and his tie was askew. He gestured with a hand that clutched a highball glass to a photo of the family on the wall in the corridor. The smell of alcohol wafting around him told Tamara the drink in his hand wasn't his first.

"She was a beautiful lady. I'm so sorry for your loss, Billy."

Pain filled his eyes, and he took another gulp of his whiskey. "Thanks, Tam'ra," he slurred.

She couldn't blame him for wanting to numb himself to the ache. She hurt for him and his obvious grief. Still, she hated to see her friend get publicly drunk at his mother's funeral. She reached for his glass. "Can I freshen that up for you? Maybe with iced tea this time?"

Billy frowned at his empty glass. "Yeah. Whatever."

He followed her into the kitchen where Jewel Mayfair and Becky French had their heads together murmuring quietly as they arranged finger sandwiches on a tray. They glanced up when Billy and Tamara entered the room.

"Oh, Billy," Becky said, "I was just telling Jewel how much I hate that Doc Mason missed the funeral. I know your mother was a dear friend of his."

Tamara's stomach lurched, and she busied herself pouring Billy some tea. She kept her eyes cast down, hoping her expression gave nothing away.

"From what I hear, though, he's earned this vacation," Jewel added. "You know, he came out to the Hopechest Ranch in the middle of the night a few months ago when one of the girls spiked a high fever. He seems like such a nice man."

"He is. And he truly cares about his town and his patients." Becky bustled past Tamara to take a jar of relish from the refrigerator. "Billy, he's going to be heartbroken about Tess."

Billy grunted acknowledgment and leaned drunkenly against the door frame. "Yeah, I s'pose he would've been. He and Mom went way back."

Tamara looked at the tea she'd poured Billy and wondered if coffee might be a better option.

Becky held the tray of sandwiches out to Billy. "Here, darlin', have one. I haven't seen you eat anything all day."

Billy waved the food off. "Not hungry, thanks. Think I'll go outside for a smoke."

After he left, Becky sighed heavily. "Poor fella. I remember how much it hurt when my mother died a few years ago. He's taking it so hard."

Jewel pulled back the filmy window sheers and cocked her head as she watched Billy outside. "Grief affects us all differently. I'd say as long as he expresses his grief, he'll be all right. It's when a person tries to suppress their emotions that problems can arise. It's unhealthy. If they—" Jewel laughed self-consciously. "Good gracious, listen to me prattling on like Dr. Phil."

Tamara gave her a grin. "It's okay. You're allowed."

"And you're right," Becky chimed in. "This town has always been supportive when one of our own is in need. And Jack and Billy are going to need us in the coming weeks. We'll pull them through this."

Tamara glanced out the window at Billy and decided to give her friend a few moments alone, away from the cloying attention of the people gathered in his house. Instead she went in search of Clay, who was now chatting with Nick and Georgie beside the spread of food on the dining-room table. She gave Georgie a small smile of greeting when Clay's sister hugged her. "Who's watching Emmie while you're here?"

"Jewel suggested we let her stay with the girls at Hopechest for the afternoon." Georgie grinned. "When we left, she was embroiled in a no-holds-barred game of crazy eights with Ana Morales."

Jack Akers approached the table and cast a strained smile to the group. "Eat up, people. Even with Billy's appetite, I don't know how we'll use all this food before it goes bad." He shoved a cookie toward Clay. "Try these, Colton. Macy Ward brought them. They'll melt in your mouth."

Clay flicked a dubious glance to Tamara then took the proffered cookie. "Thanks."

"Georgie, how's that little cowgirl of yours?" Jack asked, his voice unnaturally loud and overly bright.

Though Tamara couldn't see any evidence that the father had been drinking like the son, his forced upbeat conversation was uncomfortable. He seemed strung tight and ready to snap. As if the only thing keeping him going was maintaining the illusion of cheer.

Grief affects us all differently, Jewel had said. Perhaps Jack thought he had to keep smiling, convince everyone he was fine, or he'd break down. Whatever his reason, the widower's stilted smiles and cowboy jokes were difficult to bear.

Tamara made eye contact with Clay and hitched her head toward the door.

"Excuse us for a minute," he mumbled and slipped away from the table with her. When they were out of earshot, he gave her shoulder a squeeze. "You ready to go?"

"Not quite yet. I want to check on Billy again." She sighed and tucked her hair behind her ear. "This would be hard enough even without knowing about Doc. But not telling people the truth about Doc feels like we're lying. I hate it."

He nodded and rubbed his knuckles along her chin. "I know. But it's just for a little while. Just buying Jericho a little time."

She glanced outside and studied Billy's slumped shoulders as he leaned against one of the cars parked on the street. "Did I ever tell you that Billy volunteered to be my escort for homecoming when I was a freshman? My date got sick at the last minute, and I didn't have anyone to walk me out on the football field during halftime 'cause my dad was working. Billy heard about it and showed up at the game in a tux." She smiled at the memory. "I told him he was my hero."

Clay gave her a lopsided smile. "Are you trying to make me jealous?"

She lifted one eyebrow. "Did I mention the tux was powder blue and had a ruffled shirt?"

Clay pulled a face and covered a laugh with a cough.

Sobering, Tamara turned back to the storm door. "I only mention it because Billy has been there for me lots of times over the years. And now when he's hurting, I don't know what to do or say."

"I think just being here says a lot." He nudged her back. "Come on. I'll go with you."

Billy looked up when the storm door creaked open. He glanced at the cigarette in his hand then to Tamara as she approached. "I know, I know. B'fore you lecture me on how bad these things are f'r me, let me say, I've been trying to quit."

She lifted her palms and grinned. "Did I say anything?"

"Didn't have to. You had that look in your eye." Billy dropped the half-smoked cigarette on the street and tamped it out with his toe. He gave Clay a nod of greeting, which Clay returned.

Tamara braced her hands on her hips. "What look?"

"The same one Doc Mason always got before he'd lecture me. He hated my smoking."

"Hmm, a doctor who doesn't want his patient to smoke. Unheard of!" Tamara grinned and bumped Billy with her shoulder as she propped next to him. "Sounds to me like you just have a guilty conscience."

Billy scoffed and crossed his arms over his chest as if he didn't know what to do with his hands. "Like he had room to talk. An addiction is an addiction. It's not easy to quit smoking. And

I have cut back. Or I had…" His volume dropped to a mumble. "Before Mom got so sick."

Tamara rubbed his arm, looking for a way to lighten the mood. "Hey, I was just telling Clay about that blue suit you wore to homecoming my freshman year."

Billy raised his head and wrinkled his nose. "Aw, man. Just don't go pulling out any pictures."

Clay flashed a lopsided grin. "There are pictures?"

Billy raised a hand. "Not if I can help it."

Tamara wrapped her hand around Billy's arm. "You were really sweet that night. It meant a lot to me."

He glanced quickly to Clay then away. "Yeah, well, don't let it get around. I have a reputation to maintain. Wouldn't want the guys thinking I'm a softie."

Silence fell among them for a moment before Billy hitched his head toward Clay. "So what's the story? Is a reunion in the future?"

Tamara's heart jumped, and she flicked a glance at Clay to gauge his response.

With a stiff laugh, Clay shrugged. "Well, I heard the cast of *Love Boat* was considering an anniversary show. Personally I think all these 1980s reunions are overrated."

Billy scrunched his mouth sideways and shook his head. Turning his face toward Tamara, he arched an eyebrow. "What do you say, Brat? You getting back with that ole cowboy or what?"

Had he not been drinking, she doubted Billy would have been so cheeky. She fumbled for a way to dodge the question as Clay had.

Forget butterflies. A flock of mallards flapped their wings in her stomach as she looked for an answer under the penetrating gaze of both her ex and her old friend. She prayed neither of them could read her confusion and anguish in her expression. She swallowed, trying to moisten her suddenly dry mouth. "I…well, I…guess time will tell."

Clay met and held her gaze, his expression hard to decipher. Tamara realized she was holding her breath and released it with a slow exhale.

"Time, schmime. Georgie will tell. I bet if I ask your sister, I'd get the real lowdown." Billy pushed away from the car where he'd been leaning and dusted the seat of his suit pants. "Think I'll get myself another shot of my friend Jack Daniel's. Clay?"

Her ex shook his head. "No, thanks. I'm driving."

Billy smiled as he excused himself with a drunken wave of his finger. "But I'm not."

Tamara opened her mouth to dissuade Billy from his drunken binge. Clay's warm hand on her arm stopped her.

"He'll be all right. May have a hell of a hangover tomorrow but don't worry about him."

She watched until Billy disappeared inside, then lifted her eyes toward the bright summer sun. She replayed their conversation with Billy, fretting over an uneasy sense that something wasn't right. She tried to dismiss the unsettled feeling that pricked her as a remnant of his bold question about a reunion between her and Clay. But her disquiet had started before that moment, had started even before they'd come outside. If she were honest, her sense of foreboding was as much what had prodded her to seek Billy out again as her concern for his well-being.

"What am I missing?" she asked aloud.

"Pardon?" Clay lifted his head with a small shake as if roused from deep thoughts.

"Something about Billy seemed…off." She chewed her lip and stared at the ground trying to puzzle through her odd sense.

"You mean besides the fact that he was drunk as a skunk and mourning his mother?" Clay stepped closer and massaged her neck with one strong hand. The warmth of his touch, the relaxing kneading of her muscles and the contradictory tingle of arousal that flashed over her skin detoured the line of thought that beckoned with a nagging urgency. As much as she hated to, she stepped out of Clay's reach so she could think more clearly.

Clay's frown didn't escape her notice.

"I need to concentrate," she said by way of apology, "and you were distracting me." She twitched her lips in a sideways grin.

"Concentrate on what?" His dark eyes queried her from under the brim of his Stetson.

Her mind backtracked through every detail of the funeral and the current gathering of mourners at the Akerses' house. Snippets of conversation, facial expressions, the food…

Her gaze landed on the cigarette Billy had dropped on the street.

What look?

The same one Doc Mason always got before he'd lecture me. He hated my smoking.

The logical part of her brain began to tick as realizations fell in place.

"He used the past tense," she mumbled to herself.

"What?"

She replayed everything Billy had said about Doc Mason, and her stomach twisted. "Every time Billy mentioned Doc Mason, he used the past tense. But you, me and Jericho are the only ones in town who are supposed to know Doc's dead."

Clay's face paled. "Jericho told me once that killers often give themselves away by referring to a missing person in the past tense before their death is officially confirmed."

Tamara raised a hand, even as panic swelled inside. "Slow down, Clay. Remember Billy is drunk, and there has been lots of talk in town lately about Doc Mason leaving town to retire. Maybe that's all he meant." But her CSI experience had already led her to more ominous explanations. Every reasoned conclusion met with heartsick denials. Her pulse thundered in her ears, and nausea roiled in her gut. She paced the street, shaking her head. "Billy's not involved. Doc Mason was his parents' friend since before he was born."

"Tamara."

She faced Clay, tears stinging her sinuses and dread knotting in her chest. Clay pressed his mouth in a firm line, but his eyes were soft with compassion.

"He's my friend," she said, her voice cracking.

"And Doc was mine."

She rubbed her arms as goose bumps rose on her skin, despite the Texas heat.

She had to clear Billy of any involvement. To put *her* mind at rest if nothing else.

She glanced around her, her mind in overdrive, and her gaze landed on the cigarette at her feet. "I need a plastic bag. A clean zip-top bag and…a clean spoon or something."

"Why?"

She locked a determined stare on Clay's dubious frown. "I can get Billy's DNA and fingerprints off this cigarette. You and I both saw him smoke it and drop it there. We have an unmatched root hair at the CSI lab and fingerprints from the trunk of the Taurus on file. With a few tests to that cigarette butt, I can clear Billy."

Her chest contracted. *Or convict him.*

Chapter 14

After bagging the cigarette butt and paying their last respects to the Akerses, Clay and Tamara left the funeral and headed for San Antonio. In the elevator, as they headed up to the CSI lab on the seventh floor, Clay cast Tamara a stern look.

"We're only dropping off the cigarette for your team. You're still on medical leave, and you aren't staying." Concern prodded him when he recalled how hard she'd pushed herself the last time they'd brought in evidence and how her fatigue had set back her recovery. Despite the progress in her healing, Clay swore not to let her endanger her health that way again.

His ex's returned gaze challenged him with cool blue determination. "Like hell. Billy's my friend, and I owe it to him to run the tests myself. I already feel like a traitor even suspecting him of something so heinous as being involved in Doc's death."

The elevator doors rumbled open, and Tamara brushed past him as she stepped off. Clenching his teeth, Clay followed her into the lab. "I wouldn't have brought you if I'd known you were going to insist on running the tests yourself."

She sent him an annoyed glance and set to work without responding.

Short of throwing her over his shoulder and carrying her from the building, he didn't know how he was supposed to get her to leave the work for her team to finish.

Clay approached the desk where her office phone sat. Several autodial buttons had been labeled with the names of important contacts. He scanned the list. Eric was the third button. Lifting the receiver, Clay punched the speed dial for Tamara's boss.

"Crime Scene Investigation, this is Eric."

"Hey, Eric. Clay Colton here. Tamara's ex."

Tamara gasped and spun around to face him, a murderous expression darkening her eyes and a bottle of chemical solution clutched in her hand.

"We just brought in some new evidence related to the case in Esperanza y'all are helping out with," Clay continued, undaunted.

Still holding the chemical bottle, she marched over to her desk and tried to pry the phone from him.

With a twist of his body and his height advantage, Clay kept her at bay just long enough to reach his desired goal. "Tamara has started the tests, but—"

"She's here? Working?" Eric sighed heavily. "I gave her a direct order to stay out of the lab until her leave was over. If there is evidence to process, we have plenty of capable technicians here who—" He stopped and grunted his frustration. "Tell her I'm on my way down."

Clay flashed Tamara a cocky grin. "Will do, Eric."

She pressed her lips in a grim line. "You rat! Are you trying to get me fired?"

"No, I'm trying to keep you from setting back your recovery by exhausting yourself like last time. Besides, you've got personal stakes in the outcome because of your history with Billy."

She pinned him with a glare. "Are you saying I'd let my

emotions get in the way of doing my job? Feelings don't influence hard scientific data. Tests can't be altered because I want—"

"Tamara, what are you doing here?" Eric demanded as he stormed through the door.

She aimed a finger at Clay's nose. "I'll deal with you later." Squaring her shoulders, she faced her boss. "I'm fine, Eric. I can start these tests and get—"

"No, you won't. You're on medical leave until Monday." Eric plucked the bottle from her hand and crossed the room with it. "You can leave any evidence that needs to be processed, but you aren't staying to do the analysis yourself."

"Eric, these tests are important. An old friend of mine—"

"Every test we run is important, Tamara. Every victim, every criminal, every witness is somebody's child or spouse or dear old friend."

A flicker of contrition flickered across Tamara's face, and Clay's chest contracted. How did Tamara, with her soft heart, do her job day after day, knowing the lives that would be altered when her analyses came to light?

Eric planted a hand on Tamara's back and scooted her toward the door. "Vamoose, Ms. Brown. Don't let me catch you in here again before Monday or else."

Tamara divided a glower between Eric and Clay. "Fine. But you better call me the minute you know anything. If you push them through as a priority—"

"Then we'll be even farther behind on the tests we've already scuttled aside when we expedited the last evidence you brought in." Eric crossed his arms over his chest and angled his chin. "Tamara, we have a mountain of work to catch up on when you get back Monday. So if you promise to go home and get rested up so we can make some progress on the backlog next week, I'll run all the analyses on your new evidence over the weekend."

"The weekend?" Tamara's impatience vibrated in her tone.

"That's the best I can promise. Esperanza isn't the only city with unsolved cases."

She opened her mouth, clearly ready to launch another plea for haste, but Clay took her elbow and nudged her toward the door. "This weekend will be fine. Thanks for helping out. Say good-night, Gracie."

Sighing, Tamara marched out of the lab and gave Clay the silent treatment for the first twenty minutes of the ride back to the Bar None.

As they reached the Esperanza town limit, she snapped a sharp glance across the front seat. "You never change. You're so bossy and controlling sometimes I could scream. You take charge even in things that are not your business."

He rubbed his chin and weighed his response. She seemed to be spoiling for a fight, but the last thing he wanted tonight was to argue with Tamara. "If I overstep my bounds on occasion," he stated calmly, "it's only 'cause I've had to take charge so many other times. As the oldest kid, I had to step up when Mom died or my family would've been split up, sent to foster homes. And the Bar None being my ranch means I'm the boss. I guess it's a habit. It's who I am."

"But a marriage is supposed to be a partnership!" Tamara poked a finger on the bench seat between them to emphasize her point.

"A marriage?" He cast her a startled glance. "This is about our divorce? I thought you were just mad about me calling Eric tonight at the lab."

She drew a deep breath and blew it out slowly. "I am mad about your stunt at the lab, but it's just an example of how you ignored my wishes when we were married. You were so busy being in charge of *everything* that I never got a say in *anything*."

"That's not true!" He squeezed the steering wheel as his blood pressure spiked. So much for avoiding a fight.

"It sure seemed that way to me. When you made decisions without consulting me, I felt like I didn't matter to you, like my opinion didn't count for anything." She pitched her volume down, but the passion in her voice caught him off guard.

"That's ludicrous," he sputtered. "I've always done everything I could to make you happy."

She aimed a finger at him. "You're doing it now! I'm telling you how I felt, and you're calling it ludicrous. But it *was* how I felt, Clay! Why can't you hear what I'm saying? Why can't you understand?"

"I didn't say—" He bit back the angry response on his tongue and searched for his composure. He didn't want this to evolve into a shouting match with his ex. When he met her gaze, the wounded look in her eyes stole his breath.

"When the tractor broke down the summer before I left," Tamara said in a calmer, softer voice that rippled over him like a balmy breeze, "you spent all the money in our savings to fix it. Without consulting me."

"I *did* tell you about it," he countered.

"Yeah, you *told* me about it. After the fact."

"We had to have a working tractor to run the ranch." Clay hated the defensiveness in his tone, hated more the way her shoulders slumped in frustration. He clamped his mouth shut and exhaled deeply. "Sorry. Please finish what you were saying."

They'd reached the Bar None, and he turned up the driveway.

Tamara stared out the passenger window as she continued, her tone more defeated, more tired. "We'd saved the money in that account to buy a new stove for the kitchen. Only one burner worked on the old stove and cooking dinner took forever. I was counting on getting a new one."

When they reached the end of the drive, he cut the engine and leaned his head back on the headrest. Matching her quiet tone, he said, "I'm sorry we didn't have the money to do both, Tee. But I thought the tractor was more important."

"And it probably was. But it was *our* money. I worked hard on the ranch helping save what little we had, and it hurt that you didn't talk to me before you spent it. The stove could have waited, yes. That's what I would've said. But when you didn't give me a voice in the matter…"

Clay's gut tightened as her point drove home. "I hurt you."

She looked at him sadly and nodded. "That's just one example."

He stared out the windshield, making no move to get out as what she'd said rolled about in his brain. "The night you left, when Quinn put Lone Star down…"

When he didn't finish the thought, she said, "I begged you to just hear me out, but you walked away. You said Quinn was the vet, and he knew what he was doing. His was the only opinion you'd listen to."

"The horse was suffering, Tee. Putting him down was the only humane thing to do. The disease had advanced to a point that all Quinn could do was treat the symptoms. Lone Star would never recover and could have spread the disease to the rest of the horses."

"Why wasn't he vaccinated? If Quinn had done his job right to begin with, Lone Star wouldn't have gotten sick!"

"He *was* vaccinated. But the strangles vaccine isn't one hundred percent effective. It was my fault for not recognizing how ill he was until too late. When the bacteria became systemic, there was little Quinn could do. Bastard strangles is nearly always fatal. If you want to blame someone, blame me. But Quinn did his job."

Tamara pulled her brow into a deep V. "Bastard strangles?"

"That's what it's called when the bacterial infection becomes systemic. That's what Lone Star had. He wouldn't have survived."

She gaped at him. "Why didn't you tell me this before? I would have understood."

"I tried to, but we were both so upset that night, I don't think either of us really heard what the other was saying. After you left, I figured the particulars were a moot point."

"Except that for years now I've blamed Quinn for something he didn't do." She nibbled her bottom lip, digesting the new information. "When you wouldn't listen to me, didn't give me a chance to be heard, it made me feel like all my contributions to the ranch and our marriage were for nothing. I figured if I didn't matter to you or to the ranch, why was I staying? I wanted to do something with my life that mattered. That's why I left."

Amber rays from the setting sun backlit Tamara and made her hair shine like spun gold. In the fading daylight, her skin glowed with subtle color from her time spent outdoors over the past week. She looked radiant. Beautiful.

Desire coursed through him. The hunger he'd held at bay clamored inside him, fed by a new understanding of the woman he'd once called his wife. He'd always known she was intelligent, but seeing her on the job at her CSI lab had given him a new respect for her sharp mind. The maturity and perspective they'd both gained in the past five years allowed them to finally begin to settle issues that had once torn them apart. And her time at the ranch had reminded him of the friendship and sizzling attraction that had drawn him to Tamara from the beginning. A tender ache swelled inside him along with his restless sexual appetite. Love and lust packed a powerful one-two punch.

Was he falling in love with his ex-wife again? Had he ever fallen out of love?

"Clay, do you suppose it's too late for an apology?"

He cocked his head, trying to remember what they'd been talking about before his mind had wandered, distracted by the play of sunlight that made her shine all the brighter.

"To Quinn," she added.

He shrugged. "I don't think it's ever too late to set things right."

Tamara's eyes widened then, shifting on the seat, she stared down at her hands. She opened her mouth to say something then seemed to reconsider. With a little shake of her head, she reached for the passenger door. "I hope you're right."

That evening as they ate a late dinner, Tamara poked at her food, ruminating on the events of the day. The funeral. The question of Billy's possible involvement in Doc Mason's death. Her spat in the truck with Clay.

No wonder she had no appetite. The day had been an emotional roller coaster.

"You feeling all right?" Clay asked as he stabbed a bite of Marie's glazed ham.

"Hmm, yeah. Just thinking."

"About?"

"Lots of stuff. The Akerses, for instance. I wish I could do something to help them. I know how hard it is to lose a loved one." She scoffed and set her fork down. "But what do I do instead? Cast suspicion on one of my oldest friends."

"No, Billy did that to himself. The facts will speak for themselves, and you shouldn't feel guilty about doing your job." Clay cut himself another bite of meat and furrowed his brow. "Speaking of the Akerses, did Jack's attitude at the funeral seem weird to you?"

"You mean all his false bravado and forced cheer?"

He pointed at her with his fork. "Exactly. His wife had died and yet he was telling jokes and acting like folks were gathered at his house for the Super Bowl instead of a funeral. It was creepy. Pitiful."

"I agree. But Jewel said today that everyone has their own way of grieving. He's from the generation of men who were raised to be tough and strong. The real-men-don't-cry crowd."

"Yeah, maybe so. But if it had been my wife who died—" Clay jerked his gaze to hers, his expression shaken, as if he'd only then realized what he was saying. The blood drained from his face leaving his work-tanned skin ashen. "I— Never mind."

"No, finish. What if it had been me who died?"

Shaking his head, he put his fork down and shoved his plate away. "I don't even want to think about that."

Tamara put herself in Jack's place, imagining how she'd feel if Clay died. The onslaught of gut-wrenching grief brought a flood of tears to her eyes. She choked on a ragged sob. "Oh, Clay…I'd be devastated if anything happened to you."

He raised a startled glance from his plate, a dark scowl hardening his mouth. The shock her assertion brought to his eyes softened to sympathy and compassion. Moisture sparkled in the rich brown depths of his gaze, and the intensity of the stare that clung to hers burrowed into her soul. Fear, grief and desperation reflected in his eyes, mirroring the anguish ripping her apart.

When she tried to speak, emotions squeezed her throat, and her voice was no more than a strangled rasp. "I'd want to die. I can't imagine this world without you. It'd be... I'd be—" Her shoulders heaved as sobs racked her body.

Clay's chair toppled as he bolted from it. In a heartbeat, he'd folded her in his arms and buried his face in hair.

Tamara was crying so hard, her ribs ached. As she gasped for breath between her tears, she tried to shove down the spontaneous tears. But the dam had opened, and all the seesaw emotions of the past week poured from her in a cleansing flood.

She felt safer in Clay's arms than she had in years. Nestling closer, she inhaled the familiar earthy scents that were far sexier than any store-bought cologne. Fresh air, clean straw and mellow leather combined in an aroma that was pure Clay, all male strength and raw appeal.

His grip tightened around her, and he kissed the top of her head. As he murmured comforting words in his low, rumbling bass voice, a quiver started low in her belly. She pressed her ear to his wide chest and heard the steady thump of his heart. On the heels of the horrid notion of Clay's death, the life-affirming sound reverberating in his chest was sweet music, a seductive tango. After admitting how devastating his death would be, all pretenses and excuses were stripped away, and denying the depth of her feelings for this man seemed pointless.

A desperate need clawed at her, a yearning to rediscover the physical bond that they'd once shared. She curled her fingers into his back, wanting more of him, needing to be closer. He moved his soothing kisses to her temple, still whispering words of reassurance, calming her in the same hypnotic timbre he used to quiet a spooked colt. She tipped her chin up, met his eyes. And was lost. His dark bedroom eyes held her spellbound.

As he framed her face with his callused palms, his moist gaze drank her in. "I've missed you, Tee," he rasped, his deep voice stroking her, building the clamoring need inside her.

With a low rumble in his throat, he pressed soft kisses to her eyelids, and she sagged against him. His warm lips skimmed her cheek, the hollow of her throat, her chin. He moved his mouth to hover above hers, his breath fanning her skin as he waited.

"Make love to me, Clay," Tamara whispered, barely able to speak as anticipation tightened her lungs and stole her breath. She rose up on her toes to close the distance to his lips and sealed the invitation with a kiss.

With a growl of approval, Clay angled his head and swept his tongue into her mouth. His fingers twisted loosely in her hair, and he walked her backward until he'd anchored her body against the wall. Tamara raked her fingers down the muscles of his broad shoulders, reveling in the taste of his lips. Her tongue tangled with his, and she strained upward to deepen the kiss. While they were married, she'd kissed Clay thousands of times, yet tonight the sweet pull of his lips on hers held a magical newness, the thrill of rediscovery.

Clay raised his head, his dark eyes gleaming with passion, his breathing a light, staccato rhythm of desire. His hands restlessly stroked her face, her hair. "I don't want to hurt you."

Tamara's pulse missed a beat. Did he mean physically? Was he worried about her ribs?

Or was he worried about the emotional attachments making love would inevitably bring?

Either way, the reward was worth the risk. She needed to feel Clay holding her, needed have his warm skin next to her, needed the spiritual connection she'd always experienced when they joined their bodies. She'd been away from Clay too long, and she needed new memories to tide her through the lonely days to come.

"I'll be fine," she told him, praying she was right. Could she really make love to Clay again, then walk away unscathed when it was over?

Holding her gaze with a dark piercing look smoldering in his eyes, Clay scooped her into his arms and carried her upstairs. Once in his bedroom, he lowered her gently onto his bed and followed her onto the mattress.

"You're beautiful, Tee. Even more lovely now than when we were first married." He traced the line of her jaw with a crooked finger, and a sensual shiver slid through her.

"When you look at me like you are now," she whispered, "I feel beautiful. I feel safe. I feel…" *Loved.*

She swallowed the word that sprang to her tongue. Was it love she saw in Clay's eyes or just her own wishful thinking? Clay had devoured her with his hungry gaze many times when they were married, but she'd had little similar evidence of his feelings outside the bedroom. He still hadn't said anything to indicate he felt more than basic affection.

As he released the buttons on her blouse, Tamara shoved aside the pang of regret that twisted in her chest. Tonight she simply wanted to savor the intimate pleasure of this man who still owned a piece of her heart. She tugged at his shirt, pulling the hem from the waist of his jeans, and smoothed her hands over the warm skin of his back. As his fingers skillfully freed her of her blouse and bra, he captured her lips again for a soul-shaking kiss.

One by one, more articles of clothing were shed, and the fire that had smoldered between them the past week burst into flame. Every touch, every sigh, every heated glance heightened her anticipation. Erotic sensations swamped Tamara's body and left her languid and breathless.

Clay remembered all of her most sensitive and erogenous zones as if five years hadn't come between them. He licked her earlobes, teased her nipples, kissed the back of her knees.

Months of heartache and loneliness melted away.

Tamara returned his tender ministrations, nibbling the curve of his throat, sliding her body along his and stroking every inch of his warm, taut skin. Their limbs tangled, and their mouths explored, renewing the sizzling passion that had been a hallmark of their marriage.

By the time he'd donned a condom and braced on his arms above her, ready to join their bodies, he'd reduced her to a puddle of quivering nerves and tightly coiled desire.

When he nudged her with his erection, she nearly shattered. Lifting her hips, she wrapped her legs around him and dug her fingers into his buttocks, urging him to complete the union her body desperately craved. Finally, with a long, slow stroke, he entered her.

"Clay!" Tamara cried, a maelstrom of sensation washing through her.

He captured her lips and groaned his pleasure. His arms trembled as he braced above her, and she realized that his restraint was in deference to her injured ribs.

"Hold me tighter, Clay. You won't hurt me." She wrapped her arms around his back and clung to him. "Please, hold me tighter."

Nuzzling her ear, he hugged her closer and buried himself deeper. His arms squeezed her body against his, tightly enough that she could feel the pounding of his heart against hers. In the circle of his arms, she savored the completeness, the safety and the heartfelt connection she'd missed the past five years. The sense of destiny and peace she'd known only with Clay.

As he brought her to a shattering climax, tears pricked her eyes. She was falling in love with him again. Maybe she'd never fallen *out* of love with him.

But she could never love him enough to make up for the shortfall in his feelings toward her. She had no doubt he desired her, was sure he had affection for her. But without the unconditional, soul-deep love she needed from him, they were no better off than the day she'd walked away from their marriage. She needed to know, really *know,* that she mattered to him. That she was truly important to him on every level, not just as a sex partner.

Long minutes passed before Clay loosened his grip and eased away from her. His ragged breathing calmed, and he rained gentle kisses on her cheeks and chin. She met his dark eyes and smiled at him. "Well, some things don't change. You still make the earth move for me."

A sexy laugh rumbled from his throat. "Back at ya, darlin'." He tucked a wisp of her hair behind her ear, and his expression sobered. His voice husky and quiet, he said, "No one has ever been as special to me as you are, Tee."

Her heart gave a hard thump.

Special? Hardly the declaration of undying love she'd hoped for, yet even the watered-down, vanilla affirmation fed her hungering soul.

A hollow ache she'd known well in the last days of her marriage returned in force. Perhaps *special* was all she was to Clay. The sooner she accepted that fact, the sooner she could move on with her life.

But for tonight, she wanted to treasure the precious moments she had left with Clay. She snuggled under his arm and stroked a toe down his leg. "Stay with me tonight? I want to know you're beside me while I sleep."

He pressed a kiss to her hair. "Wild horses couldn't drag me away."

She sighed and closed her eyes.

Maybe wild horses wouldn't steal him away tonight, but in the morning she would have to face the cold truth. Clay was no more hers now than he had been the day they divorced.

Chapter 15

Two mornings later, Tamara rose early with Clay and accompanied him to the stable as he did his chores. The routine was so familiar, yet strangely foreign. Perhaps because she and Clay had never done the ranch work *together*. When she tried to help separate the flakes of hay for the mares to eat, Clay stopped her. "You're supposed to be resting."

"I'm tired of resting. Besides, ranch work is cathartic in its own way."

He pulled a frown. "I thought you hated ranch chores."

"I never said that. Being back on the ranch has been good. I missed the Bar None."

He leaned on the pitchfork he'd been mucking stalls with and cocked his head. "Ranching has a way of getting in your blood."

She gave him the raspberry. "You have to say that. It's your business."

His expression grew thoughtful. "Naw, it's more than a business for me. I love it. I love the work, the fresh air, the horses." He propped the pitchfork against the wall and stepped closer to her. "I've been thinking about the conversation we had the other day. About Lone Star."

She raised a hand. "Let's not argue about that again."

He caught her fingers and kissed them. "Not argue. But I want you to understand."

She tipped her head and eyed him warily. "Understand what?"

"If I shut you out that night, it was largely because I didn't know what to do with my own grief. Seeing your pain only made it harder to do what I had to. The horse was suffering. Quinn couldn't save him once the disease went systemic."

She nodded. "I know that now, but—"

"I was hurting, too, Tamara. Losing my best stallion was a tremendous blow to the ranch when we were already struggling financially. I didn't know how we would survive without a breeding stud."

"But you did."

He closed his eyes and nodded. "Yeah. But my point is, I wasn't hurting that night because of the loss to my business. I hurt because I was losing Lone Star. I'd raised him from birth. I'd groomed him and fed him and spent hours working with him. I know I'd told you not to get emotionally attached to the animals, that ranch animals aren't pets. But I wouldn't be in ranching if the horses didn't matter to me. I was grieving for Lone Star the same as you."

Tamara stared at Clay with moist eyes, a tender ache filling her chest. She moved closer, wrapping her arm around his neck. "Thank you for telling me."

"I know it doesn't change what happened that night." He sighed and brushed a kiss across her lips. "But I wanted you to know." Planting his hands on her hips, he levered away from her. "Now quit distracting me, or I'll still be mucking stalls when my family arrives for the barbecue."

"So let me help." She reached for the pitchfork, and he pried it from her hand.

"Uh-uh. You overexerted yourself yesterday doing chores, and it took its toll. I saw the pain you were in, so don't try to deny it."

She arched an eyebrow. "I wasn't too tired to make love to you, and I had several hours' rest last night."

She'd only intended the statement to support her argument, but mention of their lovemaking the past two nights changed the atmosphere in the stable like a flash of lightning from the blue sky. Immediately the air seemed charged, and Clay's body tensed.

A muscle in his jaw twitched, and his eyes darkened with the same heated desire she'd seen in them last night and the one before. The mild abrasions his stubbled cheeks had left on her skin tingled again with anticipation, and a heady sensation spun through her and made her tremble. Clay stepped closer, still holding the pitchfork. With his free hand, he stroked her cheek, and her blood flashed hot.

"You got a big day ahead of you. My family will be here in a couple hours. Don't you want to go back to bed for little while?"

Her mouth went dry. "Depends. Will you be joining me?" Her attempt to add a note of levity to the challenge came out as a husky croak.

Clay drew a deep breath, his nostrils flaring and his eyes zeroing in on her mouth. "Tempting as that offer may be, these chores don't finish themselves." His hand curled around the nape of her neck, and he pressed a kiss to her temple. "Maybe a rain check?"

Tamara opened her mouth to agree then stopped. Her pulse fluttered. A rain check implied there would be a future opportunity for redemption. After the barbecue, what excuse did she have for staying with Clay any longer? The simple fact that she'd felt well enough to make love to him the past two nights proved she'd healed enough to return to work on Monday. To be alone at her apartment. *Alone.*

Her heart gave a painful kick. She hated the idea of her lonely apartment after the past few days in the welcoming comfort of Clay's ranch, surrounded by family and friends from Esperanza. Even the presence of the ranch hands and horses made the Bar None feel more homey, buzzing with life and love.

She smiled wistfully at Clay. "Rain check." She'd keep that promise if only for the chance to store away a few more precious memories with Clay. She gave him a peck on the cheek before backing toward the stable door. "I'll see if Marie needs help in the kitchen."

The ensuing hours were a frenzy of preparation for the Colton barbecue. As time for the rest of the family to arrive neared, Tamara found herself pumped with anticipation and humming.

Jewel and Meredith were the first to arrive. As Clay welcomed his aunt and her niece with hugs, Tamara marveled at how much Jewel resembled her mother's twin sister. Other than age and the fact that Meredith wore her golden hair in a chic bob now, the two favored each other in almost every way, right down to the stately and dignified way they carried themselves.

Tamara smoothed a self-conscious hand over her own casual ponytail before stepping forward to greet Meredith.

"Tamara, honey, it's so good to see you!" The older woman air-kissed her cheeks.

"Wow. To think, I could be hugging the future First Lady," Tamara said with a laugh.

"From your lips to God's ears!" Meredith crossed her fingers and held them up.

Emmie burst through the front door without knocking. "We're heee-re!"

The adults chuckled as the spitfire skipped into the family room.

Clay scooped her up for a hug. "Hey there, squirt. Did you bring your mom and Nick with you or did you drive yourself?"

Emmie rolled her eyes. "I don't have my driver's license yet."

He tweaked her nose. "Then you better not let Sheriff Yates catch you behind the wheel."

Clay's rapport with his niece spread a gooey warmth inside Tamara. How many times in their marriage had she pictured him bouncing a child of their own on his knee?

Giggling, Emmie squirmed out of his arms and greeted Tamara with a hug. "Hi, Aunt Tamara!"

Aunt. Tamara's heart turned over. If only…

Georgie and Nick bustled in, giving the front door a perfunctory knock as they entered.

"Did anyone see a little kid come in here? Four years old. Red hair. *No manners.*" Georgie directed the last to Emmie with raised eyebrows. "You didn't knock, and then you left the door wide open. Were you raised in a barn?"

Emmie flashed a sassy grin. "Yes! The rodeo barn."

Clay cocked his head. "She got you there, sis."

"I hear there was a bit of excitement here a couple nights ago? Your foal arrived?" Nick offered his hand to shake Clay's.

"Yep," Clay said with the grin of a proud new father. "And he's a beauty. I was just out to check on them a few minutes ago and mom and baby are doing fine."

"Wonderful," Jewel said.

Her smile seemed genuine, yet Tamara detected a note of sadness in her eyes.

"Mama, can I go see the new foal?" Emmie asked, tugging on Georgie's arm and dancing from foot to foot. "Please?"

"I'll take her," Jewel said then hesitated and glanced to Georgie. "If that's all right?"

"Fine by me." Georgie aimed a finger at her daughter. "Remember, you have to be quiet and calm. Don't stress the baby or her mother, young lady."

Emmie gave a dramatic groan. "I know. I know."

A bittersweet pang twisted in Tamara's chest as Emmie skipped out the back door with Jewel. Clay's niece was as precious and precocious as they come. She wished she could be around to see the girl grow up. But despite all she and Clay had shared in recent days, nothing had been said about her staying. Too many obstacles still stood in the way of making a go of their relationship this time. The past days had been a sweet diversion, an emotional walk down memory lane, but by Monday morning, she would be back in San Antonio, back in her lonely apartment, and burying her heartache in her job.

"Clay," Marie called as she came in from the backyard. "If we're going to use that table outside to eat, we'll need a big table-cloth. You have one big enough to fit?"

He stared at Marie as if she were speaking Greek then shrugged. "I have no idea. Anything I have would be in the closet by the mudroom, though, if you want to check."

"Let me do that," Tamara volunteered, glad for a task to occupy her and get her mind off all she'd miss, not being part of this family in the years to come.

"And a large platter for the meat?" Marie added.

Clay hitched his head toward the back hall. "Same place, if it's anywhere. In the kitchen, anything beyond a cereal bowl and the microwave is out of my domain."

Georgie snorted. "You're not kidding. I remember your attempts to cook before I took over to save us all from starva-tion." She hooked her arm in Tamara's. "Come on. I'll help you."

They made their way back to the large walk-in storage room at the back of the house, and Tamara pulled a dangling string to turn on the bare lightbulb overhead. "I can remember getting a large checkered tablecloth as a wedding gift. It's bound to be around here somewhere."

Assuming Clay didn't get rid of it when he got rid of every-thing else from their married life. An arrow of resentment shot through Tamara. The stripped-down, highly masculine version of the Bar None ranch house was a far cry from the warm home that was a blend of their personalities when they were married. One more reminder that Clay had moved on, had eliminated Tamara from his life.

"Holy cow! I'm afraid to move anything," Georgie said with a laugh as she looked around the crowded storage area. "Pull one thing, and the whole closet becomes an avalanche!"

Tamara roused from her dreary thoughts and blinked at the stuffed shelves and clutter-lined floors. "Good grief! How are we supposed to find anything? We never had this much in here when we were married."

"Cripes, when did my brother become a pack rat? He never used to keep so much stuff around."

Tamara appraised the miscellany, wondering where to begin. As her gaze traveled down the top shelf, a familiar pattern caught her eye. She gasped.

"What?" Georgie said, drawing her arms close to her chest. "Is it a spider? A roach?"

"My curtains," Tamara murmured as she reached for the top shelf. Intent on recovering her homemade window dressing, she ignored the pain that streaked through her when she stretched her arms above her head.

Pulling the dusty curtains down, she stroked a hand over them then clutched the folded material to her breast. Her mind buzzed, and her heart thumped a wild cadence. She lifted a stunned gaze to Georgie as tears pricked her eyes. "He kept them."

Georgie tipped her head and pulled at the cotton fabric to see what Tamara had found. "Hey, I remember these. They used to be in the kitchen. Didn't you make those in home economics class with Mrs. Akers or something?"

Tamara nodded, still shaken by her discovery. A more intentional scan of the storage closet revealed more surprises. Propped in the back corner were the lithographs she'd selected for the living room. On the shelf below the curtains, she found various knickknacks that had been conspicuously missing from the family room. And carefully boxed and stored on a bottom shelf were her dried flower arrangements.

Tamara's gaze darted from one item to the next, recognizing wedding gifts, high-school memorabilia and keepsakes from the first years of their marriage.

Clay had kept everything.

Right down to the tattered scrunchies she'd used to keep her hair back when she did her ranching chores. The tears that had threatened all day rose like a flash flood. With a choked sob, Tamara sank to the floor.

Georgie knelt beside her, concern creasing her brow. With a

cool hand, she pushed Tamara's long hair away from her face. "Tamara? What's wrong?"

"He saved it all. Everything. I thought he'd cut me out of his life, but he kept everything of mine." She blinked, clearing the puddle of moisture in her eyes. "Why would he do that?"

Georgie barked a laugh. "I'd think that was obvious. Certainly anyone who has seen the change in Clay these past few days wouldn't have to ask."

Tamara narrowed her gaze. "Changes?"

The redhead chuckled. "Heck, yeah. He's smiling again. Even at the funeral the other day, despite his polite somberness, he just seemed...happier. Whenever he looked at you, I saw a spark in his eyes that hasn't been there for five years. Today his grin is downright contagious."

Tamara frowned skeptically. "Because his family is here. He loves his family."

Georgie's shrug didn't deny Tamara's assertion. "Because you're here. He loves *you*."

Breath backed up in Tamara's throat. She tried twice to speak before any sound would come. "But if that's true..."

Her thoughts spun. As much as she wanted to believe Clay loved her, he hadn't said anything about his feelings for her. Even after they'd made love, the best he could say was that she was *special* to him. "But he hasn't given me any reason to think he wants anything to change. If he wanted me to stay and try again—" She hesitated.

What would she do if Clay asked her to stay, to give their relationship a second chance?

Georgie tugged on the curtains Tamara still held with a white-knuckle grip. "Here's your proof, crime lady. Clay only keeps things that are important to him. Do you really think these curtains matter to him because of the lovely print? No. He kept them because you made them. He kept them because you matter to him."

Hope fired in her soul, tempered by the logical side of her brain that needed hard evidence. Her pulse fluttered an uneven cadence, wavering between joy and denial.

"Just because he kept the things I chose for the ranch, doesn't mean he wants me back. Maybe he's saving them to give to charity. Or to give back to me. I left in a rush that night and never asked for any of the things from our marriage. I wanted a fresh start. It was easier to start over without painful reminders around me of what used to be."

"And why were the reminders painful?" Georgie asked, then plunged on before Tamara could answer. "Because you loved Clay, right?"

After a moment to consider how honest she could afford to be with Clay's sister, Tamara nodded slowly.

"So why would Clay be any different? He moved the reminders of you out of his sight, because he cared so much it hurt."

Georgie's argument made sense, but accepting it as truth meant turning everything she'd ever believed about Clay's attitude toward her on end, smashing every assumption she'd made about his cool reserve during the agonizing days of their divorce.

Georgie pulled a tissue from her pocket and wiped the moisture from Tamara's cheek before handing it to her.

Tamara blew her nose and gathered her thoughts. "So what do I do?"

"I think the only real question is whether you still have feelings for Clay and are willing to give him another chance." Georgie squeezed Tamara's hand and met her gaze with a probing scrutiny. "Do you love my brother? Will you stay, or are you going to leave him again?"

Tamara drew a shaky breath. "It's not that simple. I have a job I love in San Antonio."

"So? Nick loved his job with the Secret Service, but he loved me and Emmie more. He quit and moved to Esperanza to be close to us. But you don't have to quit. I mean, San Antonio is—what?—a half-hour to forty-minute drive? Big-city folks spend that much time in traffic or on a bus each morning. You *could* commute from the Bar None. It's doable."

Tamara blinked as the possibilities she hadn't let herself

consider began percolating, bubbling like champagne and lifting her hopes.

"Georgie? Tamara?" The sound of footsteps accompanied Meredith's call. "Did you get lost? Clay's afraid the closet swallowed you."

"In a way, it did," Tamara said under her breath. She dashed the tears from her eyes and schooled her expression just before Meredith appeared at the storage-closet door.

Clay's aunt wasn't fooled. "Oh, dear! You've been crying. What happened?"

"We're fine." Georgie pushed to her feet. "Just girl talk."

As Tamara blew her nose again, she saw Georgie mouth to Meredith, "Tell you later." Tamara lifted a corner of her mouth. In a big family there were few secrets. She couldn't begrudge them that, though. Families shared each other's travails because of the love they shared. To be included in the Coltons' circle of affection and acceptance after five years by herself...

Fresh tears welled, but Tamara quickly stanched the flow. Tapping the strength she'd developed to face a crime scene objectively, Tamara got herself back under control. She had plenty to think about, thanks to her discovery of the curtains and Georgie's angle on what the contents of the storage room meant.

A second chance with Clay? The idea both thrilled her and scared her silly.

Regardless of her interpretation or Georgie's, what mattered were Clay's feelings for her *now* and whether he wanted another chance to make things work. He still hadn't said that he loved her as Georgie claimed, and Tamara refused to make the mistake of assuming anything this time around. She needed hard evidence, not hearsay.

As she awkwardly climbed to her feet, she spotted the red and white checked tablecloth they'd been sent to retrieve at the back of a lower self. "Here it is. Not sure I would have seen it if I hadn't been at this angle."

Georgie gave her a knowing grin. "Amazing what you discover when you look at things from a new perspective, huh?"

With a long-handled spatula, Clay poked the coals in his barbecue pit and added another handful of mesquite chips to the fire. The woody scent of the smoke curled up around the slab of ribs he'd started slow-roasting a couple hours earlier, and Clay's mouth watered. Texas barbecue, in his opinion, was like nectar of the gods.

"Oh my, that smells great! Joe is going to be so sorry he missed this," Meredith said as she approached from the house. "The girls found the tablecloth." His aunt held the checkered cloth up as proof. She hitched her head toward the table. "Come help me with it, Clay?"

"Sure thing." He wiped soot from his hands on his jeans and strode over to the picnic table he and Tamara had set up that morning. Mention of his uncle Joe reminded Clay how Georgie had recently been falsely accused of threatening Joe Colton's bid for the presidency.

"How is Joe doing? Any more harassing e-mails or threats to his campaign?" Clay asked.

Meredith unfolded the tablecloth and flicked a corner to him. "Joe's in California, working, and no more threats, thank goodness! Maybe that terrifying chapter of this campaign is finally over. I'm so relieved. It was pretty scary to think someone was out to sabotage Joe's campaign—or worse, hurt Joe."

Clay nodded. "Scary for us, too. The fact that the threats have stopped supports the fact that the real culprit was Rebecca Totten, not Georgie. It was plenty nerve-racking at this end knowing Georgie's identity had been stolen to frame her for the campaign threats."

Meredith tsked and sent him a worried frown. "I can imagine. Poor Georgie." Together they shook out the table cover and smoothed out the wrinkles. "While it is great to see you and Georgie—and this barbecue was a wonderful idea—I guess you know the real reason I came to Esperanza."

He cast a quick glance toward the corrals where Jewel and Emmie were watching the horses. "I have a good idea."

"And how is my niece doing?" Meredith flipped her hand in inquiry.

"I've kept an eye on her like I promised."

His aunt smiled. "I knew you would. Is Jewel adjusting to Texas? Does she seem happy?"

Clay scratched his freshly shaved chin and decided how best to be honest without alarming Meredith. "She seems…content. When I ask how she is, she always assures me she is fine. Lately she's been bringing girls over to the Bar None to ride horses. The progress she is making with the girls clearly makes her happy. But…"

Meredith's gaze darkened. "But?"

"Well, I'm concerned she might be working too hard. She looks tired to me most of the time, as if she's not sleeping well or she's pushing too hard and doing too much."

"Have you mentioned it to her?" Meredith asked.

"I didn't feel like it was my place to get too personal, but whenever I've asked if I can do anything else to help her out, she's told me she's fine." He shrugged. "I don't know that she'd confide in me, though."

Shoulders drooping, Meredith replaced the salt and pepper shakers and stack of napkins she'd moved to cover the table. "Well, thanks for looking out for her. I feel better knowing she has you nearby." Her scowl deepened. "The poor girl has been through so much with the loss of her fiancé and baby. I can't help but worry."

Clay's chest constricted, remembering the conversation he'd had with Tamara concerning how devastating it'd be to lose the other. The possibility was too painful to consider.

Yet Jewel had lost the love of her life and her unborn child as well.

He sent another glance toward the corral where Emmie was bouncing excitedly on her toes, and Jewel smiled at the little girl wistfully. He prayed that someday Jewel would find someone to bring her the kind of happiness that Tamara gave him.

His heart stuttered.

Holding his breath, Clay replayed the last thought. Tamara made him happy. She made his life feel complete, meaningful. With an ache in his chest, Clay realized that come morning, Tamara would return to San Antonio, leaving him alone again.

As if mimicking his thoughts, a cloud passed in front of the June sun, casting a long shadow over the ranch.

"Clay, did you hear me?" Meredith touched his arm, jolting him from his melancholy musings.

"Huh, no. Sorry. What did you ask?"

"I said, how is Ryder? Have you heard from him? Written to him?"

His gut tensing with guilt, Clay's mood slipped another notch. He busied himself placing condiments and silverware on the table. "No. I haven't heard from Ryder since he went to prison."

"At all?" Meredith's dismay was clear in her tone.

Unable to meet her gaze, he shook his head. "I gave up trying to get through to him when he was arrested this last time. I had to accept that I'd failed my brother, that there is nothing else I can do for him now that he's in jail."

"Clay Colton!" Meredith's stern tone caught him off guard. He glanced up and met an equally chastising stare from his aunt. "I would have never pegged you for a quitter. Why, you didn't build this ranch from nothing by giving up when it got hard. Making the Bar None a success was a labor of love for you. And sometimes family relationships take the same effort and sacrifice. If you love your brother, he deserves better than for you to turn your back on him."

Clay sat on the end of the picnic table bench seat, stung by the truth of Meredith's rebuke. "I don't know what else to do for him."

"Love him. Let him know you are still there for him." She sighed and sat down across from him. Reaching for his hand, she added, "Don't forget, I had a sister who hurt and disappointed me, too. Now I wish I'd tried harder to reach out to her before it was too late. But it is not too late for you and Ryder. You've only failed when you quit fighting. Isn't your family worth fighting for?"

Meredith's question smacked Clay between the eyes.

He sat straighter, pulling his shoulders back as a tingle of fresh insight washed over his skin. "Of course they are."

No wonder he had such guilt regarding his brother. For a man who hated failure and worked his fingers to the bone making his ranch a success, his decision to walk away from Ryder, to quit fighting for the brother he loved went against everything he espoused.

"It's not too late for you to save your relationship with your brother. Regrets are a miserable companion, Clay." Meredith squeezed his fingers before getting up and heading toward the corral where Jewel and Emmie were patting the mares.

Resolve coalesced inside him. He had to reach out to Ryder again.

Why had he given up on his brother so easily? Did he hate the taste of failure so much that he'd chosen to abandon his brother rather than feel his continued efforts to reach Ryder were in vain? In truth, his real failure had come when he'd given up. His guilt was over his quitting, not his lack of success with Ryder. Clay removed his hat and plowed his fingers through his hair. He blew out a slow cleansing breath.

"You all right?"

He jerked his head up to see Tamara standing a few feet away, holding a bowl of Marie's potato salad. "Yeah, I just had an…enlightening talk with Meredith. She gave me a lot to think about."

Tamara's cheeks drained of some of their color. "About what?"

"Uncle Clay," Emmie called as she charged over and flopped against Clay's lap. "When do we eat? I'm a growin' girl, ya know. I need to eat to get bigger."

Clay ruffled her hair. "Well, by all means, let's eat then. I think everything's ready now. Wanna help me round the crew up?"

Emmie bounced on her toes. "Yeah!"

"We'll talk later," he told Tamara as his niece dragged him by the hand toward the house. She nodded, her eyes burrowing into him with a bright intensity.

"Race you!" Emmie shouted and took off.

As Clay broke into a jog behind the girl, a heart-stopping new thought filtered through his brain.

Had he given up too easily on his marriage and Tamara as well?

The question nagged him as his family gathered around the table and joined hands to say a blessing over the food. When he lifted his head at the end of Meredith's prayer, his gaze collided with Tamara's. Her eyes were red and her skin looked a little blotchy as if she'd been crying. He frowned and mouthed, "Are you all right?"

She twitched an uneasy grin and nodded as Nick tapped his fork on his glass to get everyone's attention. "Since we have all of you, our family and friends, gathered here today, Georgie and I decided this would be an excellent opportunity to make an announcement." Curious eyes turned toward the former Secret Service agent. "A few nights ago when we were discussing our plans for the future, Georgie and I—"

"You're getting married!" Emmie squealed excitedly, bouncing on her seat.

Georgie sent her daughter a wry grin. "Way to steal our thunder, Em."

"Then she's right?" Clay asked, dividing a glance between his sister and Nick.

A glow radiated from Georgie's face as she glanced to the man at her side and wrapped his hand in hers. Nick leaned over and gave her a kiss.

"Yes, we're getting married," Georgie said.

A collective cheer went up around the table, the most boisterous coming from Emmie.

"When? I want to be sure Joe and I are free to attend," Meredith asked.

"July." Nick stared into Georgie's eyes, and the love Clay saw in the man's face filled him with reassurance that his sister was in good hands.

Excited conversation buzzed around the table as dishes were passed and plates filled until Emmie stood up on her chair and waved her hands.

"Wait a minute. Wait a minute!" A look of horror washed over his niece's face.

The adults quieted.

"Emmie, what's wrong?" her mother asked.

"At the wedding," Emmie said, scrunching her nose in disgust, "will I have to wear a...dress?"

Laughter bubbled like champagne around the table.

Georgie shook her head. "Not if you don't want to, honey."

Chapter 16

On Sunday morning after a late breakfast together, Clay and Tamara went to the small nondenominational church where most of the citizens of Esperanza gathered faithfully each week. The peaceful setting, the inspiring sermon and the familiar hymns usually proved a respite for Tamara from her inner turmoil. That morning, though, she couldn't get out of her head the Akerses, the pending DNA test results on Billy's cigarette or the inevitable end of her stay at the Bar None.

"I want to take some of the extra food from the barbecue over to the Akerses this afternoon," she said on the drive back to the Bar None. "They weren't in church, and I'm worried about how they're doing."

Clay gave her an unreadable glance then nodded. "Sure. Give me a chance to check on the new colt and talk to my foreman about a couple things, and I'll drive you over later."

She smiled her appreciation then dug in her purse for her cell phone. Switching it back on after having it silenced for the service, she checked her messages.

Nothing.

"I'd hoped I'd have heard from Eric by now." She shoved the phone back in her purse and sighed. "I know he said he was busy but…"

"What will you do if the tests show that the hair your team found in the tunnel matches Billy's DNA?"

She turned to stare out the side window. "I hadn't let myself even think that far. I've been so busy praying I was wrong in my assumptions and suspicions." She angled her head to look across the front seat to him. "I'll have to turn him in to Jericho, I guess. What else could I do?"

"Maybe we should have told Jericho about the things Billy said at the funeral and your theories about his involvement."

She shook her head. "Not until we have proof. I could be totally misconstruing things Billy said, and he was drunk, after all."

Clay reached over and squeezed her shoulder. "Let's hope you're right."

When they got back to the ranch, Tamara gathered up the extra uncut apple pie she'd made for the barbecue, large helpings of smoked chicken, potato salad, baked beans and thick slices of Marie's homemade bread. She wrapped and packed all the food to take to the Akerses then checked her cell for messages again.

Still nothing.

Clay came in from the stables and did a double take when he saw all the food she'd fixed. "Don't you think they'll still have a full refrigerator from the funeral? Every family in town had to have brought a full meal's worth of chow."

"And now it's my turn. Besides, I hate to show up empty-handed."

Clay shrugged. "Whatever. Ready?"

She stowed her phone in her handbag, and he helped her load the food in his truck.

On the way to the Akerses, she checked her cell for messages twice more.

Clay chuckled. "You've heard the saying about a watched pot, haven't you?"

She jammed her phone in her purse again and twisted her mouth in a frown. "I know. I'd just feel better about this visit if I already knew Billy had been cleared."

As they pulled up to the Akerses' driveway, Tamara noticed a *for sale* sign in the front yard. She exchanged a dubious look with Clay. "Did Jack or Billy mention selling the house when you talked to them at the funeral?"

Clay opened the driver's door. "Naw. This is news to me."

They headed up the sidewalk as Billy came out the front door carrying a large box.

"Need a hand?" Clay asked, hurrying up to the porch to hold the door.

"I got it, thanks. What brings you folks by today?" Billy propped the box on the porch railing and wiped his brow with his arm.

"Well, we didn't see you at church this morning and thought we'd stop in to see if you were all right. And we brought food." Tamara lifted the pie toward Billy. "Made it myself. Well, with some help from Clay's housekeeper."

Billy arched an eyebrow. "Say, Brat, that looks good enough to eat. Thanks."

She returned a withering glance. "You're welcome. I think. Where should I put it?"

"Anywhere you find a spot. Go on in. I'll just put this in the car and be right back."

Clay held the door for Tamara, and she headed for the Akerses' kitchen, weaving through the collection of boxes, stacks of books, piles of clothes, and general clutter that had taken over the Akerses' home. Not only were the Akerses selling their house, they were packing their possessions as if their departure was imminent.

An uneasy jitter chased down Tamara's spine. Why were the Akerses leaving so abruptly, and where were they going? She didn't think she'd like the answer. She silently conveyed her concern to Clay with a meaningful glance.

He arched an eyebrow and mouthed, "Suspicious."

She bit her bottom lip and strode into the kitchen.

Jack Akers stood by the sink wrapping glasses in newspaper and packing them in a box. He sent Tamara a startled glance when she breezed in with the pie. "Tamara, uh, hi."

"I hope you like apple pie. And Clay's bringing in plates of barbecue." She forced a note of casual cheer in her voice.

Blinking, Jack set aside the glass he held. "Love apple pie, hon. Thank you."

Clay set the dinner plates on the counter next to the pie and offered his hand to Jack. Mr. Akers glanced at the ink on his fingers and shuffled his feet before shaking Clay's hand.

Tamara gestured around the room. Keeping her tone light and curious, not accusing, she asked, "Mr. Akers, what's all this?"

The man hesitated, blinking rapidly again, then turned his back on them. "It's, uh…Tess's things. We're just giving some of her stuff to charity."

Tamara glanced at Clay who, with a slight nod of his head, directed her attention to the box at her feet. Fishing trophies and hunting gear filled the plastic crate.

"Mrs. Akers didn't hunt, did she?" Tamara picked up a reel and turned it over, examining it.

Jack faced them, a puzzled look on his face. "No, why'd—" His gaze dropped to the fishing items, and color suffused his face. "That's, uh…"

Billy bustled back inside and met the deer-in-the-headlights expression on his father's face. "What's going on? Dad?"

Jack cleared his throat. "I was just telling Tamara and Clay that we're packing up a few of your mother's things to give away."

Billy drew his brow in a frown and narrowed a dubious gaze on Tamara. "That's right. And we're rather busy with it so…"

"Billy, we saw the *for sale* sign in the yard." She stepped closer to her friend and placed a hand on his arm. "Why would you move? You've lived in Esperanza your whole life. This town is your home."

Hands fluttering against his legs, he shrugged. "Maybe with Mom gone, Dad and I decided it was time to move on. See more of the country."

"But why not give it more time? Your mom *just* died. Don't make any rash decisions while you're still staggering from that loss. Wait a couple months and give yourself time to think it over."

Billy jerked his arm from her touch and paced across the room to start slamming his mother's cookbooks into a box. "No need to debate it, Brat. We've done all the thinking we need to. We want to make a fresh start. Now's as good a time as any."

Tamara exchanged a worried look with Clay. Clearly the Akerses meant to be packed and gone in a matter of days, maybe even hours. But why the rush? The obvious conclusion didn't bode well.

"Doc Mason apparently thinks Arizona is real nice. You might consider giving that area a try," Clay said casually.

Tamara tensed.

Billy paused mid-motion as he loaded another book in the box. He frowned and glanced at Clay then his father.

An awkward moment later, Jack scoffed loudly and slapped Clay on the back. "Naw, I'm tired of this heat. I'm ready for cooler summers and maybe a little snow at Christmas. I'm thinking Missouri, maybe Nebraska."

Billy went back to stacking the books, but his motions were stiff and jerky. He kept a wary eye on Clay as he worked.

"We'll miss you. You've been good friends for a lot of years. I hope you'll keep in touch." Tamara rubbed her hands on the seat of her jeans, looking for a way to break the tension in the room. Or was she only imagining the nerve-splitting vibes zinging around the Akerses' kitchen? She prayed the mood she detected was simply remnant grief, more of the odd reaction Jack and Billy had had to Tess's death.

Her phone jangled in the ensuing silence. Startled by the harsh ring, she flinched. Jolted with adrenaline, her hands shook, and her heart thumped. The eyes of the three men flew to her, as she fumbled to dig her phone from her purse.

Already heading for the hallway to take the call, she flicked the phone open quickly to stop the ringing.

"Tamara, I've got the results of those DNA tests on the cigarette you wanted," Eric boomed over the line before she could even say "Hello."

She stifled a groan, praying her boss's voice hadn't carried as much as she'd feared.

"Hi, Eric," she replied in a lower tone, hoping he'd follow suit. "Can I call you b—"

"It's a match. Same DNA as the hair from the tunnel," Eric blurted.

Because she was trying to cover the bad timing of the call, the news took a split second to register. When the significance of the results crashed down on her, she gasped. Instinctively her gaze flew to Billy's.

He stiffened and narrowed his eyes warily. Cast his father a warning look.

Too late she realized how telling her actions had been. In a fraction of a second, the damage had been done. She worked to school her face, hoping she could still smooth over her reaction somehow. Her mind scrambled.

"What's more, the fingerprints we lifted from the cigarette match the partial print that was on the trunk of the Taurus abandoned in your ex's pasture," Eric continued, snapping her attention back to the call.

"Oh, that's a relief!" She faked a smile and divided a quick glance between the men, gauging their reaction. "I'm so glad no one was hurt."

Clay's jaw tightened, and a muscle in his cheek twitched. Billy opened and closed his fists, shifting his weight as he kept a keen watch on her. Jack hung his head, his eyes closed and his shoulders drooping.

"Uh, Tamara? What are you talking about?" Eric asked. "Did you hear what I said about the prints?"

"Right, of course. Sounds like a close call."

"Someone's in the room with you?" Sure. *Now* Eric chose to lower his volume.

"Yeah."

"I've already called Sheriff Yates's office," her boss continued more quietly. "Figured he needed to know ASAP."

"Right. Thanks."

"And I'll see you back here at the lab in the morning, right?"

"Okay." She noted Billy's suspicious expression and Jack's dark look, and she added, "Tell Brenda accidents happen and not to blame herself. Give her my love. 'Bye."

She disconnected the call before Eric could respond and gave the room's occupants a forced grin. "My boss. He and his wife were in a fender bender. No one was hurt, but he needs us to come pick him up."

She met Clay's eyes, needing the reassurance of his steady composure. She drew a deep breath and headed back to retrieve her purse from the countertop where she'd left it. "Sorry we have to run."

Billy took a long step and blocked her path. In a flash, his arm snaked around her waist. Grabbing her wrist, he twisted her around and hauled her up against his chest. "Not so fast, Brat. Who was that on the phone? What did they tell you?"

"Get your hands off her," Clay growled. He took a threatening step toward Billy, his posture vibrating with barely harnessed violence.

With one hand clamped around her wrist, Billy dragged her back a couple steps and snatched open a cabinet drawer.

Black metal flashed in her peripheral vision.

"Stay back!" Billy yelled. "I swear, Colton. I'll pop her if you so much as blink."

Cold steel kissed her temple.

A gun.

Denials flooded her brain even as her knees buckled. Her childhood friend could *not* have a gun to her head. Not Billy. Not—

But the stark terror in Clay's eyes told the truth.

Bile rose in her throat, and she swallowed to shove down the bitter taste of fear.

Clay raised his hands, palms out. "All right. Easy."

"William!" Jack barked. "For God's sake, put that gun down now! You'll only make matters worse for yourself if you hurt the girl."

"No, Dad, I'm not gonna let them take me down. It was an accident!" Billy's grip on her wrist tightened, and pain shot up her arm as he wrenched it to an unnatural angle behind her. "An accident!"

"Wh-what was an accident?" Tamara kept her tone noncon-frontational, warning Clay to back off with her eyes. Her ex's face had blanched to a pasty gray. He wore an expression between rage and panic.

Billy scoffed. "I know you've figured it out, Tamara. I sus-pected as much as soon as Colton cracked that comment about Doc Mason liking Arizona."

"I didn't—" Clay started.

"Shut up!" The muzzle of Billy's gun jabbed harder.

Tamara's heart jolted, and her mouth dried.

Keeping his eyes fixed on her, Clay reached slowly for his hip and fumbled there. Did he have a weapon hidden under his shirt?

Please don't let him try something that will get him hurt.

"I think we all know Doc never made it to Arizona, so quit pretending. I heard your friend on the phone. You have some kinda DNA evidence against me, don't you?"

"Billy, I—" Tamara considered lying, but she didn't want to anger Billy further.

Jericho knew of the new evidence against Billy. Eric said he'd called it in. Surely the sheriff was on his way to arrest the Akerses' son even now. If she could just stall…

"Don't you?" Billy shouted, the gun in his hand poking harder.

"Billy, don't!" Clay gasped, lunging forward another step, desperation written in his dark eyes. "You said it was an accident. I'm sure if you explain that to the cops—"

"I ain't talking to the cops! If she's got proof I did it, they'll send me away for life. Maybe give me the chair." Raw fear rolled off Billy in waves. She heard it in his voice, felt it in the tremble in his hands, smelled it on his skin.

Frightened, trapped criminals reacted much like cornered animals. They could panic. Be unpredictable. Turn deadly in a second.

"Tell me what happened, Billy. Maybe we can find a way out for you." She forced calm into her tone, hoping to defuse the situation.

"It was my fault," Jack said, tears in his voice. "I asked Doc to help Tess. I begged him to end her suffering."

Clay scowled and glanced at the senior Akers. "Assisted suicide."

Jack squeezed his eyes shut, and fat tears rolled down his face. "Yes. I couldn't stand to see my Tess ravaged by that horrid disease."

Shaking his head, Clay glanced back at Billy. "Doc would never—"

"He didn't. He told Dad *no*." Disgust soured Billy's tone. "Until we offered him money."

Tamara gasped, remembering the money that had been in the trunk of the Taurus. "A hundred thousand dollars."

"That's right. He sure enough paid attention when we produced that cash. Said it'd come in handy to pay for some swanky rehab place in Arizona he wanted to go. Seems Doc got himself addicted to pain pills after he hurt his back last fall."

Clay's face registered recognition, acceptance. At least parts of Billy's explanation rang true for her ex, even if that truth was hard to hear.

"But Tess only died a couple days ago. And Doc…" Clay looked to Jack now, confusion knitting his brow.

"He backed out once he got the money, the sorry thief," Jack grumbled. "He took off with the cash we gave him and headed out of town."

Billy's grip on her arm had slackened. But the gun at her head still posed the most immediate threat. She listened to the Akerses explain their actions while she mulled possible means of disarming and subduing Billy. He was desperate, and their friendship would mean little if he thought she'd betrayed him, if he panicked and tried to escape.

"Even before Mama got sick, we didn't have that much money," Billy picked up the tale. "As it is, we cashed in most of my account and Dad's retirement savings to get Doc the money he wanted. I couldn't just let him take off out of town with all our money!" Billy's breathing grew more rapid and shallow. Tamara felt his hands shake harder. "So I followed him. He must have been stoned that night 'cause his driving was erratic. He was all over the road, and he finally veered off across your pasture. When he crashed into those mesquite trees, I thought that might be the end of it." Billy sighed, and the gun wavered.

Tamara glanced at the Akerses' kitchen clock, trying to gauge how long it would take the sheriff to arrive. *Please, God, let Jericho be on the way!*

"I figured I could just confront him, scare him. I'd get our money back and that'd be the end of it." Regret tinged Billy's tone.

Jack wiped a hand down his face and heaved a ragged sigh. "Oh, Lord, it wasn't supposed to end like this. It was all just an accident, Tamara. Really."

Clay had a sharp eye on Billy's gun, but he coaxed, "What went wrong?"

"I grabbed a knife when I went after him." He waved the gun toward the butcher block on the counter.

Tamara saw Clay stiffen as if getting ready to pounce on Billy now that the gun wasn't aimed at her head. She caught his eye and gave her head a subtle shake. She wanted Billy's full confession. Wanted to keep him distracted until help could arrive. "But you never intended to hurt Doc, did you, Billy?"

"Of course not! I'm not a murderer! I only wanted to scare him, make him give the money back. But he tried to grab the knife from me, and we struggled. Like I said, he musta been stoned 'cause he was really unsteady on his feet and, well, he fell." Billy's grip tightened again, and his rapid breathing told Tamara how reliving the nightmarish events stressed him. Billy's voice sounded choked, and she knew without looking that he was crying. "H-he stumbled and fell. He landed on the knife."

"You see," Jack pleaded, his hands spread in appeal. "It wasn't Billy's fault! My boy's not a murderer. It was all just a tragic accident!"

"Why didn't you call the police?" Tamara asked. "You could have told them the truth."

"What truth? That we'd bribed the doctor to help my mother die? That I'd brought a knife along to scare the man into giving our money back?" Billy scoffed. "Not stuff I wanted to admit to, Brat."

"Better than murder charges," Clay said.

Billy tensed and swung the gun toward Clay.

Tamara sucked in a sharp breath, fear for Clay turning her blood to ice. "No! Billy, just put the gun down. Please! Don't make things any worse for yourself."

"They're already worse." The gun moved back to her temple. "Thanks to you." He scoffed. "As a kid, you were always running to tattletale to our parents and getting your brother and me in trouble. And you couldn't leave this alone either. I saw you pick up my cigarette the other day at the funeral. I knew you were up to something. That's why Dad and I were getting out of town. I knew it was only a matter of time." Billy huffed his frustration and shoved the gun against her head. "If I'm going down for murder, I at least oughta make it worth my trouble. What do ya say, *Brat?*"

"William, stop this now!" Jack sobbed. "Let her go. Please."

"I'd covered my tracks," Billy grated as if not hearing his father. "I hid Doc's body in a tunnel I remembered playing in as a kid, wiped up the car, even faked a call to his switchboard to make people think he'd gone out of town. I had everything under control…" He grunted, and his grip on her wrist wrenched tighter.

A lightning ache flashed up to her shoulder. She gritted her teeth against the pain.

"If you went after the money, why did you leave it in the trunk of the Taurus?" Clay asked, edging a step closer.

Tamara held her breath, trying to signal Clay not to try anything that could backfire. *Where was Jericho?*

"After I moved Doc's body to that old tunnel, I heard something. Thrashing or crashing. And something sounded like voices."

Clay nodded. "Probably when my neighbor came to investigate the commotion he'd heard and found a steer caught in the fence wire."

Billy harrumphed. "I thought I'd been found out, and I panicked. I just wanted to get the hell outta there. I was already home by the time I realized the money was still out there. I'd planned to go back the next night after it was dark to get the money, but by then the cops were already crawling all over the scene. The money was in police custody.

"Then when I saw you at Doc Mason's clinic, and you said you'd fallen in a hole on Clay's property…" He groaned. "I knew I had to move the body. I went straight out there, wrapped it in a sheet to move it. Buried it in a shallow grave out by the landfill."

Clay rubbed a hand down his face. "Doc deserves a decent burial. Do you think you can find the place again?"

Billy jerked a nod.

Jack wiped his face on a sleeve. "When he told me, I… I didn't know what to do. Billy's my son. I love him and had to protect him. I… It's my fault. I started this mess when I asked Doc to help Tess die. I never thought…" He sniffed and turned away.

Billy drew a long deep breath and muttered a curse. "I'm sorry, Dad. I let things get out of control. I only wanted to help. Only wanted to get the money back—"

A knock from the front door reverberated through the house.

Billy jerked. Tamara could feel every muscle in his body stiffen and vibrate with tension.

Then Jericho's voice rang loud and strong. "Open up, Akers! Sheriff's Department!"

Chapter 17

Before Clay could register relief that backup had arrived, all hell broke loose.

Billy panicked. His face flushed with rage.

"No! I'm *not* going down for this! It was an *accident!*" Hauling Tamara up against his body with an arm across her throat and the gun at her head, he stumbled back a step toward the door.

Stark cold terror flooded Clay's veins. He needed the sheriff and his service revolver in here—now!

"Jericho!" Clay shouted. "In the kitchen! He has a gun!"

"Damn you," Billy hissed, his eyes narrowed to snakelike slits. "Damn both of you!" He dragged Tamara back another step, his gaze flickering restlessly around the room. "I won't let you do this to me!"

Tamara's eyes bulged as she gasped for air against his stranglehold. Her fingers scrabbled at Billy's arm, trying to loosen his grip.

Her gaze found Clay's, and the pleading in her expression raked his heart with sharp claws. Until now, he'd given Billy a wide berth because of his weapon and Tamara's signals to proceed with caution. But the stakes had changed.

Caution be damned.

He wouldn't stand by and let Akers hurt his wife. He'd lost Tamara once when he'd been foolish enough to let her walk away. When he'd deferred to what he thought she wanted years ago, he lost everything that mattered. But this time, he would do what he had to. He'd take the necessary risk to save the woman he loved. Clay would rather die than let anyone use Tee as a human shield.

The front door opened with a crash.

Billy bolted for the back door, hauling Tamara in his wake. "Let me go, or I swear I'll kill her!"

Tamara's lips were turning blue. She didn't have time for Clay to hesitate.

Billy shifted his attention for a split second to find the doorknob behind him.

And Clay pounced.

Seizing the muzzle of the gun, he swung it toward the ceiling. As he lunged forward, his momentum and weight brought Billy and Tamara crashing to the floor with him in a tangled heap. The gun went off. Tamara screamed. Adrenaline pumped through Clay, numbing him to all but defending his woman.

With all his strength, he battled Billy for possession of the gun, struggling to keep the weapon aimed away from them. He'd wrestled calves into submission at the rodeo that put up less fight. But Tamara's life had never been on the line before. He wouldn't fail her. Couldn't lose her.

Moments later, the weight of another body crushed him to the floor. A third pair of hands joined the fight for control of the pistol. Clay took an elbow in the jaw, a knee in the gut, but he held on. The rodeo had taught him how to handle pain and keep going.

"Drop the weapon! Lie on your stomach with your hands on the floor!" a voice repeated over and over.

"It was an accident!" Billy screamed.

"Stop fighting. It's over, Billy. You're under arrest," Jericho grated, and Clay realized the sheriff was responsible for the added body and subduing hands.

"Billy, don't get yourself killed over this! Please stop!" Jack Akers begged. "It's too late to change things now."

As if someone had drained the life out of him, Billy grew still. With a scuffle of hard-soled shoes, Jericho's deputies surrounded them and snapped handcuffs on Billy's wrists.

Clay groaned and rolled aside. Every muscle in his body hurt.

Lifting his head, he searched frantically for Tamara. "Tee?" he rasped. He spotted her sitting a few feet away in the mudroom. She stared at him with wide blue eyes and tears streaming down her cheeks.

Joints aching, he half crawled, half dragged himself toward her. She lunged forward and landed in his arms. "Clay! Oh, thank God. I was so scared you were… I thought the shot…"

"I'm all right." He clasped her against his chest.

As Jericho dragged Billy to his feet and a deputy read the Akerses their rights, Clay met the sheriff's eyes. "Did you get all that?"

Jericho patted the cell phone clipped to his hip. "Every word."

Relief spun through Clay, and he pressed a kiss to Tamara's head.

Thank God she was all right. Clutching her tighter, he held her close—with no intention of ever letting her go.

"Once you've read over your finalized statements and signed them, you're free to go," Jericho told them hours later at the sheriff's office.

Tamara chafed her arms. A chill she couldn't blame on the air conditioner had settled deep in her bones.

Beside her, Clay scribbled his name at the bottom of the typed statement he'd given Sheriff Yates regarding everything the Akerses had said and done this afternoon. "What's going to happen to Billy now?"

Tamara sighed and signed her statement. Her childhood friend's future was grim. A trial. A jury. Almost certain jail time, even if he worked out a plea agreement with the district attorney's office. Jack would face much the same, thanks to his silence. What he'd done out of fatherly concern and protection made him an accomplice in the eyes of the law.

Jericho shrugged and stroked a hand over his mustache. "They've got a good lawyer. Beyond that, it'll be up to the courts."

Tamara slid her signed statement across the desk to Jericho. Compunction pressed down on her. Knowing evidence she'd gathered would be key in convicting Billy and Jack weighed heavily in her thoughts.

Clay reached for her hand and squeezed her fingers. "Hey, Miss Long Face, they brought this on themselves. They had ample opportunities to come clean about what happened with Doc Mason and earn themselves some leniency. Instead they tried to cover it up, and their trouble snowballed."

"I have to wonder…" when Clay stroked the inside of her wrist with his thumb, Tamara almost forgot the question on her tongue "…why Doc was in a stolen car that night?"

Jericho grunted and crossed his arms over his chest. "Good question. We may never know for sure, but best we can figure, he'd already decided he was going to take off with the Akerses' cash and head for Arizona. In case the Akerses reported him, he didn't want to be in his own car. Guess he thought the stolen car would give him anonymity a while longer. But if he was hopped up on drugs as Billy claims, there's no telling what his warped reasoning was."

Clay shifted uneasily in his chair, shaking his head. "I should have realized there was more to his odd behavior and shaky hands than just fatigue. He denied anything was wrong, and I believed him. If I'd been a better friend—"

"Clay, he hid his addiction from a lot of people," Jericho countered. "Easy to do when you live alone like Doc did. From what Dr. O'Neal and his nurse told us earlier when we questioned them, they only learned of the addiction recently themselves when drugs started disappearing from the locked narcotics cabinet at the office."

Tamara raised her gaze to Jericho's. "That's what I overheard them talking about the day I was at the clinic."

He nodded. "I'd say so. O'Neal said he was trying to keep his suspicions on the down low to protect Doc Mason and the clinic's reputation. Dr. O'Neal was buying into the practice, planning to take over for Doc when he retired. He was afraid of how revelations of the lead doctor's drug addiction might affect the negotiations and the insurance company's willingness to cover them for malpractice."

Clay tapped his Stetson back and scratched his head. "That's why they were so jumpy when we asked questions about Doc's whereabouts."

Jericho quirked an eyebrow. "Likely. They did mention they were afraid all the questions about his long absence were related to a drug investigation. They truly believed he was in Arizona, getting clean."

Deputy Rawlings approached the sheriff and handed him a sheet of paper. "Sheriff, this just came in. Thought you'd want to see it."

"Thanks."

While Jericho scanned the report he'd been handed, Tamara and Clay exchanged a long look. He squeezed her hand again, and she sent him a tremulous smile.

She had so much she wanted to tell Clay once they were alone. When she'd had Billy's gun at her head, thinking she could die at any moment, her main concern had been for Clay. She'd seen the damage a gunshot wound could do at point-blank range. If Billy had shot her, the sights and sounds for Clay would have been nightmarish. She shuddered at the thought, and Clay's eyes darkened with concern.

Jericho glanced up. "This is the autopsy report on Tess Akers. ALS didn't kill her. She had a massive heart attack."

Turning her attention to Jericho, Tamara digested the news with a heavy heart. "It's just as well she died when she did. Learning of Billy's part in Doc Mason's death and his attempts to cover it up would have devastated her. At least she was spared that grief."

"Or *did* she find out and the stress of it brought on the heart attack?" Jericho suggested.

Tamara gasped, and her chest squeezed at the possibility.

Clay glanced from Tamara to Jericho and scowled. "You couldn't have just kept that theory to yourself?"

Jericho winced and raised a palm. "Sorry. Guess I'd better get back to it. Lots of paperwork to do before I go home tonight."

Clay shook his hand. "Thanks for everything. I hate to think what could have happened if you hadn't shown up when you did."

"Well, we were already on the way over after talking to Tamara's lab about the tests they'd run. But thanks to your smart thinking and that cell phone trick, we knew the volatile situation we were facing when we arrived, knew the urgency of getting to the Akerses quickly."

Tamara scowled. "What cell phone trick?"

Jericho grinned and shuffled away. "I'll let your ex explain."

She tilted her head and gave Clay a querying glance.

"Jericho was the last person I'd talked to before we headed to the Akerses. I had my cell clipped on my belt as usual, so when I saw how things were getting out of hand with Billy, I punched redial and left the line open. Jericho heard everything Billy said, knew what was going down in the Akerses' kitchen."

A grin warmed her face. "I always knew you were smart."

He touched the brim of his hat. "Why, thank ya kindly, ma'am." He slid his lips into a lopsided grin. "Shall we go home?"

Home.

A rock settled in her stomach, and her smile faded. She wished she could consider the Bar None her home again. But the simple truth was, she no longer belonged there. She may have made love to Clay, but he'd never said he loved her. She may have indulged in a walk down memory lane these past several days, but her future didn't include Clay. Not if his attitude toward their relationship and his feelings for her hadn't changed.

She ducked her head and stared at her fidgeting hands. "Yeah, I should go home. To my apartment in San Antonio."

Clay didn't answer. Didn't move.

Finally she mustered the courage to meet his penetrating dark

and I knew there was a good chance I'd lose the ranch and not be able to provide for you. You'd already spent too much of your life doing without, and I was so afraid of failing you."

She opened her mouth to counter his statement, but he placed a finger over her lips. "I believed you'd want more than me and the ranch one day, and so I was afraid to give you my whole heart. I pulled away, built a wall to protect myself."

She released a huff of frustration. "But that distance, that wall was what made me feel I didn't matter. You stopped saying you loved me, stopped asking for my input, stopped sharing your innermost thoughts with me. I felt alone, lost. When you withdrew from me, what else was I supposed to think but that you didn't care anymore? Especially when you didn't do anything to fight the divorce."

Conviction flared in his eyes, and his jaw tightened. "Not fighting for you was the biggest mistake of my life. Like with Ryder, I didn't fight, because I thought I'd already lost you." He plowed his fingers into her hair, and his dark gaze drilled into hers. "But my real failure was in letting you walk away without telling you how much I wanted you to stay. I did love you, Tee, but I was afraid my love wasn't enough for you."

Her heart tripped. "Clay…"

"All I ever wanted for you was your happiness. I thought leaving the ranch and following your dreams was what would make you happy. That's why I let you go."

A tear spilled onto her cheek. "All I really wanted was your love, to feel I mattered to you as much as the ranch. That I was important to you."

His fingers curled against her skull, and he pulled her face down to his. "*Nothing* is more important to me than you," he rasped.

His warm breath teased her lips, sent a wave of longing rippling through her.

"The past few days," Clay murmured, "I've learned that sometimes you can make painful choices—even difficult sacrifices—for all the right reasons, for the good of the people we love, but the decision is still wrong. You can make mistakes even when you have the best of intentions."

She closed her eyes and sighed. "Like the Akerses. They wanted to spare Tess the pain and deterioration of her ALS, but went about it all wrong. One bad choice led to another until they'd created a nightmare for themselves."

"Tamara, tell me it's not too late to try again. Forgive me for not fighting for you, for ever letting you think I didn't love you. I'll do whatever it takes to win you back."

Fresh tears streamed from her eyes, and she pressed a kiss to his lips. "You don't have to win me, Clay. I've always been yours."

"But what about your job? I don't want you to give up your career. You're good at forensics, and it's obvious what it means to you."

"My work *is* important to me, but not as important as you. I love you, Clay Colton, with all my heart. I'd give up my job to be with you."

Clay pulled back and scowled. "Tee, you can't."

She interrupted him with a kiss. "I'm not! I'm just saying I *would.* For you." She smiled broadly and ran her fingers through his hair. "As your very wise sister pointed out, San Antonio is close enough for me to commute. I can live on the ranch *and* keep my job with the CSI."

A seductive grin spread across his face. "Then you're staying?"

"All I need is to know you love me, and you want me in your life again."

His mouth opened then closed. Without warning, he shifted her off his lap and dropped to one knee in front of her. "Tamara Brown, I've loved you since high school, and my love is deeper now than ever. I've made some terrible mistakes in the past that hurt you, and for that, I'm truly sorry. I promise never to let another day pass without telling you, without showing you how important you are to me."

Joy like golden rays of sunshine spread its warmth through her. If his words weren't enough to convince her of how he felt, the passion and sincerity that shone in his espresso eyes vanquished any lingering doubt. But he wasn't finished.

"The past five years without you have been the darkest of my life, Tee, and I want nothing more than to have you back on the Bar None with me. I want to ride the range with you and make babies with you and grow old with you. Will you marry me…again?"

The eager anticipation that lit his face tugged her heart. Did he really think she could say no to a proposal like that? "Well…" She fingered the collar of his shirt and angled a coy glance at him. "Do you think you have a place at this masculine ranch for my dry flower arrangements and homemade curtains?"

He caught the hand that toyed with his shirt and pulled her close for a kiss. "Absolutely and forever."

She leaned into his broad chest and stole another kiss. "Then, yes, I'll marry you…again."

Her cowboy's eyes were suspiciously damp as he drew her into his arms. "Welcome home, Tee."

* * * * *

THE SHERIFF'S
AMNESIAC BRIDE

BY
LINDA CONRAD

Linda Conrad was inspired by her mother, who gave her a deep love of storytelling. "Mum told me I was the best liar she ever knew. That's saying something for a woman with an Irish storyteller's background," Linda says. Winner of many awards, including the *RT Book Reviews* Reviewers' Choice and a Maggie, Linda has often appeared on the Waldenbooks and BookScan bestseller lists. Her favourite pastime is finding true passion in life. Linda, her husband and KiKi, the dog, work, play, live and love in the sunshine of the Florida Keys. Visit Linda's website at www.LindaConrad.com.

Chapter 1

Uh-oh. Big trouble.

"Shut up, lady." One of the two men in the front seat swung his arm over the seat back and smacked her across the cheek. "You're in no spot to argue. You say you can't remember? Well, that ain't my problem."

The driver didn't turn around, but muttered, "When we get back, the boss'll make you talk. And he won't be as nice as we are. You took something that didn't belong to you, and that's a no-no."

"But…but I really can't remember." She rubbed at her stinging cheek. "I don't even know who I am." Tears welled up and she fought the panic that was quickly crawling up her spine. She didn't dare cry. Hardly dared to breathe.

Caught in an internal struggle for clarity, she'd been trying to bring up memories from her past. She was desperate to remember anything at all. Even her own name escaped her, and it had been this way for what seemed like hours.

Where there should've been something, there was a huge void. Darkness. A little pain. But nothing even vaguely familiar.

She didn't have a clue as to why these men had forced her into the backseat of this speeding car. Or where on earth they were heading. Everything out the window seemed as alien as everything in her mind. She didn't know what she was doing here. Or who these horrible men were who kept insisting she tell them where "it" was.

The only thing she did know was that these two goons were carrying guns. Big ones. They'd waved them at her when she tried to tell them she couldn't remember.

Oh, God, help her. She was going to die if something didn't give soon.

Putting her hands together, she silently prayed for a break. Some way of escaping this car and these two men.

As if God had answered her prayer directly, a church spire appeared out the front windshield. The car slowed.

"What the hell is all this traffic about?" The driver sounded irritated as he slammed his foot on the brake. "It ain't Sunday, damn it. Get out of our way, you idiots!"

Oh please, let me find a way out, she silently begged. Let this be the time. Let this be a place where I can find sanctuary and someone who will save a desperate woman with no memory.

Then, quietly, an answer came to her from out of the emptiness in her mind. *The Lord helps those who help themselves.*

Sheriff Jericho Yates glanced up toward the Esperanza Community Church steps looming directly ahead and slowed his pace. He wasn't chickening out of his own wedding, but there was truly no sense in getting there before the bride-to-be would be ready to start.

"You're sure you want to go through with this, bro?" Fisher, his older brother and the best man, slowed his steps too.

With a serious face but eyes that always seemed to be laughing behind his sunglasses, Fisher Yates, U.S. Army captain home on leave, rarely showed any emotion. But at the moment, it was Fisher who looked panic-stricken by the thought of this wedding.

"Hell, yes, I'm going through with it," Jericho muttered as an answer. "I gave Macy my word. But I don't want to piss her off by showing up too soon. We've been best friends ever since I can remember, and I couldn't hurt her feelings by embarrassing her like that."

"Well, I remember when there were three of you best friends—back in the day. You and Macy and Tim Ward. I thought the whole idea of two guys and a gal hanging out and being so close was a little weird at the time. And sure enough, it was Macy and Tim that eventually got hitched. So what were *you* all those years? The dorky third wheel?"

Jericho straightened his shoulders under the weight of his rented tux and rammed his hands into his pockets. He would not let Fisher get to him today. His slightly shorter big brother, who was only just now back from his third tour of duty in the Middle East, could be a pain in the ass. But Jericho felt he needed to make allowances for Fisher—for possible psychological problems. Or whatever.

He opened his mouth to remind Fisher that the three of them, he and Tim and Fisher, too, had all been half in love with Macy in high school. But then, Jericho thought better of jamming the truth in his brother's face right now. Tim had been the one to win the prize. Jericho also remembered that Fisher had taken off in a hurry to join the army after Macy picked Tim to marry—and his brother had never looked back once.

"No," Jericho finally answered, forcing a grin. "I was the best friend and glad about my buddies hooking up and being happy together. I was also the friend who stood by Macy when Tim got sick and died six years ago. And today, I'm the friend who's going to marry her and give Tim's teenage son a new father."

"Yeah, you are. And right friendly of you, too, bro. But as you said earlier, you and Macy aren't in love. What's the real deal? I'm not buying this friendly daddy-stand-in story."

Jericho wasn't sure he could explain it to someone like Fisher, a guy who'd never had anybody depending on him—except, of course, for the men in his squad. Well, okay, his brother probably would understand loyalty and honor, but not when it came to women or kids or best friends. Fisher had never let any of those things into his life.

"The real story is that I'm not *in* love with Macy...."

"You said that already."

"But…I do love her and want the best for her. And that kid of hers and Tim's already seems like family to me. I'm his godfather, and I think I can make a bigger difference to his life as his stepfather. I mean to try."

T.J. was the foremost reason Jericho had been so determined to go through with this wedding when Macy had brought up the subject. As kids, Fisher and he had done without a mother after theirs had abandoned them. But they'd had the firm hand of a father to raise them right. As a tribute to his dad, Buck Yates, still by far the best father in the world, Jericho would bring T.J. into the family and do for him what Buck had done for his two sons. Give T.J. the greatest start possible.

"Act like a best man, why don't you, and just shut up about love and real stories." He poked Fisher lightly on his dress-uniformed arm. "We need to waste a few more minutes out here, bro. If you've gotta keep yakking at me, tell me what your plans are for after your leave is over."

Just inside the Community Church, waiting behind closed doors in the vestibule with her maid of honor, Macy Ward fidgeted with her dress. "What do you think everyone in town will have to say about me wearing off-white? Maybe I should've worn a light blue dress instead."

The dress was of no consequence, but Macy didn't want to say what she really had on her mind. Her maid of honor, Jewel Mayfair, was also her boss. And although she really liked Jewel, being too honest in a case like this might not be the best idea. Even though Macy was about to be married, she still needed the job.

So as devastated as she felt by the nasty looks she'd received from Jericho's brother at the rehearsal last night, and as much as she would love to pour her heart out to another woman as kind as Jewel, she would instead keep her mouth firmly shut on the subject of Fisher Yates. Anyway, he was about to become her brother-in-law. So the two of them would just have to find a way of getting along.

But Macy felt nervous and jittery about more than just an irritating old boyfriend in uniform. She was dwelling on something much more important. Her son T.J. had been giving her fits over this upcoming marriage. He'd said he didn't want anyone to take his father's place. Though her boy liked Jericho well enough, and eventually Macy felt sure he would come to love and respect the man as much as the rest of the town.

What was not to love? Jericho Yates was the best man she knew. He was kind, loyal and so honest it almost hurt her heart. His honesty had recently made her feel guilty because she had not been absolutely honest with him or anyone else in such a long time.

"What's wrong, Macy? You don't look happy. You should be ecstatic. Today's your wedding day."

"I'm okay, Jewel. Honest. It's just…" She decided to confide in her boss, at least a little. "Jericho and I aren't in love. Not like a man and woman who are about to be married are supposed to be."

"No? But then why get married?"

"My son." Macy plopped down in the nearest chair, disregarding the possible wrinkles to her dress. "T.J. needs a father badly. And Jericho will make such a great dad. I'm the one who convinced our poor county sheriff to take pity on an old friend and do me the honor. I knew he would never tell me no."

"But now you're having second thoughts?"

"Second, third and fourth thoughts actually. I'm about to ruin a good man's life and saddle him with a wife he doesn't love and a kid who's a handful.

"I like Jericho," she added hastily. "A lot. I don't know if I can do this to him."

Jewel knelt on the carpet beside Macy's chair and spoke quietly. "If you ask me, he'll be getting the best part of the deal. You don't seem to understand how really beautiful and special you are, and I'm not sure why you don't get it. You're a terrific mother and a fine employee. I'm both your boss and your maid of honor, a double threat at the moment. So I'm the one who's here to remind you of what everyone else already knows. If you decide not to go through with this wedding, it'll be Jericho's loss, not yours."

Macy's eyes clouded over with unshed tears, but she bit them back. Jewel had become the dearest friend. But when everything was said and over, Macy just could not go through with this sham wedding. At least not today.

"Jewel, will you back me up if I postpone the wedding?"

Jewel put an arm around her shoulders. "Sure, honey. But why don't you go out and talk to Jericho about it first? Maybe you can catch him on his way in."

"Come with me?"

"All right. But we'd better hurry. The guests are already arriving. There's a major traffic jam outside."

* * *

Outside under the cottonwoods and next to the church, standing with his brother Fisher beside him, Jericho had been biding his time. He turned when he heard someone calling his name.

"Sheriff Yates!" The voice was coming from his deputy Adam Rawlins.

Jericho watched as the man he'd hired not long ago hurried toward him. Adam was dressed in his full deputy's uniform because he'd been on duty today and hadn't planned on attending the wedding. Rawlins was a good man who had come to them with terrific references from a deputy job in Wyoming. And Jericho was mighty glad to have found him.

"Sheriff, we've got ourselves a traffic tie-up out here on the highway. Someone called it in and I thought I'd better come over and direct traffic."

Geez. The entire county must be planning on attending his wedding. Who all had Macy invited? He'd left the plans up to her because he'd been so busy for the last few weeks. What with that case of identity theft a while back and then an actual dead body and a murder investigation out on Clay Colton's ranch that had just been put to bed, the sheriff's business was booming lately.

"All right, deputy," he told Rawlins. "Thanks for the quick thinking. I'll be out of pocket here for a few more hours and then I can help you out."

The deputy nodded and raced back toward the highway, apparently all ready to set out traffic cones and organize traffic lanes.

"Aren't you and Macy going on a honeymoon, bro?"

Fisher laid a hand on Jericho's arm, reminding him of his presence and of the upcoming nuptials.

Jericho winced and shook his head. "Not funny, bubba. You already know the answer to that. Besides, Macy and I are planning on spending some quality time with T.J. over the next few days. I thought I might take him hunting like Dad used to do for us. I hear the wild boar hunting has been good up on the north Gage pasture."

"Yeah, wild boar hunting the day after your wedding does sound romantic." Fisher scowled and rolled his eyes.

Jericho shook off his brother's sarcastic comments. He didn't care what Fisher or anybody thought of this marriage to his best friend. Macy was a great lady and a great friend, and Jericho vowed to do right by her and her son—regardless of anyone else's opinion.

Still twisting her hands in the backseat and waiting for a good opportunity, the woman with no past and a questionable future bit her lip and stared out the car's window. There was so much traffic here. Surely one of the people in these other cars would see her predicament and come to her aid.

"Son of a bitch, the traffic's even worse now." The car wound down to a crawl as the driver turned around again to speak to her. "Don't get smart, lady. You call out or make any noises like you need help and we'll shoot you. I don't give a rat's damn if that special item the boss wants is ever found or not. The choice between you giving us the answer and you never being able to answer again ain't nothing to me.

"You got that?"

She nodded, but the movement seared a line of fiery pain down her temple. Another couple of pains like that and she might rather be dead anyway.

"Terrific," the goon sitting shotgun said. "Just look at that, will ya? A local smoky. Out in the middle of the highway, directing traffic. Crap."

"What's going to happen, Arnie?" The man in the passenger seat was beginning to sweat.

"We're not doing anything wrong," Arnie answered with a growl. "We're regular citizens just driving down the road. Nothing to worry about. Stash your gun under the seat until we pass him by."

The driver bent and buried his own gun, then twisted back to her. "Remember, sis. No funny stuff. I swear, if you call out, you're dead."

Shaking badly, she wondered if her voice would work anyway. But right then, the miracle she'd prayed for happened. Their car came to a complete stop, almost directly in front of the church.

She bit her lip and tried to guess whether it would be closer for her to head for the sanctuary of the church or to run for the policeman in the street ten car-lengths away. The truck in front of them inched ahead and she decided to break for the church—it was her only real choice.

For a split second she stopped to wonder if she might be the kind of person who made rash decisions and who would rather fight back than die with a whimper. But then, whether out of fear or out of instinct, she knew it didn't matter.

If she were ever going to find out what had happened to her in the first place, she would have to go. Now.

* * *

Jericho heard a popping sound behind his back. Spinning around, he scanned the area trying to make out where the noise had originated.

"Was that a gunshot?" Fisher asked, as he too checked out the scene in front of the church.

In his peripheral vision, Jericho spotted a woman he'd never seen before. A woman seemingly out of place for a wedding, dressed in fancy jeans and red halter top. And she was racing at top speed across the grass straight in his direction. What the hell?

Another pop and the woman fell on the concrete walkway. From off to his left, someone screamed. Then tires squealed from somwhere down the long line of cars. When he glanced toward the sound, he saw a sedan with two men sitting in front as they roared out of the line and headed down the narrow shoulder of the highway.

Chaos reigned. Car horns honked. People shouted. And the sedan spewed out a huge dust plume as it bumped down the embankment.

Jericho took off at a run. He dropped to one knee beside the woman, checked her pulse and discovered she was breathing but unconscious and bleeding.

"Is she alive?" Deputy Rawlins asked, almost out of breath as he came running up. "I got their plates, Sheriff. But I didn't dare get off a shot with all the civilians in the way. You want me to pursue?"

Son of a gun. It would figure that he didn't have his weapon just when an emergency arose.

"Stay with the woman," Jericho ordered. "You and

Fisher get her to Doc O'Neal's as fast as you can. My rifle's in the truck, and…" He looked over his shoulder toward the church door. "Tell Macy…"

Right then Macy appeared at the top of the church steps and peered down at him. He was about to yell for her to get back out of the line of fire. But within a second, he could see her quickly taking in the whole situation.

"You go do what you need to, Jericho," she called out to him. "Don't worry about us. Just take care of yourself. The wedding's off for today."

Chapter 2

It was one of those spectacular Texas sunsets, but Jericho had been too preoccupied to enjoy it. Now that the sun had completely dropped below the horizon, he retraced his steps to the Community Church and the pre-arranged meeting with his deputy.

"Sorry you didn't catch them, Sheriff. I searched the grounds like you told me when you called in, and I came up with just this one bullet casing. From a 9mm. Pretty common, I'm afraid."

Jericho felt all of his thirty-five years weighing heavily on his shoulders tonight. "Yeah, but just in case there might be anything special, send it off to the lab in San Antonio. Okay?" It wasn't often that a trained lawman witnessed an attempted murder and couldn't either catch—or identify—the perpetrators. So why him? And why on his wedding day?

The deputy nodded and put the plastic evidence bag back into his jacket pocket.

"What happened with the victim?" Jericho asked wearily. "Is she still alive?"

"Last time I checked she was sitting up and able to talk, still over at Doc O'Neal's clinic. But she wasn't giving many answers."

That figured. Why make his job any easier?

"Did you run the plates?"

Deputy Rawlins frowned. "Stolen. Not the car. The plates were stolen in San Marcos day before yesterday."

Jericho's frustration grew but he kept it hidden as he rolled up the sleeves of his starched, white dress shirt. "When I checked in the last time, everyone else was okay. That still true?" He was concerned about Macy. How had she handled postponing the wedding?

"I never saw an assemblage of people disband so quickly or so quietly." The deputy removed his hat and fiddled with the brim. "Mrs. Ward was amazing. Once we were sure the immediate danger was over, she told everyone to go home and that she'd notify them when there would be another try at the wedding. Had everybody chuckling pretty good…but they went."

"I'd better call her."

"Yes, sir." With a tired sigh, Deputy Rawlins flipped his hat back onto his head. "Doc O'Neal needs someone to take charge of the woman victim. Says her condition is not serious enough to send her over to the Uvalde hospital, but she isn't capable of being on her own, either. You want me to handle it, Sheriff?"

"No, Adam. You've had a long day and you've done a fine job. You go on home. I'll clean up the odds and ends."

The deputy nodded and turned, but then hesitated and turned back. "Sorry about the wedding, boss. Don't you think that whole shooting scene was really odd for broad daylight? What do you suppose it was all about?"

When Jericho just raised his eyebrows and didn't answer, Adam continued, "Wait 'til you try to question that woman victim. She's a little odd, too. Wouldn't say much to me. But she's sure something terrific to look at."

"Thanks. Good-night now." Jericho would talk to the victim, and he would take charge of her and this case. But he had a mighty tough phone call to Macy to make first.

As Jericho stepped into Dr. O'Neal's clinic, his shoulders felt a thousand times lighter. Macy had been wonderful on the phone—as usual. She'd tried hard to make him feel better about ruining the wedding. She had even told him that she'd been considering postponing anyway. When he asked her why such a thing would occur to her, she said they would talk tomorrow.

In a way, he was curious and wondered if he'd done something inadvertent, other than being the sheriff, to make her mad. But in another way, his whole body felt weightless. He had meant to marry Macy today. Still did, in fact. He'd given his word. Besides that, recently he'd come to the conclusion that it was important for him to become a family man in order to honor his father.

But before Macy had suggested it a couple of weeks

ago, he had never planned on marrying anyone. He'd begun thinking of himself as a lone wolf. The idea of turning into the old bachelor sheriff had somehow taken root. He'd had visions of ending up like his father and having a girlfriend or two stashed away—ladies he could visit on Saturday nights. But in general the single life suited him just fine.

Now that Macy was hedging, Jericho felt ashamed to admit that her change of heart would seem like a reprieve. His only sorrow if they didn't marry would be T.J. But maybe things around the county would settle down enough now for him to spend more time with the boy despite not being his stepfather.

"Sheriff Yates." Dr. O'Neal met him just inside the front door. "I'd like to speak to you in private before you see the patient. Let's sit out here in the empty waiting room."

Jericho followed the doc. "What's wrong? Did the bullet do serious internal damage?"

Dr. O'Neal sat down on the flimsy, fake leather couch and removed his glasses. "No. Her gunshot wound is superficial. The bullet went right through the flesh on her left side and completely missed her ribcage. She twisted her ankle when she fell, but it's not broken or sprained. She also has some old bruising and a few nontreated cuts that appear to be at least twenty-four hours old. All things considered, her physical condition is unofficially 'beat-up' but not serious.

"That's not the worst of it, though," Doc added thoughtfully.

Jericho leaned against the edge of Doc's desk. "What are you trying to say?"

"She can't tell me how she got the bruises or the cuts. In fact, she doesn't remember a thing before this morning. I'm no expert in head trauma, mind you. But even with the small bump on her head, I don't believe she's suffered any major jarring of the brain. Certainly there's not enough outward damage to suspect a physical blow caused her amnesia.

"There *is* a condition known as a *fugue* state or psychogenic amnesia," he continued. "It's caused by a traumatic event so frightening to the patient that they flee from reality and hide themselves in another, safer life— one with no memories. I don't have a lot of training in psychology, but I do remember learning that this kind of state may last for months or years."

"Amnesia? But it's just temporary. The memories will eventually come back, right?"

"Hard to say," Doc hedged as he blew dust from his glasses. "I understand that in some cases snippets of memories will flash through the mind and memories may fade in and out until the full picture emerges. Sometimes…nothing comes back at all."

Jericho took a breath. He couldn't imagine how hard that would be. To never be able to bring back the memory of growing up or the memory of his mother's face. What would that do to…?

He jerked and straightened his shoulders. Whatever would possess him to think such a thing? His mother had been a drunk and had left the family when he was only a kid. Truth be told, he hated her. Why would he care to remember what her face looked like? That was one memory he wouldn't mind losing for good.

"Let's go talk to the patient, Doc. What's her name?"

Dr. O'Neal shrugged. "No clue. She doesn't remember and your deputy said he couldn't find any ID in her clothes or at the church scene."

Now, that was *one* thing Jericho would hate to forget. The Yates name meant something. There were generations of Yates men who had been lawmen, sportsmen and land-owners. It was a name to be proud of and to do right by.

Sheriff Yates. He'd worked hard to get that title. He'd paid his dues as deputy, been appointed when the old sheriff retired, and finally had been elected on his own merit. He anticipated continuing to be a man worthy of everyone's respect. And it was high time to do his job.

As Jericho walked through Dr. O'Neal's office door to meet the mystery woman, he didn't know what he expected to find. But it was definitely not the most gorgeous woman he had ever beheld.

Yet there she sat on one of Doc's plastic chairs. Miss America, Miss Universe and Venus de Milo all wrapped into one—with a bad haircut and wild, sky-blue eyes. Jericho had to swallow hard in order to find his voice.

"Good evening, ma'am. I'm Sheriff Jericho Yates. How're you feeling?"

She lightly touched her temple, but continued to stare up at him, those strange electric eyes boring holes straight into his. "The headache and the four stitches in my side are the worst of it. No, I take that back. Not knowing my own name is the worst of it. Did Dr. O'Neal tell you that I can't remember anything? He says I have amnesia."

"Yes, ma'am. I understand. But we need to talk about what you *do* remember. Can you start with your first clear memory and tell me everything that happened up until the time when you were shot?"

"Um…I guess I could do that." She reached up and rubbed the back of her neck. "But can you sit down first? I'm getting stiff just looking up at you. How tall are you anyway?"

Jericho found a chair and dragged it over while Doc moved to sit behind his desk. "Six-three." They both sat. "There you go, Red. Is that better?"

"Yes, thanks." Lost and feeling vulnerable, even in the presence of someone as safe as the sheriff, the woman had to take deep breaths in order to calm herself down.

"Did you just call her 'Red,' Sheriff?" The doctor was scowling over his desk pad.

The sheriff looked perplexed. "Well, I suppose. We've got to call her something. 'Hey you' just won't do and she has all that bright red hair. Seemed to work."

"Bright red hair? Do I?" She put her hands in her hair. "But that doesn't feel right."

"Don't upset yourself by trying to force the memories of your lost past," the doctor said soothingly. "Not yet. Give it some time." He turned back to address the sheriff. "Jericho, I want you to take things slow. Pushing her to remember will only make it worse.

"Oh, and I don't believe 'Red' is the least bit feminine," the doctor continued. "It doesn't fit this beautiful young woman and it doesn't sound respectful to me. Can't we come up with something else?"

Still with her hands in her hair, she worried that more

seemed wrong with it than just the wrong hair color. Though God only knew what she meant by that.

"Okay, Doc," the sheriff conceded. "How about 'Rosie?' That's in the same color type."

"Rosie's okay with me," she agreed quickly. The name didn't nauseate her nearly as much as the wrong feeling about her hair.

"Okay, Rosie," the sheriff said with a deliberate drawl and a tight smile. "You can call me Jericho. Now tell me what you do remember."

She wasn't sure she could do this. Every time she thought of how terrifying those men had been, her whole body started trembling. Looking up at Sheriff Jericho for support, she was surprised to find an odd softness in his eyes as he waited for her to speak.

She'd thought he had looked so tough. Scary-tough, with all his hard angles and rough edges, when he'd first walked into Dr. O'Neal's office. Now, it seemed that at least his eyes held some empathy toward her, and the idea made her relax a little.

"The...um...first thing I remember clearly is two men pushing me around. One was pointing a gun at me while the other kept shaking me by the shoulders, hard. I felt as though I'd just woken up from a deep sleep. But now I'm not sure that was the case."

"And these two men didn't look familiar?"

"Not at all."

"Where was this? What do you remember of your surroundings?"

"After a few minutes, I decided it had to be a cheap motel room. But I...never found out whose."

"Okay," the sheriff said as he rubbed a thumb across his neat mustache. "Don't strain for answers. Let's just take this nice and easy."

She must've been wearing a frown as she'd tried to bring the images to the front of her mind because that tender look had returned to Jericho's eyes. "Can you tell me what the men said to you?" he asked gently.

"Oh, yeah. They wanted to know where some special thing was." At his curious expression, she shrugged her shoulders. "I never found out what the 'thing' was they were looking for. But they said I had stolen it and their boss wanted it back."

"You believe what they were saying was the truth? Like perhaps you had stolen something?"

Yeah, God help her, it kinda did. But with that strange thought, she began shuddering again. A lone tear leaked from the corner of her eye. "I don't know."

"Sheriff…" The doctor cautioned him with his tone.

Jericho scowled briefly then nodded. "Sorry, Doc. I won't push.

"Okay, Rosie, what did the men say or do after you couldn't give them what they wanted?"

She sniffed once and wiped her hand across her face. "They beat me up a little. You know, like slapping me and punching me in the arms and shoulders. And the whole time they kept demanding that I talk. I was so scared they were going to kill me that what they were doing hardly even hurt."

The doctor cleared his throat. The sheriff fisted his hands on his knees.

"What did they say then?" Jericho asked in a rough voice.

"Finally, they looked at their watches and said I was going to go with them to see the boss. That he would make me tell where it was. Then they pushed me outside and into the backseat of their car."

"Did anything outside look familiar?"

Dr. O'Neal huffed and opened his mouth to chastise the sheriff's choice of words.

"Oh, yeah. Sorry again," Jericho put in quickly. "What I meant was, what did it look like outside the motel room?"

"I couldn't see much. But what I did see wasn't anything special. Like the poor side of lots of small towns, I guess." Now how would she know that? She couldn't even come up with her own name and yet she knew what the poor side of town would look like?

The sheriff gave her an odd look. "Do you know where you are now?"

"Your deputy told me. Esperanza, Texas."

"Does that hold any meaning for you?" Jericho glanced over at the doctor and then held up his hand in self-defense. "Don't answer that, Rosie, not unless something comes to you. I shouldn't have asked."

Jericho was more than a little frustrated. He didn't want to hurt her by asking the wrong questions. But the only way he could help her was by getting answers. He promised to think longer before he opened his mouth.

"Okay. Let's get back to the men. Can you describe them?"

"I guess so."

But while Jericho watched her open her mouth to try, he noted her wincing as another one of those slashing pains must've struck her in the head. "Never mind. Give it a rest for tonight. We'll try it in the morning. In fact, if you're feeling well enough by then, you can go through mug shots."

Rosie sighed and her shoulders slumped. She glanced up at him from under long, thick lashes with a look so needful, so vulnerable, that it was all he could do not to sweep her up in his arms and keep her bogeymen at bay. He'd never before acted as some female's sole link to the world and to safety. He was just a county sheriff. But whatever had frightened her badly enough to erase her memories needed to be dealt with soon. He vowed to be the one to take care of it.

"Jericho," Doc interrupted his thoughts. "Rosie needs a good night's sleep. We've determined that she doesn't have a concussion, but we haven't got any place to make her comfortable here. What can you do for her?"

"Leave this place?" Rosie folded her arms over her very generous chest in a self-protective move that stirred his own protective instincts even further.

There were no motels in Esperanza. The nearest one was a half hour away. It was too late to call anyone in town to find her a place for the night.

"But what if those goons come looking for me again?" Rosie's voice was shaky and her eyes wild and frightened again. "Will they? Do you think it's possible?"

Hell. It actually was a possibility that those men might double back and finish what they'd started. Rosie needed to be in protective custody. But where could he be sure she would be safe and comfortable? The deputy's substation in town had only a small holding cell. That would never do.

"Don't you worry, ma'am. You're coming home with me. You'll be perfectly safe and comfortable there. I've got a spare bedroom and it's all made up." Had he really just said that? He stood up and stretched his legs.

"Your spare room should be okay, Jericho," Doc said. "But there's something I must tell you both first.

"I haven't said anything to Rosie about this yet," the doctor continued. "Because I don't know if it might spark a memory and cause her some pain. But both of you need to know that there should be *someone* who cares about her and should've missed her by now."

Rosie sat forward in her chair. "What do you mean?"

"While I was examining you, I discovered you're around two months' pregnant." The doc said it carefully, gently, but there was no way to make that news go down easy.

"No." She put a hand to her belly. "Can't be. How could I forget something like that?"

The doc went over to put his arm around her shoulders. "It's possible that you didn't realize you were pregnant before you lost your memory. Two months isn't very far along. If you don't start getting your memories or haven't found a family by the time you're feeling a little stronger, come on in and see me for prenatal instructions.

"And in the meantime, watch your diet. No caffeine. No alcohol, and definitely no smoking. My examination tells me you've never carried a baby to full term before, but I'm sure you won't have any trouble. There are just some things you'll need to know."

"Yeah," Rosie said. "Like who I am and who the baby's father is." She shot Jericho a rolled-eye smile.

It was such an intimate gesture. As though the two of them already shared some gigantic secret from the rest of the world. In that split second, her smile miraculously swept away one of the invisible shackles to his normal restraint.

He could almost hear the snap of an old, half-forgotten anguish relinquishing its hold on him.

With a competent smile, he offered her a helping hand at the elbow. "Let's go. All of this will look better in the morning."

She stood and he did something he hadn't done in so long he could barely remember the last time. As they walked out of the doctor's office, he pulled her closer and they walked arm in arm together toward the truck.

Chapter 3

The moment Rosie stepped into Jericho's huge log-cabin home it seemed clear she'd made a mistake. Oh, the place was beautiful, with its handcrafted furnishings, sleek open spaces and heavy-beamed ceilings.

After taking a few steps past the wide front door, she spied a state-of-the-art kitchen, including dark granite countertops and stainless-steel appliances, that appeared prominently just beyond the stone fireplace.

Decorated in tans, browns and natural woods, the place certainly looked comfortable. And since Jericho was sheriff, it should be safe.

But where were the feminine touches? The walls held few decorations, save for a large fish mounted on a brass plaque and a couple of birds, or maybe they were ducks, stuffed and stuck on wooden planks. A bronze statue standing on a hand-hewed coffee table was the only other decoration she saw. Even the kitchen seemed stark and empty. This was definitely a man's home. A single man.

"Uh," she began. "Aren't you married? Where's your wife?" Why hadn't she thought to ask that before she agreed to stay here?

"I'm not married." He walked to the grand, airy kitchen and opened the refrigerator. "You want something to eat or drink? There isn't much. I was, ah, supposed to be on my honeymoon tonight."

She relaxed a bit. At least he had a girlfriend. "What happened? What stopped the honeymoon?"

He turned from the open fridge. "There was a shooting right outside the church. The wedding was called off."

"Ouch." She winced and slid onto one of the barstools at the counter. "I screwed it up, didn't I? I'm so sorry."

Leaving the refrigerator door standing open, Jericho crossed the kitchen and leaned over the counter in her direction. He laid a hand on her shoulder and the electric jolt his warmth caused against her skin both shocked and surprised her.

"Don't be too hard on yourself," he said. "Seems the bride-to-be was about to call the whole thing off. Temporarily, anyway. I'd bet she might even be grateful that you gave her the perfect excuse." He took his hand away and stared at it, as if he too had felt the sizzle.

With his hand gone from her shoulder, Rosie decided she could almost breathe again. "You don't sound very upset. Are you heartbroken?"

Turning his back, Jericho cleared his throat and went to the open fridge. "Naw. It was going to be one of those whata-you-call-'ems? Marriages of convenience. Macy Ward has been my best friend since we were kids. I volunteered to marry her and take over being the father to her out-of-control teenage son."

He glanced around the kitchen and then back into the nearly empty refrigerator as though he had never seen them before. "But I'm not sure where I figured we would make a home together. This place isn't set up for a wife and kid. I built it with my own hands, me and my dad, and I certainly don't want to move out of it and go to town.

"I guess I hadn't really thought the whole thing through well enough."

Maybe it was because of her jumbled state of mind, but she was having trouble processing everything he'd said. "You mean you two don't love each other but you were going to get married anyway? I didn't know things like that really happened." She shook her head. "Just so you could be a father to her son? Wow."

What was that she'd been spouting? How would she know anything at all, let alone about marriage? Was she married? She didn't feel like she was. Damn. The harder she thought, the hazier everything became. She must be more disoriented than she'd thought.

"Yeah, I guess that's about right." Jericho shrugged a shoulder. "You want tomato soup? I've got a can or two I can heat up and soda crackers to go with it."

Was this guy for real? "Sure. Soup will be fine." Maybe the whole thing was some terrible dream she'd been having. Any moment now she would wake up and find herself back to being…

Nope. The best she could do was to remember she'd been running for her life and had fallen at the feet of one deadly gorgeous, *single* Texas sheriff.

And tonight she would have to adjust herself to a whole new persona. Mother-to-be. Without so much as a smattering of memory of her own mother.

Not to mention, without having the first clue as to who the baby's father might be.

Hmm. All that might be more than she could handle for one night. Maybe she'd be better off doing what the doctor said and just go with the flow. At least for tonight.

So far she'd learned this Sheriff Jericho guy might be too good to be true. Marrying the best friend he didn't love in order to give her son a father? Good for him. And by the same token, that ought to mean she wouldn't have to worry about him forcing her to do anything against her will. Mister Knight in Shining Armor must be the ultimate good guy. Who woulda thunk a man like that really existed?

Rosie tried to let her mind go blank as she watched Jericho fumble around in the kitchen. But she couldn't get the idea of him being unattached out of her head.

As she looked down at her left hand, it made her chuckle to think that she would know about married women wearing wedding rings on the third finger of their left hands but she didn't know whether or not she was married herself. Her fingers bore no rings at all. But that didn't tell the whole story. What if she'd taken off her rings? What if they'd been stolen?

Sighing in frustration, she went back to studying the man.

Then wished she hadn't.

Wide, muscular shoulders flexed as he reached for dishes in the cabinets. His dark blond hair and sexy hazel eyes made him as handsome as any movie star. Her glance moved down along his torso as it narrowed to lean hips. She forced herself to turn away from the sight of his fantastically tight butt. But she didn't completely lose sight of his long arms and even longer legs. The whole picture was developing into a hero, all lean and formidable. Like the sheriff in a white hat from an old-time movie.

The good guy. The *sexy* good guy.

He set a bowl of steaming soup in front of her and sat across the counter with his own. "This must be tough on you."

Heartfelt concern shone from those deep hazel eyes as he gazed intently in her direction. The more she watched them, the darker the irises became. Soon they were steel gray, and suddenly sensual. Hot.

She quickly took a sip of the soup and nearly burned her tongue. "Uh, yeah. It's hard not knowing where I came from or who I am. I wish I knew what those men were after."

Jericho lifted the spoon to his mouth and blew as he studied the beautiful woman across the counter. He was having trouble keeping his mind from wandering. Wandering off to things he would love to do to her, for her, with her.

Her stunning eyes had lost that wild, crazed look, so

he'd been studying the rest. The body seemed made for sex. At five-foot-ten or so, she wasn't quite his height. But she also wasn't a dainty little thing, one who might break if he didn't watch his step. Somewhat on the thin side, she looked like a model. But unlike the models he'd seen on magazines, her lean body just made those fantastic breasts seem all the more voluptuous. And those legs. Don't get him started on those long, shapely legs. Even encased in designer jeans, he could tell how they would look naked—wrapped around his waist and in the heat of passion.

The mere sight of a good-looking woman had never done things like this to his libido in the past. He couldn't imagine why she was so different. But the why didn't seem to matter all that much. She just was, and he had to find a way to stop thinking about her like that.

She was pregnant. No doubt she belonged to someone—somewhere.

"Is the soup okay?" he asked, trying to push aside the unwanted thoughts. "Is there anything else I can do for you before I settle you down for the night?"

Ah hell. Just the word *night* made him long for things he had no business even considering.

"Soup's fine." She took another sip and a bite of the crackers. "But I feel so…I don't know. Like I'm not grounded. Like I'm flying around in midair. It's probably because I can't recall my past and my family. And this baby thing… That really threw me.

"Maybe it would help if you told me something about your family," she went on to suggest. "Would you mind? I think just hearing that someone else can remember and knows who they are will give me hope that someday I'll get my memories back. Does that seem too nosy?"

He was good at questioning victims and criminals. And he'd forced himself to become a decent politician in order to get elected. But talking about his life to a complete stranger was totally out of his realm. He had a strong instinct to keep his mouth shut, but she looked so vulnerable, so needy.

"There's not much to tell." But he guessed he *could* give her a few basic facts. "I was born and raised right here in Esperanza. My dad is Buck Yates, and he was born right here in town, too. Dad spent years in the service and now he owns the farm-supply store in town. Of course around here, that means he sells mostly guns and tack, some deer blinds and a lot of game feeders."

Jericho let himself give her one of his polite, running-for-office smiles as he continued. "My older brother, Fisher, is a captain in the U.S. Army, just home on leave from his third tour of duty in the Middle East." He shrugged and ducked his head, not knowing where to go from here. "That's about it for the family. Want to hear about my friends?"

"You didn't mention your mother. Has she passed away?"

If only she had simply died. "Our mother took off when Fisher and I were kids."

"Took off?"

"Disappeared. Haven't heard a word from her in nearly thirty years. She might be dead by now for all I know." Good riddance if she was.

He stood, picked up his empty soup bowl and eyed

Rosie's almost empty one. "You want another bowl of soup? Or anything else?"

Without answering, Rosie glanced up at him and he spotted dark, purplish circles under her eyes. The lady was whooped. His protective instincts kicked right back in again.

"Let's get you into bed for now. We'll have a fresh start in the morning. Okay with you?"

"I am tired. Thanks." She slid off the barstool and he watched her hanging tightly on to the counter as if her legs were about to give out on her.

He dumped the dishes into the sink and went to her side. "Here, take my arm. I won't let you fall."

For a moment, it seemed that she would refuse. Jericho saw her try to straighten up and steady herself. But within a split second, she started to slide.

There was no choice. He bent to pick her up in his arms. A lot lighter than he'd imagined, her body hugged his chest as she threw her arms around his neck and hung on.

"I feel ridiculous. I can't even remember my own name and now I can't walk under my own steam. It's a good thing you're here, Sheriff."

Yeah, maybe. Or maybe this was going to turn into his worst nightmare.

Jericho carried her down the hall and into the spare room. Setting her down in the corner chair, he pulled back the covers from the double bed.

"This should be comfortable enough." He had to turn away from the sight of clean, fresh sheets just waiting for bodies to mess them up.

"It looks great," she told him. "But I wish I had a pair of clean pajamas. These clothes are getting gamy."

He stood there for a second, picturing her naked again. Finally, making a tremendous effort, he started thinking with his head instead of another part of his anatomy.

"How about I lend you one of my T-shirts? I've got one or two older ones that've turned soft from washing and I don't wear them anymore. Would that do?"

She nodded and gave him a weak smile.

When he brought a shirt back into the room and handed it to her, his sex-obsessed brain produced another thought. This one worried him.

"Are you going to need help getting undressed?"

"No, I'm feeling stronger, thanks. I think the food helped."

"Great. The bathroom is right across the hall. There are towels in the closet and an extra new toothbrush. Use whatever you need."

"Thanks again, Jericho. I'll be fine. See you in the morning."

Glad to know she would be okay for the night, Jericho eased out of her room and headed for his own. He probably wouldn't fare as well with his own night. The thought of Rosie lying in bed in the room right next to his would keep him tossing and turning.

Sighing, he shrugged off his by-now-filthy dress shirt and tried telling himself it would all be okay. He had a plan. He would just start thinking of her like he would a roommate.

Well, that plan didn't work out so well. Jericho dragged himself into the shower the next morning and turned the faucets on full cold. *Roommate, my foot.* When had a roommate ever kept him lying awake for half the night with daydreams of long, silky legs and ripe, sensitive breasts?

Irritated at himself, he swore to do better today. And it would serve him right if he was too tired and miserable all day long to concentrate.

After his shower, he stood before the mirror, preparing to shave. A couple of things were going to have to change today, he silently demanded of his image. He needed to get a line on Rosie's relatives. Somewhere people must be missing her. The sooner he found them and returned her to her previous life, the better off he would be. Let someone else protect her.

The second thing that needed to change was the way she dressed. She didn't have a change of clothes, and she needed to cover herself up real soon.

But the thought of how she dressed reminded him of something else. Another chore he must do, first thing. Maybe he could combine the two. Yeah, that should work.

Rosie opened her eyes when a dash of sunlight hit her eyelids and irritated her enough to wake up. She glanced over at the bright sunshine peeping through the wood-slatted miniblinds and wondered what time it was.

Rolling over, it hit her. A gigantic black void. The gaping abyss in her brain suddenly threatened to swallow her whole.

Gasping for air, as though someone had been choking her, and flailing her arms against a sea of nothingness and nausea, Rosie let her mind grab hold of the only thing it could. The one thing she saw clearly. The memory of Jericho Yates.

Immediately her heart rate slowed and warmth replaced the stone-cold numbness she'd felt when she awoke to find nothing familiar. Jericho had made one hell of an anchor last night. He'd tethered her to the earth with quiet concern and a sensual smile.

Fighting to remain in the moment and trying not to think either backward or forward, she sat at the edge of the bed and took stock. First was the physical. Her head wasn't pounding as it had been last night. The stitches in her side were barely noticeable. She rotated her ankle and found only an echo of the pain she'd experienced.

Okay, so she felt a little achy and sore, but she would live. Well, unless the bad guys came back.

Her second concern—and the real question—remained the same as before: How was she going to get her memories back? The doctor said not to push it. The moment she'd tried to find some thread of memory, panic had set in.

Taking another deep breath, she came to the conclusion that she had no choice. To keep from going stark raving mad, she had better just go along minute by minute. Living hour by hour and feeling her way.

Standing in the kitchen drinking coffee, Jericho heard Rosie opening the spare room door and going into the bathroom. The sudden jolt of anticipation at seeing her again competed with the practiced calm he had almost perfected during the hours since his shower.

But just then someone knocked on the front door.

Jericho figured Rosie's goons wouldn't have the guts to confront him in broad daylight, and they definitely wouldn't be knocking when they came to call. So this must be the person he was expecting.

He checked out the window and saw her car. Yes, it was his best friend. He wiped the smile off his face and went to let her in.

"Morning, Macy. Thanks for coming." He stood aside and allowed her to come in.

When she entered the room, everything felt easy, even somehow more homey. "Good morning, Jericho. I had every intention of talking to you this morning anyway. It's my pleasure if I can be of some help at the same time."

As a best friend, Macy Ward couldn't be beat. As a potential spouse…he would just as soon skip it.

"I wanted to say how sorry I am about the ceremony, Mace. You know I wouldn't have ducked out on it if I'd had any choice."

Macy went straight into the great room and dumped her armload of folded clothes on the nearest chair. "I know. You're a good man, Jericho Yates. That's one of the reasons I twisted your arm into agreeing to marry me."

"Now, Mace. You aren't holding a gun to my head. I volunteered to help you out with T.J."

"Yes, you did. And I love you for it." She turned and touched his arm. "You are really a good guy, my friend. Too good to get saddled with a wife who won't ever love you the way she should. I can't do it to you.

"I'm calling the wedding off permanently," she blurted. "You're off the hook for good."

Relief mixed with sadness and kicked him in the gut.

He didn't want to get married, but he would do anything to help Macy out in her time of need.

"What about T.J.? How are you going to take control of him now?" When she didn't answer, Jericho stepped up again. "Look, I can make some extra time for him this summer. Just as soon as I find a link to our mystery woman, my schedule should lighten up."

Macy smiled softly. "T.J. is a big part of the reason I'm canceling our wedding. You know he's in the middle of doing that community service project you arranged for him over at the state park this week. He's not pleased about having to make up for the toilet-paper and mailbox mangling incidents, but I hope he's learning his lesson and is staying out of trouble.

"And then earlier this week Jewel agreed to let T.J. work at the Hopechest Ranch for the rest of the summer." Macy's smile brightened. "The hard work should be good for him. But that means you don't have to worry about making time for him. He'll be plenty busy."

Several emotions flitted through Jericho at breakneck speed. Disappointment came first. Then another level of relief. Finally, a streak of annoyance came and went. Now he would have no excuse for not spending all his time with Rosie and working on her case.

"Do you think T.J. is going to be broken up about the change in marriage plans?" He hoped not. Deep down the kid was really good and Jericho hated to see him hurt.

Macy shook her head. "Don't worry about it. Actually, he's been pretty antsy over us getting married.

I imagine he'll be happy to hear his mother will continue being single."

Jericho didn't like the sound of that. "Is he still upset over my giving him community service? I only did it to keep him out of the juvenile system. I…"

"No, Jericho," she interrupted. "You did the best thing for him. You're not trying to be his friend. Me neither. It's our job as adults to do the right thing. I really believe T.J.'s biggest trouble with the wedding is Tim's memory. He saw you as Tim's friend for so long that he couldn't quite get past the changeover to having you take Tim's place."

"But I wasn't…I wouldn't."

Macy chuckled at his mumbling protests. "I know. And T.J. would've found that out if he'd had the chance.

"But calling it off is for the best," she continued. "For all of us. This way, you'll have the opportunity to find someone who you can…"

At that moment, Rosie cleared her throat to announce that she was interrupting. She still had on his old T-shirt but she'd slipped on her jeans underneath it and her hair was wet from the shower. The sight of her in the hallway simply set his veins on fire.

The difference between how he'd felt seeing Macy and how he felt right now seeing Rosie seemed extreme. And he didn't care for it one bit.

Chapter 4

"**Y**ou must be the one Jericho's calling Rosie. I'm Macy Ward." The woman rushed over and reached out to capture her hands. "Jericho's old friend. It's gotta be terrible for you, not having any memories. I was so shocked when I heard. You poor thing."

Taken aback by such an effusive greeting, Rosie felt torn between laughing and running for her life. But there was just something about Macy Ward that made her want to smile.

Slinging her arm around Rosie's shoulder, Macy hugged her close. "I brought you some decaffeinated teas and a few things to wear, honey. Just to get you by for a day or two. I can't imagine not having a closet or even a purse to call your own.

"Oh, makeup," Macy added with a start. "Darn. I should've thought of that, too."

"Um. That's okay. I don't know if I wear any." With that thought, Rosie lifted the back of her hand to her mouth in an effort to hold off what might turn into a sob.

But she stopped in midair, struck by the wayward idea that she might be a nail biter. Checking, Rosie was relieved to find her nails seemed intact. And manicured and polished at that.

So she was a woman who took care of her appearance. Spent money and time on it. Not that anyone could judge by the way she looked this morning. One glance in the bathroom mirror after her shower, and Rosie had nearly fled screaming. In addition to the bruises and cuts, her disaster of a hairdo could not possibly be normal. Not only didn't it look like she'd spent any money or time on it, but it just didn't *feel* right.

Rosie nearly broke down again as she wondered how long it might take her to get a clear idea of what her hair was really supposed to look like. Would that ever happen? It was possible, she supposed, that the memory would never return. But thinking that way made her knees weak.

Macy turned back to Jericho, who had been standing there with his mouth gaping open. "Jericho, fix Rosie this tea and us some coffee, will you? Maybe you could even scramble Rosie a couple of eggs. You *do* have fresh eggs?"

Being called down by Macy seemed to shake Jericho out of his reverie. "I've got a few eggs, and the coffee's already made. What are you going to do?"

"I'm going to help Rosie change. The things I brought should be a close fit to her size. She's a little taller and thinner than I am, though. So we'll have to see." With that, Macy spun them both around and headed down the hall.

Rosie heard Jericho mumbling from over her shoulder. "Well, sure. Y'all help just yourselves. I'll cook."

Fifteen minutes later and she was still feeling a bit weepy. Macy had been trying to brush her awful hair into some semblance of a style. Of course, without much luck.

Rosie thought things in general seemed a lot better. Macy bringing clean underwear had been a real blessing. Putting clean clothes on made Rosie feel almost human again. They'd discovered Macy's slacks were about an inch too short and the shoulders of her blouse were big enough for a Rosie and a half—yet the buttons in front barely closed. Still, clean clothes had made a world of difference in how Rosie saw her situation.

"I'm sorry I messed up your wedding yesterday, Macy. Are you upset? Can you reschedule?"

The other woman turned and captured her in a big bear hug. "You're a sweetheart for thinking of me when you have so much trouble of your own. But not to worry. The wedding is off for good. You didn't mess up a thing."

Rosie's curiosity was piqued and she decided she didn't care about sounding too nosy around this sweet woman with the blazing white smile and two tiny dimples. "Why did you call it off? Did something happen between you and Jericho?"

"Come sit down with me for a moment," Macy said as she led her back into the spare bedroom and plopped on the bed. "Let me tell you something about the man who's taken you in."

Curious, Rosie eased down beside her. She didn't remember a thing about her past, but maybe it would be smart to know a whole lot more about her present.

"When I was born in this small town," Macy began, "there were several boys who lived on my block. I guess I was kind of a tomboy as a kid because two of those boys who were my age became my best friends. I never had much to do with the other little girls in town."

It was nice hearing Macy talk about her past. Somehow her story seemed to be grounding Rosie.

"One of those two best guy friends was always acting as my protector and big brother. Countless times he saved me from bullies and rescued me from runaway horses and from out of trees." Macy's dimples showed at the memories. "By the time I was twelve, though, it was the other one who'd captured my heart. I developed a huge crush on that one and it quickly turned to love. We married the minute we were old enough."

"Jericho was the big brother of the two." Rosie was sure Jericho hadn't been the lover.

"Of course. He's still doing it, too. My husband, Tim, died about six years ago and Jericho stepped in to make sure my son T.J. and I were okay. I'm not sure what we would've done without him."

"But Jericho's never been married?"

Macy's smile dimmed slightly. "No. But in my opinion, it's just that he's never found the right woman. Everyone who knows him loves and respects him. He could've had his pick of any woman in the county."

"But not you? You're sure?"

It was a sad smile that Macy wore by the time she answered. "I wish I felt differently. But no. I'm sure. Jericho and I are like brother and sister. We'll never get past that. I know he's relieved to be getting out of our marriage agreement. But he's still the best man in the entire county.

"Who else would've agreed to marry his best friend just so her son would have a father?" Macy shook her head sadly and patted Rosie's hand. "Enough about me. How are you feeling? You look a bit pale. Are you queasy? Let's go get you something to eat."

For a split second when Rosie appeared out of the bedroom wearing Macy's clothes, Jericho had been absolutely positive the image he saw was all wrong. This mystery woman did not belong in cotton slacks and long-sleeved, button-down shirts, of that he was sure. He envisioned her as being more into silks and fancy designer duds. But then when he blinked once, the lost woman with no past was back and it didn't matter what she wore, his heart went out to her.

As the three of them sat around his kitchen table and Rosie ate breakfast, Macy babbled on about the current happenings in her life. Jericho suspected she was doing it to make Rosie forget her predicament.

"My boss, Jewel Mayfair—you'll love her when you meet her, Rosie. Well, anyway, she's had a kind of rough life. But her uncle is Joe Colton. He's that senator in California who's running for president, you know?"

Jericho cut in, "Macy, Doc O'Neal said we shouldn't

expect Rosie to bring back memories just yet. She's supposed to relax and just let things come to her on their own."

"Oh, but…" Rosie interrupted. "The name Joe Colton does ring a bell. He must be really famous."

"Or maybe you were just interested in politics." Macy added her own conjecture. "I know that the presidential campaign has been really heating up on TV. Jewel says her uncle has lots of influential backers. But since our Texas governor entered the race against Senator Colton, Jewel says things haven't been going so well. And I can imagine that's right. Governor Daniels is really hot. I voted for him for governor, and he can probably count on my vote for president, too. But don't tell Jewel."

Rosie chuckled, but then put her head in her hands. "I don't know. Everything sounds familiar but nothing is. The harder I try…"

Jericho would've liked nothing better than to take Rosie in his arms to comfort her just then. But Macy leaned over and lifted a gentle hand to Rosie's shoulder.

"Then don't try, sweetie." She turned to Jericho. "Maybe you could help Rosie by finding out the kinds of things she likes to do when she's relaxing. For instance, you know I love to read romance novels. I'm positive that wouldn't change about me even if I couldn't remember anything else."

Okay, Jericho had always figured he made a pretty good detective when it came to catching criminals. But this kind of detective work seemed a little over his head.

"Uh, what kinds of things would you suggest she try?" he asked Macy.

Macy raised her eyebrows and then tilted her head to study Rosie. "Most women would love a good relaxing day at a spa—along with some chocolate. But there aren't any spas around here. And I always love a good relaxing day of shopping, which is also in limited supply in Esperanza, Texas, I'm afraid.

"Um…" Macy looked around the great room as though something might come to her. "Maybe she has a hobby. Like sewing or knitting. Or…" She swung her arm around to indicate Rosie should look at the room. "Decorating. Does anything about this room speak to you?"

Rosie blinked a couple of times and then glanced over Jericho's furnishings. "It just says *man's man* to me," she said with a shrug. "Except I guess for the Frederic Remington bronze on the table over there, and that antique Navajo rug on the wall behind the leather couch that I suspect is worth several thousands. Those aren't museum-quality pieces, by any means, but they're nice examples of the style."

Jericho knew his mouth was hanging open. And judging by Macy's silence, she too had been surprised by Rosie's sudden show of knowledge. He'd almost forgotten he'd even bought the Remington at a charity auction. And the Navajo blanket had been a housewarming present from his father that he barely noticed anymore. Those were the only two things in the whole house except for his rifles that were worth much. Rosie had spotted them right away.

He finally got his voice back when Rosie turned to him. "Hmm," he said for lack of anything more definitive. "I suspect you've been either an art collector or a museum volunteer at some point in your life, ma'am. What do you think?"

"I don't know," she said with a heavy sigh. "I don't seem to know anything. I can't explain why those things just popped out of my mouth."

Macy stood and bent over Rosie to cuddle her around the shoulders. "Jericho, this poor girl needs to relax and not think too hard so her past can ease back to her. You've got to find something to help her."

He stood, too. "My job is to keep her safe and alive first, Mace. I'm worried that whoever tried to kill her will come back around for another try. We're just going to have to let the memories come as they will and see how she does."

An hour after Macy left, Rosie's head was still buzzing with Jericho's words. *Those men might come back for another try? Oh, God.*

"You awake?" Jericho poked his head inside the spare room where she'd been trying to take a nap.

Just the sight of him made her stomach muscles flutter.

"Yes," she said as she sat up at the edge of the bed.

"I've been on the phone with my deputy. And he's gathering some mug shots off the Internet for you to look at later today. You willing to give it a try?"

"Of course I am. I want those men caught." Thinking of those awful goons made her body shiver in dread.

"Easy there." Jericho took her hand and helped her stand. "I've also been giving some thought to hobbies that might make you relax. You still don't have a clue as to what you like, do you?"

"No." But having said that, Rosie's mind tricked her into thinking about one way to relax she wouldn't mind trying at all. Sharing a relaxing kiss—with the man whose soft hazel eyes were gazing into hers right now.

On second thought, Rosie admitted that kissing Jericho might not be as relaxing as all that. Just standing next to him now was shooting jazzy little sparks of lust right down her spine. Kissing him was bound to become more intense than relaxing.

How could Macy have turned him away? He was so hot.

"When I want to relax," Jericho began in his fantastic Texas drawl, "I always find being outside with nature is a great way to shuck your stress. Does that sound like something you might want to try?"

She shrugged, not able to concentrate on anything much more than a pair of to-die-for hazel eyes that were turning a gorgeous shade of sea-mist green that matched his shirt.

"What did you have in mind to do outside?" she asked. But in the next moment she wished she'd kept her mouth shut. She sure knew what she'd like to be doing—either outside or in.

"Well, usually I fish or hunt," he answered as though he had no clue what was on her mind. "Both real relaxing. But I suspect those might be too tricky for someone without memories. And it would take us too long to get out to the right spots for them, too.

"I was thinking, though," he added. "That you might be willing to take in some fresh air at the same time as I gave you a small lesson in self-defense. I have a target set up behind the house in the woods so I can practice with my service weapons when I need to. Think I can talk you into trying a little target practice? Maybe you'll find that relaxing."

"Self-defense?" Oh, Lordy. Just the idea made her anything but relaxed. "Do you really imagine that I might need to know how to shoot a gun?" Her stress quotient jumped at least a hundred percent.

Jericho grinned at her. "What makes you think you don't already know how?"

"I…don't… Maybe you're right. I should try lots of things before I just say no automatically.

"But do you truly think shooting somebody might be necessary?" she added warily.

"Slow down." He took her hand and slid his arm around her waist. "We'll go nice and easy. Just give target practice a try. Probably never going to need a weapon for any reason, but I'd just as soon you were comfortable around them all the same.

"Besides," he added with another grin. "I want you to meet my two hounds. I've been keeping them outside in their dog run for your benefit. But I know they'd like meeting you. Maybe you're a dog lover. You might even find out you've always liked target practice. Some people find it totally relaxing."

"Damn it all to hell, Arn." The hired goon called Petey swore again and spit out the window of their idling car, almost hitting a willow tree. "Unless she's dead, we can't go back without the chick. We'll be the ones in dead trouble. So what're we going to do?"

"The boss just now told me on the cell that he's sure she ain't dead, stupid." Arnie pocketed his cell phone and ran a sweaty hand through his hair. "No body looking like hers has showed up in no morgues. She's not even been booked into any hospitals round here. The boss can find out that kind of stuff."

"Crap! Can we skip then? Maybe get lost in Mexico?"

"Listen, you idiot, don't you know the boss has contacts in Mexico? He has contacts where you wouldn't even believe. There's no place you can hide from him. Just calm down and let me think."

"So where could she go?" Petey wasn't calm and he couldn't seem to keep quiet. "I know I plugged her at least once. I'm not that bad a shot, and I swear to God I saw her go down. There was a bunch of people around the church. Too many for her to crawl off into some hole to die."

"Shut up a second." Arnie rubbed a hand across his face and tried to think.

In a few seconds, Arnie was trying out his thoughts aloud. "Okay, so we know there was some kind of smoky at the traffic jam. He maybe made the tags. But we dumped them right away, so no sweat there. No chance in hell he got a decent look at our faces, either. I figure we're golden on that score, too. We're still just a couple regular dudes with nothing to hide.

"But the chick…" Arnie screwed up his mouth to think harder. "Somebody helped her. Took her in. Probably the smoky, or maybe some kind of doctor do-gooder in that crowd."

Petey started to whine, "But if somebody's helping her, she'll turn us in. Turn in the boss, too."

Arnie nearly cracked his imbecile of a partner across the mouth. "Weren't you paying attention, idiot? She said she couldn't remember nothing."

Petey shrugged. "I figured she was lying. Trying to save her skin."

"Yeah? Well, what if she wasn't? What if some sucker is helping her and she can't tell them nothing?"

"Then we're in the clear. Let's get out of here."

Huffing in frustration, Arnie rolled his eyes. "We've gotta find her. The boss ain't gonna give up just 'cause she's lost her mind. I'm guaranteeing you, we don't bring her back, and we're dead meat. Finished. You understand?"

Petey nodded his head but couldn't get a word out of his trembling lips.

"Fine," Arnie said almost absently. "So we're gonna go see what we can find out about her. Somebody will know something in a town as small as Esperanza, Texas."

"How? Who's gonna tell a couple of strangers anything?"

"Shut up, Petey. I'm doing the thinking. In every small town there's a couple of places where people know stuff and don't mind spreading it around. If you was a woman, we could go to the beauty parlor. You find out all the gossip in them places."

Petey opened his mouth as if to complain, but Arnie threw him a sharp look.

"I saw just the right place for us back down the road a ways," Arnie said. "You know, I think you and me are in need of new hats. I've been meaning to get me one of those cowboy hats, anyway. Pulling the brim down over my eyes will make a perfect disguise. And I'm thinking you'd look pretty decent in a John Deere cap."

"Aw, crap, Arn. I don't like caps. Can't I get the cowboy hat? Where are we going get this stuff anyway?"

Arnie put the sedan in gear and pulled out of the roadside park. "Do me a favor, idiot. Do not say one frigging word while we're in the store. Not one, you hear?"

"Yeah. Yeah. But where?"

"Where every old codger in town usually shows up every day," Arnie told him with no small pride in his voice. "And all of them cowpokes can't wait to spill their guts around so they don't have to go back to work too fast."

At Petey's frustrated look, he gave it up. "At the farm-supply store, of course."

Chapter 5

"Is this the correct way to hold it?" Rosie asked as she grasped the weapon with both hands and pointed it at the target. "It doesn't feel right."

Jericho scraped both his sweaty palms down his pants legs and tried to figure out how he'd managed to get himself into this fix. It was one thing wanting the woman to be able to defend herself and quite another completing the mechanics of the thing without touching her.

He'd been standing a minimum of six feet behind her, spouting instructions at the back of her head. Now he lowered his eyes to take in her slender back, narrowing to the tiny waist. A little lower and his gaze stuttered across her small but firm butt encased in Macy's old jeans. Then his wayward eyes strayed further to look their foolish fill as his stare wavered on down those

long, sexy legs. Holy mercy, but those long legs could
sure give a man dreams he ought not have.

His attraction to her could not be tolerated or indulged.
Too close, and he was bound to give in. She was too
tempting, with her sexy body and her vulnerable but
bright eyes. He knew with his whole being that if they
ever made love, he might find he wanted to keep her
forever. Or some other such nonsense in the same vein.

Jericho had a good life here. His father lived and
worked nearby and they talked nearly every day as
family should. He'd grown up with all the people of this
town. People like Macy and Tim, Clay and Tamara
Brown and Clay's brother, Ryder, and his sister, Mercy.
Some of them were gone now, either dead or moved
away. But still Jericho's roots here were strong. He
didn't need anything else in his life.

The people of this town and county knew and respected
him. Depended on him. That was where his energies
should be focused. Not on a pair of lost, sky-blue eyes.

Okay, so maybe on some particularly lonely nights,
being single in a small town wasn't all he'd ever wished
for. It could be stark and depressing. That was a fact.

"Jericho?" Rosie turned to see why he hadn't
answered. "Is this right?"

Tamping down his hormones, Jericho stepped up to
the task. He slid in close to the warmth of her back and
wrapped his arms around her in order to show her the
correct stance by example.

The zing of electricity between their bodies almost
knocked him back again. But the sheriff of Campo
County had to be stronger than all that.

"Not exactly," he murmured into her ear. "Here, I'll put my hands on top of yours to show you the right way. Just relax."

The minute the words were out of his mouth, he knew they were both in trouble. Each of them took a deep breath, straightened up and cleared their throats.

Rosie's body trembled against his chest, but he felt he had to finish what they'd started. After a few more minutes, he couldn't have said how he'd ever managed to stand his ground and show her the correct way of pulling the trigger while keeping her eyes open and aiming at the same time. But, he had, and she'd hit the target—twice. So he backed off and took back his weapon.

"You seem to be a natural at shooting," he told her as he clicked on the safety. "But to tell the truth, you don't seem very familiar with guns. How does it feel being outside?"

"Weird. Like maybe I don't get out in the sunshine too often. But I kind of enjoy it." She stared into the woods behind the tree where he'd set up the target. "I'm not crazy about the wild though. Isn't it kind of scary in the woods? I don't think I'd care to go in there."

Jericho chuckled and took her elbow. "Okay, then. We'll cross hunting and fishing off our list of possible ways to relax." He headed them back toward the house. "Let's go to town and see if Deputy Rawlins has some photos for you to look at."

Rosie smiled at Jericho's deputy as he shook her hand. At just about six feet tall, Adam Rawlins seemed to be in great physical shape. But even with all his muscles, the deputy still didn't appear as formidable as the sheriff.

"We'll catch those bastards," Adam told her with a polite smile. "Don't you worry, miss."

She walked with Adam toward a computer that was stored in an alcove at back of the sheriff's office. Meanwhile, Jericho went to one of the two large desks in a different section of the large room. Even just a few yards away, Rosie felt bereft without him by her side.

Adam pulled two folding chairs up in front of the computer and motioned for her to have a seat in one of them while he sat down beside her. "Let me show you how to work this. It's pretty easy."

The deputy smiled over at her and she knew he'd intended to put her at ease. But his perfect brown hair with every strand in place and his sympathetic brown eyes that were studying her carefully didn't come close at all to settling her nerves. His hair wasn't the same dark blond color as Jericho's and didn't occasionally go astray due to having strong hands stab through it with frustration. Not like Jericho's. And the plain brown eyes of Deputy Adam weren't at all the same as Jericho's hazel eyes that could change from gray to green—all depending on the weather and what the man was wearing that day. Nothing about the deputy sitting next to her did a thing for her nerves.

Trying to hide a secret sigh, Rosie returned her attention to the computer. "Yes, I think I've got it," she told Adam. "The program doesn't look all that complicated. You don't have to sit with me. I'll call you if I run into trouble or if I spot anyone who looks familiar."

"Yes, ma'am." The deputy gave her a half smile as he stood and walked toward his own desk.

Rosie shot a quiet glance in the direction of the tall man wearing a long-sleeved white shirt and uniform tie standing across the room and bending over a desk loaded with paperwork. In contrast to sitting beside the deputy, just the sight of Jericho sent her pulse racing and her stomach bouncing. Whenever Jericho touched her, little firecrackers exploded inside her chest. Her palms grew damp, and her thighs trembled. Learning to fire a gun at the target this morning beside him had been a trial of fighting lustful thoughts and urges.

Things were so unsettled in her mind. But one thing stood out clearly. She wanted that man to want her. Badly.

"Is she all right over there by herself?" Jericho asked his deputy.

Taking a quick look in the direction of his boss's gaze, Adam nodded his head. "Yep. Frankly, I think the lady's better at using that computer than I am. Seemed to pick up on it right away."

"Yeah? Well, that should tell us something about her. I just wish I knew what it was besides the fact she knows computers."

Adam threw his boss a hesitant smile. "Yes, sir. Do you have any ideas regarding how we should go about starting our investigation? Where we should begin if she doesn't spot anybody from those mug shots?"

Jericho released a breath and turned away from the sight of Rosie's long legs bunched up under her as she sat at the desk. He rubbed absently at the back of his neck.

"Start with missing persons. Check all the wires to see if someone of her description is listed.

"She's a real looker, don't you think, Adam?"

The deputy nodded. "Except for the hair, I do."

Jericho frowned at Adam's truthfulness, but then shrugged it off, believing the choppy cut and unnatural color only added to her appeal. "So someone in this county or nearby must've seen her at least once before she ended up shot at the church's doorstep. She didn't just appear in the back of a car in Esperanza out of thin air.

"Why don't you start asking around?" he suggested. "Check the gas stations and the truck stops. And go on over to my dad's feed and supply store. Everybody in the county shows up there sometime or other during the day. Find out if any of the ranchers spotted her or one of those goons driving through or stopping to ask directions."

"You bet, boss. I'll go right now. You can help the woman with the computer if she finds anyone familiar, can't you?"

Yeah, Jericho thought. He could help her. And he would, damn it. Nothing else mattered quite as much to him at the moment.

Frustrated and tired, Rosie clung to Jericho's arm as they strolled down Main Street and prepared to cross at the corner, heading toward Miss Sue's town café. It seemed as if over the last couple of hours she'd stared into the faces of hundreds of men, all terrifying and snarling at her from the computer monitor. But none of them had been the ones who'd hurt and kidnapped her.

Worse, being outside in the fresh air now after

studying all those criminal faces was giving her the creeps. Every man who either drove by or walked in her general direction made the hairs on her arms stand straight up. Some kind of internal instinct must be calling out, demanding that she run and hide. Stay out of sight.

Definitely someone somewhere wanted an unknown thing from her badly enough to send goons after her. She was positive they wouldn't give up so easily.

"You okay?" Jericho asked as she took a couple of deep breaths. "Still want to grab a bite at Miss Sue's? You wouldn't want to miss her pecan pie."

"Um…yes. I guess so." Rosie looked up into Jericho's face and found a concerned expression, half hidden by the brim of his uniform's cowboy hat. "It's just that I can almost feel someone watching me. Waiting for me."

Jericho stopped directly in front of the café's door. "I take gut feelings seriously, ma'am. So I can't say for sure it's not possible that those guys are in town and waiting. But I guarantee you they won't be inside the café. And I promise I'll be guarding your back when we leave.

"All right with you?" he asked. "We have to eat sometime, and while we're here I can check with some of the folks about your case. What do you say?"

She threw a quick glance over her shoulder and saw nothing but an ordinary small-town street and loads of bright sunshine. "I say, I'm with you, Sheriff. Lead on."

Jericho did just that. He walked them inside, and hesitated long enough to flip his hat on a peg next to the door. He then found an empty table in the center of the room, away from the huge curtained windows that looked out on Main Street. Rosie could've kissed him for being so thoughtful. In fact, she could've kissed him just for being so broad-shouldered and steely-eyed. And, actually, she intended to find a time to test his kisses as soon as she could get him alone.

The tough but friendly sheriff greeted every person in the café with a smile and a personal word. Rosie guessed he must know them well since he'd lived here all his life. But no one looked the least familiar to her.

The café itself seemed old but spotless and well cared for. Homey. The mismatched wooden tables and chairs were all full of smiling, happy people who seemed to be enjoying their food. Shouldn't a place as comfortable as this feel as though she'd been here before? She'd wanted it to be familiar. But it wasn't.

Jericho ordered for them, since she hadn't a clue what she might like to eat. Within minutes their lunches were delivered.

"Why do I have a salad?"

"Well now, that's easy. I've found that pretty, thin ladies like you seem to go for salads at lunchtime. Does something else sound more appealing? If so, Becky will be happy to fix you anything you want."

Without warning, her eyes filled with tears.

Swiping at them, she tried to explain. "I hate this. I hate not even being aware of what I like to eat. I hate looking into people's eyes and not knowing if I've ever met them before." She gritted her teeth and fought back the sob threatening in her throat.

He put his hand over hers on the table and squeezed. "It's hard, I know. But the doc said for you to take it slow. Pushing could make things worse."

"Forgive me, but the doctor doesn't have goons hiding nearby in the shadows who want to kill him," she said with a whine in her voice she didn't care to hear but couldn't seem to help. "None of you can know how hard this is."

"True," Jericho said with another light squeeze of her hand. "But most of the people in town will be happy to watch out for you once they learn about your problem. Give them a chance."

Somehow certain she had never been able to depend on anyone the way Jericho was saying she should depend on the whole town, Rosie heaved a heavy sigh. "I'll try."

"Good. And in the meantime, why don't you give the taco salad a chance, too. You might be surprised."

That made her smile. And relax a little. At least, she relaxed enough to discover that the taco salad tasted pretty good. And that she'd been really hungry.

Just as they were contemplating ordering the pecan pie, a nicely dressed woman with short golden-brown hair stepped into the café and looked around. Her warm eyes skipped over every table as though she were searching for someplace to sit. The sight of someone like that who looked a little lost, got to Rosie. She immediately thought of this woman as a kindred spirit.

When Jericho spotted her, he stood and issued an invitation for the woman to join them at their table. Instead of being frightened, Rosie warmed to the thought of getting to know the lady with kind eyes and a friendly smile.

"Rosie," Jericho began after the woman had been seated with them and they'd all ordered pie, coffee and a glass of milk for Rosie. "This is Jewel Mayfair. She's Macy's friend and her boss at the Hopechest Ranch."

He tilted his head toward the woman he'd introduced as Jewel. "This here's our mystery lady, Jewel. I've been calling her Rosie because we don't know her real name."

Jewel extended her hand across the table. "Hi, Rosie. I've heard about you and what happened yesterday from Macy. I was certainly sorry to hear about your troubles. Are you feeling okay now?"

"I'm okay. It's just…frustrating…not knowing anything."

"I'll bet. But I'm sure it will all come back."

As she'd said those words, Jewel's expression had turned melancholy. She looked so depressed and forlorn suddenly that Rosie couldn't help but reach out.

"Are you all right?" Rosie stared into the other woman's face for a moment and discovered deep circles under her eyes. "Aren't you feeling okay?"

"Oh, yes," Jewel told her quietly. "I just haven't been sleeping well lately. That's all."

"Is there something wrong out at the ranch?" Jericho asked. He turned to Rosie. "Jewel runs a new state-of-the-art facility designed specifically to help troubled teens. She tries to give them a stable home base and good hard outdoor work while they're in treatment. I think it's a great idea. Been needed in these parts for a long time."

Returning his attention to Jewel, he said, "There's nothing wrong with any of the kids, is there? Or anything I can do to help?"

Just then the waitress brought out their plates of pie and drinks.

Jewel emptied a sweetener packet into her coffee mug and took a breath before she answered. "It's nothing, Jericho. Just my same old nightmares finally getting the better of me, I guess."

"Nightmares?" Rosie hadn't thought about dreams. Would she have any? Would they be scary or about the good times from her past that she couldn't remember in the bright light of day? "Are they horrible? What do you dream about?"

Jewel looked startled by the question. Rosie could scarcely believe she'd asked such a nosy, none-of-her-business type of thing.

"Sorry. I shouldn't have asked."

Turning to Jewel, Jericho gently put a hand on her shoulder. A dart of jealousy flew into Rosie's chest before she could block it. Such silliness. What was wrong with her? She'd only known Jericho for about twenty-four hours. She simply could not have any feelings for him this fast. And besides, she'd been wanting to take Jewel's hand for support herself.

"You don't have to talk about this, Jewel," Jericho told her. "It's too personal."

So Jericho knew about Jewel's past. Maybe that was just normal for a small-town sheriff. Or maybe they shared something special between them.

"No, it's okay." Jewel tilted her head back to Rosie. "I'm a psychologist. We believe that the more you talk out your demons, the less hold they'll have over you. So I don't mind you asking.

"It's all ancient history, anyway," Jewel continued. "Not something I should be afraid about now. But I still have these nightmares that I…"

"I think I'd rather not remember the bad stuff," Rosie blurted.

Jewel actually lifted the edges of her lips in a half smile. "Sometimes I wish I could have a little amnesia—just about this one thing from my past. But unfortunately, it was a too-real car accident. When I close my eyes, it still seems as clear to me today as it did when it happened a couple of years ago."

"I'm so sorry," Rosie wished she could drop into a hole and cover her head. She didn't want to hear the details. "Were you injured?" she asked anyway.

The other woman sighed. "Yes. And hospitalized for a long time. But that wasn't the worst of it. My fiancé had been driving us out on a date in my car that night. He was killed instantly—along with our unborn child. I…"

Rosie couldn't stand to hear any more. She leaned forward in her seat and whispered, "But you're a psychologist. Isn't there something you can take to make you sleep without the nightmares?"

"No, there's nothing you can take for nightmares," Jewel told her with a note of familiarity that indicated she felt a bond to Rosie. "I've gotten in the habit of taking strolls around the ranch when I can't sleep. It's nice out—usually. The stillness of the night. The vastness of the stars in the heavens. The stock softly baying in their pens. Something about it soothes me. If you have bad dreams, you might try walking."

"Absolutely not." Jericho had been quietly listening

to their conversation, but now he broke in. "And you need to stop going out alone after dark, too, Jewel."

"Oh, Jericho…" Jewel began, skepticism showing in her voice.

"Listen to me," he interrupted. "Remember, it wasn't that long ago a body was found on Clay Colton's ranch land—in a spot right adjacent to the Hopechest. And you—"

He turned to Rosie. "Just yesterday someone shot at you in front of a ton of people at the church. I'd rather you didn't walk anywhere alone. If you need to walk, then let me know. I'll be there to watch your back."

Chapter 6

Rosie's eyes went wide, but then she ducked her head and quietly sipped her milk.

Okay, so maybe he'd come on a little strong. But the idea of anything else happening to Rosie had gotten him all riled up.

Jewel sat, looking down and ringing the edge of her cup with a finger. "I've invited my teenage half brother, Joe Colton, Jr., to come visit for a couple of weeks. I'm hoping the company will help, if that makes you feel any better, Jericho."

An awkward silence spread over the table and Jericho decided he'd be better off to step away from it. He looked around the room and spotted a couple of county road workers that he might be able to question.

"You two be okay here?" he asked, but without expecting an answer. "I'll take care of the bill. Y'all sit as long as you like. I'll just be right over there."

As he strode across the room, Jericho thought he heard the two women whispering behind his back. But he was glad Jewel had befriended Rosie. Jewel's California sophistication seemed a better match to whatever Rosie had been in her past than his rural upbringing would ever be.

He was still trying to puzzle the mystery woman out. She wasn't an outdoors girl, that's for sure. Though, she had definitely taken to the dogs. Both old Shep and the collie puppy Chet nearly loved her to death when she'd stopped to pet them on the way to target practice this morning. He'd been left standing to the side, wishing he could've joined in the fun.

Whatever relationship was developing between him and Rosie had become a primal pull that he was having difficulty ignoring. But giving in to it just wasn't like him. He'd always been a right-is-right kind of man.

After a few minutes of questioning the two county road workers as they ate their lunches and finding himself getting nowhere, Jericho was relieved to hear his name being called out. He turned to find the deputy coming his way.

"Glad I caught up to you, Sheriff." Adam looked calm and cool, even though he'd just come in from the heat of the day. "I wanted to give you an update."

Jericho thanked the road crew and found an empty table so he and the deputy could talk more privately. "Any of the missing persons reports seem promising?" he asked.

The deputy shook his head. "Sorry, boss. I went back through the files for the last six months but didn't come up with anyone who even looked close to our mystery woman's description."

The waitress brought them glasses of water, but they declined anything else. "All right. That's fine, Adam. We'll keep checking around. When you get back to the office, why don't you put out a bulletin to the neighboring counties concerning Rosie and her situation. Something should turn up shortly.

"What else did you get done on Rosie's case today?" Jericho asked.

"I went on over to the feed-and-supply store like you said," the deputy answered as he picked up his water glass. "By the way, your dad says to say 'hey.'"

Jericho nodded, imagining his father's Texas drawl and the casual way he always held his body to make sure everyone felt at home.

"And your brother Fisher asked about the wedding," the deputy added. "I guess he's staying with your father while he's in town, right? Anyway, he wanted to know if the ceremony has been rescheduled. Told him it wasn't any of my business."

Chuckling to himself, Jericho could just imagine Fisher's attitude with the deputy. "If anyone asks you again, Adam, you can say the bride has called the wedding off."

"Yes, sir." The deputy sipped his water. "I left word with your father to check with everyone who comes in the store to see if they can remember anything about the woman or that car.

"But I'm thinking now I'd better get back to the office," Adam added. "On my way home later I'll swing by the truck stop and check with a few of the drivers. See if anyone remembers seeing a woman with crazy red hair."

"Fine. Good work. Something is bound to turn up eventually. Maybe by tomorrow."

Jericho wasn't exactly thrilled about having Rosie stay at his house for another night. Either Jewel or Macy probably would've taken her into their homes for a few days—and maybe he should've asked them for the help. But he'd rather not take the chance of putting anyone else in jeopardy. Someone was still after Rosie. He could feel it in his gut.

Having the mystery woman stay with the sheriff ought to keep her safe. No one would be crazy enough to attack her while she was with him.

Rosie sat back in her chair at the table as she listened to Jewel and Becky French, the café's owner, discussing the first stages of a pregnancy. Maybe she ought to be more attentive to their discussion since she'd been the one to start the conversation by asking questions. But she couldn't muster a whiff of interest in the subject.

In her mid-sixties, Becky was short and plump and seemed like the perfect embodiment of a grandmother. In fact, the first thing the woman had done when she sat down in Jericho's place was to drag out pictures of her own grandchildren in order to show them off.

Something felt familiar about Becky. Rosie stared at her over the rim of her milk glass, willing herself to remember. But whatever had caused that spark of recognition in the first place blew away like a smoke trail in a strong wind.

Did she have her own grandmother somewhere who looked like this one?

Whenever a wisp of a half-remembered memory strayed just out of her reach, she immediately thought about not having anyone. The feeling of being all alone in the world overwhelmed her again and again with paralyzing fear.

What kind of person had she been? Did she have a big family? Lots of brothers and sisters, friends and neighbors? She could only hope that she'd at least been a good person. All that talk from those goons about her having stolen something was worrisome. Was she a thief?

She supposed that if she'd been dishonest the police would have some record on her. Perhaps the deputy had come up with something already. It was a scary idea, but at least then she would know who and what she was.

Looking toward the table where Jericho and his deputy were temporarily seated, Rosie wondered what they'd found out so far. If she was some kind of criminal, she wanted to know for sure. Even if that meant having to face justice somewhere.

She watched Jericho closely. Every single person she'd seen interacting with him so far seemed to have the ultimate regard for the man.

What she wouldn't give to have people think of her in that same way. Was it possible she'd been like that in her previous life?

Maybe she would never remember who she had been

before. Maybe they would never be able to put a name to her face. Then she could build an entirely new life. Starting from today.

If things went that way, Rosie wanted her new life to be like Jericho's. She vowed to make every moment count from now on.

Jericho and Adam rose from their places and walked toward her table. As he came closer, Jericho looked so strong and dependable. It made her want to curl up in his lap and let him protect her from everything. From everybody.

She wanted him. Wanted him to be her sheriff and protector. Wanted him to help her build a new life and become her family. She just plain wanted him.

"Everything good over here, ladies?" Jericho grinned and straddled an empty chair to sit down. "Maybe we should be on our way if you're done."

"Y'all stay as long as you want," Becky told him with a friendly smile.

"Well, that's very nice of you," Jewel said. "But I have to get back to work."

Jericho turned to speak with Becky while Adam took Jewel's elbow and walked with her toward the restaurant's front door. Rosie was left sitting there. She got up and eased toward the door herself so she could bid Jewel goodbye, too.

"I was wondering if you might be willing to join me for supper this Friday night?" Rosie could hear Adam talking quietly to her new friend and she slowed her steps to give them a little privacy.

She couldn't hear Jewel's response, but the other

woman was smiling sadly and shaking her head. Looked like Jewel must be turning the deputy down.

In the next second, Jewel turned and glanced longingly back at Rosie. She seemed to be asking for help.

Rosie walked over beside the other two. "I didn't get a chance to say goodbye, Jewel. Wait up."

Adam nodded his head at the interruption, excused himself and turned away to join the sheriff. Jewel hustled Rosie out the front door of the café so they could say goodbye and not be heard.

"Are you going out with him?" Rosie whispered.

"I can't. I know it's been almost two years since my fiancé died, and Adam seems like a nice enough guy. But I'm just not ready."

Rosie felt terrible for her new friend. "You need to start living again, Jewel. Look at my circumstances. If I don't find out who I am, I'm going to have to build an entire new life. And I won't be able to do it by hiding my head—even if that's what I'd rather do.

"If I can do it, so can you." Suddenly, Rosie's eyes welled with tears and she was forced to flick them away with the back of her hand.

Jewel took her other hand and squeezed. "You're such a dear person. But I suspect you're a lot stronger inside than I am. For me, it's just too soon."

Rosie felt ridiculous being so weepy all the time. Had she always been like that? She straightened up.

"I don't know why I'm so emotional," she told her new friend. "It doesn't seem like I was that kind of person before. But how can I know for sure?"

Jewel patted her shoulder. "Maybe it's because

you're pregnant. Anyway, that's how I felt during my first few months, too. I cried at every little thing. Then after the accident…. Well, I can't possibly have any tears left at this point. I must've cried an entire ocean."

Rosie wanted to hug her friend, but her instinct told her to back off for now. "Maybe you're right to be cautious about dating," she hedged.

She should give herself the same advice. But with Jericho… Well, it was just different with him somehow. She felt like they'd known each other forever. And when it came down to reality, perhaps it would eventually turn out that her *forever* had started yesterday.

"I'd better go check and find out if Jericho wants to go," she said quickly to change the subject. "Will I see you later?"

"I'm really busy at the ranch right now. But maybe Jericho can bring you out to see our operation and meet the kids sometime."

Rosie hoped so. This life might not be her real life, but she was feeling more and more comfortable here and in her new skin.

She said goodbye to Jewel and then returned to the café—only to find Jericho and Adam donning their hats and getting ready to leave themselves. Jericho was still busy saying goodbye to Becky.

But the deputy turned to her and then slid a glance over her shoulder. "Did Jewel go already?"

The tint of a blush rode up Adam's neck. Rosie thought the idea of the tough deputy having a crush on Jewel was sweet.

"Jewel said she had to go back to work, Adam." The

man's crushed expression made her feel bad and urged her to keep on talking, hoping to take the sting out of his rejection. "Did you find out anything about my past so far?"

The deputy shook his head sadly and took her by the hand. "Sorry, ma'am. Nothing yet."

Not as much a surprise as a wake-up call, she found that Adam's hand in hers lacked the same energy as Jericho's. There was no zing with the deputy. No sizzle.

"I wish there was something I could do to help," she said. Then she thought of those goons' scary words about stealing and quickly decided it was time for her to push the issue, even if it meant learning an unfortunate truth. "Have you checked to see if I'm wanted by the police somewhere?"

The deputy reared his head back slightly, narrowed his eyes and dropped her hand. "No, ma'am. Should we?"

She opened her mouth to say yes when suddenly Jericho stepped in close and answered for her. "We've been operating under the assumption that she's the victim, deputy. And I still believe that'll turn out to be the case. But maybe we should cover all the bases. Rosie and I will come back to the office on our way out to my cabin and let you take her prints and a mug shot. Then run them through the Texas system and also through AFIS."

Jericho's eyes were dark and bright as he watched her closely. He looked dangerous as hell. Rosie really hoped she wasn't on the other side of the law from this man. He was probably deadly against his enemies. And she would much rather remain his friend.

The deputy nodded curtly and went on his way.

Jericho took a deep, cleansing breath. He was trying

his best to get his inappropriate jealousy under control. When he'd turned and found Adam's hand on Rosie, his temperature had flared. But feeling this possessive of a mystery woman was just insane. What if she turned out to be a criminal and was faking the amnesia?

No, his gut told him that wasn't right. She couldn't possibly be anything but a victim. Her eyes said that much.

"Come on," he told her.

As he took her elbow, electricity ripped through his hand. His fingertips burned with the mere touch of her skin. He felt more alive and dynamic standing next to this woman than he had in longer than he could ever remember.

"Let's go back to the station and get this over with," he said gruffly. "Then I think we'll stop out by my dad's store on the way back to the cabin. Okay by you?"

She nodded and slipped a hand into his. The sparks exploded between them again. Every time he touched her, no matter how casually, he felt as though he had been branded. He wanted desperately to make her his own. To brand her in return so that everyone would know to keep their hands off.

Unfortunately, the ideas of what he *should* do and what he *must* do were beginning to merge in his mind. Right and wrong had always been clear before. Now all he could visualize was the gray lying in between the black and white. Lust was making him think in ways he'd never done before.

Stupid. Stupid. Stupid.

The handsome and powerful man excused himself from the lavish party and slipped outside to the terrace.

As he went, a dozen beautiful women watched him walk by with lust plainly apparent in their eyes. Too bad he couldn't take them up on their unspoken offers. He had too much to lose right now to give it all up just because he couldn't keep his fly zipped. No matter how tempting.

Checking his cell messages, he found the one from his hired man, Arnie, he'd been expecting. It was about time. After listening for a few moments, he lit an after-dinner cigar and returned the call.

"But, boss." Arnie was hedging with a whine clear in his voice after being chastised for not completing his mission. "She's staying with the sheriff himself. We don't dare try to take her as long as she's with him."

"I said to make your move *now*. Before things get any further out of control. And I expect you to follow orders. I want that woman here within a few hours."

"But boss…he's the sheriff."

"How many men does he have guarding her?"

"Just the sheriff."

The boss *tsked* aloud and chewed on his cigar. He never had trouble controlling his irritation. That's how he had gotten this far. But now he felt a pang of pure anger beginning to crawl up his spine. It made him weak. Unacceptable.

He blew out a breath and vowed to keep his cool this time, too. "Then do as I say. A small county sheriff in Texas is nothing to me. He won't cause you any trouble. Do whatever you need to with him. I can fix it later.

"But I want her back here by tomorrow," he added. "Or else. And no excuses this time. Do you understand me?"

Chapter 7

Rosie waited in the back of the farm-supply store with Jericho's father, while Jericho joked around and told stories with his brother. The two over-six-footers were standing in an aisle near the front windows. Afternoon sun hung low in an orange sky and flowed through the windows, bathing both men in a warm glow as they spoke quietly together.

No customers were in the store at this hour. Just the three Yates men—and her.

Jericho's father made her feel comfortable. Like she almost belonged here. She didn't mind waiting for Jericho and getting to know his father at all. At six feet tall himself, Mr. Yates was still in great physical shape. He wore his gray-streaked hair cut close to his head, and his tanned, leathered skin spoke of a lifetime of outdoor living.

"You sure have two fine-looking sons, Mr. Yates."

"Call me Buck, please. Everyone does." The older man shot a quick glance at his two boys and then turned to study her. "I always tried to raise them with strong values of patriotism and service, and that much seems to have taken hold. But raising good-looking, community-minded men hasn't helped me a bit in getting grand-children. I had hopes that Jericho might be on the right track with Macy, but…"

"Oh." Did Jericho's father blame her for getting in the way of their wedding? "Maybe it was all my fault that the wedding didn't happen. But Macy said…"

"Hold on there." Buck interrupted her with a grin. "I know those two weren't really meant for each other. Not over the long haul. As a matter of fact, my son never once in his life looked at Macy the way he looks at you. It's a good thing he didn't ruin two lives by marrying the wrong person before the right one came along. I did that myself and have regretted it ever since."

"The way he looks at me? He doesn't even know who I am for sure. What do you mean?" She pulled herself up a little straighter and held her breath. It had always seemed to her that Jericho's eyes were questioning her, so Buck's answer seemed all-important. But she wasn't entirely positive why.

Buck patted her shoulder. "He looks at you as if he could eat you in one gulp. As if the sun had never shone on the world until you showed up. It don't matter how long two people know each other. That kind of feeling only comes along once in a lifetime. And my son's got it for you."

Did Jericho feel the same things for her that she'd been feeling for him? How could something like that happen so soon? And in the middle of such terrible confusion and terror.

"I...uh..." Buck started to speak, but his expression had changed from pleasant and hopeful to wary and sad. "That is...I didn't do my sons any favors by not remarrying after their mother left us. I was so sure I could be both mother and father to them that I didn't believe we needed anyone else.

"Trouble with thinking that way, though, is that Jericho was too young at the time to do without a mother." Buck shook his head and frowned. "He never understood why she'd left and never quite forgave his mother for not coming back. I'm sure he blamed himself, but that couldn't be further from the truth. I think he must still have a lot of anger inside him that needs to come out before he can ever be really happy. That's why he's never found anyone before now."

Anger? But that certainly didn't sound like the Jericho Rosie was beginning to know. All right, so maybe he thought of himself as a dedicated bachelor. But was he single because he wanted to be or single because he didn't trust a woman not to hurt him?

Geez. Rosie suddenly decided she was thinking too much. Where had all these crazy amateur psychology ideas come from anyway? Was that what she had been in her real life? A psychologist?

No, that didn't sound right at all. But on the other hand, how could she know anything anymore? Her whole life before Esperanza, Texas was a big fat blank.

Just then, Jericho and Fisher came up the aisle toward them. "You ready to go back to my place?" Jericho asked her.

The warmth Jericho caused by standing so close flamed across her skin and made her wonder if going back to his house was such a good idea.

Yes, she suddenly decided, it was. Getting closer to him was all she wanted. There was nothing she needed more than to plaster herself as close to him as possible. Had Buck been right about Jericho's desire?

There were so many things Rosie couldn't know because her mind had blocked them. But Jericho's desire for her was one thing she had the power to discover in the here and now. And she vowed to force the issue if she had to.

Twilight had arrived. In the parking lot behind his father's store, Jericho unlocked his pickup and turned to help Rosie climb into the passenger seat. But when she stepped closer, he was hit by a blast of yearning so forceful it nearly knocked him to his knees. He wanted her. Badly. Yet he'd known that before. This time, though, it seemed like something more than lust.

As he took her arm, he tried to come up with why this need felt different. *Safe.* That was the only word he could think of to define what he was feeling. He'd been trying so hard to keep her safe that it never occurred to him she might be the one to make him long for security. But as he looked into her eyes, it was like nothing he'd ever experienced before.

Family. For the first time in his life, someone besides

his father and brother made him yearn to be part of a family. This lost woman and her unborn child needed him in a way no one else had—including Macy and T.J. On more of a primitive, survival level.

"Jericho?" Her eyes searched his.

He'd been standing here staring for too long. Abruptly, he threw his arm around her waist to help her into the truck's cab. But he stumbled in his haste, and she reached for his shoulders to steady them both.

Inside, he was anything but steady.

Too close, their gazes locked as a sudden change came into her eyes. She fisted a hand in his shirt and dragged him even closer, though the whole time her eyes stayed intent upon his. Automatically, one of his hands went to her hair, stroking, soothing, until it finally eased its way down to cup the base of her neck.

Time hung between them, like the magic first star in the night sky that hovered just above the horizon. Then came another change. She murmured something low, clamped her hands on both sides of his head and dragged him down for a kiss. Many kisses.

She nibbled and nipped. Licked and sucked with such desperation that Jericho could barely keep up.

His mind went blank. Nothing was making any sense. Nothing but the surety that if he didn't return her kiss right now, this minute, he was going to die.

Giving in to his own desperation, he slanted his mouth over hers and kissed her as if it were the last thing he would ever do. But instead of the end of something, he wanted this kiss to be the first kiss she remembered. His kiss—not some dude's from the depths of her murky past.

As he returned Rosie's wild lust, he put his whole being into it. He ran his hands along her body, drinking in every curve. Soft. Yielding. Sensuous. Jericho absorbed the details, wanting to experience them all.

His hands burned as he touched her everywhere. His lips were set afire by her kisses.

"I want you, Jericho," she whispered against his mouth. "I feel alive with you. What's between us is right. I know you feel it too. Show me. Please."

The sounds of her urgent pleas knocked the sense back into his muddled brain. Thankfully, just in time. Another minute and they would've been sprawled together across the front seat of his pickup. And though it was getting darker by the minute, they were still in the brightly lit parking lot of his father's empty store.

Jericho gently took her by the shoulders and set her back from him. "This isn't right." He eased her up into his arms and slid her into the pickup's front seat.

Striding around the cab, he slipped behind the wheel and started it up. "You must belong to someone—somewhere. If we give in to our hormones tonight and tomorrow your memory comes back, along with a husband, you would never forgive yourself—or me. I won't take that chance."

"What? But…" Her voice trailed off as he put the truck in gear and pulled out of the lot. She folded her arms over her chest and stared out into the night.

Gritting his teeth, Jericho silently fought an internal struggle with fluctuating ideas of right and wrong. And he also battled to bring his overheated body back into line.

Frustrated as hell. He couldn't wait to get home and into a shower. A cold one.

The ride back to Jericho's cabin through the dark countryside was long and silent. Rosie stared out into the night, wishing Jericho would say something. Every now and then, the lights from someone's house shone in the distance. She took those opportunities to sneak a glance over at the man doing the driving.

He gripped the wheel with both hands, so tightly that even in the darkness she could see his knuckles turning white. He had wanted her. She didn't know very much of anything right now, but that had been clear when he kissed her.

Perhaps his father was right and Jericho did want her in a way he'd never wanted anyone before. That knowledge would help her because she couldn't even say the same for herself. She wanted him, all right—but had she wanted someone else the same way once before?

Damn, this was so frustrating. She began wringing her hands in her lap. Needing to think this romance thing through better, Rosie ticked off the few points in her favor as the black night flew by outside her window.

The two of them were attracted to each other. That was good. They seemed to have a definite chemistry. That was also very good. So what was stopping them?

Jericho had been about to be married when she'd fallen into his life. That could be bad. But then Macy and Jericho had both made it clear they didn't love each other and the wedding was off. Good for her again.

So now how about her own past? She was pregnant

with someone's child. And of course, that had put a serious damper on Jericho's desire a few minutes ago. But deep down Rosie didn't feel that there was anyone else, even though someone had obviously been with her—at least once. She'd thought and thought, scoured her feelings, but the only emotions she felt from the fog of her past were scary. Fear. Not love.

And if there had been someone, why hadn't he reported her missing? That was the number one unanswered question making her feel positive she was alone.

"Hell." Jericho took his foot off the accelerator and peered through the windshield down his own long asphalt driveway as the outside lights from his cabin burned through the darkness before them.

Rosie looked up, too. "What's the matter? Is something wrong?"

Jericho left the truck idling for a moment. "Everything looks fine. But…" He rolled down his window. "The dogs aren't barking. And there's just something—not right."

He put the pickup into neutral, flipped off the headlights, and reached around to eye his rifle, which was hanging in a rack in the back window. "I'm going to turn the pickup around, drive to the main highway and leave you there parked and locked in the truck. Meanwhile I'll call the deputy to come meet you while I hike back here to check things out."

He turned forward without unracking the rifle. Instead, he pulled his cell phone out of his pocket—just as a loud ping sound hit the truck's front bumper. Dropping the phone, Jericho rammed the truck into gear, hit the gas and spun in a one-eighty.

"Someone is shooting at us!" Rosie shouted above the noise of the engine revving.

"Right. Get down!" He flipped open her seat belt and shoved at her back.

She slid all the way to the floor and covered her head with her arms. Rolling into a tight ball, she squeezed her eyes shut and prayed.

Jericho cursed under his breath as he straightened the wheel and stomped on the accelerator again. He wished for the cell phone that was now out of reach on the floor somewhere. They needed help.

Hoping he could escape, he raced wildly down his own driveway. Good thing he knew every inch of this asphalt drive. He'd built it with his own hands.

But just when his pickup was within a hundred feet of the highway, moonlight picked up the shadow of a massive SUV pulling into the driveway from the road and blocking their exit.

Slamming on the brakes, Jericho came to a stop. Sweet mercy. They were surrounded.

Another series of blasts, sounding like they must be coming from an assault weapon of some sort, exploded through the air. The shots completely missed them, but Jericho didn't figure they'd be so lucky a third time.

"Yipes!" Rosie screeched from the safety of the floor.

How many were there? At least two. One in the SUV and one nearer to the house. Jericho was fairly sure they hadn't managed to break through his carefully constructed security and gotten into his home. But he needed to get inside there himself. Inside was a way to call for help and plenty of firepower to hold them off until help arrived.

Reaching over, he grabbed a handful of Rosie's shirt by the back of her collar. "Take your seat again and buckle up tight," he ordered.

"What are you planning?" she asked shakily as she rose to her knees.

Even though he didn't answer, when he jerked upward, she pushed herself back into a seated position. Then he waited one more second to make sure she had the safety belt tight enough.

"Hang on and stay low." Without considering other consequences, he swung the wheel to the right and pointed his truck off the driveway toward the empty fields. Then he hit the gas. The pickup jerked and roared ahead, breaking through a wooden fence he'd only just finished building last month.

Jericho plowed his truck through the rangy field. With the headlights still off, he prayed silently that none of the pickup's tires would hit a recently dug prairie-dog hole. Damned varmints never stopped digging, no matter how he had tried to stop them.

He and Rosie were lucky on this night. He heard the pickup's four-wheel drive cutting in as needed, and on a few occasions, the tires spun in the dirt before he slowed and allowed them to catch again. It didn't matter that they were bashing through prickly pear cactus and past tall, spindly wildflowers. His good ole truck made short work of it. He refused to think about what this wild ride might be doing to the paint on the sides and fenders. What was a new paint job when it came to saving Rosie's life?

At last they'd almost crossed the open field and reached the tree line beyond. There was only a half-moon tonight, but he wasn't having any trouble seeing where he was going. He knew it all by heart.

"Stop! Watch out for the woods," Rosie shouted from her seat next to him.

Apparently she wasn't having much trouble seeing in the moonlight, either. Jericho hoped to hell the bad guys' positions had been far enough away that they weren't seeing their escape route quite as well. And God help them if these goons had night-vision goggles.

He slowed the truck just a little at the tree line and drove right between two tall ebony trees. Hearing Rosie gasp, Jericho wished he had time enough to explain. But for his plan to work, he had to keep concentrating on his driving.

If the bad guys were smart enough to listen, they would certainly be able to hear the pickup's engine, even though the truck would be hidden by the woods. Because of that, he should turn the pickup off as soon as possible. But fortunately, he knew that people unfamiliar with rural areas would not think to step outside their vehicles and pay attention to the noise. He had to hope these perps were city boys.

Dodging through the sparse trees, Jericho judged their position and decided it must already be close to his destination. Sure enough, another few feet and he felt the front tires making contact with caliche. The ancient road through the woods that ran from an abandoned homesite—situated maybe a few hundred yards behind his cabin—to the main highway might be overrun with weeds and pockmarked by the weather. But it would take him where he wanted to go.

And where he wanted to go was not back to the highway. He was counting on that being what the bad guys would figure. That he would make a beeline for the highway, trying to escape. But Jericho knew the stretch of highway running in front of his acreage was always pretty deserted at this time of night. So he turned his truck in the other direction and headed toward the old homesite.

He spared a swift glance toward Rosie and saw her hanging on to the door with all her might. She was badly shaken by this bumpy ride. But at least she was alive.

As the pickup neared the relic of the ancient cabin, Jericho cut the engine and let it glide up to the clearing. When he thought they were in the best spot not to be seen through the woods, he parked and took the first breath he'd had since the original rifle shot had hit the truck.

"We're right behind my cabin—out a few yards behind those targets I set up." He shifted and drew his service weapon. "Here. This is similar to the gun you were using to practice this morning. I want you to keep it and stay with the truck." He handed the Glock over and then turned to bring down his rifle.

"You're not leaving me here." Even in the darkness he could see her trembling.

"You'll be safer here. I'm going to sneak up to the house and get in through a hidden basement door. I won't be able to move as fast or as quietly with you in tow. Stay here where I know you'll be safe."

"Why are you going to the cabin? Why aren't we running for our lives in the other direction?"

"Trust me," he said. "They won't be expecting me

to head right for them. This'll be the best way—a real surprise."

Hefting the rifle with one hand, he quietly eased open the door but flipped off the overhead light. Then he reached around under his seat with his free hand.

When he straightened, he held up something small. "Here's my cell phone." He shoved it at her. "Call 911 the minute I'm out of sight. Tell them Sheriff Yates needs help at his cabin. And also tell them you're waiting in my pickup by the old Gaston place. They'll come, but it may take twenty minutes."

Before he stepped out, Jericho shifted close and seared a quick kiss across her lips. "Please stay put. No matter what you hear. I'll come back for you as soon as I can."

She blinked a couple of times and then stared down at the weapon still fisted in her hand. "Okay," she answered in a shaky voice.

Rosie watched Jericho slide noiselessly out of the truck and shut the door behind him. Within seconds he disappeared into the darkness.

She called 911 and the operator also told her to stay where she was. After hanging up, she was all alone again.

Her heart thudded so loudly in her chest that she was afraid it would give her away. Her eyes had adjusted to the darkness, but every shadow seemed to move. The black night began closing in on her.

She couldn't just sit here. If one of those men happened to spot the truck, they'd have her captured in an instant. Not sure she could use the gun and sorry she had promised to stay put, Rosie made the decision to move. To hide in the trees, away from the pickup.

Easing out her door, she carefully shut it again. Then, putting the phone in her pocket and holding the gun with both hands, she tiptoed across the caliche and into the forest in the same direction as she'd last seen Jericho.

Shaking badly and with her back against the rough surface of a tree, she stopped to catch her breath and listened for any sounds. Nothing. No night noises of any kind. No car engines. No whispers or footsteps close enough that she could hear.

She closed her eyes and tried to calm down. But then it happened. A loud click sounded through the night. Close by. Had it come from over by the truck? Was it the sound of a weapon being prepared to fire? Or was it someone's footsteps breaking a twig beneath their shoes?

It didn't matter which one. She had to get away. Adrenaline shot through her veins, giving her false courage and agility as she stepped out and made her move.

Chapter 8

Rosie had been holding her breath for the last fifteen minutes. Hadn't she? Hiding behind the largest target Jericho had set up in his backyard, she exhaled and peered toward the back of his cabin through the spotty moonlight.

Suddenly staccato bursts, which she thought must be guns firing, echoed through the night. But they seemed a long way away. Were sounds deceiving out here? And who had been doing the shooting—and who may have been shot? The next moment brought total silence again.

Weren't there outside lights in the back as well as the front of the cabin? It seemed as though this morning she'd noticed a few tall posts at the edges of Jericho's backyard that she'd assumed were lights or electricity. Now there was nothing but darkness.

Curiosity got the better of her. She had to find out what was going on.

Creeping out from her hiding place, Rosie wondered if she would be too exposed even in the dark by cutting across Jericho's yard. She slipped the gun into her waistband and dropped to all fours. Crawling might cause her hands and knees some damage, but maybe she would live longer by keeping a lower profile.

After slithering a few feet, her hands were covered in nasty burrs from the sticker bushes. Another yard and her skin began to sting. Ants! Cripes.

Was it worth it to stay low? Someone from above must've been watching out for her, because right then she felt the raindrops start against her back and neck.

Rain would be a good cover, she thought. So she stood, dusted off the ants and stickers as best she could and moved on through the windy mists, hopefully still in the direction of the cabin.

Did she know how to pray? Had she been a churchgoer in her previous life? Rosie couldn't say, but still, she tried begging for mercy in the only way she could imagine.

Please, God. If I was a bad person, then don't help me now for myself. But keep me safe for Jericho's sake. She knew the sheriff well enough by now to know if he lost her, it would devastate him.

The rain began coming down in sheets then, and she gave thanks for the shield it provided. But in the next moment she found herself totally turned around. What direction was the cabin? Rosie could barely tell up from down.

Frozen in panic, she swiped the water out of her eyes

and tried to reason. Should she keep on going straight ahead? Had she turned her body at all after she'd stood up and the rain started?

A disturbing noise reached her ears through the sounds of rain splashing against the dirt. It sounded for all the world like someone moaning. Jericho?

Had he been injured? If so, he would need her help.

Sucking up all her courage, Rosie put her hands straight out in front of her body to run interference in case she smashed into any trees or walls. And then she took her first tentative steps, going in what seemed to be the same direction as the moaning sounds.

Shuffling along, she went quite a few yards, totally blinded by the rain. Then the weather eased up a bit, allowing her to see the dark shape of the cabin straight ahead. She stopped to listen.

There. The same unsettling moans. Closer to the cabin's back wall. She inched ahead again.

Nearby. She felt she was almost on top of the sounds now. Did she dare call out?

Dear Lord, what shall I do?

Out of nowhere a siren's scream pealed through the night. Help was coming! Thank heaven. They were saved.

"Jericho," she rasped in as loud a whisper as she dared. "Where are you?"

Another blind step and Rosie tripped over something large and inert, lying on the ground. She put her hands out in front of her body to take the brunt of her fall. But it wasn't any use.

Down she went. In the next instant, her nose buried itself in mud and muck. Ugh. As fast as possible, she pushed herself up and tried to roll over to catch her breath. The mud clung to her, sucked her back down.

Damn it. All she could think was had that inert object been Jericho's body? Rosie forced herself up to crawl backward. She had to find out.

Quickly losing his grip on self-control, Jericho slammed the door to his empty pickup, still sitting exactly where he'd left it, and cussed under his breath. Where the hell was she? She'd promised to stay here.

He knew the bad guys hadn't had a chance to kidnap her. He'd been keeping them plenty busy over the last half hour. First with the surprise of having to fight off his firepower. And then with trying to get away after they'd heard the sirens heading their way.

At least they hadn't gotten away totally clean. He'd winged one of them as the guy had been making a dash toward his buddy in the SUV. Jericho was sure of it. He was also positive their SUV had taken several hits as he'd fired at their retreating backside.

Both Deputy Rawlins and a deputy from another part of the county had arrived at the scene at the same time. The other deputy had taken off in pursuit, but Jericho didn't figure he would have much of a chance of catching the SUV that'd had a few minutes head start.

Now where the hell was Rosie?

"Lend me your cell, Adam," he said to his deputy.

"Sure thing, boss." Adam threw him a phone and then began edging around the clearing with his flashlight studying the ground.

"There won't be any decent prints left after that rainstorm," Jericho told him. "I'm going through the woods toward the rear of my cabin. You go on back to the house by way of the highway and see if you can spot Rosie anywhere along the road."

They split up and Adam retreated carefully down the ancient caliche road in the direction of the highway. Jericho flicked on his own flashlight and headed into the woods at approximately the same spot where he'd gone in an hour ago.

In a few minutes, he came out at the edge of his property line. Going left, he found the emergency shutoff for the outside lights and turned them back on. Earlier darkness had saved his ass. Now it was keeping him from finding Rosie. She had to be somewhere close.

He stood for a second, letting his eyes become accustomed to the floodlight. Then, thinking he heard a snuffling noise, Jericho moved closer to his cabin. In the direction of that noise. Pulling out his deputy's phone, he put it to his ear and punched in his own cell number.

It began to ring, but the ringing was much clearer in his free ear than in the ear next to the phone. His own phone had to be somewhere nearby.

"Hello?" He heard Rosie whispering into the phone.

"Where are you?" he demanded. "You were supposed to stay put."

"Jericho? I need you. I'm out behind...."

Her sentence was interrupted when Jericho's flashlight beam roamed across her face. "Here I am. Help me, please."

Through the beam of light, Jericho saw her sitting on the ground in half shadow just a few feet behind his cabin. She looked like someone had covered her in mud and weeds. Her tear-streaked face was caked and intense. If he wasn't mistaken, she also seemed to be holding his old shepherd's head in her lap.

"What the hell?" He bent on one knee. Sure enough, Shep's body lay perfectly still and Rosie was murmuring something quietly in the old dog's ear.

"I think he's still alive," she said. "But…but…"

"They poisoned him." Jericho's blood raged. He had to grit his teeth against the idea of anyone hurting his animals.

Thrusting the flashlight into Rosie's hand, he carefully scooped up the dog. "Lead the way toward the kitchen door. As soon as we get him inside, I'll call for help. Then I'll need to come back out and look for Chet."

At the mention of his name, the collie appeared out of the shadows. With his tail between his legs and shaking his head as though to clear it, the collie didn't look all that strong, either.

"Good boy, Chet. We've got your buddy now. Don't worry. Come inside."

Rosie opened the door, flipped on the kitchen overhead light and stood aside so he could bring both dogs across the threshold. Jericho took one look at her in the bright light, and his heart sank.

Not only hadn't he managed to keep his dogs safe, but the one person he'd been determined to save tonight looked like she'd been dragged through hell.

Nice night's work, Sheriff.

"Thanks, Quinn. I appreciate it." In the early hours of the morning, Jericho stood at his front door, saying goodbye to his neighbor, Quinn Logan, a large animal vet. "I know dogs aren't really your business, but I'm not sure mine would've made it without your help."

Rosie stood back a few feet and listened as Quinn prepared to leave. She ached all over. And even though she'd washed her face and hands, her body was still covered in mud. However, she was much more concerned for her host than for herself. He'd been so pale and quiet as they'd tried to make the dogs comfortable and waited for the vet.

At first, after they'd come into the dry, safe house, he'd been all business and strong as he'd dealt with the deputies and made phone calls about their attackers. Then a little later, when they were sitting on the floor with the dogs in the kitchen, she'd caught Jericho trembling while he stroked the coat of his old shepherd. She almost knew how he felt. If Shep died because someone was after her, she would never be able to live with herself.

"Well, I didn't do much," Quinn told Jericho. "I wish I could've done more for the shepherd. Your collie should be fine by tomorrow. But it may be touch and go with the older dog for a few days."

"What kind of poison do you think they used?"

Quinn, a man about Jericho's height but with an easygoing manner and sensitive eyes, shook his head and took a breath. "Not sure. But if I had to guess, I'd say it was probably an illegal human drug. Maybe something like PCP, which is easy to get on the street, and acts like an anesthetic in animals. As a powder, it would've been simple to add it to hamburger and feed it to the dogs.

"If it'd been anything like a real poison, the dogs wouldn't have lived for this long."

Jericho cleared his throat and looked down at his boots. "Yeah, well…"

Quinn clapped him on the shoulder with a gentle hand. "There's nothing else you can do but wait. Get some rest yourself."

The vet tilted his head in Rosie's direction. "I'm thinking the humans in this house need as much attention as the animals. Both of you look like a strong wind might blow you over."

Jericho shot her a quick glance. His eyes softened as they took in her messy appearance. Then he turned to finish telling the vet good-night.

After he locked the door and set the security alarms, Jericho took a few steps in her direction. He held his hands out, and Rosie thought he might take her into his arms. But something stopped him and he dropped his hands limply to his sides, shaking his head with hesitation.

"Why don't you take a shower and hit the sack?" he said as he brushed past her, heading for the kitchen. "You heard Quinn. I'm just going to check on the dogs once more then collapse myself."

"Aren't you worried about those men coming back?"

"Not tonight." Jericho's lips actually quirked up into the semblance of a smile as he stopped and turned. "I'd bet those goons are going to be busy finding a way of tending their wounds without going to a legit doctor who would be bound to turn them in. They won't even think of us again tonight. Then, for tomorrow night and every night until we come up with answers, I've already lined up a watch system. My brother, Fisher, and a couple of deputies from other parts of the county have already volunteered to stand guard in shifts. I'm sure a couple of our neighbors wouldn't mind helping out, either."

"Oh, no. That's too much trouble because of me. Maybe I should leave. Go…" *Where?* Where could she go?

Jericho's expression tensed as he shook his head. "You're safer here than anywhere else. Let us watch out for you while we figure out where you came from. None of the people around here mind taking up the cause of your safety. It's what we do in these parts. We watch out for each other."

Rosie brushed her fingers over her burning eyes. "Thank you, Sheriff. I suspect your friends and neighbors will help because of you, not me.

"But I don't seem to have a lot of choices, do I?"

He stood watching her intently for several moments without answering. "Go on to bed. We'll figure out something eventually. And in the meantime, just remember you're safe."

Turning his back then, Jericho headed into the kitchen to look after his animals. Miserable, but out of both choices and energy, Rosie forced one foot in front of the other and made her way toward the shower.

At the very least she could clean up. It was one of the only things she could do to help herself.

A half hour later, Jericho stood barefoot in front of his bedroom mirror, staring at his own image. Naked to the waist, he bent over the dresser and beat his fisted hands against the top. What a jerk he was.

Damn it! He'd been so scared when he'd thought he might've lost Rosie. It made him sick to his stomach to think of it.

Gulping in air, he wondered what the hell was the matter with him. She wasn't his to lose. She didn't belong to him. In fact, she clearly belonged to someone else.

His dogs were resting easy now. He couldn't worry too much about them for what was left of the night. But he had a feeling he wasn't going to be faring as well as they did, what with Rosie right next to him in the other bedroom.

After he took a couple more deep, calming breaths, an odd noise reached his ears. Someone seemed to be in trouble nearby.

He stepped out into the darkened hallway and stood still to listen. The noise was much clearer from this spot. What he'd been hearing with the door closed was definitely the sound of a woman's sobs. Coming from his bathroom.

He'd thought Rosie was already asleep in her room. Something must be wrong with her. But what should he do about it?

It sounded for all the world as if her heart were broken. But maybe she'd been hurt. What if she'd cut herself and really needed his help?

Hell.

In three big strides, he was at the bathroom door. He tried the knob, hoping to peek in and check on her without her noticing him. The door was unlocked, so he held his breath and opened it.

When he could see inside, he found the bathroom

awash in limited, flickering light. Just the two night-lights were burning, but the overheads had been left off.

Rosie stood in front of the bathroom mirror, looking at herself through the dim light in the mirror. And sobbing uncontrollably.

"You okay?" he whispered. "Do you need help?"

She gasped, and it was only then he noticed she didn't have on any clothes. She didn't turn around but grabbed a towel and held it to her body, trying to cover the intimate parts.

But she couldn't cover her long, lovely backside. And he let himself take it all in. From the crown of her strange red-colored head, down her slender neck and past the slim torso all the way to her perfectly rounded buttocks and those mile-long legs. My God. She was perfect. He'd known she would be. But this was better than all his idle dreams.

"Go away. I'm…okay," she began with a stutter. "No, that's not true, Jericho. I do need help. I need…"

She started to turn, but then their eyes met in the glass and she halted. She blinked and licked her upper lip. "The doctor said it was all right to shower, but not to get the bandage too wet. It seems I got the dressing all muddy earlier. So then I tried to change it myself, but I…can't reach."

Jericho watched as the tears began again. They glistened against her cheeks in the low light and swamped her beautiful blue eyes.

"Let me," he said and took a step closer.

Rosie tried to stem the flow of her tears. What an idiot she must be. It was a simple thing. Just changing her bandage after a shower. But when she couldn't seem to help herself, she'd remembered how all alone she was and the tears poured in earnest.

Jericho was being so nice. But nice wasn't really what she wanted from him. She wanted—well, she wasn't sure.

Glancing up into the mirror over the sink, their gazes met—and locked. Oh, yes. That's what she wanted from him. Whatever that was, there in his eyes. Was it a hunger? A wanting so desperate he looked ready to pounce.

"Give me the bandage and show me where," he demanded roughly.

Her heart pounded wildly as his gaze lowered to the edge of her towel in the mirror. She could feel her nipples tighten painfully in response to that look. She wanted him to touch her there, relieve her aching.

"The bandage is on the counter," she said, but was surprised at how deep her voice sounded. "And the wound is on my side, under my left arm."

"Show me," he repeated slowly, and put his hand on her shoulder.

Her skin sizzled at his touch. It was too much temptation. She nodded and dropped the towel.

Rosie didn't know what to expect. Would he turn away? Every moment the unspoken question hung in the air her passion spun higher. Yet, so help her, she could not have blinked as much as an eyelid if her life had depended on it.

He didn't turn. He didn't budge. He didn't seem to be breathing.

Part of her wanted him to whisk her up and carry her to bed. But the part of her that could've moved stood transfixed as his hand finally…finally…flexed and began caressing her shoulder as he bent to place kisses against her neck.

Even in the shadowed lighting, the sight of his darkly suntanned hand, contrasting against her pale body, was exciting. The skin lying under his fingers grew heated and began to tingle.

He stepped in closer and she could feel his warmth against her back. Her sensitive skin flamed and flushed, igniting at every point they came together. She could also feel the hard ridge under the placket of his jeans zipper poking into the small of her back. The juncture of her thighs flooded with moisture and she watched her own eyes going wide in the mirror.

She opened her mouth to beg, but no sound came out. Wanting to face him, to touch him, she started to turn. But his right hand came up under her arm to her ribcage and pulled her back into his chest.

"Stay," he growled.

He rubbed his palm upward so that his fingers were in position to trace her taut peaks. She moaned. Wanted to squirm. Instead her head fell back against his shoulder as he pulled and lightly pinched her sensitive nipples.

Every movement felt so wonderful. So perfect. Had sex ever been good before? Not like this, she was sure.

Jericho's other hand slid around her hips, flattening against her belly. A downpour of sensation raced straight to the spot between her legs that ached for him, as his hand slowly inched lower through the curly hair under her belly button.

Her eyelids drooped and her knees trembled.

"Watch," he gasped.

Her lids popped open and she stared straight ahead at the sight of the two of them in the mirror. While with one hand he rubbed and provoked the tips of her breasts, his other thumb flicked over her feminine nub— stroking, tempting, tormenting.

The woman in the mirror looked so wanton. She was sensual, heavy-lidded, breathing through an open mouth and with startling rosy nipples that grew higher at every caress.

But as Jericho continued to tighten the string on her reserves, Rosie decided she didn't care how it all looked. She only wanted to experience an end to this growing pull inside her.

"Jericho, please." How sexy she sounded to her own ears. Every movement of Jericho's and every sound she made only served to build the tension higher and higher inside her.

He began murmuring soft words of lust into her ear in that lazy, erotic Texas drawl of his. Stroking and caressing, his fingers worked faster, harder, until she thought her whole body would burst into flame.

At last the tight rubber band inside her snapped in a flood of sensation as the orgasm washed over her. In the mirror, her eyes widened impossibly and her mouth dropped open in a very unfeminine scream.

Pulsating aftershocks hit her in waves of pure pleasure. Her knees buckled and Jericho lifted her into his arms.

He turned to carry her into the bedroom as she whimpered against his chest. This was going to be a long but fantastic night. She couldn't wait.

Chapter 9

"Hang on." Jericho carefully laid her down on the guest bed, flipped on the bedside lamp then turned and strode back out the door.

Hang on? What could he mean, and where was he going?

Rosie's senses still reeled. But she suddenly felt cold without him. He should be here beside her. She needed to touch him and make him feel every bit as good as he'd done for her. Together they were going to be spectacular. So why wasn't he here?

Minutes dragged by before he reappeared in the doorway, carrying something in his hand.

"If you're worried about protection," she began, "I can understand your concern. But the doctor's tests would probably have caught anything I might've had. And if it's for the other reason, wouldn't that be like locking the prison door after the criminals already escaped?"

"Turn on your side." Ignoring her comments, he slid a hand beneath her and urged her to turn on her right side, facing away from him.

Hmm. Was this usual? she wondered. Why couldn't she remember having sex? This was like being a virgin— at least in her mind.

Instead of sliding his body into the bed behind her, he raised her arm above her head and began rebandaging her wound. "This won't take but a minute. Then you can get some sleep."

"What? Aren't you coming to bed with me?" She couldn't see his expression as he worked on her side, but his tight silence told her everything.

"Jericho, I don't want to go to bed alone." She heard the tones of exasperation mingling with her near desperation and tried to calm down. "I want you to come to bed with me so we can finish what we started. You didn't…I mean, you didn't have your…um…turn. Let me touch you. Let me feel you inside me."

Instead of answering, she felt him patting down the edges of the tape around the bandage. Then he gently placed her arm down at her side and turned her over on her back. Staring up at him, Rosie became so frustrated she wanted to scream.

Jericho's eyes gleamed bright with what she would swear must be desire as he gazed down on her naked body. He reached over and placed his palm flat against her belly. The fire his hand caused seared her there and set her aflame once more.

She groaned and reached her arms out to him.

"No." He grimaced but left his wide hand gently but firmly against her flushed skin. "Tucked safely under my hand is someone else we have to consider. We can't just act without thinking through the consequences for everyone. Your child has a father—somewhere.

"I shouldn't have taken advantage of you like that," he went on. "The two of you need to know where you belong—*before* making any decisions you might come to regret. Tonight was all my fault. I've promised to protect you, and I mean to, even if it has to be protection from me."

He took a deep breath. "You've had a bad night. Mostly due to my mistakes. I'd appreciate it if you would sleep now."

Too stunned at his little speech to speak, Rosie blinked up at him as he lifted the covers and tucked her in. This guy was definitely too good. Or was that more like so good it could be bad?

As he turned off the light and backed out the door, she worked to bite back her neediness, closing her eyes and wishing a dream to come for what she really wanted.

But when the images came into her mind, she couldn't tell if they were dreams or not. Everything seemed so familiar. But then again…it might not be her own reality.

The soft evening air, tenderly perfumed with the scent

of flowers, ruffled her hair. The sounds of an orchestra played in the background. Gentle laughter and conversation floated lightly on a sweet breeze.

How strange.

She was floating, too. In a long blue gown. Shimmering up a staircase that appeared out of nowhere. A staircase that looked as though it must belong in a castle.

How amusing. And how thrilling.

Before her appeared a prince. Wearing a tux, his royal bearing quickly became a powerful aphrodisiac. Tall and lean, with dark brown hair combed in an impeccable style, he stood out above all the rest. She felt a tiny pang of regret, somehow missing dark blond hair that grew over the collar and always appeared messy.

But then the prince gave her a generous smile that eased into a deep dimple on his left cheek, and her heart fluttered. Thoughts of any other smiles flittered away as his eyes filled with romance, passion and sex.

The prince held out his hand to her, and she stepped into his arms. Music filled her head with sparkling, erotic diamonds of pure passion as they danced across a ballroom floor like a royal couple.

Was she a princess? Looking down at herself, she saw glass slippers on her feet. So…not a princess. She must be only pretending.

But she quickly decided she didn't care. Twirling around the dance floor, she felt beautiful—and powerful. Like nothing could ever hurt her, and like everyone in the room would want to be her.

A bolt of lightning suddenly shot golden flashes through the ballroom. With the boom of thunder that followed, spears of panic darted straight into her heart. She gasped, stepping back and holding a hand to her breast to still the fear.

Glancing at the prince for reassurance, what she saw instead sent chills up her spine. Dark, demon eyes glared at her with fury and hunger.

Sinister.

Evil.

My God. She stumbled back, turned and fled.

The music disappeared and she was barefoot, running through a field of blood. It was after her. The monster was hot on her heels.

Closing in faster and faster.

She had to hide. Ripping at her clothes, she stripped off the gown and streaked through the foggy night. Shivering now, and mewling like a wounded animal, she fell to her knees. But all around her was blood. A sea of it.

The contents of her stomach curdled with nausea as she tried to crawl away. But the simmering scarlet ocean clung to her, dragging her down. Tentacles reached around her body, tugging at her ferociously.

Dragging at her body.

Pulling her further and further down.

Clawing her way up, Rosie forced her eyes to open. Sunshine glittered into the room, nearly blinding her with its welcoming reality. She was safe. Safe in Jericho's guest bedroom.

Thank heaven. The sheets were twisted around her body, a reminder of her nightmare. They clung to her, tying her to the bed.

She fought them off and swung her legs over the side. Trying to clear the last bit of fog from her brain, Rosie stood up, took a deep breath—and nearly doubled over from the nausea.

That must be still part of the dream, right?

In the next moment, she found out that being sick to her stomach was unfortunately very real. She made a mad dash for the bathroom across the hall, praying she would make it in time.

At nearly midday, Jericho hurried his way through morning bathroom chores. He wasn't too sure he would ever again be able to spend much time in his bathroom. Images of what he and Rosie had done together last night surrounded him and punched him in the gut. Trying to shave, he'd felt himself suffocating on the visions he remembered in the mirror.

Dumb. Taking advantage of the situation last night had been a purely dumb-ass move. He'd always imagined himself to have more self-control. Guess not. At least not when it came to Rosie.

In only two days, the woman had gotten under his skin. Having her stay here in his home wasn't smart. Obviously he couldn't be trusted to keep his hands to himself. Maybe this afternoon he would be better off sneaking her over to one of the neighbor's houses to stay the night. If handled properly, the move could easily remain a secret and she should be safe.

Rubbing at a sudden ache in his chest, Jericho braced himself for seeing her again. Was she still asleep? They'd had a late night, which he hadn't done a blessed thing to help. He hoped to hell she'd been getting the rest she needed since then.

Jericho headed for the kitchen and the coffeepot. But before he could even leave the shelter of the hallway, Rosie's voice wafted through the air and met his ears. Coming to a halt, he stood and listened to her speaking softly to the dogs. In another second she began humming, sweet and low in her throat.

A disturbing memory ambushed him. He hadn't awoken to a woman humming in the kitchen since he'd been seven years old. Sharp, edgy memories of growing up and hoping against hope to hear those feminine sounds once more came darting through his conscious mind.

Waking up in his room upstairs at home, sneaking down to peek into his dad's kitchen and praying that Momma would've finally come home. He'd been so sure that any day now she would be back and tell him she'd made a big mistake in leaving him. Despite Daddy forever saying it would never happen.

Dumb again, Jericho told himself while he exhaled heavily and cleared his head. As an adult, he realized that the family had been much better off without his alcoholic mother. *He'd* been better off, too.

Still, what a surprise to suddenly find that aching need had never completely gone away. That it had just been lurking there in his subconscious. Irritated with himself for being so vulnerable, he stuffed the old feelings back into the dark corner of his mind and went into the kitchen to confront all his demons.

"Good morning," Rosie said and looked up at him as

he entered the room. She was sitting on the kitchen floor, trying to coax Shep into drinking water.

God, she was even more beautiful in the light of day than she'd been last night. If that was even possible.

Refusing to just stand and stare at her, he bent on one knee and checked Shep's eyes. They were much clearer and the old dog seemed to recognize his master.

Jericho cleared his throat. "It's nearly noon, but it looks like the day will be good one. The dogs are better."

"Yes." She gently placed Shep's head back down on his dog bed and stood. "I hope that means they're going to make it."

"I think it must. Though Quinn said it would take a couple of days to be sure." He stood too and turned to the coffeepot. "Have you had anything to eat?"

"Uh, no. I fixed myself some tea and made you some coffee. But I'm not really very hungry."

He glanced over his shoulder, really looking at her, and saw that her face was pale, her hair standing up on end as though she'd run her hands through it. "You okay?"

"I had a nightmare. But I think it might mean something. Maybe my memories will be coming back through my dreams. What do you think?"

His first thought, that her returning memory was the last thing he wanted, sideswiped him with unusual force. When she remembered, she would leave him and go back to her life. *Breathe.* After another moment, he got his bearings and mentally kicked himself for being such a fool. Of course she needed to remember. It was her life.

"It's possible," he said. "Doc O'Neal said the memories might come back in bits and pieces." Jericho tried to smile at her, to reassure her, but he didn't feel much like smiling. "What did you dream?"

"Most of it was silly—or scary. But I clearly remember looking down at myself and thinking I looked like a fairy princess. With long, beautiful and shiny hair." She reached up and tugged at her own short locks. "Not the horrible-looking mess that's there now."

He blinked a couple of times and all of sudden the image of her naked in the mirror last night sprang into his head. "You know, I believe you probably are a natural blonde. If that makes you feel any better."

She frowned. "No. That just makes things worse. I want to know for sure. I wish I had a picture. Being sure about my looks might make it easier for the rest of it to come back."

"Well, now," he said as the idea gelled in his mind. "I think we need an expert opinion. And maybe you might discover something you enjoy doing at the same time.

"Get your shoes on. I'll call one of the neighbors to come over and stay with the dogs for the afternoon. I know where we'll find just the person we need to figure it out."

Rosie once again stared intently at herself in a mirror. Only this time the mirror was at Sallie Jo's Cut N Curl, a few doors down from the sheriff's office. The person standing directly behind Rosie with her fingers sliding through Rosie's hair was the owner, Sallie Jo Stanton.

"What do you think, Sal?" Jericho asked from his spot, off to the side. "That red can't be for real. Can you tell anything about the natural color?"

"Hmm." Sallie was a woman in her early forties. Maybe a little heavyset for her bones, but her hair and makeup seemed impeccable and her clothes fit perfectly.

She combed Rosie's hair into sections. "Yeah, looky there. The blond roots are already growing out.

"Now why would you want to cover up your gorgeous ash-blond with that nasty red dye, sugar?"

Rosie lifted her eyebrows. "I don't know—for sure. But can you put it back to natural?"

Sallie shook her head and studied the hair a little closer. "The only way to totally get rid of the dark red color would be too harsh. I could strip it out, but that would ruin your hair and it still wouldn't be natural."

She lifted a section so Rosie could see it clearly in the mirror. "We can lighten it up some. Maybe end up as a strawberry blonde for a while. But the best thing will be to let me cut it shorter so it can grow out quicker."

"Shorter?" Rosie felt positive she should have long hair. All down her back, if she believed in dreams.

"This…I hesitate to call it a cut…isn't doing you any favors, hon." Sallie picked up her shears. "All these split ends and funny angles just call attention to the drastic dye job. Let me style it short for you.

"Think of it this way," Sallie continued as she combed through the hair once again. "Cutting is one way to get rid of that awful coloring job a lot faster. Then we'll lighten the rest and before you know it, you'll be blond again. What do you say?"

"Okay, I guess so."

Jericho stepped into her view in the mirror. "That's fine. You'll be good here for a while, right? I'm going over to speak to the deputy. He needs to revise his bulletin and recheck with the people around the county.

"We've been asking about a redhead when we should've been checking for any word on a blonde." With that, he tipped his hat at Sallie. "I'll be back in a couple of hours. That do?"

"Sure, Sheriff." Sallie watched Jericho leave with an admiring gleam in her eyes. "That there is sure one fine-looking man. If I wasn't already married…" Her voice trailed off, leaving no question what she'd do.

Yes, Jericho surely was fine-looking. And a fine-quality man, too.

Rosie suspected that Jericho would turn out to be the best man she had ever known. Over the last two days, between hiding for her life and almost having sex, she had fallen in love with him. And she had a strong sense that he felt the same way about her. Now all she had to do was prove it to him. There had to be some way to make him see that the two of them belonged together.

Rosie was determined to find it.

Deputy Rawlins checked his watch and discovered it was past five o'clock. It'd been a long, discouraging night last night and he should've been off the clock long ago. But he wanted to make just one more stop before he headed home this afternoon.

He'd already checked with some of the truckers at the truck stop yesterday. But today he had new information.

For fifteen minutes Adam spoke to as many of the drivers as he could find. Finally, he'd found one who claimed to know something.

"Yeah, I gave a ride to a drop-dead gorgeous blonde," the long-haul trucker said. "Five days ago. I have it in my log. A real looker, that one. She'd be hard to forget."

Adam asked for a better description.

"Oh man, hair and legs down to there," the driver said with a grin. "And a shape worth losing your job over— if you know what I mean."

Though not a perfect description, Adam figured it was close enough. "Can you tell me where you picked her up and dropped her off?"

"Sure. I picked her up sixty miles or so north on the interstate. Between Austin and San Antonio. At a joint called Stubbins Barbeque. You ever heard of the place?"

"Yeah," Adam said. He'd eaten there, the place was famous. "The food's good, even if the patrons are on the rowdy side."

The driver nodded. "Don't know that the lady ate anything. I'd eaten earlier, but old Charlie Stubbins lets drivers catch a few hours sleep in the back of his lot. So I was just about to get underway again when I spotted this babe running down the side of the highway. She looked like she'd seen a ghost. I figured a couple hours in the cab with a broad who looked like that wouldn't be such a bad thing. You know?"

Adam nodded, then continued, "Where'd you drop her?"

"I was heading across the border. Let her out just this side of the river, in the town of Rio View."

Adam got the driver's name, address and number, then sent him on his way. Jericho should be pleased with this new info.

At least now they had a handle on where to start looking. All they had left to do was ask a million questions at both ends until something popped.

And at the same time, they'd better keep watch on their backsides for an ambush. Adam didn't like it, but he guessed that this kind of thing was all part of the job.

Chapter 10

The hired gunman called Arnie eased his stolen pickup into the dark lot of a roadside bar near the Mexican border. He found a spot to park on the caliche and got out. At long past the midnight hour, and considering it was during the middle of the week, the place seemed usually packed. Dirty trucks and well-used four-wheel-drive SUVs squeezed into every inch.

Grateful to have already made it over the border and back, Arnie gave a moment's thought to his previous partner. He'd left Petey in that medical clinic in Ciudad Acuna. No one there spoke much English, but the medicos managed to treat Petey's wound and more or less agreed to keep him in the clinic until his arm healed. Arnie had just been glad it was cheap.

Also thankful that their employer had given him another chance, Arnie figured otherwise he would probably be dead right now. But this time around, the boss wanted things to go differently. And whatever the boss wanted, Arnie was willing to do. It would keep him alive a few days longer.

That's why Arnie was about to walk into this rough, sleazy out-of-the-way nightspot. The meeting had been set up for 1:00 a.m., and Arnie hoped to hell he managed to leave by 2:00 a.m. with both a new partner and a new plan. Most of all, he hoped to get out of the place alive and in one piece. If this turned out to be a setup, he would never know what hit him.

Inside, after his eyes got used to the low lighting, Arnie spotted the man he was supposed to meet. Located at a table in a dimly lit corner, the guy was sitting with his back to the wall. A group of dangerous-looking hangers-on surrounded him, leaning their elbows on his table. A chill ran up Arnie's spine as the man in the middle of things tilted his head and shot him a narrowed-eyed stare across the smoky room.

He'd seen this man before, of course. In a much different context. But even tonight in this backwater bar, the guy carried an air of respect. His dark brown hair had not a strand out of place. His lips turned up in a kind of sneer as his eyes followed Arnie's movements. But when Arnie got closer he saw that a dimple marred the strength in the man's craggy cheek. A shift in the guy's position at the table as he raised his bottle of beer caused a small beam of light to glint against the metal badge affixed to his breast pocket.

Swallowing his fear, Arnie gathered his courage as he strode through the crowds. It was too late to ask how he'd gotten himself into this.

Too late to do anything differently either. Arnie braced himself for the worst—and hoped to hell it would end with the best.

Rosie awoke sick to her stomach again the next morning. But she was no longer in Jericho's guest bedroom. Despite her protests, last night he had delivered her to his best friend's Bar None ranch for the night. Clay Colton and Tamara Brown were lovely hosts, but they simply could never replace the man she loved.

Rolling out of bed, she tiptoed into the guest bath and lost whatever was left of the contents of her stomach. Today's morning sickness was a big fat reminder of yesterday. But similar as it was, last night there had been no dreams. Not even one fuzzy glimpse of her past. She wondered if that was because she was no longer in close proximity to Jericho. Perhaps he was the catalyst for her returning memories. If so, that might be a good excuse to stay near him.

Washing her face and brushing her teeth, Rosie couldn't help feeling somewhat lost without the security of Jericho nearby. This morning Tamara had promised to take her shopping for clothes at a mall she frequented just this side of San Antonio. But afterward Rosie was scheduled to spend the rest of the day with Jericho, trying to trace her movements on the days before she lost her memory.

Checking out her new hairdo in the bathroom mirror,

Rosie was pleased with what she saw. The stylish cut and lighter color made her look almost sophisticated. Sallie had given her a little makeup, too, and as she applied a touch of lip gloss a picture began to form in her mind.

A picture of herself, in a dark gray business suit and crisp white blouse, getting ready for work. So…she must have a job. But if she did, why hadn't her boss reported her missing?

Why hadn't *anyone* reported her missing? Didn't she even have any friends that missed her?

Becoming frustrated once again, Rosie put away all her unanswerable questions and finished getting dressed. If that's the way her old life had been—no friends, a boss who didn't care if she showed up, and a husband or boyfriend who couldn't be bothered to report her missing—then she didn't want to remember.

She decided not to buy anything that looked like a business suit today when they went shopping. Getting something that was right for Esperanza, Texas—and its sheriff—would be a much better way to go.

Jericho helped Rosie up into the passenger seat of his pickup. Since he'd showed up here at Clay's ranch to pick her up a few minutes ago, he couldn't seem to take his eyes off her. She looked so different with the new haircut and new clothes that really fit.

Not bad, mind you. But different. Spectacular.

The bruises around her face had nearly disappeared, and it looked as though the long, lean woman had evolved into a real Texas stunner in her narrow dark jeans and a tight-fitting denim jacket. She seemed to belong at one of those big outdoor Texas-style charity events, held in Dallas or Houston, rather than in small-town Esperanza, Texas. She wasn't the Rosie he had been getting to know over the last few days.

But then, who was she?

"Where are we going first, Jericho?"

To find out who you really are so I can know who I'm falling in love with. "To Stubbins Barbeque. It's about sixty miles up the road. Ever heard of it?"

She put her thumbnail to her lips, lost in thought.

"For a moment…I thought…" She shook her head. "No, it doesn't sound familiar. But then nothing does. Why are we going there?"

"Someone said they thought they saw you at the place almost a week ago. I want to ask around now that your hair is lighter and see if anyone recognizes you. Okay?"

She squirmed a little in her seat. But when she turned to answer, her eyes were bright and she had a big, warm smile on her lips. "Great. Wouldn't it be terrific if we find someone who knows me?"

Past the words— Past the smile—

There was a sense of misery about her. When he looked deeper, he noticed a tiny lick of fear hiding in those brilliant blue eyes. If she was miserable because their time together might be drawing to an end, that was okay. He felt much the same way.

But the fear—now, that bothered him. He intended to protect her from those goons or any others sent in their place. Didn't she know that? What else was there for her to be afraid about?

Confused, but determined to stand beside her despite

whatever they might uncover, Jericho headed his truck up the ramp to the interstate and drove on toward the answers.

As they turned off I-35 at the exit for Stubbins restaurant, Rosie's nerves tensed and strained. Nothing looked even vaguely familiar. Still, the closer they drove down the frontage road, the more jittery she became.

"Any sparks of recall?" Jericho asked as he turned onto the gigantic blacktop parking lot.

The smells of mesquite smoke mixed with her panic and filled the air with doubts.

Yes. "No. Maybe." She rubbed at the hairs standing up on her arms. "Nothing specific. Just a bad feeling."

"I'm right here. But don't do anything that makes you too uncomfortable. Just let me know and we'll leave."

Jericho parked behind the big red barn of a building, turned off the pickup and rounded the truck to help her down. "Ready?"

Rosie felt as if she were being marched to the guillotine. "I guess so. What are we going to do?"

"We're going to find out if anyone remembers seeing you on the first of the month. That's when the driver claims he picked up a blonde."

"But…" The sign beside the entryway said the hours were noon to midnight. All the deputy had managed to get was a date. How many people had come and gone on that day?

Jericho took her hand and strode up to the cashier's booth. The woman behind the counter was bleached blond, skinny as a rail and watched them with sharp, hawklike eyes.

She coughed and cleared her throat before picking up a couple of paper placemats and raising her painted-on eyebrows. "Just the two of you?" she asked with what sounded like a smoker's rasp.

Jericho shook his head. "I'm Sheriff Yates from Campo County. We're investigating a shooting, and I'd like to speak to anyone who was working here on the first of this month."

The cashier looked a little taken aback, but she glared at his badge and the gun strapped in its holster at his side before she said, "A shooting *here,* Sheriff?"

"*Was* there a shooting here on that date?"

"We've had our share of knife fights and an occasional gunshot," she said by way of an answer. "But not last week. I worked that day—the lunch shift."

"I would imagine I need to talk to someone working later in the day. Could you tell us who worked the dinner shift?"

Rosie quietly tried to stem her unease. She shifted from one foot to the other and folded her arms under her breasts.

"Let me check." The cashier pulled a plastic-covered chart out from under the counter and studied it for a moment. "There's two waiters and a busboy who were here that night and who'll also be on tonight. Actually, they might be already in back getting set to start their shift. If they're here, I'll send them on out.

"Besides them," she added. "I'll have to check with the manager to see if I can give you a list of the others who worked that night."

The cashier asked them to wait and they stood in the small lobby, idly staring at framed pictures of prize bulls that sported blue ribbons and snorted at the camera. Rosie found it hard to think. She couldn't even manage to get a word to form.

A young man with dark hair and a big apron came out of the open half of the kitchen and walked up to them. The kid looked scared to death of Jericho, but he stood his ground and answered questions.

After one look at Rosie, though, he shook his head. "So sorry," the kid mumbled with a heavy Spanish accent before he went back to work.

Another young man, this one with his light brown hair tied back in a thong at the nape of his neck and wearing jeans, a checked shirt and a red vest that obviously was part of his uniform, stepped out of another back room. He immediately seemed to recognize her.

"Hey," he said. "You cut your hair. Shame. It was cool all the way down your back like that."

"You've seen me before?"

"Sure. You were in the other night with another woman. Older broad. Maybe your grandma? Don't you remember me?" He went on as if he didn't expect an answer. "I remember the two of you paid in cash. Not something we see a lot around here what with truck drivers and business people using credit cards and all. You two weren't bad tippers, either…for two single women."

A picture of an older woman who looked something like Becky French, only she was wearing a business suit, glasses and a worried expression, flashed in and out of Rosie's mind. She started to sweat. Trying hard, she couldn't bring back anything more.

Jericho asked the young man another question or

two but suddenly Rosie's ears were ringing. Her legs became spongy and she found herself leaning on the sheriff for support.

He slung his arm around her waist, thanked the waiter and pulled her outside into the sunshine. "What's wrong with you? Aren't you feeling well?"

"Something…" One look around the parking lot and a flood of images flashed in her brain like a movie on fast-forward.

Darkness and fear. Someone chasing her across the blacktop. A gunshot. A thud from behind her.

Blinded by fear, she couldn't breathe. "Ahhh." The muffled scream came unbidden from Rosie's mouth but it originated somewhere deep, primal. "Is she hurt? I have to run. Hide."

Suddenly Jericho had her in his arms, rocking her gently. "You're okay. What do you remember? Who was hurt?"

She couldn't stop trembling and found herself shaking her head as though that might clear up the images. "I…I can't make it come back." The tears started to flow. "For a second back there, I saw another woman sitting across the table. A friend, I think. But now I can't…the pictures in my mind won't come back."

"What about out here in the parking lot?"

Swiping furiously at her cheeks in frustration, Rosie glanced around the lot. "It's just bits and pieces. Something that sounded like a gunshot—or maybe a car back-firing. Dark shapes moving through the shadows. Damn. Why can't I remember?"

Jericho half dragged her over to his truck, opened the

door and helped her in. "Stay here. Lock the doors and stay put. I'm going back for a couple more questions then we'll head out. You'll be okay?"

She nodded her head. But without her memories, she wasn't sure she would ever really be okay again.

Jericho spent the next half hour talking to the manager of the restaurant and then driving himself and Rosie over to the local county sheriff's office. He'd only met the newly elected sheriff of this county, Richard Benway, once. But had heard Benway was a good man.

Rosie's color had come back by the time they finished at the sheriff's office. It had been decided that Benway would open a full investigation as to what exactly had taken place in the restaurant's parking lot on the night of July first.

Jericho had loads of unanswered questions. The truck driver who picked up Rosie hadn't seen another woman, so what happened to her? Had she been hurt? Had anyone witnessed what took place? And how exactly had Rosie arrived at the restaurant in the first place? Driven? If so, what happened to her car?

Luckily, Sheriff Benway was willing to do the legwork. He had the authority and the extra manpower. But there were no guarantees the investigation would be successful.

Back in the truck, Rosie turned to him and asked, "What's next? Are we going home?"

It was a shock to his system to hear her calling Esperanza home. But he found he sort of liked it.

"This time of year," he began easily. "The sun doesn't

set until nearly 9:00 p.m. I thought we could drive on to the border. Check out the town where the truck driver says he let you out.

"You willing to give it a try?" he added thoughtfully. "Are you too tired?"

"I'm okay. If there's any chance of finding out who I am by going, then I'm there."

Jericho nodded and pushed down on the accelerator. This time they would play it smarter and start at the county sheriff's office.

But, unfortunately, he knew this county's sheriff. Knew him only too well.

There'd been rumors for years about how Sheriff Jesus Montalvo had gotten rich by turning his back to the forty-mile stretch of border that his county shared with Mexico. Like Jericho, Montalvo's county had no big cities and a small tax base. But unlike Jericho, Sheriff Montalvo of San Javier County had managed to accumulate an enormous amount of land and a few heavy bank accounts. The only difference between counties was a wild forty miles of Rio Grande riverfront.

Still, Montalvo *would* help. He had a large staff of deputies and knew where all the bodies and secrets were buried in his territory.

By the time they arrived in Rio View it was suppertime. Rosie didn't think she was hungry until her stomach started rumbling and she remembered that she hadn't eaten anything today. Jericho called ahead and Sheriff Montalvo agreed to meet them at a truck-stop restaurant near where the truck driver had claimed he'd let Rosie off late on the night of the first.

As they entered the crowded diner, that same uneasy feeling from before began to niggle around the edges of Rosie's mind. She forced it aside, determined this time to either ignore the images and feelings or capture them whole and place them properly in her memory.

A waitress pointed out the booth where Sheriff Montalvo was waiting. They worked their way through the loaded tables and past row upon row of full booths made with brown plastic seats and linoleum-covered tables. Everywhere Rosie looked were men. Long-haul truck drivers. Cowboys and ranchers. Rugged-looking men who seemed too busy eating to pay much attention.

Until…she walked by. Then every set of eyes studied her carefully. It gave her the creeps.

She'd thought she would be glad to slip into the booth across from Sheriff Montalvo and get away from the stares. But when she came near enough to the table to get a good look, there was something about him that seemed darkly familiar.

Not knock-you-down familiar. But close.

The man sat slouched in the far corner of the booth, but the power of his position glowed around him. He wasn't wearing a hat and his brown hair was combed in a perfect style. His white shirt looked starched and crisp under his badge.

A couple of waitresses stood beside the booth, like two virginal handmaidens. Rosie could just tell that everyone in the place, probably everyone in the county, would treat this sheriff with deference.

She grew uneasy again. Did she know this man? And if so, would he be able to tell her who she was?

Easing her way into the booth in front of Jericho, Rosie suddenly surprised herself by wishing that Sheriff Montalvo would not be able to tell her a blessed thing.

Chapter 11

"Is it very far from here?" Rosie stared out the windshield into the growing silver-gray dusk.

Jericho watched her body tensing with every mile they drove and his gut twisted from wanting to do something for her. Montalvo hadn't turned out to be of much help. The San Javier County sheriff told them he hadn't gotten any reports of trouble or missing women. But something about Montalvo's body language had been saying that he at least knew of Rosie, though he swore he'd never laid eyes on her before.

As they'd waited for their supper, Montalvo prompted Jericho and Rosie to ask around the restaurant to see if anyone recognized her. No one did. But Jericho's instincts had screamed at him through the whole search. The diner crowd had looked at her with hints of recognition in their eyes, yet not one would even meet his gaze with their own as he'd been asking questions. Liars.

After supper, Montalvo had also encouraged him to check with a motel on the outskirts of town that might match Rosie's description of the one she'd seen on the day she had lost her memory. Montalvo even called ahead to get them an appointment with the manager/owner.

As they pulled up in front, Jericho decided Rosie's original description fit the place perfectly. A cheap motel on the poorer side of a small border town. Just as she'd described it.

The deepening purple shadows of nightfall obscured his view of Rosie's face as they walked to the motel office. But he could feel the nervous energy radiating from her.

At the office door, he stood still for a moment, holding on to the handle as the fluorescent light from inside shone out through the glass. "Something's coming back to you, isn't it?"

Her eyes were wide and bright and her face flushed. "This is the place," she whispered. "From that morning when those two goons grabbed me. I remember the neighborhood."

"Yeah. I figured it was. Anything else coming back?"

She shook her head and bit her lip.

"Okay, let's see what we can find out from the owner." He let her go in ahead of him so he could watch the reaction of the man behind the desk.

The owner turned out to be a portly guy in his fifties, dressed in shorts and a T-shirt turned gray from washing. The bald spot on the man's head was almost covered over by several thin ash-brown strands of hair. But not quite. From Jericho's viewpoint, towering over the man's five-foot-eight frame, the guy would've been a lot better off leaving the bare patch alone.

As they stepped into the room, the owner never blinked an eyelash or showed any recognition of Rosie. But then once they came closer, Jericho caught a glimpse of the man's pupils widening involuntarily at the sight of her—right before he quickly glanced away. The man knew her all right. Even if he wasn't going to admit it.

They introduced themselves. The motel owner seemed put out at having to answer questions. Too bad.

"So, you're sure you don't recognize this woman?" Jericho asked after the man had just said he didn't. "Take another look."

"Once is plenty, bud. The answer is no. Back off."

Jericho lost it in that instant. He grabbed the owner by the front of his shirt and lifted him off his feet and halfway over the counter.

"It's Sheriff Yates to you, *bud.* And Sheriff Montalvo said you would cooperate. Let's have some of that cooperation right now.

"This woman was here in your motel no more than four days ago. Take a better look."

"Jericho…" Rosie put her hand on his shirtsleeve and her expression said she didn't want this much trouble.

Jericho lowered the owner back to his feet but refused

to open his fist. In fact, he still held the man's shirtfront in a death grip.

"Oh…oh, yeah," the owner stuttered as he took another look at Rosie. "Ya see, I didn't recognize you. You've changed. You're the broad that had the long, blond hair.

"You left one hell of a mess in the bathroom of one of the units when you dashed outta here, you know? There was hair and blackish-red dye everywhere. Ruined a couple of our good towels, I can tell you that."

Jericho let him go and then threw a couple of bucks from his pocket onto the counter. "That should take care of any damages.

"Was she registered here?" he added, putting a demanding tone in his words. "Under what name?"

The guy shrugged. "I don't remember. Or, maybe I just wasn't on duty when she came in."

"You want to take a look at the register anyway?" Jericho's patience with this character was running thin.

After another ten minutes of avoiding giving any actual answers, the owner shrugged again and said, "Look, we're not in the business of asking questions about our guests. This place isn't located on any main highway. The people that come here do it for their privacy."

"And I suppose your guests all pay in cash?" Jericho was ready to pound this sucker into the ground if he hedged one more time.

"Sure. In advance. We don't take credit cards and only take checks from the people that live around here."

"Well…" Frustration was making Jericho steamy. "How did she arrive then? Not on foot, surely."

The manager narrowed his eyes at Jericho. "None of my business. There's a bus stop about a block down. Maybe that way. How should I know? Ask her."

Jericho's hands fisted once again, but just then Rosie touched his shoulder. "This isn't doing any good," she told him. "I'm not getting any flashes of my past here. Let's just go."

"Hey," the manager said as he tilted his head to give her another look. "What're all the questions for? Don't you remember?"

The way he had said it told Jericho the man already knew very well that Rosie couldn't remember her past. And probably knew why not. Someone had already told him. Or warned him. Sheriff Montalvo? The sheriff was the only one who could've let the owner know what was going on.

If that was the case, then Rosie was right. They weren't going to get anything else out of this guy. In fact, all of a sudden it seemed like he'd had been deliberately hedging his answers in order to keep them here longer. If the sheriff were somehow involved, then whatever was going on in Rio View and with Rosie went far beyond dangerous. It would have to involve something bigger and more secretive than just a woman who'd been kidnapped.

Jericho's gut was telling him he needed to get Rosie out of San Javier County. Fast.

"Let's go." He took her by the arm and rushed them both outside and into his truck.

Buckling up, Jericho mentally ticked off the various routes he could take that would get them back to Esperanza the quickest. Menacing darkness began closing in around the pickup as he pulled out of the motel parking lot and kept an eye on what was going on in the rearview mirror.

Rosie cast a sideways glance at Jericho's profile in the glow of the dashboard lights. His jaw was set and a slight tick pulsed under his right eye. The man must still be furious.

She had never seen him as mad as he'd been while he questioned the motel owner. He'd controlled it in the office as long as she stood by his side, but the whole time she'd been afraid that the thin string binding up his anger would snap at any moment.

But why should he still be mad? He had no reason to be mad at her. She couldn't help it if her memories were lost. Yet he seemed furious.

With no clue as to what he was thinking, she looked out the pickup's window as the few remaining buildings on the outskirts of Rio View flew past. Rosie noted that they'd begun picking up speed. When the city-limits sign sped by and nothing but black, moonless night took the place of outdoor floodlights and lighted billboard signs, she all of a sudden realized they were zipping down the highway way too fast. Good thing the roads seemed deserted at this hour.

She cast a quick look over to the speedometer and was stunned to see the gage touching the ninety mark. Asphalt rushed under the truck as she tightened her seat belt. She was not ready to die tonight just because Jericho was a little miffed.

"What's wrong?" she asked him, and was embarrassed by the squeak in her voice. "Are you mad at me?"

"No."

Well, at least he'd answered. But that wasn't enough of an explanation for her. "Then what's up with you?"

It was then that she finally noticed him checking the rearview mirror every few seconds. "Someone is following us." She'd answered her own question.

He shot her a sideways glance then went back to concentrating on the road ahead. "Not yet."

"Yet? How do you know for sure that…"

"Crap." Jericho must've stepped down harder on the gas pedal just then because the truck gave a roar, bucked and unbelievably the speedometer needle eased up past one hundred. "There they are."

Rosie twisted her neck so she could look out the rear window. About a half a mile back a set of headlights could be seen in the distance heading in their same direction.

"What makes you think that car is following us?"

"Gut feeling. That guy in the motel kept us there for far too long. He set us up."

"Well, what do they want?"

Jericho spared her one, quick glare. "Guess."

"Me? Oh, God." Her voice almost left her in the dust as the truck flew down the highway into the dark. "What are we going to do?" she rasped out.

"We're going to lose them."

But even through those determined words, Rosie could hear the other vehicle's engine roaring up right behind them. She turned again and saw a huge set of headlights bearing down on them. They were close. Too close. How had they caught up so fast?

"All we need is another mile..." Jericho's words were interrupted by a loud thump and a terrific jerk.

"They're ramming us," Rosie screamed.

Were they crazy? Ramming people while doing a hundred miles an hour could get them all killed.

While Jericho struggled with the wheel, downshifted then hit the gas again, Rosie turned back to see the other vehicle losing ground. Apparently they'd had to fight the effects of the bump themselves.

"There it is." Jericho tapped the brake, cranked the wheel in a ninety-degree angle and downshifted into second. The engine whined and the tires squealed, but the truck responded in a perfectly executed wheelie, hitting the hidden side road back on all fours.

Rosie thought her lungs would explode. The truck barreled down a narrow paved road with barbed-wire fence whizzing by on both sides. She gasped for breath, closed her eyes and hung on.

"Do you know where you're going?" Blinking open her eyes, she screeched past the engine's whine. This might turn out to be a dead end. Then what would they do?

Jericho was keeping one eye on the rearview mirror as he answered, "My dad and I used to hunt the leases in this section. If nothing's changed since then, I know every inch. There's a couple of places to lose them up ahead."

If nothing's changed? That might be a big if when their lives depended on it. Rosie shivered and prayed for all she was worth.

Jericho drove on through the darkened fields, forced to continue using his headlights and pushing his truck as much as he dared. But they hadn't gone far enough to be safe when he picked up the other guy's headlights once again in his rearview mirror.

Finally spotting what he'd been waiting for, he slowed just enough to make the turn onto a caliche farm-to-market road. The tires clanged over a cattle guard and spun briefly before they caught again. Stepping down on the gas after the truck righted, he noted that the fencing was gone from the left side of the roadway. *Open range.* Dangerous driving in the dark.

Figuring they had about five miles to go before they made cover in the woods just past Gage's Arroyo crossing, he hoped to hell they made it that far.

Jericho threw a fast glance toward Rosie and vowed they would make it, at least that far—and beyond. The other choice was unthinkable. Once they hit the woods he would find some place to hide the truck, for long enough to call for help. But that was presuming his cell would work out here. He counted on those woods being located in the next county over. A county with a sheriff he could depend on to come to their aide.

Taking his eyes off the road for a millisecond, he checked on the woman sitting next to him. Her body was stiff. Her breath coming in short staccato bursts, and her fists bunched and ready to strike. He approved. She was scared but ready to fight.

That was his girl. Beautiful as always, but tough when she needed to be. Good for her.

The road got rougher, and he peered out as far as his headlight beams would reach. Pockmarks, potholes and deep ruts kept his speed down to a roar as the truck behind them began gaining ground.

Holding his breath and gritting his teeth against the violent shaking from his truck, Jericho hit the gas again. The next time he looked into the rearview mirror, he'd gained a little ground.

Son of a gun, that was one gigantic mother of a truck. Taller, wider and faster than Jericho's, the thing loomed out of the darkness like a huge beast with blazing eyes. Resembling a fantasy dragon in this darkness, from a distance it even appeared to be snorting smoke out its sides as dust and caliche spewed from under the tires.

He wasn't sure if that description was bad news or good. Bad news because he couldn't outrun them. Good news because he should be able to outmaneuver them on the narrow, slippery back roads.

Wondering if the driver was more, or less, familiar with this range road than he was, Jericho fought the wheel as he tried to bring their surroundings into better focus. Where were they now? How far from the bridge?

There should be a couple of bends in the road up ahead where the packed caliche wound around the edge of a deep arroyo off to his left. He blinked and stared into the star-filled night, trying to judge how far.

At the distant edge of his headlight beams and seemingly right in the middle of the road, he caught the shadow of a mesquite tree. That told him the first bend in the road was coming up. Downshifting enough to take the curve on four wheels, Jericho held his breath waiting for the second curve.

"Jericho, watch out!"

Rosie must've seen the hulking outlines in the road a second before he did. A half dozen cattle had wandered out onto the caliche and were lying around soaking up the day's lingering warmth. Son of a bitch!

Jericho jerked on the wheel and went right, knowing the arroyo was to the left. And hoping against hope to miss any more of the cattle that might be off to that side.

The minute the pickup was off-road, it skidded in the sandy dirt and he lost control. The truck did a one-eighty all by itself. He hung on to the wheel anyway, stepped lightly on the brake and prayed for a clear path.

But tonight they were not going to be so lucky. Out of the darkness loomed a hefty-sized cactus. Dead ahead.

He slammed down on the brake, holding out his right arm in a vain attempt to keep Rosie backed into her seat. But it was too little, too late as the truck's momentum pushed them forward.

In the next instant, he heard his front bumper crunching against the cactus, and the truck came to an abrupt halt, though his body was still violently jolting in the seat. He vaguely heard the air bags deploy—immediately after his head smacked hard against the driver's-side window.

Then it was suddenly all over. Pain shot through his temple and everything faded to black.

Chapter 12

Rosie fought her way around the deflating passenger air bag, coughing at the dust in the air and battling with her seat belt. She scrambled over the center console to reach Jericho's side. His moans, coming from behind the driver's wheel, meant he must be alive. She was okay, so he should be all right. He just had to be.

Everything had gone so quiet. The truck's engine was still running, but it had stopped whining. When she reached Jericho, his inert body took the breath from her lungs with fear. She quickly checked him over and placed her ear to his chest. He wasn't conscious, but he also wasn't bleeding. His breathing seemed heavy but nevertheless steady. Thank heaven.

Just then she heard another noise that sent chills

running down her spine. Leaning over, she turned off the engine, listening intently. Yes, it was the other truck, and it was getting closer.

She tried to keep her head. What should she do? Run into the night and hide? But what about Jericho? She would never, ever leave him here, and there was no way she could carry or drag him away in time.

Without really thinking it all the way through, but minus a moment to consider, Rosie unbuckled Jericho's seat belt. That left her room to undo the safety cover on his holster. She carefully lifted his service weapon from its place, and tried to remember everything she'd learned from him about guns.

Stepping out of the pickup, she faced the road the same way they'd come and listened as the other truck's engine noise got louder and louder.

"Jericho?" she whispered, turning her face to him and silently begging him to wake up and take over for her.

But his soft moan told her that wasn't to be.

Standing in what she hoped was relative safety behind the pickup's open door, and holding Jericho's gun with both hands, Rosie pointed it in the direction of the oncoming engine noise. In the next instant, headlights caught her in their glare as the huge truck navigated the first curve. Petrified, but determined to save both Jericho and herself, she aimed right above the headlights and held her breath.

Hold off, she cautioned herself. Let them get a little closer. That's what Jericho would do.

But Rosie could see that the truck was already slowing and turning more directly toward her as they no doubt had seen Jericho's headlights off the road. There wasn't going to be enough time for perfect shots.

She fired. But must've missed them. They were still coming. Firing once again, she heard a ping and knew that this time she'd at least hit the body of the truck.

That ended up being her last shot because right then the driver apparently caught sight of the cattle in the road. To avoid Rosie's bullets coming from his right and to miss colliding with ten tons of cow dead ahead, the driver dragged his wheel hard to his left.

For a moment or two more, Rosie could see headlights bumping off the road away from her. And then all of a sudden they disappeared. Disappeared!

After a crashing noise that sounded truly terrible to her ears, another unholy silence filled the air. Then, at last, Jericho called her name. She turned and scrambled back to his side.

"Who was doing the shooting?" he asked weakly as he shook his head and fought to untangle his own deflated air bag.

She heaved a deep sigh, so glad he was conscious and seemingly okay that she almost wept. "Me." Holding out his gun to show him, she began to shake. "Are you injured badly? What hurts?"

He gave her a curious look, took the gun and then turned to stare out the window past the cactus. "I'm okay. Where's the other truck?"

"I don't know. After they spotted the cows, the driver went off on the other side of the road. Then I heard a crash."

"The arroyo is over that way," Jericho said darkly. "It

was pretty damned steep and rough down in that spot the last time I saw it."

"Do you think they're still alive?"

Once again, Jericho's answer scared her. "It doesn't matter right now. We have to get out of here. This is still San Javier County. We're in danger every moment we stay here.

"I wonder if my pickup will still run," he added as he put his gun back in the holster, buckled his seat belt and straightened up in his seat.

"I turned it off," she told him. "And the motor was still going then."

He cranked the ignition and it roared to life. "Buckle up again, sweetheart. We're getting out of here. Only this time at a slightly safer speed."

"But shouldn't we check on…whoever that was? Maybe they need help."

"I'm real proud of the way you stood up to those bozos," Jericho said as he put the truck into Reverse and eased backward. "But you don't go sticking your hand in the hole, wondering if the rattlesnakes are doing okay. If they're still alive, that's the last place you should go. If they're not… Well, we'll call the sheriff in the next county and let him find out. Just as soon as we make it there safely ourselves."

Jericho listened from the bedroom of their suite at the bed-and-breakfast as water began running behind the closed bathroom door. Rosie was preparing to take her shower while he tried to sort through his emotions. It had been a very long night so far.

Thankfully, the sheriff in this county was an old friend and had been ready and willing to help. A crew of deputies was dispatched to Gage's Arroyo in the middle of the night to search for survivors. But when they'd found the smashed monster truck at the bottom of the dry arroyo bed, the driver and any passengers had been missing. The questions now seemed centered on whether any survivors had left the scene under their own power or had been thrown clear in the crash. A better search of the area would have to wait until daylight.

Meanwhile, Jericho could hardly arouse any real interest in those bastards. It was Rosie and his feelings toward her that had been hogging all his thoughts.

His old friend Sam Trenton, the sheriff of this county, had seen how beat up and tired he and Rosie had looked after all the questions were answered to the best of their abilities. Sam had called around and found them this one lone vacant suite in an entire county full of summer tourists who'd come for an arts-and-crafts festival.

Driving for a few hours to Esperanza had been out of the question. The pickup would run, but the tires were completely shot, the air bags needed to be replaced, the right front fender was crumpled and the headlight broken.

And the two of them needed rest.

From behind the bathroom door, the sound of running water changed over to the stronger noise of shower spray. Jericho sat down on the edge of the bed to consider what was going to happen when Rosie came out of the bathroom and they found themselves exhausted and alone together in a room with only a king-size bed and a sitting room with one tiny sofa.

His life had changed forever in one intense moment back there on that dark road. Gone was the guy he had once been, the one who'd wanted nothing more out of his life than a bachelor's existence. In his place was a man who would give anything to trade in his old ways for a chance at one red-hot lady who couldn't remember her baby's father. A lady who also easily remembered her weapons' training and thought nothing of wielding a weapon when backed into a corner.

For the last couple of hours, while he'd been checked over in a local clinic and had taken his own shower, he'd found himself thinking not about bad guys but about how best to remodel his cabin. How to change the house he'd built into a real home.

He looked over to the bathroom door. She was there—just on the other side. The only woman he'd ever met for whom he would gladly give up the rest of his life.

For her and for her child. He'd been thinking of her little one, too. More than anything, he wanted to be that child's father. He would make a great dad. He'd had the best example in the world.

For some reason, Jericho discovered he wasn't afraid of Rosie leaving him. Always before, when he'd come close to a serious relationship with a woman, he would call a halt to things sooner rather than later. Mostly due to his worrying about how long it would last before the woman up and left. Maybe that kind of thing was a legacy from his damned mother.

But not this time. If Rosie hadn't left him unconscious in the truck to save herself, and she certainly had not, he was positive she would never leave him at all. Not once she fully committed.

So that was what he was sitting here thinking about. How to go about making her *want* to stay as much as he wanted to keep her. But as usual, whenever he thought of her, the testosterone took over and he quit using his brain altogether.

In fact, right this minute his pulse pounded with need and his senses were on overdrive just knowing she was naked on the other side of that door.

Then with no warning, the door opened and Rosie stood on the threshold to the bedroom wearing nothing but a towel. Like a zombie he stumbled toward her with his arms outstretched.

Those brilliant sapphire eyes of hers swam with need, but she held out one arm to fend off his advance. "Jericho, wait. We have to think this through. I may be a terrible person. At the very least, I'm probably a thief. And obviously I slept with someone who didn't care enough about me to look when I went missing."

"You are my fantasy." It was all he could think to say. "The one I've waited for all my life." He took another step closer.

She backed into the bathroom. "But getting involved with me might bring you lots more trouble. Someone is still after me."

"Too late," he murmured. "I'm already involved. You stayed. You stayed and I don't care who or what you were before. I'll find a way to protect you from anything.

"And what's more," he added with a deep breath. "I hope we never find out who you were."

Her eyes went wide and she dropped the towel, holding out her arms to beckon him closer. It was all the invitation he would ever want.

She was stunning and he was breathless as he dragged her into his arms and pushed them both up against the bathroom counter. He slanted his mouth over hers and stroked her waiting tongue with his own.

Kissing like this, with him half dressed and her totally naked was pure torture. But also pure pleasure. His senses soared as he touched her everywhere. He craved her like a thirsty man craved drink.

Bringing a hand up to caress her breast, he reveled in the soft, weighty feel of it in his palm. She had such fabulous breasts. The joy of touching them intensified. His blood fired as he bent his head and took one rosy tip into his mouth.

She moaned and bucked against his hips. It was such a luxurious gift to hear her moaning under his touches and kisses. He spent another indulgent moment in licking and sucking her deep into his mouth, while at the same time letting his other hand slip easily between her legs to cup her.

Another moan came from her parted lips, and he lifted his head to kiss her again. To swallow her little sounds of pleasure and to push his tongue deep inside her, mimicking what he wanted them to be doing in other ways. He held her tight and felt himself growing harder.

Jericho wanted this to happen, more than he'd ever thought possible. But he also wanted to go slow. To draw out every precious moment—for both of them.

Nibbling his way down the satiny column of her

neck, he found her so sweet-smelling and fresh after her shower, and so compelling with her moist skin and soft moans that it nearly threw him off. He steeled himself against a too-soon ending to all this intimacy.

Rosie felt damned good under his hands, and he wanted her to experience something so special with him that she would never forget it. He needed to become familiar with every inch of her body. It seemed imperative to learn everything that she liked. What turned her on. What brought out those tiny mewling sounds of pleasure. What caused her to jump and shove her hips hard up against him, begging for more.

His fingers sought the nub to her core and rubbed there gently. Testing, exploring. Finally, teasing and tormenting.

"Jericho." His name came out like a whispered prayer. He was so turned on he almost missed that she was starting to come.

Crying out, she buried her hands in his hair and hung on. Her breathing came in short pants. He pulsed with anticipation next to her and gave an instant's thought to slowing her down just to bring her up again.

But in the next moment, when her body went taut and she jerked against him with a whimper, he knew this was so much better. To be able to watch her come apart in his arms was the ultimate pleasure. He'd done it once before but this time was even sweeter. This time there would be another and, he hoped, even another chance to make this happen. They had the time and he definitely had the desire.

Rosie trembled, clutching at him as he lifted her chin and kissed her. Kept on kissing her and touching her and rubbing up against her until she groaned again and reached down for his zipper.

"Please, don't leave me again," she whispered hoarsely as she fumbled with the button on his jeans. *"Please."*

He heard all the words she didn't say. *Come inside me. Become one with me. This is meant to be. I will never leave you.*

Helping her out, he slid out of his boots and shed his jeans while she leaned her bottom against the bathroom counter and watched him from under heavy lids. Then he was there. All for her.

Lifting her hips, he filled her. Pushing deep. Her head leaned back on a moan and her hips jerked forward, shoving him ever deeper.

She gripped his shoulders as he thrust once... twice...until his head was literally spinning. Her internal muscles tightened around him, clenching and stroking. Her body pulled at him, drawing him, locking them together in a primitive way and making sure he stayed with her.

Oh, he would stay with her, all right. Stilling, he looked down at her beautiful face, with her eyelids half-closed and with an expression that said she was lost in sensation. Her lips were parted and her breathing shallow.

Breathing deeply himself, he smelled sex, exotic and compelling. Both masculine and feminine shades of lust combined within the scent and drove him mad.

There was no time left. As much as he would've liked to go on forever, when she rubbed her hips to his again, he was undone.

He belted his arm around her waist and pulled her hard against him, thrusting again. The next few moments whizzed by in a blur of thrusts—deeper, deeper, again and again.

Higher and higher, lost and crazed, his muscles tensed and strained as he fought to hold on. He heard her scream, then curse something unintelligible as she twisted and lurched. She plastered herself to him, seeming to want the melding of the two of them into one entity.

That was all he needed. His climax surged through him like an earthquake. His whole body shook with the force. He braced his trembling legs and went along for the ride.

Bending nearly in two, he brought his mouth down on her neck, nipping and grazing and loving the sweetness and softness of her. One last thrust and his head came up as he gasped for breath.

Talk about your life-changing experiences.

He picked her up in his arms and headed for the bed. All he wanted now was another few hours. *Or* maybe, a whole lifetime of feeling this damned good.

Chapter 13

Rosie stretched out beside Jericho's sleeping body. Only moments before he'd laid her down on the bed and crawled in after her. Feeling limp and sated, she was amazed that her body still pulsed with pleasure. Surely there had never been anything in her previous life to compare to him and the things they'd done.

From that very first moment when he'd echoed her thoughts and said he hoped they never uncovered her past, she'd been all his. Forever. Whatever he wanted. For however long he wanted.

Still, at the beginning she'd felt compelled to tell him she loved him. That he was the only one there would ever be from this moment on. It had seemed so important to say the actual words. But quickly she'd come to the conclusion that words didn't matter.

He'd been such a master at telling her everything he was feeling without words. She'd felt his need throbbing inside her. She'd known his thoughts, begging her to never leave him as he'd worked hard to make sure she was fulfilled before taking his own pleasure.

For this short time with him, she'd forgotten all about her fears and the tension of having people after her. And now she wanted to find a way of forgetting them for good. To let Jericho become her permanent protector, so that together they could conquer all the bad things in the world.

He wanted that, too. She was positive. But just now she lay quietly racking her brain for the best way of communicating their mutual needs.

When he softly snored, she found the sounds of him beside her, seemingly so comfortable and sated himself, terribly endearing. He'd been through so much for her. He needed a little sleep.

Easing out from under his arm, she inched away and stood, turning back to look at him on the bed. So beautiful. She vaguely knew that wasn't how you were supposed to describe a man, especially a tough guy like this one. But she thought Jericho was simply gorgeous.

The strong chin. The hint of stubble. Those long lashes lying against the high curve of his cheek.

Whew. Despite the cool air-conditioning in the room, a trickle of sweat beaded at her temple and slithered down her neck. Rosie walked to the bathroom, found a glass and drank water, trying to cool off.

But knowing he was there on the bed, naked, brought her back to the doorway so she could stare at him some more. Just to look at those broad shoulders that had been absolutely perfect to hold on to during the throes of passion. They narrowed down to lean hips. And it was all sleek, flat muscle in between.

Half the time she thought he was some kind of throwback to the old West. The strong, silent type. But when they were alone together, his eyes told her something entirely different as they changed colors with his moods.

Granite when he was mad or taking his job seriously. Amber when he was being sincere or teaching her how to shoot. And almost jade-green when he was in the midst of giving her passion. That last image, the one of him gazing intently into her eyes with those fantastic green eyes, made her actually shiver as the heated desire skittered down her spine.

How could she explain that she wanted forever from him without scaring him or turning him off?

He stirred, rolling onto his back. The sight of all that manhood moved her to action. Thinking simply stopped.

She slid into the bed beside him, tempted beyond restraint. Taking him into her hands, she stroked and played and massaged. First she ran a forefinger down one long, smooth side. Next a tender touch to the rounded, slick tip.

When his body began to respond to her ministrations, she leaned in and took him into her mouth. A soft groan came from above her but what she was doing felt so indulgent, so right, that she refused to give it up.

Jericho came awake with a jolt of erotic sensation. When he looked down at the top of Rosie's head and realized what she was doing to him, he reached out for her. But she shied away from his hands.

Sweet mercy. The vibrations alone nearly caused him to come three feet off the bed.

Very much more of that and it would be all over. And though one day that might be a good plan to follow, it wasn't what he had in mind for tonight.

He wanted tonight to be all about her pleasure. Needing to make her see how much she meant to him. Desperate to make her understand that he did want her to stay with him forever. Tonight was supposed to be hers.

Tunneling his hands through her hair, he firmly eased her back. She lifted her head and looked at him and the sight of her glazed eyes and satisfied expression was a bigger turn-on than what she'd been doing.

Rock hard, he moved fast. Twisting their bodies with a roll and a plunge, he found himself inside her again. Right where he wanted to be.

Her body was slick with sweat but so was his. A momentary thought of moving this show into the shower came and went. Later. The next time. And there would be more. Lots more. Until both of them were weak and weeping and had no more questions about a future.

He eased out of her and then back inside again with a slow draw, setting up a rhythm he hoped to continue for a good long while. Hot damn but this was heaven.

She rocked hard against his hips, sending another blast of pure pleasure spinning through his veins. He reached down and cupped her bottom, holding her tightly to him.

Their bodies were on fire everywhere they touched. So damned hot he figured they might combust.

"Jericho, you feel so good."

"Back attcha, darlin'." *Good* didn't seem adequate. But so help him, his brain must be melting. Words were impossible.

He leaned down and kissed her, moving in and out and loving the feel of silky wet heat. Hoping somehow to make her see.

But he wasn't exactly positive about everything he wanted her to know. Except that he needed her to stay. Was that enough?

"I love you," she said on a moan as her body began tightening around him.

He thrust again on a long slow glide. Was this really what love felt like? Was that what he needed to say?

But before his mouth could catch up, she arched her back and her whole body went rigid. "Jericho!"

Nature took over then, freeing him from thinking, as his own movements came faster and faster. Pounding hard into her, too soon the orgasm broke through him on a flood of flashing sensation. He barked out a unintelligible curse and went with the flow.

Collapsing beside her afterward, he rolled them until he had her captured in his embrace and spooned against his chest. He lay there for a few seconds, smiling into the back of her head.

He breathed in the smell of her shampoo, and thought it might be the nicest scent ever invented. Not sure if it was some kind of flower or just the smell of clean, he figured he could certainly get used to it.

Running a hand along the smooth skin of her arm and amazing himself by becoming hard again so soon, Jericho figured he could certainly get used to this part, too. They were sure good together. Idly he wondered if they had the stamina to keep it up all night.

Then Rosie moaned, turning in his arms and moving in close. He felt her breath, hot along his neck. Her breasts pressed tight and hard against his chest. And without question he knew there was one thing for certain.

He had all the strength he needed for this night.

Rosie leaned back against the bed's headboard, a silly grin plastered across her face, and listened as Jericho shaved and finished getting dressed in the bathroom. What a wonderful night it had been. She didn't know if she'd ever had one quite like it before, but it didn't matter. Not now that she was sure she would be spending many more nights in the same way.

Well, that is if she could hold up. She probably hadn't gotten more than an hour's worth of sleep during the whole night. But at the moment she couldn't possibly feel any better even if she'd slept for days. She wasn't sick to her stomach and it was midmorning already. Maybe sex was good for that too.

She was in love. And though Jericho hadn't said it in so many words—that he loved her and wanted her to spend the rest of her life with him—he'd made his feelings perfectly clear in all the things he'd done and the ways he had treated her.

Hmm. *Mrs. Jericho Yates.* That seemed as good a name as any for her to take. In fact, a lot better than most.

Thinking about her missing name brought up a subject she would rather not consider. Her past. But more than her past, who was chasing her and why. Had she stolen something? If only she could remember.

She thought back to the one and only breakthrough to her past that her mind had yielded—the dream of a prince turning into a monster. The prince from her nightmare had looked a little like Sheriff Montalvo, only taller and much more sophisticated and suave.

Sheriff Montalvo. Her skin crawled just at the thought of him. Now *there* was someone to worry about. Rosie wondered what he was doing this morning. Had Jericho's friend, the sheriff from this county, contacted Montalvo about the attack and crash already?

Curious, she picked up a remote from the bedside table and turned on the television that was housed in a beautiful antique armoire across the room. Maybe there would be some news about the missing men. Flipping through the channels, trying to find a local station, Rosie caught the tail end of an image that stopped her cold.

Her mouth sagged open as she backed up the channels until the picture came onto the screen once again. Then all of a sudden, there he was. Her nightmare prince.

No mistaking him. The tall regal bearing. The dark brown hair combed in an impeccable style. Conveniently, the fellow was even wearing a tux. Whoever the man on the TV screen was turned then and gave the camera a generous smile. A deep dimple on his left cheek was all it took to make some things click into place for Rosie.

The man she was staring at, her nightmare prince, was also most definitely her baby's father. And there he was, live and in color, right on the television. Oh. My. God.

* * *

Jericho turned off the water and folded his towel. From behind his back he heard the TV running. Rosie must've turned it on while she was waiting for him to finish getting dressed.

The fleeting thought of her caused his lips to spread into another of the big, stupid grins that he'd been plagued with all morning. She was perfect. He could barely wait to begin their lives together. He wanted lots more nights. Lots more time to find ways of telling her how much he cared.

But not until after they got a few other things taken care of today. He needed to borrow a truck to get them back to Esperanza, and he wanted to go long before dark. His friend Sam had called a while ago to say Sheriff Montalvo had taken over the crews searching for crash victims in the arroyo. After all, the scene was located in his county.

But that knowledge did nothing to calm Jericho's nerves. He was positive Montalvo had had something to do with those men in the first place. And he didn't like knowing a man as powerful as a sheriff might be after Rosie.

Rosie. Another smile crossed his lips. One thing he needed to do today was tell her how much he wanted her in his life for good. Maybe while they were driving back to Esperanza would be as good a time as any.

He picked up his clean shirt, freshly laundered courtesy of the staff of the bed-and-breakfast, and shoved his arms into the sleeves. As he buttoned down, he tuned into what was happening on the television behind his back. It sounded like a news story. Had Rosie found a story about the attack and crash?

Turning and taking the few steps out into the bedroom, Jericho was shocked with what he saw. Rosie sat hypnotized by something she was watching on the screen. He glanced at it but didn't see anything exciting. It was nothing but a national news story about the presidential candidates. Still, Rosie's face had gone pale. Her eyes were glazed and her mouth hung open. She seemed paralyzed. Completely lost in something on the screen.

"What's the matter?" he asked as he moved to her side. "Is everything okay?"

No reply.

"Are you okay, darlin'?" He took her by the shoulders and gently forced her to face him.

He could see her fighting to bring his features into focus. Her features were contorted with fear. What on earth could be the matter?

"Rosie. Honey. Talk to me."

"It's him. I…I mean… It's starting to come back." She grabbed for his hand and he captured both of hers. They were ice-cold.

"What's coming back?"

"Jericho, look." She pointed at the television screen but all he saw there was the Texas governor, giving what seemed to be an ordinary political campaign speech for his run for the presidency of the United States.

"Governor Daniels?"

"Allan Daniels. Yes. That's him. That's my baby's father. I'm positive."

Worried about her growing hysterical state, Jericho

sat at the edge of the bed and gathered her close. "Calm down, sweetheart. I know you may think this is real, but it doesn't seem possible. Allan Daniels? How? Why?"

"I don't know." She frowned and knitted her eyebrows. "I can't remember any of that. My own name isn't even coming back. But I know this for sure. Allan Daniels is the man I was with. The only man. I know it."

Standing in tall grass at an isolated bend in the Rio Grande River, Arnie watched in the distance as a marked sheriff's SUV drove down the dusty side road, heading for the clearing. Montalvo. It was about time.

Glad his bleeding had stopped some time ago, Arnie fingered the cut across his cheek. Damn it. The thing would probably leave a deep scar.

Arnie needed help to cross the border so he could find medical assistance, and Montalvo was going to provide that help. The *boss* had said the sheriff would do what he could. And what the boss said, happened.

After all, it was Montalvo's brilliant idea that had gotten him into the big mess last night. What the hell had Arnie, a big-city guy, known about the range land after dark? Or of that arroyo area. Or of stupid dumb-ass cows for that matter.

Nothing. Zip. But he did know how to climb out of a busted SUV and scramble up the side of a brush-strewn arroyo to save his butt. And he also knew enough to drag the driver's dead body free and hide it good.

Most of all, Arnie had known to call the boss and beg for forgiveness and help. After all, there was no one else on earth who could help him if the boss refused.

The sheriff's SUV pulled into the clearing and stopped, the engine still running. A blacked-out side window rolled down and Montalvo stared at him from behind huge aviator sunglasses.

"It's about time," Arnie said. "I've been waiting."

"Shut up."

A chill rode up Arnie's spine and he secretly fingered the .45 hidden under his shirt. This was not going down well. Montalvo was always a snake anyway.

"Did the boss tell you what I need?" Arnie tried once more to be heard. "I just want an easy way across the river without the U.S. Border Patrol shooting me on sight. Nothing else. I swear."

"I know what your boss wants," Montalvo said menacingly and reached down as if for a weapon.

Uh-oh.

To hell with it. Arnie palmed his gun and fired point-blank exactly at the moment he twisted and headed for the river, going at a dead run.

Only thirty or forty feet from the steep riverbank to start, he knew he could make it in a few seconds if he wasn't shot dead before getting there.

For those few seconds nothing happened behind him. No sounds or shouting. No lights from Border Patrol units. Maybe he was home free. Maybe he'd plugged Montalvo. And maybe Montalvo had agreed to meet here because he knew this place had a gap in the Border Patrol area. Maybe.

That son of a bitch Montalvo. He'd meant to kill him.

If Arnie hadn't actually finished Montalvo with his lucky shot, he vowed to come back and do the job right. After he found safety in Mexico, of course.

Arnie hit the river running and never stopped. Splashing across the two-foot-deep water, it occurred to him belatedly that Montalvo would never have had the nerve to ambush him if the boss hadn't agreed. Hell. If the boss wanted him dead, he might as well stop breathing.

At the Mexican side of the river, Arnie took a huge breath and figured he had a few more hours to live. He would try to figure out something.

But then he looked up the bank and spotted a whole squad of Mexican *federales* staring down at him. Or at least they looked like they were part of the Mexican army.

Until…they pointed their AK-47s in his direction and began firing.

Chapter 14

"So what'd you do to her, man?" Clay Colton stood on his own front step with his hands on his hips, scowling down at Jericho.

Clay might be his best bud, and he'd been nice enough to let Rosie stay here at his ranch again last night. But Jericho would be damned if he would let Clay interrogate him. He stuck his hands in his pockets and looked away.

"It's none of your business," Jericho said through gritted teeth. "Is she ready to go?"

"Tamara is with her. Apparently she cried all night and has been sick to her stomach all morning. So what happened? Where are you two going today? 'Cause I heard her tell Tamara that she didn't want to go."

Yesterday Jericho had heard all Rosie's reasons for not wanting to go to Austin and confront the governor. But he was just as determined to show up for their appointment with Allan Daniels as ever. She was the one who'd insisted Daniels was her lover, after all.

Jericho would never forget it. Not if he lived to be a hundred. After their fantastic night, and just as he was trying to find a way to tell her he wanted her to be his forever. That's when she'd burst out with the news.

In so many words, she'd said, "Oh, by the way, thanks for saving my life and for one really great night. But I see my old life on the TV. And there's no way for you to live up to its sophistication and power."

Hell.

From that moment on they'd disagreed about calling the governor and arranging a meeting. But though it had taken him all afternoon and most of the night, Jericho had been determined that Rosie needed to confront her past—if Daniels really was that past.

He'd finally done it, too. Found an assistant to an assistant who agreed to get Rosie a moment with the governor. Between Daniels's regular duties and his busy campaign schedule, it had not been easy. And for the whole time, Rosie had begged him not to make her go.

Jericho didn't understand her. If she really was happy here with him, as she said, why bring up her past at all? He'd come to the conclusion that she wasn't happy and contented here. Either Daniels was her child's father and deserved to know about it. Or he wasn't and Rosie had invented the whole Daniels thing to ease out of a relationship with Jericho that had grown pretty intense.

Eventually, early last evening, he'd brought her out here to stay with Clay and Tamara for the night and then spent his own night brooding at home.

"Well?" Clay was waiting for some kind of answer.

"We're driving to Austin to check on a lead to her past. I don't know why she's saying she doesn't want to go."

"Maybe she's scared," Clay offered. "She's been kidnapped and shot at a couple of times. I know that would give me more than a moment's pause about driving around the countryside with you."

Jericho frowned again. "Thanks for the vote of confidence. But I think she might be okay from now on.

"Last night Sheriff Montalvo in San Javier County was found shot to death in his official sheriff's unit, parked down by the Rio Grande. They also found the body of a known hitman nearby in the river. The theory is that it was some kind of Mexican drug deal gone sour."

"Montalvo? Rosie said something about how creepy he seemed and that maybe he was behind the attack against you down by Gage's Arroyo the night before last."

Jericho nodded and heaved a sigh. "Yeah. I've come to the conclusion Rosie must've been somehow involved with Montalvo in her past. And that he was the one who hired those goons to come after her.

"I intend to keep investigating what his motives might've been and what precipitated the kidnapping. But with Montalvo dead, I think she should be okay."

He figured maybe she would be *more* okay with her old life rather than with him in a new one. At least she wouldn't have to keep looking over her shoulder. She could relax and heal. And while he worked to get over her and figure it all out, he wouldn't have to keep worrying about saving her life.

Twisting her hands together nervously, Rosie peered down the hall as they stepped out of the elevator. They were on the sixth floor of the Austin office building that supposedly housed the governor's campaign head-quarters. She really didn't want to be here. But Jericho had insisted.

She still couldn't figure out what had gone so suddenly wrong with him. All during their fabulous and intimate night, Jericho had given her everything. He'd made her every wish come true. She'd been so positive the rest of their lives would stay that way.

But right after she'd had the vision of her and Daniels, um, making a baby, Jericho had changed into someone else entirely. Someone angry and withdrawn.

He'd barely said a word to her since then. His attitude had surprised the devil out of her. After all, he had to have known *someone* else was the baby's father. But he'd suddenly started insisting they go to Austin and confront the governor rather than talk it over, figure out the truth and learn why no one had reported her missing.

Rosie wasn't too sure why she didn't want to see Daniels. But maybe it was for just that very reason. Why hadn't he cared enough to report her absence? Why weren't the Texas Rangers and all the county sheriffs out looking for her? He was the governor. He had the power to find her anywhere, if he wanted to.

She took a couple of steps along the rather ordinary-looking hallway behind Jericho and hesitated. Yes, this place did seem vaguely familiar. But it also seemed scary. She didn't like it.

"What's the matter? Come on." Jericho turned, and she wished she could see his eyes better but they were hidden under his broad-brimmed sheriff's Stetson. He took her by the elbow and gently tugged her forward. "We just barely managed to get this appointment. We can't be late for it."

"I don't…" She was shaking so badly that she couldn't speak. What if she'd been wrong and Daniels didn't even recognize her? They shouldn't be here. Everything just felt bad.

But right then Jericho stopped in front of the door marked as the Daniels's campaign headquarters. He opened it and drew her inside with him.

A couple of women stood at a reception desk. Both of them were engrossed in something on the desktop and didn't glance up. Directly behind them was a big open room with rows of long tables, all empty at the moment. Off to each side were a couple of office spaces with closed doors. Everything had a temporary and bare feeling.

Both of the women were dressed in pantsuits, very businesslike. One was in her twenties, blond and pretty. The other must've been in her fifties. She had salt-and-pepper gray hair, but it was cut with sophistication and made her face look fragile. Jericho cleared his throat to get the women's attention.

The older one looked up first. "Olivia! You're back. It seems like you've been out forever. How're you feeling? Are you finally completely well?"

Olivia? Rosie took a step backward, but Jericho held tight to her arm and kept her beside him.

The second woman had lifted her head by then. "What on earth did you do to your hair?" She tilted her chin to study Rosie. "I simply loved all your long blond hair, Olivia. It always made me so jealous. This style isn't too terrible, though…I guess. It frames your face. But the color. Why in heaven's name did you darken it? That shade doesn't do a thing for you."

Jericho moved forward a few feet, dragging her along. Rosie's feet didn't move willingly. In fact, her whole body was going numb. These women weren't the least bit familiar to her, even though they seemed to know her well.

"You know this woman?" Jericho asked them.

They both looked at him as though he had materialized out of the woodwork.

The older one recovered first. "Of course we do, Sheriff…uh…Sheriff…"

"Yates. Sheriff Jericho Yates from Campo County. I called about an appointment with Governor Daniels for our amnesia victim."

"Amnesia? Our Olivia? Really?" The older woman stared into Rosie's eyes.

"Then you do know her," he interjected, taking charge of the situation, as he usually did. "How? What's her full name?"

"Olivia Halprin," the younger of the two blurted out and then also came closer to study Rosie. "And we work with her. She's Governor Daniels's campaign treasurer. She's been out sick with the flu for the last ten days.

"Or at least that's what we all thought," she amended.

Rosie's knees were trembling and she was afraid she

might be sick again. Clinging to Jericho's arm, she fought to bring images to her mind. Any images.

The name *Olivia* did sort of ring a bell. Maybe Olivia was her real name. At least it could be. But that was all there was. Nothing else was making any sense.

One of the two side doors opened and Allan Daniels stuck his head out. "What's going on out here?" He turned to her and his eyes widened. "Olivia. Sweetheart. There you are. How are you feeling? Better, I hope."

A picture formed in Rosie's head of kissing those smiling lips. Of kissing the nightmare prince.

With legs collapsing under her, she started down a long dark tunnel. Where things began growing smaller and smaller, like *Alice in Wonderland,* until her whole world simply disappeared.

Sometime later Rosie lay back on the leather couch in Allan's office with her eyes closed and listening to Jericho finish explaining to Allan how he'd found her and about everything they'd been through for the last few days.

It all sounded fantastic. But to her it was the only reality. She still couldn't come to grips with an old life. A few shadows, like old black-and-white movies moved across her consciousness. But most of it didn't stick around long enough for her to bring it into focus.

Shifting a plastic baggie full of ice that one of the women had plopped on her forehead after she'd been carried to this couch, she remained quiet with her eyes closed. But she still paid attention as the two men talked about her as if she were someone else.

"I can't believe she's been through all that just in the

time she's been gone," Allan said. "We were lucky you were the one who found her, Jericho. You don't mind me calling you that, do you? I owe you a big debt of gratitude and I hope to find a way to pay you back."

Allan hesitated and Rosie could just picture him taking off his jacket and loosening his tie, the big phony. "So you believe this Sheriff Montalvo from San Javier County was somehow responsible for the things that happened to Olivia?" The image of Allan Daniels was now firmly formed in her mind. From her past. And from her present.

Jericho must've nodded his head because she didn't hear him agree. She might not be able to see him, but she was tuned into his responses. Feeling him growing colder, more distant, with every passing moment, she wished they could leave. She couldn't really blame Jericho. With every word and movement Allan seemed more snakelike and slimy. How could she have ever let herself be conned by the man?

"Well, then," Allan said to Jericho. "I would take it as a personal favor if you'd follow up on that. I'll put you in touch with Chief Aldeen of the Rangers. He'll see you get all the help you need for your investigation."

"Thank you, sir."

"You're…"

"Allan." Rosie decided it was time to come back into this life, though truthfully she was as hesitant as Jericho. Most of the things that belonged in her previous world were still only vague images. And not all of them would apparently be full of sunshine and light. There continued to be lots of dark, black holes that she couldn't— or wouldn't—fill in.

And all of it seemed to circle around the governor of Texas, for crying out loud.

"Olivia, you're up," Allan said as he came close and helped her to stand. "Are you sure you don't need to be checked out at a hospital?"

"No," she heard herself say. "A doctor looked me over in Esperanza. I'm going to be fine."

He gave her an odd look, and Rosie wondered if he had any idea she was pregnant. She would bet not. Well, it remained to be seen whether she ever told him the truth. At the moment, chances were slim.

Like a silent beacon of hope, Rosie felt drawn instead toward Jericho, who stood behind the desk. He was her savior. Her protector. Her love.

Shooting her a rather creepy and lecherous look, Allan let his gaze linger on her breasts. Her growing unease around him became an urgent sense that she needed to get out of here. Away from this man.

Allan put his arm around her shoulders, and a disgusted shudder skittered clear down her spine. Why was she so sure this guy was not who he seemed? She inched away without making a big deal.

"I just want to go home." Amazingly, she did remember where her old condo was all of a sudden. However, she found herself dearly wishing to go to the *home* a hundred miles southwest in a blip on the map called Esperanza.

Allan's pleasant expression turned frustrated. "I can't take you home right now. I have that $10,000-a-plate fund-raiser coming up in a couple of hours. You remember—you set it up."

She did not remember. Nor did she want to. It was all wrong. Wrong. Wrong.

Afraid Allan might insist she go with him, she began, "I can get there by…"

"I'll see her safely home, sir." Jericho had moved to stand at attention by the door, but he interrupted her firmly and came closer. "If you'll give me her address, I'd be happy to take care of it."

Jericho sounded like a damned bodyguard. Was that all their time together meant to him? Just because she was on the governor's campaign staff and probably had sex with the man—

"That would be terrific, Jericho, if you wouldn't mind," Allan said in what she vaguely remembered were his normal, charming tones. Then he turned to her. "There's always been a spare set of keys to both your condo and your car stashed in your office. Just in case of emergencies. Let's go see if they're still there. Then all of us can be on our way. And I'll contact you later at home."

"I wonder what happened to my car?" Rosie said absently as Jericho unlocked her condo and ushered the two of them inside.

She lived on the twelfth floor of a downtown building with parking below and a doorman in residence. Jericho wasn't surprised at the condo's sweeping views of Austin and the Hill Country from the floor-to-ceiling windows.

"You don't remember?" he asked as he hesitated just inside the threshold. "What kind of car do you own?"

"A Mercedes S550." After a silent instant, she continued with a grin. "Wow. A few minutes ago I couldn't have come up with that answer. Things are just flashing into my brain at lightning speed."

She strolled wide-eyed through the large foyer and stepped into the sunken living room. Gracefully, she walked around the room, touching white leather couches, staring at expensive artwork on the walls, marveling at marble sculptures. The furnishings seemed to bring memories back into her mind.

Jericho wasn't too pleased to see this much opulence. No expert, he still would bet there was several hundred thousand dollars' worth of art and sculptures skillfully placed around the room. And her car was a Mercedes. Of course it was. Daniels no doubt kept his girlfriend in diamonds, too.

How could his handmade cabin and seven-year-old truck ever compete with all this? How could he ever hope to compete with the *governor of Texas?*

The answer was simple, he couldn't.

But he could do his job and also do the governor his favor at the same time. "If you'll give me your license number and a description, I'll report your car as missing. We'll find it."

She nodded idly. "Thanks."

"Are more things coming back?" he asked, hoping against hope that they weren't. That she would only ever remember him and their time together. He had to guess it was already too late for that.

"A few," she told him. "Like the fact that my birth name is Olivia DeVille Halprin. The only child of Chester Halprin and Suzanne DeVille. And before he passed away, my father built an Internet empire that's been valued in the billions."

Oh? Maybe it wasn't Daniels's money that had provided all the opulence then. But that didn't give Jericho much comfort. He still couldn't live up to any of this. Never would.

"So your father is no longer alive. How about your mother? I'm wondering why she didn't report you missing?"

Rosie turned and graced him with a wry smile. "As cold and ruthless as my father was, Suzanne is just the opposite. Beautiful and outgoing and a pillar in hundreds of Texas charitable foundations. She has just never had much time for a daughter. She's much too busy devoting her life to really good causes.

"I haven't talked to my mother in months." Rosie continued a little too quietly. "In almost a year now, I think. But I'm sure she would've missed me eventually."

Jericho couldn't imagine such a family. Okay, so his mother had disappeared and never come back. But both his father and his brother had always been the rocks in his life. What would he have become without his family?

He took a step in Rosie's...no Olivia's...direction before coming up short. He didn't know Olivia Halprin, and he had absolutely nothing in common with her. She wouldn't want sympathy from him, and he couldn't stand to have her back out of his arms when she realized the same thing.

Olivia blinked a couple of times then said, "A *bath?*"

"Excuse me?" He hadn't said anything about a bath. She shook her head as though to clear it. "What? Oh, sorry. I don't know why I said that. I never take baths. But it just popped into my head while I was thinking that things seem a little off."

"A little off? How do you mean?"

Shrugging, she turned and walked over to open one of the many doors that led off the main room. "My office is in here. Let me see if it feels funny, too."

Jericho shoved his hands in his pockets and followed. Funny feelings were not in his jurisdiction.

Olivia's office was crammed with computer equipment. It made him wonder if she'd inherited her father's genius.

"Before I became the Daniels campaign treasurer," she began as she studied the machines up close, "I was a CPA. A Certified Public Accountant. That's just what I love to do. I know it doesn't sound interesting, but I specialized in forensic accounting. Chasing bad guys around inside their bank accounts."

She turned and smiled at him. A real smile. "Maybe that's why I fell under the spell of a lawman. You think?"

He couldn't talk to her about that right now, so he shrugged one shoulder and stayed quiet.

Her smile faded slowly, then she turned and moved one of the keyboards a few inches to the left. "I swear it feels like someone has been in here since I was last in this room. I'm sort of fussy—okay *anal* would be a better word—about my workspace. Everything has to be just so. Must be the accountant in me.

"And my things have been moved. I could swear to it."

"You sure it isn't just that it's been a while?" he asked soothingly. "Your security alarm was still armed when we came in. We had to disarm it. Besides, you've been through a lot over the last few days. Especially with your memory. Maybe things are still hazy in your mind."

She looked around. "Lots of things are still a little hazy. But not this room." Sighing, she turned back to him. "I guess I need more time. How long are we going to stay here? Do I have time for a bath?"

Those seemed like odd questions, but he decided it was past time for him to get out of town. Let her have her bath and anything else she needed. The lady was home. She hardly needed him to stick around anymore, despite the fact that leaving was bound to kill him.

"You go on and take your bath. I've got to be heading back to Esperanza. Just come see me to the door. Make sure your doors are locked and the security alarm is set behind me."

"You're leaving without me? But…"

"Look, *Olivia*. You're where you belong. You have a job and people who care about you. But I sure don't belong here. Let's just cut our losses while we still can."

Her face crumbled and big tears welled in her eyes.

"I'll stay in touch," he offered. "Let you know how the investigation is coming along. And I'll be sure to work on finding your car."

She sniffed and reached out a hand to him. "But can't you see that I don't belong here anymore, either? No one in my old life even bothered to check up on me. That would never happen in Esperanza. I need…"

Jericho needed to get out of there—fast. "You'll change your mind when more things start coming back. I mean, for one, yours would be the only Mercedes in all of Esperanza, Texas. And that's just for starters. There's no place to shop. We don't have any art museums. I can't think of anybody who would need the services of a CPA."

He waved his hand as if that explained everything. And to him, it did. He could never stand to work at making a life with her only to lose her back to the big city.

The worst had happened. She was regaining her memory and that meant he wouldn't stand a chance in the long run. Just like his mother, only for different reasons, she'd be off and running before he could turn around.

"Lock up behind me," he said as he turned tail and made a dash for the door. "I'll contact you."

Maybe. *If* his heart could stand the pain of hearing her voice and knowing his house would forever stand barren and lonely without her there.

Damn her all to hell for making him believe it could happen. Believe he could get what he wanted for once.

Well, Sheriff Jericho Yates would be just fine alone.

Chapter 15

Furious at herself for being such a hormone-raging wimp, Rosie slashed at the tears streaming down her cheeks. She'd finished locking up behind the retreating Jericho, and then had come to the conclusion that she might as well have that bath, so that's where she was headed.

How could he have left her here in Austin all alone?

She *should've* said he had to take her with him. That his job wasn't done and they hadn't even had a chance to talk. She *should've* said something about her things being still in his closet and that at the least she needed to say goodbye to the dogs. She *should've* grabbed him and kissed him senseless, just to remind him of everything they'd done together.

But she'd been so surprised, so thrown by the idea

of how shallow her old life had been, that she hadn't thought fast enough to get out a word. All the should'ves in the world didn't matter when the person you counted on turned his back on you and walked away.

In her old life it had been easy to blame her distant, cold father for all her unhappiness. But in truth, she remembered now how it really was. She'd tried desperately hard to become the most beautiful and successful daughter a father could ever want. No matter what she did, though, he'd never seen her efforts—not really. So to emulate her father, make him see her, she'd learned to appreciate art, as he had, and forced herself to like the other superficial things in life that meant a lot to him. But of course, *her* list of superficial things also ended up including dating gorgeous, powerful and successful men with no scruples.

That was how she'd been drawn to Allan Daniels in the first place. But giving up her old job to please him had been the craziest part. The only thing in her life that she'd ever done that made any real sense was to work at the forensic accounting consulting firm. She'd tossed it all the minute Allan crooked his little finger at her.

Rosie turned on the bath water and thought of Jericho— not Allan. Thought of how much better her life had been with the Campo County sheriff. In just a few short days, she'd turned herself into someone who could be appreciated and respected. Because of him. He had really taken time to see her for herself. Not for only the outside.

But stupid her, she'd just let him walk away.

Sitting on the edge of the filling tub, Rosie hung her head and wept for all the things she had not done or said that might've made a difference. Might've made Jericho wait for her. Want her.

This place—this life—weren't hers anymore. So she would refuse to stay here, by heaven. After she took this bath and rested a little, she would rent a car and drive right back to Esperanza, Texas. Back where she belonged.

An odd, instant and intense urge to put bath salts into the water had her reaching for the fancy jar she'd never opened but only used for decoration. Though once she had the clear bottle in hand, she *knew*. In her mind she could actually see herself hiding something deep inside the fuchsia crystals.

Standing up beside the vanity, Rosie dumped the contents of the salt jar out on the counter. The clunk of something hard and metallic captured her attention. What had she hidden? And why?

In another moment, at least the *what* was clear. Out of the baths crystals rolled a tiny flash drive. Hmm.

Fighting to remember more, she turned off the bath water and headed to her office. It should be easy enough to find out the *why* by plugging the drive into one of her computers.

The curiosity was killing her.

Cut and run! He'd done it again.

Jericho eased on the brakes of his borrowed SUV and pulled into a roadside park off the 290 that was not quite in Johnson City. A half hour out of Austin and he was finally getting his head on straight. About damned time.

With the engine idling, he beat his fists against the steering wheel and wondered what the hell 'was the matter with him. In his whole life, every time a woman got too close, he would shut down and split. That was just who he was. Call it pride. Call it not wanting to take a chance on being hurt. Whatever. But never before had it seemed this important, or this wrong to run.

All those other times the women were perfectly fine, and maybe he could've made a life with them. But this time. This time it was Rosie and she was…she was…

Everything.

Jericho drew a deep breath and tried to think instead of letting his emotions tie him up in knots. Why was he always like this, shutting down without a fight? Could he change this time? After all, he never backed down from other challenges in his life.

But with that thought in his mind, a picture of Allan Daniels leering at Rosie with a malevolent gleam in his eye and yet another picture of Rosie begging him not to take her there, made him rethink all that had taken place.

There were several missing pieces to the puzzle of Rosie. Big missing pieces. Like, what had those goons wanted from her? *It.* They'd kept mentioning an *it.* Was Rosie going to suddenly remember what that was and then be in terrible danger again?

Jericho had walked off the job before it was done. He had never done that in his life.

Putting the SUV in gear, he prepared to turn around. Had he been so intimidated by Daniels's position as governor that he'd lost his mind? There was nothing right about the whole scenario. If Rosie and Daniels had been such great lovers, then why hadn't Daniels gone to her condo to check on her when he'd thought she was sick? He knew if she'd been *his* girlfriend and had really been sick with the flu, Jericho would've stuck to her bedside like glue.

Who the heck had reported that she had the flu in the first place?

Lots of problems. Lots of big red flags that should've caught his attention.

But the worst of it was that he hadn't listened to Rosie. He hadn't given her a chance to talk. She had become his whole world and he'd turned his back? Stupid. Stupid.

Pulling out onto 290, he stepped on the gas and retraced his route back to Austin. Back to Rosie. Maybe she would give him a second chance. Maybe he could make her see that he was willing to fight to save her—fight to love her.

He just hoped to hell it wasn't too late.

Rosie sat staring at the monitor, too stunned to move. Everything—all the secrets and terrible truths—came back in a rush of clarity.

Allan Daniels was dirty. More, Allan was an embezzler who consorted with Mexican druglords—and he was running for president of the United States. Holy moly.

She remembered well her first instance of finding these horrible facts on an innocuous-looking flash drive in Allan's office. Almost ten days ago now. After convincing herself of the reality of what she was seeing, she'd been nearly hysterical wondering what she should do next. Who to go to who would not only believe her but who could do something to stop him.

The governor of Texas was the head of the Texas Rangers. So that was out. The police? The FBI? She remembered thinking they might laugh at her—or worse—ignore her. He was, after all, a candidate for the presidency, and everyone figured all his secrets were already out.

Not by half.

After taking the precautionary step of hiding the flash drive in her bath salts and making a copy to hide in her car, she'd done the only other thing that made sense. She'd contacted an old friend, a reporter for the *Dallas Morning News,* who was honest and who could start a secret investigation that could eventually bring Allan down.

Mary Beth Caldwell. My God. What had happened to her?

Rosie remembered their secret meeting at Stubbins Barbeque. Remembered distinctly sitting across from Mary Beth, who looked a lot like Becky French, in her early sixties, short and plump. But Mary Beth was a shark. Smart and well-connected, as an investigative reporter she could not be beat.

Mary Beth had not only believed her about Allan, but had agreed to hide Rosie until the authorities could be convinced. Rosie had already realized she was in dire trouble because Allan had called her cell while she was with Mary Beth. He'd wanted to know if she'd seen anyone strange near his office. Obviously, he'd already missed his flash drive and knew she was the only one who could've taken it.

She and Mary Beth had immediately left the barbeque joint and headed for Rosie's car. But before they got there, a couple of dangerous-looking men came up behind them. Rosie remembered running, then a thud coming from behind her. Mary Beth must've been hit, but she'd been too afraid to turn back to help. Oh, God. Rosie's stomach clinched.

She remembered dropping her car keys and running. Running for her life and not looking back. A trucker had picked her up down the highway, and she'd thought she might be okay if she got far enough away. When that good-guy driver dropped her off in Rio View, Rosie had done the smart thing and headed straight to the sheriff for help. Sheriff Montalvo.

Yeah, Montalvo had helped all right. He'd helped her find a motel to hide in. And then he'd apparently called the governor to help himself to whatever clandestine reward Allan must've been offering for her.

Now Montalvo was dead. Mary Beth was probably dead. With sudden clear panic, she knew she was as good as dead, too.

Oh, Jericho, where are you? She reached for the phone to call him at the exact moment when she heard a slight noise in another part of the condo. Not much of a noise. But enough to keep her from being surprised as the voice she'd dreaded to hear came from directly behind her back.

"Put the phone down, Olivia."

She did as he demanded and slowly turned to face what looked like a silencer attached to a huge gun. "Hello, Allan," she managed without looking at his face. "I thought you were at that fund-raiser. Where's your secret-service security detail?"

Oh, hell, she was done. She hadn't remembered enough of her past in time. With just a few more minutes, she could've been out the door and gone. Of course now that it didn't help her, she remembered that Allan had access to a duplicate key and knew her security codes. That was the very last thing she'd remembered and probably the last thought she would ever have.

He chuckled. "Yeah, I gave them all the slip. The secret service thinks I'm having a quickie fling in a hotel room not far from here. Smart and sly. That's me. It'll be a great alibi in case I ever need one."

Did "ever need one" mean that he wasn't planning on killing her? Or did it mean he imagined no one would ever question the governor?

"Look, Allan, there's something important you should know." Her mind raced to find some excuse to stay alive. Give her the break she needed to get away.

He waved the gun at her, and perversely she noted he was wearing a tux. "Shut up. Now that I've found my flash drive—" He pointed the barrel at the monitor as if that said it all. "I don't need to hear anything from you. I've already got a plan. You're going to be killed by whoever's been chasing you. They broke into your condo because you forgot to lock the door and set the alarm.

"*Tsk, tsk,* sweetheart. What a shame." He leveled the gun at her and took aim.

"Wait a second," she begged. "I made a copy of the drive. Kill me and you'll never find it."

Jericho heard the voices coming from Rosie's office and crept closer. He'd been alarmed when he'd arrived back here only to find her front door unlocked and ajar. He definitely remembered Rosie locking it behind him when he'd left.

That's when, on instinct, he'd drawn his service weapon and edged inside the door instead of knocking. Was that Daniels's voice? Absolutely. And Rosie's, too, sounding scared and on the verge of panic.

She'd been right about not coming here. Why hadn't he listened? The only thing he had in his favor now was surprise. That would have to do.

Sneaking up to the office door, Jericho eased it open and peeked inside. Daniels was standing with his back to him, but he was holding a weapon to Rosie's head.

"I said, shut up, bitch." Daniels screamed, clearly out of control. "Lies won't save your traitorous ass. You stole my property. You were going to use it to ruin me.

"If you made a copy and hid it, then where is it? I've had this place searched top to bottom." Daniels rammed the barrel of the gun against Rosie's cheek. "Better make me believe you by telling the truth."

Jericho's anger came up fast and hard. He wanted to shout at Daniels to take his hands off her. It was all he could do to tamp it down and think like the lawman he needed to be.

"Hold it, Daniels," he yelled, jamming the barrel of his 9mm into the man's back. "Drop your weapon. Now!"

Daniels stilled for the moment, but said, "You won't shoot. If you do, your girlfriend here is dead. You'd better drop your gun, sheriff, and we'll have a little conversation."

Nearly blinded by his furor at the man, Jericho fought

his emotions long enough to make the right move. Daniels would have to kill both of them now. It was his only out. But there would be two of them to his one. Jericho figured those odds were in their favor.

At least, he had to give surprise a try. Otherwise, Rosie was dead.

"Okay, Mr. Governor, you've got the upper hand," he said with as casual tone as he could manage. Under his shirt, his muscles bunched and tensed. "I'm going to put my weapon on the floor. Don't be surprised." He kicked the 9mm clear across the room and under a daybed. "See there. Now we can talk."

"Not until you come over here where I can see you," the governor snapped at him. "Carefully. Move to your right. Go stand beside your girlfriend's chair directly in front of me."

Daniels still had his weapon poking into Rosie's temple. Jericho raised his arms slightly, almost offhandedly, and took a docile step to the right.

"Easy there," he told the other man. "I'm moving."

But with his second step, Jericho deliberately stumbled a half a foot closer to Daniels. Surprised and panicked by the sudden move, the governor spun and pulled the trigger without aiming. The shot went wild, off into the ceiling.

Everything happened at once then. Rosie screamed and kicked out at Daniels's gun hand. The weapon flew out of his grip. And in that instant, Jericho was on him.

The two of them were on the floor, grappling and throwing punches. Daniels didn't stand a chance. Not with the superhuman power Jericho's furor provided him.

The son of a bitch had hurt Rosie. He'd planned to kill her! Jericho landed a right and heard Daniels's nose break. Well, let's just see how he likes being hurt.

Battering Daniels's head against the ground, Jericho didn't feel any of the other man's blows and could only think about Rosie. This bastard had been planning on taking away the one woman he loved. Never!

Daniels fought with incredible strength. Still, Jericho remained on top and was numb to any pain. Finally, Jericho edged free enough to ram his knee into the other man's groin. He felt gristle crunching underneath the slacks even as the other man shrieked in pain.

"Hope it hurts like hell, you bastard." A scarlet haze of pure hatred and anger developed in front of Jericho's eyes, as he just kept yelling and punching. Never noticing the other man go limp.

Hitting. Smashing. Landing blow after blow.

Rosie came to her senses and scrambled across the room to get a hold of Allan's gun. She pointed it at the two men on the floor. That was when she saw that Allan wasn't fighting back anymore.

"Jericho, stop." She put the gun down and moved closer when he didn't seem to hear. "Jericho!" she screamed.

Inching closer, she yelled again and got the nerve to shove at his arm. "Please, honey. Don't do this. Stop."

Tears sprang from her eyes and threatened to swamp her, but she kept yelling his name and shoving at his arms and back, desperate to make him understand. *Please, my love. Don't ruin your life—my life—over this piece of garbage.*

At last, Jericho quit swinging and turned to her. Shocked at what she saw, she reached out for him.

Tears rolled down his face, his fury clear but almost spent. Reaching for her, too, he stood and pulled her into his arms.

"Are you okay?" He swiped his face across his shirtsleeve and choked back an obvious sigh.

His father had been right. There must've been a lot of anger buried in him for all these years.

She looked up into his beloved hazel eyes, now dark green with feeling. "You came back," she managed through her tears. "You came back for me."

"I shouldn't have left. If I'd been a few seconds later…" His words trailed off as she saw the deep emotions swirl across his face.

It thrilled her. Scared her. He seemed so intense. So full of concern for her.

To shake off the strong feelings she didn't know what to do about, she turned back to look at the limp body on the floor. "I hope you didn't kill him. He isn't dead, is he?"

Jericho seemed reluctant to let her go, but in a second she saw the sheriff return to his eyes. He stepped closer to Allan and checked his pulse.

"He's alive," Jericho said with authority. "He's going to live to spend a long time in prison. I can't believe how I missed seeing what a phony he was."

"Everyone missed it. The whole world missed it." She shook her head, heading toward her desk. "I'll call 911 and get an ambulance. Do you think we need to tie him up?"

Jericho reached out and pulled her to a stop. "I'll tie his hands and you can call in a second," he said gently.

"First, I have to apologize to you. I almost lost you. I should've listened when you didn't want to come here. I should've listened when you wanted to leave with me. I…" Again he seemed to choke on his words.

"You didn't know," she said, rubbing uselessly at his sleeve.

He drew in a deep breath. "No. I did know something, if only I'd just paid attention. I knew you loved me and I knew I loved you. That should've been enough."

"You love me?" The adrenaline must be spiking inside her again, because she thought she was hearing things and her whole body began to shake.

"More than anything. It would've killed me to lose you. Literally. I can't…I can't live without you.

"Whatever your name is now, Rosie-Olivia, marry me and change it. In fact, marry me as soon as we clean up here. Today. Tomorrow at the latest. I'm never leaving you again."

The tears started up again and Rosie damned her hormones. But laughing through the rolling rivers of salt on her cheeks, she managed to nod her head.

At last she would know for sure who she was. A woman worthy of respect and love. A woman so full of love for the man who provided it that she thought she might burst.

Epilogue

Pleased with himself for getting the seventy-two-hour waiting period waived and arranging for the justice of the peace on short notice, Jericho stood with his best friend and watched as his new bride talked to his father and brother on the other side of the yard.

"Are we supposed to call her Olivia now that her amnesia is gone?" Clay asked as he poured himself a drink from the temporary refreshment table set up in Jericho's backyard.

Rosie's backyard now, too, Jericho thought with a secret smile. He was simply amazed at how peaceful, how settled he felt since she'd said yes. What a lucky bastard he was.

The governor was recovering from his injuries in the

hospital jail, and many of the questions had already been asked and answered. The worst answer concerned finding the body of the reporter, Mary Beth Caldwell, in the trunk of Rosie's car at the bottom of a ravine. Rosie's testimony, the flash drive and the rest of the pending investigation would put Daniels away for good.

Tilting his head to Clay, Jericho answered, "Mrs. Yates will do for you." A little sarcastic maybe, but then he allowed the smile to show. "Really, she says she prefers Rosie. But she's willing to answer to either one."

Clay nodded as he too looked across the lawn to where Rosie stood. "It's nice your brother's leave isn't over yet so he could be here for your actual wedding. Family is so important at times like this."

Clay sounded so down all of a sudden, not like himself at all.

"You okay?" Jericho asked.

"Yeah. It's just…well, you know I've been writing to my brother, Ryder, in prison. My most recent letters came back as undeliverable."

"What does that mean?" Jericho could see that the news had upset his friend. Maybe a lot more than he was letting on.

"Not sure." Clay looked off at the sunset. "I'm planning on calling the warden to find out. But I've been a little hesitant, knowing it might be something I don't want to hear."

Jericho could understand that. Running instead of standing and listening was something he was real familiar with.

He put his hand on his friend's shoulder. "No matter

what it is, it's better to know the truth. Let me know if you need my help."

Rosie turned to him and their gazes met across the lawn. The thrill ran down his spine, landing squarely in his gut. Would it always be this way? The desperate hunger. The pulse-pounding wave of recognition when he looked her way.

As he walked toward her, he imagined it would probably last a lifetime. When he got close enough to put his arm around her waist, he was positive. This. This exhilaration and breathlessness would never go away.

"So, bro," Fisher began. "You two planning on a hunting trip as a honeymoon?"

Jericho kept his gaze locked with his bride's. "None of your business. Just let us handle the honeymoon."

Moving closer to him, Rosie felt the warmth of her new husband's love clear down to her toes. She stood, basking in both the sun and in the friendship and love she'd found with all these wonderful people.

What an amazing thing it was. Not more than two weeks ago she was a lonely, superficial woman with no family to speak of and no friends. Amazingly, if she'd given it any thought back then, she would've said she was happy. She'd had things, a prominent job and a part-time lover who had power and influence.

But deep down something big had been missing. She hadn't been able to put her finger on it then, just as she hadn't been able to come up with her past over the last days. But she'd kept on reaching—reaching for *love* as she now knew. And for family.

Family. She gazed at her handsome new husband

and then at his loving and gentle father and brother who were chuckling at Jericho's teasing. Well, she had a family now. A better one she never would've found.

Easing her hand over her belly in a protective motion, she reminded herself that there would be one more family member soon. A baby to love and cherish. How lucky could she be?

Smiling at her love, a secret smile that told him all that was in her heart, Rosie Yates decided all was right with the world at last. The sheriff's amnesiac bride had found her mind…her place…her love.

And she meant to hang on to them forever.

* * * * *

MILLS & BOON®

Want to get more from Mills & Boon?

Here's what's available to you if you join the exclusive **Mills & Boon eBook Club** today:

✦ *Convenience – choose your books each month*
✦ *Exclusive – receive your books a month before anywhere else*
✦ *Flexibility – change your subscription at any time*
✦ *Variety – gain access to eBook-only series*
✦ *Value – subscriptions from just £1.99 a month*

So visit **www.millsandboon.co.uk/esubs** today to be a part of this exclusive eBook Club!

BOOK_SUBS_2014

MILLS & BOON®

Maybe This Christmas

* cover in development

Let Sarah Morgan sweep you away to a perfect winter wonderland with this wonderful Christmas tale filled with unforgettable characters, wit, charm and heart-melting romance!
Pick up your copy today!

www.millsandboon.co.uk/xmas

MILLS & BOON®

The Little Shop of Hopes & Dreams

* cover in development

Much loved author Fiona Harper brings you the story of Nicole, a born organiser and true romantic, whose life is spent making the dream proposals of others come true. All is well until she is enlisted to plan the proposal of gorgeous photographer Alex Black—the same Alex Black with whom Nicole shared a New Year's kiss that she is unable to forget…

**Get your copy today at
www.millsandboon.co.uk/dreams**

14_ST_2

MILLS & BOON®

Why shop at millsandboon.co.uk?

Each year, thousands of romance readers find their perfect read at millsandboon.co.uk. That's because we're passionate about bringing you the very best romantic fiction. Here are some of the advantages of shopping at www.millsandboon.co.uk:

* **Get new books first**—you'll be able to buy your favourite books one month before they hit the shops

* **Get exclusive discounts**—you'll also be able to buy our specially created monthly collections, with up to 50% off the RRP

* **Find your favourite authors**—latest news, interviews and new releases for all your favourite authors and series on our website, plus ideas for what to try next

* **Join in**—once you've bought your favourite books, don't forget to register with us to rate, review and join in the discussions

Visit **www.millsandboon.co.uk**
for all this and more today!

MILLS_WEB